Praise for *The Girl*

"*The Girl from Rawblood* is a mesmerizing debut novel. It will haunt your dreams."

—Miranda Seymour, author of *Thrumpton Hall*

"Beautifully written Gothic. It is rare to find such sumptuous prose."

—A. K. Benedict, author of *The Beauty of Murder* and *Jonathan Dark, or the Evidence of Ghosts*

"A Gothic tale of love and madness, this atmospheric and chilling story drew me in from the first page, and kept me up at night, until I reached the last."

—Claire Fuller, award-winning author of *Unsettled Ground*

"A powerful contribution to the British literature of the fantastic. It's an epic family saga incorporating a great Gothic house, built upon a lyrically rendered regional landscape, from which the numinous rises as if it is a natural function of the setting. There's a touch of Ted Hughes, Emily Brontë, and M. R. James in this eerie and by turns moving story that spans generations. It filled my head for several evenings and will linger there too... A definite book of the year for me."

—Adam Nevill, author of *The Ritual*

"From Victorian ghost story to anti-war polemic and back again: I raged, wept, and hid under the bedcovers. As full of science as it is the supernatural, this is a hauntingly brilliant virtuoso performance."

—Emma Healey, award-winning author of *Elizabeth Is Missing*

"Gloriously dark and claustrophobic, *The Girl from Rawblood* is a haunting Gothic novel of intelligence and complexity. It has many echoes of the classics but is entirely its own book."

—Essie Fox, author of *The Somnambulist*

"A story to satisfy the most Gothic of hearts. I was hooked on the very first page and *The Girl from Rawblood* never let me go. Sentence by sentence, Catriona Ward made herself one of my very favorite writers."

—Kelly Link, author of *Get in Trouble*

"Elegiac in its prose and haunting in its imagery, *The Girl from Rawblood* is a precisely and beautifully woven tapestry through which threads of darkness wind their inevitable way. Ward has crafted a sweeping saga of madness in all its forms that will chill you to the bones and draw you into its murky depths."

—Charlie Lovett, *New York Times* bestselling author of
The Bookman's Tale and *Escaping Dreamland*

"Beautifully written, in equal parts both terrifying and heartbreaking, *The Girl from Rawblood* is a dazzlingly brilliant Gothic masterpiece."

—Sarah Pinborough, author of *Behind Her Eyes*

"*The Girl from Rawblood* weaves a spell that both terrifies and mesmerizes. As each layer of mystery is peeled away, more haunting truth is revealed. The book leaves the reader breathless in its Gothic tale of fear, family, blood, and love."

—Simone St. James, bestselling author of
The Sun Down Motel and *The Book of Cold Cases*

"Brilliant—*The Girl from Rawblood* is the old-school Gothic novel I have been waiting for. While it delivers everything I want from a 'haunted house/family curse' story, it is still stunningly original. I have never read anything like it, and that's saying something."

—Mike Mignola, creator of the Hellboy comic book series

"A lush, macabre, chillingly good tale. From the modern horrors of man—medical experiments, war—to the ancient power of the natural world, *The Girl from Rawblood* is not only a ghost story of the highest order but a sublime meditation on the things that hold us captive: fidelity, fear, memory, love."

—Leslie Parry, author of *Church of Marvels*

THE
GIRL
FROM
RAWBLOOD

CATRIONA WARD

Poisoned Pen
PRESS

Published by Poisoned Pen Press, an imprint of Sourcebooks
P.O. Box 4410, Naperville, Illinois 60567-4410
(630) 961-3900
sourcebooks.com

Originally published as *Rawblood* in 2015 in the United Kingdom by
Weidenfeld & Nicolson, an imprint of the Orion Publishing Group.

Cataloging-in-Publication Data is on file with the Library of Congress.

Printed and bound in the United States of America.
VP 10 9 8 7 6 5 4 3 2 1

For my parents, Isabelle and Christopher

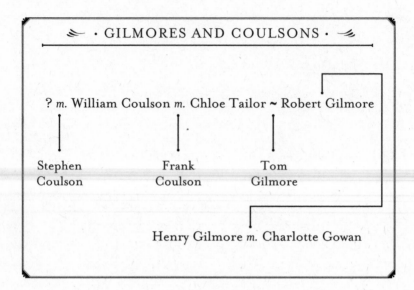

GILMORES AND COULSONS

? *m.* William Coulson *m.* Chloe Tailor ~ Robert Gilmore

Stephen
Coulson

Frank
Coulson

Tom
Gilmore

Henry Gilmore *m.* Charlotte Gowan

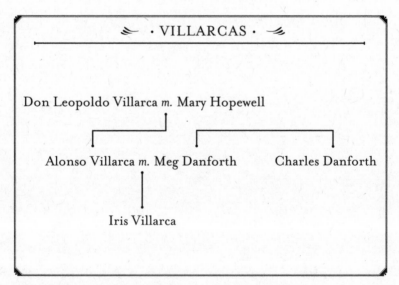

VILLARCAS

Don Leopoldo Villarca *m.* Mary Hopewell

Alonso Villarca *m.* Meg Danforth   Charles Danforth

Iris Villarca

IRIS

1910

This is how I come to kill my father. It begins like this.

I'm eleven. We find the mare shortly after noon. She's not been there long, so the foxes haven't come yet. The flies have, though. She is glossy, plump.

"Why?" I ask.

Tom's bony shoulder lifts, indifferent. Sometimes, things just die. He's learned that well. In recent months.

The mare's mane is black on the parched turf. Kneeling, I reach a finger to her. Tom pulls me away from the corpse. I expect a scold, but all he says is "There."

I don't see it, and then I do—in a clutch of bracken, ten paces beyond. Small and dark in the green shadow. Newborn.

"What will you do?" I ask.

He pushes a hand through his hair.

"Pest question, Iris. What would you have me do?"

This hurts. "I'm not a pest," I say. "I'm trying to *help*."

He gives me a gentle shove. "Pest." Since his mother died in March, Tom's voice has been blank.

We watch the foal as it lies, head tucked into itself. It sighs. Thin cotton sides heave. Its coat is still slick in places. It's too small to live, but it doesn't seem to know it.

"We could feed it," I say.

He gives me a look that means I live in a big house with floors shiny with beeswax and high ceilings where the air goes up into white silence and the linen is scented with lavender and tea rose. In the mornings, I have porridge with cream, milk from my silver mug if I am good. Tom's knees jut through the worn patches in his trousers. He lives with his silent father in the drafty farmhouse with slates missing from the roof. He is in the fields before dawn each morning. There is no *we*.

I squirm. My boots are tight, my feet bloodless like the flesh of a gutted fish. I shed my stockings somewhere near Bell Tor. Beneath petticoats, my bare legs are gorse striped, beaded with blood.

"Never works," he says at last. "They won't take it. Or they sicken. There's something not right for them in cow's milk."

"I don't want it to die."

"You're a girl," he says. "You don't understand."

So I know he doesn't want it to die either.

In a March storm, Charlotte Gilmore stepped on a fold of her skirt. I see the moment reflected in Tom's eye each day: the buffet of cold air on her face as she falls down twenty steep stairs; her dress, belling about her like a tossed blossom; the thunder that covers the sound when her neck breaks.

"Come on," he says. When he's upset, his voice rattles like a badly fitted drawer.

Our long shadows slide over the turf. The foal raises its head, questing. Tom seizes it. It twists and struggles and bats him with little hooves. Tom lifts the foal onto his shoulders, settles it there. Slender forelegs and hind legs are safely anchored in his fists. The tiny brush tail whisks, indignant. They go like that, back toward the farm.

"They'll be missing you," he tosses over his shoulder. "You go off home now. Pest," he adds.

"Wait," I say. "*Wait!*" I run on tight feet.

Henry Gilmore leans on the farm gate. His stare is wide, full of nothing. Tom stands upright before his father. At his shoulder, the foal flicks little ears. Tom asks the question once more.

"Maisie's colt weaned two days ago," says Henry Gilmore. His words are slow. He gives Tom his flinching glance. Once, he looked at you straight. Not anymore. He left his eyes in Tom's mother's grave four months back.

"Will she—" Tom stops.

Henry Gilmore shrugs. "Could be. Don't fuss her. If she mislikes it. You let her do what she will." He reaches a hand to the foal's muzzle. Its nostrils tremble, move across his skin, scent his grief.

"It'll die either way," he says. "Better quickly."

"Might not," says Tom, and the air between them grows dense.

"You'll not make a farmer," Henry Gilmore tells his son, touching Tom's shoulder with an absent hand. He leaves us, fades through the gate into the blue. Tom, the foal, and I watch him. Distance narrows him as he goes, whittles his figure to a dark drop crawling across the bones of the hill.

In the loose box, Maisie peers through a forelock the color of dirty snow. Clumps of mud cling to her tangled belly. She lifts a broad lip in our direction, shows us her butter-yellow teeth.

"You're not to go in," says Tom. "Pest. D'you hear? No matter what."

He has a twitch above his eye. His eyebrow stutters with distress.

The foal's muzzle brushes his cheek. Tom's hands tighten, sticky about its legs.

"You'll have to hold it," he says. "Can you? If you… Yes."

A flurry of little hooves, and the foal shrieks like a cat. At length, it subsides in my arms. Its pounding heart, its thin new bones.

Tom says, "We have to make them smell the same."

Pressed together, the foal and I shiver under the sun. I can't see where Tom has gone. There's the crack of his boots on the dry earth, the puzzling intricacy of wood, metal, catches, clasps, doors. He is back quickly.

"This'll do."

The tin is squat and burly. He pries the lid up with his knife, plunges a hand in. It comes up a shining paw, gloved in treacle. Dark shining loops. He covers the foal's head and withers. He puts the stuff on its hindquarters, smooths it over the heaving flanks, over its belly. When he's finished, my arms are crosshatched as if by the path of snails.

"She won't hurt it," says Tom. His hand cradles the foal's jaw. Its eyes close. Long lashes on sooty lids. "She won't," he says again, not to me.

Over the stall door, Maisie shakes her massive head, blinks a bashful eye, lifts her rubber lip.

"No," I say, "she wouldn't. Good Maisie."

The surface of the cart horse is vast. Her flanks ripple like a quiet sea. Tom watches. His eyes show the blue iris, ringed with white.

"Won't do to wait," he tells himself, or me. Maisie offers flared nostrils to his sticky hands. "Yup," he says to her. "All that. Soon." He slips into the stall, bolts himself in. His hands move to and fro, between light and the straw-scented dark. They coat Maisie's muzzle and mouth with treacle. He works backward along the colossal sculpture of her, moves out of sight into the dim. She stands, but her head follows him, the glassy brown trail.

I pick up the foal. It lies like a sack in my arms. It has given up. Its hooves are no larger than shillings. The thud of its heart on my wrist. It smells of freshly crushed nettles, sharp against the farmyard.

"Will it be all right?" I ask.

Tom says nothing. I carry the foal to the stall door. It is quiet, leaden. He reaches, takes it through the crack into the dark. Then he's out. He blinks in the sudden, honeyed day. His dark eyebrow quivers. I put fingertips to my wrist. The flesh there holds the memory of the foal's heartbeat, weaving over my own. We wait, silent.

"I can't," Tom says.

So I look.

In the dim light, Maisie's nostrils traverse the lineaments of the foal's body. She licks the treacle from its muzzle, eyes. Her tongue sweeps down its length, a thick banner. The foal mews, a high complaint. Maisie levers it upright, nose under its stomach. Her ponderous head is as long as its body, an edifice of teeth and bone. The foal stretches. Its neck elongates beyond possibility, reaches upward in a graceful line. It can't reach. It makes the high sound again. Maisie bends her legs, collapses, groaning, into the straw. Her eyes close. The foal feeds, a tiny, resolute shape by her monstrous belly. The tail whisks. Maisie breathes. Hayseed whirls in the slanting light.

"It's all right," I say. There is no reply.

Tom's lips are moving silently. I shove a finger into his ribs. I fold a damp hand around his thin brown wrist.

Tom whips his hands from his ears where they have been painfully pressed. He goes to the stall door.

"Good," he says in a rush. "Good. Oh, well done, pest."

"Don't call me *pest* anymore," I say. "I don't *like* it."

"I know," he says. "Sorry. I don't mean it, Iris. You're not a pest. It's just…remember how you felt when the dogs got your rat?"

Sorrow comes, and anger, hot.

Tom nods. "That's how I feel all the time now," he says. "Every day."

I think about this. "All right," I say. "You can call me what you want. I don't mind."

For the first time since his mother died, Tom takes my hand in his. We watch the mare and the foal. Bees hum in the falling afternoon. Sound bleeds back into the day.

"Come on," Tom says at length. "Home for you."

"No." I am not ready to face Papa.

"We'll catch it if you don't."

I'll catch it anyway, but I don't tell him that. "I don't know the way home," I say, triumphant.

"You always say that."

"I'll probably end up in *Belgium*."

"All right, I'll walk you," he says, as I knew he would. "Back to the Home of the Difficult Pest!"

"That's not its name." I leap on him, pummeling. "Or my name!"

"I thought you didn't mind anymore!" he shouts through the blows. "Pest! No, ow, no biting, pest!" We roll, joyous, in the dusty yard.

∽

I slip through the hedge. My eyes water from the sunlight, the breeze. But within the yew walls, there is stillness. The scent of lavender hangs in the air.

On the green, my father dreams. Banks of gray and purple frame him in his black suit. Open on the table beside him lies a moldering book, spine broken. There's a lime-green jug, where glassy water shines. By the jug, a soft leather wallet, half unrolled on the warm wood. I can see the gleam of metal within: sharp, inviting. I look away. I must not go near my father's pouch; I am never to touch it. That is one of the Rules. Behind him, the house rears up, warm and gray.

Rawblood. Home. It sounds like a battle, like grief, but it's a gentle name. "Raw" from *sraw*, which means "flowing," for the Dart River that runs nearby. "Blood" from *bont*, a bridge. Old words. The house by the bridge over flowing water. It has been in my family since I don't know when. Rawblood is us, and we, the Villarcas, are Rawblood.

It's a bulging, ungainly thing. Windows poke out along its lengths at no set distance from one another. Crazy angles of warm slate roof are purplish in the sunshine. It's old, and everyone who has lived here has built something or taken something away. Like its name, it has shifted through time. But the house has its own sort of will. It has preserved its long U shape quietly, with the minimum of fuss. When I try to think of Rawblood, to draw it with words, a muffling whiteness comes. I can't describe it any more than I can my own bones, my eyes. It simply is. It hangs in the foreground of everything like blindness.

These are among the first things I recall my father teaching me: that I must keep quiet and may not go among many people or to towns, because of the disease, and that Rawblood is written into us. Sometimes, I think Tom knows about the disease. Sometimes, he looks at me as if he knows something. Or perhaps I could tell him, and he'd still be my friend after all. I don't care to test it.

I come near to watch my father sleep. His head nods to inner music. His lids shiver. I am near enough to see the low sun single out each silver whisker like a filament of steel.

A hand uncoils itself into the air between us, grasps my forearm, pulls me close. It happens fast and smooth, like the whip of sapling wood.

"What have I caught?" he murmurs, eyes still hidden. "What can it be? A lion?" He tightens his long fingers, and I shriek and say no, no, I am not a lion.

"I don't believe it. You *must* be a lion. I am a famous lion catcher, you know."

He makes a show of feeling my arm, looking for paws, looking for claws. "So. Not a lion. How's this?" He hums. "A badger, then. A striped, snouty badger."

"No!"

"A fish. A lovely, silvery fish for my supper." His fingers slide over my ribs, a rapid accordion, and the laughter takes all the wind out of me.

"A person," I gasp. "I am a person!"

He opens his eyes. "So you are. Well. I must let you go, then."

But he doesn't. He looks me over, sharp. I had not considered my appearance. I'm covered in treacle, pony hair, and dirt. My pinafore is streaked with green, with black. The wind has teased my hair into peaks and horns.

My father says, "Is it…horse that you smell of? What have you been doing, Iris? Where have you been?"

I'm caught. So I tell him. About the foal, about Maisie, about the farm, backward, words stumbling over themselves.

He dips his handkerchief in the water jug, smooths the cool, wet linen over my arms. The ring on his finger gleams red and white and gold. The imprints of his fingers are white ghosts on my wrists.

"Gilmore's boy, who is *not* a farmer," he says. "Iris."

I wait. The hairs on my arms stand to attention.

He says, "Gilmore's not managing. No. Not at all." He takes my chin in the white wing of one hand and looks. His vast eyes shine like varnished wood. Now he'll tell me I'm not to. He'll say I mayn't because of the Rules… I can't bear it. The lavender is sooty in the air, my lungs. When Papa and I fight, it is always about Tom.

"Don't say I mustn't have him as my friend," I say.

"I do say so, but plainly, it has no effect," he says. "You are heedless, and you are growing. I do not know what to do. Lock you up? We cannot continue to differ on this, we cannot…"

The handkerchief falls to the table. I am new, damp, clean. I slip from his grasp and sit beside him on the lawn.

My father does not reprove me or mention my dress. He puts his hand to my head again, light and sweet. It strokes, gently picks bracken and

straw and burrs from my indignant hair. "Ragamuffin," he says to himself.
Cushioned turf tickles my unstockinged calves. Nearby, sparrows quarrel
in a rhododendron. Against the hedge, lying in shadow, a single daisy
breaks the immaculate green of the lawn. It will be gone tomorrow.

I pick up the collapsed book. A ledger, really, like the one I have seen
for the household accounts. It falls open in my hand. Some sharp scent
rises from the spoiled pages. They are damp, oily to my touch. Faint lines
of copperplate.

*She does not trouble me; the fact being so plain, perhaps, that I am
already damned. Other things haunt my dreams. A small blessing, given
to a fiend.*

"What does it mean?" I ask.

Papa's fingers drum the paper, a soft tattoo. He says, "Highly unsuit-
able." He takes the book, puts it from me on the table. Something
is frightening.

I wipe my fingers on my dress.

My father says, "So."

I look up, inquiring. He is giant against the sun.

"If he is good with horses, it is settled. We need another groom;
Shakes is getting on. We will have the young not-farmer. And"—his
hand cups my neck—"Miller's wolfhound has six pups. I will take you
down to choose one in the morning. He will sleep at the foot of your bed.
How do you like that?"

Light fingers in my hair. Inattentive, sun-dazed, the words will not at
first connect with meaning. Why would Tom sleep at the foot of my bed?
Then I understand. I scrub my hand across my eyes, across the grass.

"No," I say.

"No?" he asks. "I have given you two presents; all you have for me
is *no*?"

"Thank you, Papa. I don't want the presents." I know this will upset
everything, though the reasons are just out of my reach.

He regards me mildly. "Iris, I am surprised at you. It will be good for the boy, and the Gilmores have mouths to feed, whether you like it or not. But you need not have the puppy if you do not want it."

"He's my friend," I say.

"Now he will be your groom," Papa says. "And you will treat him as such."

"Yes," I say, because that is what one says to Papa. I'm dazed, ears ringing. "But I will have no one. It will be hard to remember that we're not friends anymore..."

"You will accustom yourself to it," he says. "We are adaptable animals. When you have called him Gilmore a few times, it will come more naturally. When he has been your groom for a year or so, you won't remember he was ever anything but."

"Papa..."

"You are disobedient, Iris, and you force me to act. You will not stay quiet; you will not stay under my roof or my eye. You *court* the disease and will not abide by the Rules." His hand strokes the soft leather case. His eyes have found the distance.

I rise to leave Papa there, warm and solid on the bench, silver head already nodding. I know my love for him. I am surprised by my hate. It comes like the shaft of a splinter on the smooth grain of wood.

Horror autotoxicus. The disease. Papa does not say, but I think it kills us, the Villarcas, and that is why we two are the last.

1908

I meet Tom the day that Papa tells me of the disease and makes the Rules.

I'm nine. I've never been away from Rawblood alone before. Papa wouldn't like it. But he's asleep in the garden, one hand swinging heavily in the sunlit air, pince-nez clinging to the end of his shining nose. I slip away like water. The lane to Manaton is quiet, dappled, hot with the last of the day. The hedgerows are high, filled with green and secret light.

My hands are crammed with two large, fragile pieces of apple tart, stolen from the kitchen table. The sweet, warm scent. I am alone in the world. Beyond Rawblood, beyond the reach of Papa's stare. My arms swing long and free. Summer light. Sleepy birdsong clear as glass. The sandy shale good under my boots. Distant voices from the neighboring fields. Harvest is nearly over.

I walk slowly, digging each toe in, dragging it behind me as an injured bird drags a wing. I kick a cloud of fine grit into the air and squeeze my eyes closed. The rhythm of my feet—drag, shhh, kick... I have a strong sensation of dreaming, though I know I'm awake. Under my breath, I sing a song I have made up, about badgers. It has no set tune. When the time comes, I will find a stone to sit on or climb a tree, and then I will eat my two pieces of tart, but not yet... The rhythm of my feet on the road.

I stop. I am no longer alone. Behind me, there's a girl, as if from nowhere. She stands in the bend. I think she's been following. She's thin, bigger than me but with a worried face, as if she's left something at home. Two brown buckteeth peep between white lips. We stare.

"Hello," I say.

She makes a noise and sticks her hands in her pinafore pockets.

"Do you want some?" I ask. I offer a fist. Apple slides between my fingers. Perhaps she will be my friend.

The girl looks at the pastry in my hand. Her teeth pull on her lower lip. She keeps worried eyes on me and points up the lane. "Where you from?" she asks. "You from there?"

"Rawblood," I say. I try not to say it *too* proudly. I look at the two pieces of tart in my two hands. "One each," I say with some regret.

"From there," she says. "It's probably poison." Her eyes are on the tart. "Does it have poison in it?"

"No," I say, offended. I raise a hand to my mouth. Sweet, crumbling crust. Sharp, green.

The girl bites her lip and stares. Then she bends quickly, fumbles in the sand. Something curves through the air. The sharp edge of the flint strikes the corner of my eye; everything bursts. Something else hits my temple with a crack. The world swings backward out of balance. The girl throws and bends and throws with perfect concentration, loading her hands quickly from the road. They all land. Some are small and sting. Some are large and make thuds on my flesh, sharp sounds on bone. I show the girl my back and hunch up small. Stones strike fiery on my kidneys, ribs, spine. Something hits the base of my skull and splashes white across my mind and eyes. Everything tastes of tin.

My cheek strikes the road with a thump. It stretches before me like a landscape. Through the pulsing in my ears, I hear the soft give, the crunch of road as she comes. I try to get up. My arms and legs are buckets of damp sand. She comes on with soft steps. Hot stuff trickles from my scalp to my chin, warm red drops. The sounds I make, like kittens drowning.

Her shadow. Her feet are before me, bound tight with rags. No shoes. She bends. Her grubby, shaking fingers uncurl my fist, lift the remains of the tart from one hand and then the other. I try to bite her; my teeth graze her arm. She turns quickly, the hedge quakes, and she's gone.

I sit in the warm road. I don't know what to do. I can't go home; Papa will see blood and cuts and know I disobeyed. I should never, ever have left… A tooth is loose. I cry in hitching sobs.

Around the bend, footfalls. I push into the hedge, through the hawthorn, the bramble, to the gray, cold stone wall at the heart of it. Sharp, unkind branches tear my dress. Something living crawls in my ear. I hold my breath. It's quiet. The wood pigeon murmurs. The breeze moves, brings the first scent of evening.

The footsteps stop just by.

"Bit of blood," says a voice to itself. It stutters a little on the consonants, like a badly fitted drawer. "All right in there?"

Something brushes through the leaves like a monster. I bite.

"Ow," the voice says. It withdraws. "No—ow."

I feel a bit sorry. And I hate and fear the dark hedge. So I come out.

The boy stands in the road, clutching the red place on his arm where I bit him. He's about my height, with bare, brown feet and a fishing pole. "You bite pretty nicely," he says. "Why you all bloody?"

"Girl came and took my tart," I say. "It was apple." I show him my hands, fragrant with crumbs.

He nods, serious. "Oh, yup," he says. "That's a stinker."

"Stinker," I say, enraptured. "What's your name?"

"Tom," he says. "You?"

"Iris." It's the first time I've told it. It's strange and a little powerful.

"There'll be some taste left," he says. So we sit on the verge and lick my gummy fingers. There's earth and little bits of bark mixed in, but it still tastes like apples. I've never shared anything before. His tongue tickles. I laugh. It hurts.

He sees. "Took a right pasting, you did," he says.

I say, "I don't want Papa to see the blood."

"All right," he says. "Come with." He takes my hand.

The stream runs shining over fat stones into a small pool of deep green. Rowan trees lean across it. The banks are covered with blackberry bushes. Midges dance in the cooling air.

The cold water shocks our bodies. We scream and paddle. Tadpoles and minnows flee from our white feet, corpse-like in the river water. The blood spirals off me, away into the stream. We eat shiny blackberries until we're stained purple. We wash it from us. My dress dries crumpled in the sun while Tom fishes. He doesn't catch anything.

"Should have a trout to show for it," he says. "Might not get it *too* bad if I have a trout."

"You ran off," I say. "So did I."

"Meant to be getting the hay in," he says. He tells me about his dad, his ma, where they live, which is a farm with cows.

"I love cows," I say. "Big eyes and eyelashes."

"They kick," he says. "Lots."

When the midges have risen all about us and the skyline has cooled to a milky gray, Tom says, "Home, I suppose."

I say, "Come home with me!"

"Can't," he says, and I catch his apprehension.

"With me, with me," I sing. "Come home with me…" I dance around him and pull tufts of his dark hair. I dance and sing loudly, because I don't want to be alone in the dark lane.

"Pest," he says. "Well, I'll walk you."

Papa sees us as we come down the hill in the last of the light. He comes out of the door like a bull. "Iris, what were you thinking, to leave me so? Do not go off! Do not! The mist could come down!" He trembles.

"There is no mist, Papa! I promise." He is always thinking there will be a mist, and it is very frightening for him.

Papa looks at me, the cuts and bruises, the dirty dress. He takes Tom by the scruff, lifts him clear off the ground. Buttons spring from Tom's shirt as Papa shakes him.

"What was done to her?" Papa says. "Speak. What hurt?"

"I didn't," Tom is saying as Papa shakes, and I shout, "No, no, it wasn't him!"

"Who are your people?" Papa asks. "They will hear of this. And now a hiding, the worst of your life."

"Tom Gilmore," he says, teeth clicking as he's shaken. "Trubb's Farm."

I tug at Papa's sleeve. "He helped me," I say. "Papa! It was the *other* one who threw the stones…"

Papa drops Tom like a sack of wheat. Tom sits surprised on the ground. Papa covers his face with his hands. "Tom Gilmore," he says.

Tom says nothing. Trying to guess which answer means trouble.

I say, "Papa, please leave him alone."

Papa makes a noise. "I forgot," he says. "I promised, and I forgot." He stares at Tom. "You may feed him, Iris. But out here. Not in the house." He turns and goes back toward Rawblood, his back shaking up and down.

Tom and I stare after him. "He's crying," Tom says.

"I know." There seems little else to say. It's no more or less peculiar than the other things that have happened today.

"Might be some tart left," I say, and that thought eclipses all others.

❧

Papa dresses me with tincture of iodine. The scent is strong and red. My bedroom is very snug. The fire is lit, as if I am not well. It leaps busily and crackles in the grate, warm on our faces. The night is outside. We are inside.

"Why were you crying, Papa?"

"I was reminded of a promise I made once," he says. "To your mother. I had forgotten, which is very bad, as one must keep promises. But not only that—I was angry, Iris, because I fear for you. I have always been careful to guard you, have I not? I have tried to teach you right, as a father should?"

"Yes," I say, stricken. "Why, Papa? Why did the girl throw the stones? Why did she think the tart was poison?"

"Others fear us," Papa says. "Our family. Dear heart, they will hurt you if they can. We have…a disease. Like Rawblood, it has run in our family forever. It lies dormant within us like a sleeping foe. It is named *horror autotoxicus*. Servants do not like to work at Rawblood because of it. So we have Shakes only. Even he does not stay at Rawblood but lives above the stable. No servants sleep in the house." For a moment, his face is faraway and blank, and then he goes on, "*Horror autotoxicus* is unusual; it is not caused by contagion or by a virus. It is caused by feeling."

"That is strange," I say, thinking of a cold I had last summer. "What does it do?"

"It makes you very ill," Papa says. "It makes you hot with fever, and visions come to you of terrible things. You slip into a dream, where monsters roam. In the end, you lose your mind, so that you no longer know the places that you love or the faces of your family. Sometimes, it causes you to harm others."

"No! I will always know your face, Papa; I will always know Rawblood…"

"I wish it were so, Iris. You must keep very calm and live quietly, because *horror autotoxicus* can come on if you are excited or upset. If you have a strong feeling that you cannot control, you must tell Papa at once. It could be the first sign."

"All my feelings are strong," I say. "I cannot possibly tell you *all* of them!"

"You must try," he says. He tuts and dries my face. "But do not despair. We can prevent it. You are in no danger as long as you live quietly at Rawblood and do not run off. It is a rational thing, which we can approach with reason. I see that I have expected too much of you, Iris. Your disobedience shows me that you cannot be trusted to apply your own judgment. So I have made Rules, which you will follow and which will keep you safe."

Papa takes a piece of paper from his pocket. He reads it aloud to me, then pins it to my bedroom door.

1. Other children: not friends.
2. Servants: not friends.
3. The disease: a secret.
4. Papa's medicine pouch: forbidden. When Papa takes medicine: leave room.
5. Eight o'clock to noon: reading with Papa.
6. Afternoons: play in the garden. Not out of the garden.
7. Bed: at seven.
8. Books: as good as people.
9. Tell Papa everything.

"These are like promises, Iris. Do you understand?"

I nod. The loveliness of the sun and the water and Tom have dissolved into tiredness, and I hurt everywhere. I had not known my body could hurt so. I am no longer eager to see the world. I am not sure it's a friendly place. *Horror autotoxicus…* Even the name is horrible. But I will be all right. Papa will make sure of it.

"I will obey all the Rules," I say. "But I will keep Tom! It's called a bargain, Papa."

Papa looks at me long. "You are your mother's daughter," he says. "It is not possible, Iris." He cradles my head in a long, white hand. He holds me in a gentle vice and looks into my eyes. "Say them after me," he says. "The Rules."

I squirm. "Papa, too tight…"

"Say them, Iris. I must be sure that you understand."

"Other children," I say. "Not friends…" I say the Rules, again and again.

Eventually, Papa releases me, puts a hand on my head, and I know I am forgiven. He says, "Very well. We will read."

"Hervor!" I say.

"Always Hervor. Such violent tastes. Very well." He takes the book from where it's open by the bed. We read.

☙

It is not really called Hervor, but *The Waking of Angantyr*. It goes like this. Hervor's father, Angantyr, dies, and he is buried with a famous sword called Tyrfing. It means "measurer of fate," or sometimes, it is called "bane of swords." Hervor is a fighter. She wants the sword. She is quite bad-tempered about it. I like this, because it seems to me people are often too good in stories.

Hervor goes to her father's grave and opens it like a door. She goes into the underworld, which is a dark place full of bonfires. She wakes Angantyr from his sleep. This is another reason it's my favorite. If my Papa died, I would go and wake him. Angantyr is angry at being woken. He says that Tyrfing is a terrible sword that is cursed. It will perform evil deeds. And both sides of the blade are poisoned, so if you touch it, you die. Hervor says, *I am your only daughter. I am heir to the sword. I'll take it and cut myself on the edges. I will walk through all these fires. I'll risk the curse. I'm not afraid.* So her father is very impressed with her bravery. He gives it to her and tells her she must go back to the living world before daylight. If the door to the land of the dead is left open at dawn, the dead vanish forever. Where to? No one knows.

She runs back with Tyrfing through the raging fires, across the black land. She reaches the door as the sun is casting its first rays across the ground. She slams the door shut. Her father is safe. She has the sword. All is well.

After that, she travels all over the world dressed as a man, riding the horses of the sea. She has many adventures. I have longed for adventures.

Papa's voice, the warm fire. I still love the story, but I have understood, today, that I am not Hervor, and that books and life are not the same.

1912

I'm thirteen.

In the pink light of the closed curtains, Henry Gilmore's skin is gray birch bark, his cracked lips trembling over yellow teeth. Constant sound comes from him, like a kettle nearly boiled. It's called farmer's lung, or hay catarrh. The land's repayment for a life's work. There's no doubt he's dying.

I look to my father where he stands by the bed. He gives me no sign. I don't know what comes next.

"I hope you are better soon," I say to Tom's father and put the basket of plums on the bed. It lands with a soft thump.

Henry Gilmore winces and breathes, a bubbling sound. He lies back on the pillow. Strands of yellowing hair cling to his brow like waterweed. A narrow bar of sunlight falls across his sunken cheek. Breath moves through his parted lips, effortful. He turns his clouded blue eyes on me. There's something stony and seeking in his look. For an instant, I can trace his younger face, buried deep beneath the old, a dark reflection on water. His bones are fine and beautiful in the afternoon light. Henry Gilmore and I see each other, and the air stretches thin between us. Time narrows and draws out.

"Do you know," asks Henry Gilmore, "that you have the devil for a father? Your father is the devil in the night."

Something touches me once between the shoulder blades, light. Papa is at my back. "You go now," he says.

I go down through the house's dusty innards, down the breakneck stairs. I go fast, eyes squeezed shut, listening for Charlotte Gilmore's ghost.

I wait, kicking at the fat white ducks that wobble across the yard. My skin prickles. *The devil in the night.*

I go around the corner of the house to the livestock stalls. At the end, past the milkers, the tip of a velvet muzzle crests the stable door. The pony makes a soft sound. She thinks I'm Henry Gilmore.

When I come close, she lays her ears down flat on her head. She backs into the far wall, trembling. She's grown now. Sleek and stout. But she's never liked me, since the day we took her from her dead mother's side. So, actually, she's hated me since the day she was born. I have a grudging respect for it—the strength, the consistency of her dislike.

I put out my hand to her and chirrup. "I *saved* your life," I tell her. "Tom and I did. *He*, Mr. Gilmore, would have left you." The filly stares, nostrils flared. I think about Tom, and smarting wells in the rims of my eyes.

As I cry, I feel the velvet of the pony's muzzle on my arm. She is delicate; her lips fondle my sleeve. I feel the warm kindness of her breath, the comfort, the solid strangeness of her presence, her silken face. I have enough time to feel all this before her blunt mouth seizes my forearm in a bruising vice. I feel every one of her narrow columns of teeth. She shakes me, watching my pain. I punch her on the poll, hard between the ears. She smiles and tightens her jaws. Her dark horse eyes are bright as I beat her about the head.

∽

My father casts pitying looks at the broken fences, strides delicately through the cow dung that covers the cobbles, dark and pungent. He goes to the trap and places a box under the backseat, calls me to him as if not quite sure of my name. Eyes dark and occupied with something.

"What's in the box?" I ask him. "That you put away."

"Money," my father says.

"Why?"

"To settle his debts."

"Why should you?" I am indignant. "What he said…"

"Pay it no mind, Iris. He is dying. And I have wronged him, in my time. It is good," he says but not to me, "to make peace if one can."

I saw the quick shift in Henry Gilmore's wasted face. I know that look, that blue contempt. I've seen it before, in another pair of eyes. Henry Gilmore found no peace from us.

In the trap, we're quiet. My arm sings with the dark, rich bruise left by the pony's mouth. I open my mouth to the wind. It rushes in, cold and dry. It takes away the taste of the hot sickroom and Mr. Gilmore's words. Fear is all through me. *Disease.*

"It will not harm you, Iris," Papa says. He sees my thoughts, as always. "It will not harm as long as you obey the Rules."

∽

In the black, my feet find the narrow ledge beneath my window. Light snow patterns my hands and face. I crawl across the slate. In the stable block ahead, one window throws out a weak guiding light.

Fingers dug into crevices, I move across. Below is the long drop and then the flagstones. It pulls at me like the tide. The world is peculiar, pitched at a slant.

At the second gable, I grasp the ridge and throw a leg over. Something skates away from my foot, and I'm sliding at great speed toward the drop. The night land rushes up. Cold streams run down my spine.

My boots meet a yielding surface. I come to rest. Needling pain in my fingertips, which are rough, wet. The shaky gutter creaks. I'm ankle-deep in old mulch and the bones of dead birds.

At the window, his hands reach to catch me. I scrape over the sill, inside. Something drums wetly in my ear. A heart.

Tom says under his breath, "Made such a clatter, you did."

We are still. I think of Shakes at the other end of the stables. I think of my father and the Rules. A board groans under my soaked feet. The stables sigh beneath. Warm movements in straw, patient horse breath. Mice rattle lightly in the eaves. A spiral of snow puffs gently through the window. No one comes.

"Getting too big for that," says Tom at length.

"No fear," I say. I am still loose, weak. "Fine talk from you anyhow."

Tom overtops me by a head now. His wrists shoot out of his sleeves like vines. "Blood," he says, uneasy. "Smell it."

"The roof. Scraped a bit."

He takes my hands in his.

"Just fingers," I say. "It's—"

He pinches my arm for quiet, and I stop. He goes to the corner and does something. Soft sounds. Presently, a cool sliding on my hands. His fingers slip around mine. The cut-grass smell of horse liniment.

Tom lives above the stables at Rawblood. Our friendship has slipped from day into night. Crossing the roof is crossing into another country. I break the Rules every night, like this.

I want to ask him, *Does it make you sad? Do you wish you were at home still?* But I don't. What would be the use? Tom has no mother, and I have no mother. Soon, his father will be gone, and he will have no one. I don't know much about the world and so on, but I do know this: the scales are already heavily weighted in my favor, and this will tip them further.

Too much goes unspoken between us lately. There's too much untruth. My father, the disease… I am pulled in opposing directions. Strong, complex bonds. I don't know what to do, so I test them all. I defy my father. I lie to Tom. I flout the Rules and court the disease. One day, something will give, but what?

Tom says, "Stink."

I ask, "What?"

"Wait."

Now he's said it, I can smell it. The scent of decay. My boots are thick with mud and gutter rot.

There's rustling. He hands me straw in a musty clump, takes a rag. I stand like a heron, one-legged. He crouches at my feet. I bend, and we scrub, wrinkling our noses. I sway, and my hands clutch for balance. I seize Tom's hair in fistfuls.

"Let me. Leave it, pest, or we'll both go down. Leave it." We tip slowly to the floor in silent, shaky laughter. My fingers curl weakly through his hair.

There's no trouble on the way out. We move through the dark stable into the open air. When we're clear, at the foot of Sheeps Tor, we shout. Our voices are high and silly. The air is fine needles. The last of the cloud is clearing. The stars are out, and the moon is up. It shows the bowl of white-dusted land.

"Trout?" I ask. "Be rising."

Tom says, "Didn't bring the line." His chilly fingers find mine. They flutter, then hold. "Come on," he says. "Show you something."

We climb. Above us, the rocks are flat and black against the sky.

"Here." Tom pulls me down into a shallow defile between the boulders. A narrow strip of turf snakes away, a path through the bulbous granite. The world is far overhead. It's clammy, frozen, the rock closing in like teeth.

"What?" I ask.

"Down here," he says and vanishes.

I follow, but he's gone as if into air. My hand slides along the lines of the slick rock passage. I turn and stumble, crack my shin on hard, cold stone. My breath hovers white before me. I think, *I'm alone. He's gone.* My heart hammers, fit to burst.

A black slit hovers ahead, dark against the jumble. An arm emerges from the crevice. "That's it," he says, guiding me in.

Inside the cave, the match gutters far up above to where the walls taper to a point like a tiny steeple. The air smells of turned earth and the faint old tang of fox. The walls are bright green, covered in moss that shines and moves under the light as if under a caress. The chamber is wide enough for five men to lie full-length on the pale floor. Near the back, in the shadows, a tall crooked stone like an altar. On the dark stone lies a small button, bright red. A child's shoe worn thin. A wooden spoon. A horseshoe, and something old and moldy that may have been bread. Behind, something gleams in the slanting shadow, something white and misshapen. It shivers. My heart is cold.

It's a trick of the light, of course. A lump of old quartz bathed in candlelight. But for a moment, it looks like bone and dead flesh. A corpse curled at the foot of the altar.

Tom's face is branded with shadow, dancing. He grins. The match fizzes. He says, "Listen."

Behind the walls, within the rock, shrill voices rage in unknown tongues, hammers ring on steel, the sound of distant slaughter. Thin sobbing, a whistling shriek, then whispers soft as breath. The sounds enclose us.

"It's the river," Tom says, "running through the ground. It won't harm." It sounds like all the harm in the world. The match flares and spits.

"Don't let it go out," I say. "Tom—"

"Wait," he says. "I've a… Wait." He fumbles in his pocket, and the little flame dances, dims. Shadows lick up; the dark is coming. What happens to the white stone in the dark? Perhaps it is not always a white stone.

"*Tom*," I say, but flame rears up from the little candle stub, brave, scattering light. The walls leap into being, green and shining. He makes to put the candle on the altar.

"No!" I say. "Not there." We sit side by side on the cave floor. It's sandy and friendlier than expected.

"Who would make this?" I ask.

"No one made it—it's here, that's all."

"People come here," I say. The small shoe lies quiet on the stone beyond.

"Old folk," Tom says. He rolls the vowels, lengthens the Devon in them. "Turn your coats inside out to keep Saint Nick away. Walk three times widdershins 'round Bexley Tor under moonlight." He sniffs, shrugs, draws his finger in a circle on the sandy floor around the candle. "*Lo,*" he says in a high pinching voice like Mrs. Brewer, who's married to the butcher in Dartmeet. "For I have drawn the line in the sand, and no one shall touch this candle now, lest they die." He looks at me and grins. "No one can put it out now. See, pest? *Magic.*"

"What's that noise?" A scratching, a faint sound in the distance, like stone rubbing against stone.

"The river," says Tom. "Told you already."

But it's different. Stealthy. I look up, around. Shadows flicker. "What does it do?" I ask, looking at the crooked altar stone, the glistening quartz behind. I don't like to take my eye from them somehow.

"Now, you may give gifts here, pest, that the one you love mayn't ever die." Tom's still in Mrs. Brewer's voice. He takes a brown glass bottle from his coat pocket and drinks, grimacing, then stands and goes to the altar. He puts something crumpled on it. We sit and look at his father's glove where it lies dirty, limp-fingered on the granite.

Tom says, "Just in case." He rubs his face hard. His cheek flushes red under his palm. "It's nonsense," he says, "like all those things." But he leaves the glove where it is.

I say, "We go to see him once a fortnight."

"I know," says Tom. "Tom the stable boy harnesses the horses, shoves old Shakes up on the box of the trap. I know everything you do, pest."

"Don't call me that," I say automatically. There's a strange, thin bite to his words. The line between our daytime and nighttime selves blurs and wavers. I have the beginning of a headache. It's so mournful, the sound. Stone grinding against stone.

"What is it between them?" Tom asks. "Between your father and mine?" The bottle clinks on the floor.

"I don't know," I say.

"Bad blood," Tom says. "Mystery! Intrigue!"

"Curses," I say. "Ancient wrongs." Our hilarity is brittle and raucous, the joke a feather's breadth from truth. It's thrilling, like walking on the clear ice where it's thinnest over the pond.

"They say things in the village," Tom says. "About him, you. Rawblood."

"What?" I ask. The clear ice, and beneath—what? Cold, deep dark.

"There's a murdered girl buried at Rawblood." He runs light fingers up the back of my arm. It gives me shivers, not entirely unpleasant.

I bat him off. "Stop. Where? It's not true."

"Some say she's under the cellar floor," Tom says. "*Some* say she's in an attic, the pieces of her anyhow, in a chest bound with iron… But most likely she's under the cedar tree. Buried beneath. The roots feed on her corpse." The hairs on my arm rise to his light fingers. "It can be seen from a certain window of Rawblood. Her grave. It's always freshly dug. Wet earth. You see it if you're about to die."

"Ugh," I say. His fingers stroke; they raise delicate chills.

"Yup, it's all rubbish," says Tom. He shifts away a little on the sandy floor. I rub my prickling arms. "I know of someone who really—" he says, stops, and starts again. "My uncle Rob was a butler. The butler at Rawblood, as it happens."

"We don't have a butler," I say.

"No," says Tom with intonation I cannot place. "Not now. My dad was older than Rob by nearly twenty years. He took care of him. More like a father than a brother, I suppose. He doesn't talk to me much, Dad. But he'll tell stories about Uncle Rob. Anyhow, one morning, Rob had not come down to servants' breakfast. And when they went up into the eaves of Rawblood to look for him, he was there, cold, dead in his bed.

Eyes wide like pebbles, like he'd seen something. And you'll never guess, pest—it was on the day that you were born. How d'you think that plays in the village? My dad sets a store of anger on it. Daft ideas. Says it was Rawblood that killed him. That Rob's life was taken, because he did something, something to displease your father..." Tom starts, recollects himself, looks at me wide-eyed.

I shrug, my heart beating fast.

Tom says, "I look like him. Like Uncle Rob." The drink's in his voice now, a little. "Apart from his red hair. And now you're thinking, 'Oh, that's why they can't get on: makes the old man sad to see his son look so like the brother. I understand now.' But you'd be *wrong*, pest. That's not why he hates me. It's worse, because there's no reason to it. 'Rawblood's ill luck for the Gilmores.' How many times have I heard it from him? But he sent me off there all right." The bottle clinks softly in the sand. "Sold me like a pony."

I take his hand. The candle flickers. The shadows move. Tom's words hang in the dark between us, mingling with others I have heard. *He did something to displease your father. The devil in the night.* I see him in my mind: Robert Gilmore, who I never set eyes on. Quick one moment and dead the next. Perhaps it was the disease. Perhaps it killed him. The ice is thin, thin…

Tom clips me over the head. "Thought you might turn tail, pest," he says, "when you first came in here." He's strained, light. "Eyes like a barn owl." His hand holds mine tight.

"Didn't though," I say, flooded with relief. The world shivers and rights itself. The dark tide retreats.

"No," he says. "Too right. You didn't. Here."

The liquid catches in my throat. It's like drinking gas lamps. I cough and drink again. Candlelight falls, beautiful and restless, on everything.

"I like it," I say. I mean the cave, the drink, the moor outside, the light within. I mean the warmth at my side where he sits. His messy head haloed in the candlelight. I am giddy with the reprieve—from what? I play with Tom's bootlace and imagine his foot within. Shapes dance on the shining green walls. The dim roof above is infinite.

"What would it be," I ask, "not to die, ever, anyhow? If by putting a glove on a stone, you could do it? Might be awful."

"People shouldn't die," Tom says. "Just *shouldn't*." When I look, I see something is happening. He's stiff, pale, arms locked around himself. He shakes with something violent. "Put out the light, Iris." The whites of his eyes gleam.

"Magic," I say. "Remember? Can't put it out." I don't want the dark. I am strange of a sudden. As though my mind is growing, pushing gently at my skull. The sound. It's like the earth is moving. Readying itself to bury us. Or as if the stone is breathing. I don't like it.

"Just—put it out." His voice thick and cottony, his mouth awry like a child's. The candle hisses on my licked thumb. The dark drops down on us like a weight. He's gone, the cave is gone… Am I gone? Behind us, within the rock, the battle rages; gurgling voices speak long incantations. Beneath it, Tom is crying, small sounds.

He says, "I should be minding the farm." He doesn't say *home*. "I should have been there, these years, learning to mind it. But I wasn't, and now all I know is horses, so I'm no good."

I put my hand into the dark. It comes to rest on his face, which is hot and wet. I find odd bits of him to hold—a collar, an elbow—and take them tightly. Sadness comes from him like breath.

Tom folds his arms about me. He breathes by my ear. He smells of drink, thick and acid, filled with juniper. His hand on my back is large and flat, then small and insistent. "No point in it. He's done," Tom says into my hair. "It's as good as finished."

I think of Henry Gilmore's drawn, translucent face. The afternoon light on his dying skin. "I know," I say. I cannot say *it will be all right*.

His heart thumps hot against my collarbone. I want to climb inside his flesh and pluck the suffering from him. I fumble for his hand. His warm palm closes on mine. Around us, the river rises in a torrent, burbling mad. Voices like stone grinding on stone. I don't mind it now. Something good moves between us like a living thing. Tom starts. He says, "Look, look."

The cave is full of moonlight. Juddering, shivering. Bars of silver scatter as if we're underwater—across the cave entrance, Tom's spiky head, his face, his ear, his shoulder, caught in moments of clarity. Light glances off the corner of the altar, chases across the walls. Shadows of far-above clouds scud across the white floor.

"Oh," I say. It is insane; it is beautiful.

Slippery light plays about the altar stone. I squint. The white stone at the base, half in shadow. I edge closer to Tom. His cheek on mine. His voice warms the air. "Iris? You could tell me your secrets. They'd be safe. I wouldn't ever, ever tell."

"What a shame," I say with sympathy. "He's touched in the head." I punch him. To break the strangeness. He punches me back, hard.

"All right. I suppose you won't." Tom's finger slides lightly on my throat; it comes to rest in the notch of my collarbone. That punch didn't work; the strangeness is everywhere. He says, "I do feel a bit...touched." We shake, laughing, gripped tight to one another. I breathe the soft place under his ear.

The moonlight plays about the cave. It glances over the pale stone at the foot of the altar. In the shifting light and dark, it could almost, almost be a very thin pale person, curled on the floor. Glimpses of things that could be bony fingers, spread wide, a bare skull peeping through baby-fine hair. The blink of a black, mad eye. The white stone uncurls. The white thing stands slowly upright. The cave goes dark.

It's all right, Tom is saying. *The moon went in. Iris, it's all right.* But he's wrong. The rock and the river, high and terrible. Beneath, stealthy sounds of someone coming. Padding soft across the sand, across the cave floor, coming closer in the dark. Desire.

I seize Tom's calloused, puzzled hand in mine. I drag him roughly up and go, bent double, stumbling. Something groans like stone collapsing. The cave shudders. Something cracks and bursts underfoot—the bottle? a white bone?—and flattens into crushed shards. The sound of the river rises, harsh and rusted. Tom calls out, and I pull him faster; we're clattering and slipping in the dark. Something grazes my back. Light and thin like a finger. Traces the length of my spine. We're out. Behind, in the cave, something moves.

On the hill, I haul the clear night into my lungs and vomit. Tom is anxious, fond. I can't answer him. His hand is on my brow; I shiver at his touch. The warmth that suffused our bones and flesh, which drew us together, is gone. What is he to me anyhow? I see with dreary clarity that everything lovely has been stripped from the world.

"There was someone," I say. "In there." My breath is still too fast. The world tilts.

"Iris," he says. "I don't think there was. My fault—I was telling tales. Trying to frighten you." But he's frightened now. I hear it. His hand is on my brow. "You're very hot," he says. "You're ill… Iris…"

Diseased.

"Keep away," I say. "You'll die."

"Don't shout," Tom says. "And I doubt it."

"Don't touch me." I'm hot and cold by turns. The fever dream is all around. White shapes drift across the gauzy sky. I thought something horrible was in the cave. But the horrible thing is inside me. Here it is at last. *Horror autotoxicus.* The disease.

At his window, in the poor, ill-lit room above the stables.

Tom's the same. The room is the same. The straw, the cloth we used to clean my boots—both lie in the corner by the door. Vague scents of gutter muck and a trace of liniment still touch the air. But nothing is as it was. The world is a slippery, raw place, stranger than I knew. No one's laughing now.

Tom's puzzled. But he tries again. He trusts me. "Iris, you look bad. Let me…"

He must be kept away. Even in my feverish state, I know the thing to say. It's been waiting to be said between us all these years. "You were right before," I tell him. "I'm getting too big for this. Too old to play with the stable boy."

I don't wait to see his face. I go back across the roof, head ringing.

In my room, I lock the door. I close the shutters. I lie in lavender-scented sheets and spin. I am cold, cold. Moonlight lies cold across the floor. The curtains are cold. The lines of the furniture are cold against the dark. Rawblood sighs around me.

I think of Tom's stutter, which comes when he's unnerved. The dark line of his brow like a swallow in flight. These things are what they are, but they are now also something else. Lightly, I touch the notch of my collarbone—my flesh remembers his finger resting there. *Horror auto-toxicus* is woken by strong feeling. I hadn't understood. I have broken the Rules. I have risked our lives.

The fever is very high now. The world whitens and broadens until everything is a flat, white soup. White shapes dance before my eyes. I seem to hear a gong somewhere. The white is deep and welcoming, and I sink in. By the time they break down the door, I don't know names or anything else. Cold, cold.

CHARLES DANFORTH

3 October 1881

I first laid eyes on Alonso the day we laid knives to our cadavers. Memory has played a curious trick in the intervening twenty years, for I recall it as if it were a tintype; the image is inert and dull colored—perhaps because the memory lives in my intellect and understanding, rather than in my eyes.

There was no horror in that room. I was put in mind of York Minster, which I have seen once, and the cool effigies that lie there in the sanctified air. The corpses were washed and bound in cheesecloth. There was little in the waxy figures before us to revolt. They lay like brides, each on their bier, the white forms barred by a little sunshine that strayed through the high windows of that echoing hall.

We set to work, with the stentorian tones of the lecturer in our ears. We began on a leg. The shape, the roundness of the calf, the muscles preserved so tight and solid beneath the waxy skin—there is a peculiar pleasure to it. The knife went in; the dermis and layers of muscle were revealed like a flower, petal by petal. There were such colors and shapes; I had not known. The muscle is a rich, purpled red, encased in marbled flesh the color of a baked salmon. The sinews and tendons are white with a yellowish tinge. The component parts lie tight together in symmetry, as if designed by a master craftsman, bound and run through by the lacework of corded vessels. The graceful long saphenous vein, from which other veins branch like winter trees against the sky. The rippling surface of the gastrocnemius muscle.

I was bemused by the vomiting and the distress that was engendered in my fellows. Unclothed, these forms retained their modesty. They were not awesome but simply the carcasses of men, sloughed away when need for them was done. The corpses were strongly preserved in formaldehyde; their flesh bore little relation to that of a living being. There could be no kinship to oneself: I could not think *There but for grace go I* or *One day I shall lie thus.* Perhaps I should have thought these things. Perhaps I was too sure and young to truly understand the condition of these cold figures, which submitted to the outrage of our knives.

Afterward, we sought the Lamb and Flag like hounds. Those of our party were seized by hilarity, commensurate to their previous unease. These young men shed their fear and talked loudly and bravely. Beer went down, and so did gin. Faces grew rosier, lips wetter, eyes brighter; their memories of the blood and the bones and the delicate layers of subcutaneous flesh were transmuted, and the company waxed lewd.

Presently, we were increased by a party fresh released from their lectures at Pall Mall East, and there was further frantic passage to and fro between tables and bar; we were busy as rats in an old cheese loft. One Irish gentleman whose name I cannot now summon besought me in plaintive accents to lay bets for the bare-knuckle fight in the yard later.

"For we have not enough entries, Danforth, for a book, and it is

Murchison, you know, fighting against a Black, and the Black is sure enough to win."

I demurred, for I have always abhorred and avoided all forms of gaming and violence; here, the two were promised to be mingled in fine anarchy. My finances were somewhat straitened anyhow. I could not have paid my shot. He would not relent, however, and shouted that not for nothing were we drinking in the "Buckets of Blood" (for this was the casual name given to the establishment in which we sat). We were to see a little fisticuffs and make up a book, so that he may buy ribbons for his little sister after all! The mention of ribbons had the happy effect of diverting his talk, and he began then to describe a house he had patronized the night before, with entertainments I would not believe, he assured me. He began to tell me a tale of a pair of little twins, as perfect as they could be, who would do something with a live snake, but as he went on, his urgency and his consonants would not ally together with the drink he had taken. His breath carried an odor of halibut and sorrow. It was no trouble to get away now, and presently, I saw him collapsed on a settle, mouth open, forelock damp, sleeping like a child.

As the sun fell, the light grew orange and straightened its beams through the casements. Without, ladies had begun to show themselves in the street, fresh from their couches, to take the evening air. Through the rippled glass, there could be seen gloved hands and the pale silk of dresses. They did not linger by the house, and I cannot blame them for it. I imagine our hullabaloo could be heard perfectly well as far as Covent Garden.

One man alone I observed, who sat quiet and played with a penny on the rim of his glass, producing a tuneful sound, never loud enough to attract notice, but so that the gathering became accustomed to the gentle noise running beneath the babble. I thought he had arrived with the others only that minute, then I thought I had seen him in the hall that morning.

This man was sallow and vast. His hair stood up at the back of his neck like the ruff of a bird. His linen was ragged at the collars and stained with ink, which also covered his hands like blemishes. He hunched in the settle chair like a crouching beast; he was fixed on his task, which he performed with movements that were precise and small. The great fingers manipulated the penny with a dexterity that confounded the eye, ran supple and light around the dirty rim. An image, a memory perhaps, arose unbidden to the surface of my mind: of him holding a knife, face solemn in the dim air.

No, I thought, he had not, after all, been with us this morning, for I was sure I would have noted him. I shook my head to clear it of the heavy punch fumes and moved closer under the cover of the shrieks. One bright spark had donned the tavern madam's bonnet and was discoursing in a theatrical voice on her "pullets" and "spiced wares" for sale. This was enough distraction for the company, who rocked with laughter.

As I moved my stool, I was clumsy and made a business of it. The wooden legs screeched on the flags; the penny man lifted his eye to mine. It was that of a blackbird, bright and deep. Like a glimpse of the bottom of a well. His finger sent the coin singing once more around the rim.

"They hear it," he said, "but they do not mark it. It is a constant; they have accustomed themselves. But if I increase the pitch so"—he poured ale into the glass, and it sang out higher—"and so on, eventually, the glass will shatter. That, they will note. There will be a great fussing with cloths and restitution and a new glass, as if it were a surprise. But the warning has been sounding"—he made the glass sing again—"all along. Do you understand?"

"I do not, I confess." I was held by the lights that moved in his eyes.

"It is so that death sits beside us every day, until it is forced upon our notice. Until the vessel breaks open and life flows out, we must be blind and deaf to its presence, or we could not conduct our carnival as we do."

He gestured at the youth who entertained the company. That individual was now bright red. The bonnet lay askew over one eye, and he had begun a series of high kicks, as the Parisian dancing girls do. The penny man regarded this with kindness, but absently, as if it were an effort by a child to imagine a giraffe when they have not seen one.

He went on, "But there are some who choose to listen to the song of mortality, which underlies it, lies beneath everything—the long note beneath the cacophony. For those who can hear death, whistling always, underneath, who do not fear him, but see his part in the music"—he grasped my arm as if in sympathy—"for them, it is a vocation of the loneliest, and the highest order."

We looked on one another. The finger turned, and the glass whistled its distress. The pitch soared and enclosed us in its sphere.

"It will break," I said.

"Ah. Not it," he said. "Not yet."

I offered him my hand, then, and told him my name.

The memories of one's youth are potent. Twenty years—but our talk, the sensations are there, as fresh as if preserved in aspic. How will it be when I am confronted with the man? I expect to find Alonso changed; I expect to find him the same.

Somehow, I think his years in Italy will not have altered him too much; he was always of a Mediterranean temperament. Ludicrous, but I am somewhat shy at the thought of our meeting. We meant so much to one another then.

I am eager for the journey to pass, which it is doing slowly. The rather circuitous and testing two thirty-five from Paddington! I cannot see the point of it—stop, start, stop, start—and no one gets on or off for the better part of three hours. We call at station after station, vacant in the sunshine. Box: no living soul. Nailsea: similarly deserted. And so on.

There is great pleasure in a new diary. (Although this resembles more a ledger that clerks write in. I prefer it so; there is more space to a page.) The paper is smooth and virgin. It smells unaccountably, but not unpleasantly, of turpentine. The cover has a soft shine and a pleasing stiffness to the boards. I am a great believer in clinical observation. I have a row of ledgers on the shelf by the window at Marylebone Lane, containing records of cases of particular interest or anything I think may be suitable for publication. I keep a small brown moleskin notebook in which I jot down any little thing that occurs to me. However, in my haste this morning—for I did not rest well and rose late—I left my own, familiar diary on the nightstand. I can picture the book where it sits, the green cover worn soft and stained a little with bromide, propped in front of my Sunday collar studs, to the left of my tooth powder. Bereft! I had intended this ledger for proper observation and records, not for my own maunderings; it will have to serve for both.

Reading this over, the knowledge is forced upon me that I have left behind also the tooth powder. D--n.

Once more, we slow. Where in heavens do we halt now? Minety. Deserted. As deserted as the *Mary Celeste*.

I neglected to bring reading matter. My wrinkled railway timetable invites me to purchase an "invisible peruke." I am asked to consider whether I would not like to acquire, for the sum of twenty shillings, an illustrated compendium of British moths. I am offered Parr's Life Pills, which "clear from the body all hurtful impurities, promote appetite, aid digestion, purify the blood, and keep the bowels regular."

This is famous news. I can retire from my profession.

Upon my return, I *must* put my mind to finding new lodgings. Mrs. Healey's conscience is as stiff and unworkable as her knees. I pay the woman thirty shillings a week for food and board! If I were sensible, I would buy out some country practitioner, find a wife, and spend the remainder of my years tending to small farmers, landed gentry, and the cottage hospital.

Yes, by rights, I should go out of the town, be rural and comfortable. And yet, I know I will not but will merely pass from one Mrs. Healey to another. Why does London hold me so? Very well. Let me diagnose.

It is not a reasoned thing but a series of impressions. The bite of the fog, the bawling of the street peddler, early on a January morning, the smell and bustle of the wharf—these things thrill my blood in the way that the first drink affects those addicted to spirituous liquors. The straining limbs of the thin mud larks, the shouts of the Covent Garden sellers, the *basso profundo* calls of the bargemen to one another—they are elixir to me.

Perhaps these sights and sounds have a greater value, in that they remind me how far I have come from my beginnings. If I could, I would excise Grimstock from the face of England, even from remembrance. I cannot put enough distance between myself and That Place. The place of my birth: a small village in Lancashire where folk still leave saucers of milk outside their doors on Samhain. Were He not everywhere, I would say that God does not know Grimstock. Where bare living is scratched from the hard, black land, where the wind moans and cuts your face. The people die young and bitter. It is a place that chills the heart and mind.

Not long. Two hours, a little more. I feel the beginning of an appetite. Travel is a great strain on the person. It produces fatigue, the migraine, or nausea; in me, it also produces hunger. With Alonso, I will have days of good wine and good food. For myself, I am content with a simple life, but it does not mean that I hold such things in contempt. Yes, it will be a pleasant respite from Mrs. Healey's tender mercies. I recall some trick of Alonso's cook, most successful, with juniper berries and a teal duck.

I will try to compose myself for sleep now, so as to be alert for my arrival. If rest eludes me, I shall watch the fields pass until dusk falls and be content.

Later

Rawblood

I disembarked at Exeter in a state of confusion, having fallen into a deep sleep. My bewilderment drew comment from a robust country child who stood on the platform, throwing stones at the sky. I regret to say that his observations earned him a sharp clip on the ear. While taking careful inventory of my belongings, I was tapped on the shoulder and saw that Shakes was there to greet me. I would not have thought he still lived; to me, he looked old when I was young. But the eyes of youth see nothing as it is.

Shakes has worked in Alonso's service for so many years that some familiarity of manner is only to be expected, but he shook my hand like an acquaintance as he took my portmanteau. I hid my perturbation.

As it is a considerable distance to Rawblood, I settled myself with the hot brick at my feet and resigned myself to the last part of my journey. I was not concerned; on a clear night with a full moon, one may drive as safely across Dartmoor as in daylight.

We drove through a cool evening, scented with grass and the honeyed tang of heather, and my spirits rose somewhat. I do believe that the air in this part of the world carries with it healthful properties. Familiar shapes rose from the dark. There was Hamel Down. And there was Hay Tor. The stones at Scorehill could be seen on the crest of a hill beyond. This is grand country, soft and carved by age. With each mile, my heart lifted. I am not fond of rural places in general, but these hills hold the imprint of affection. I have missed this land. I have missed my friend. His letter was a welcome peace offering indeed.

The carriage lamps picked out the eyes of startled rabbits as we went, and I began to consider my dinner once more. Alonso was in times past particularly fond of a kind of rabbit stew.

We came to a halt. I peered out but could discern no lights nor anything familiar. Shakes appeared at the carriage door with my portmanteau.

"What?" I cried. "Is something amiss? Have we lost a wheel, or has one of the leaders cast a shoe?"

"Naw," he said in that lackadaisical way he has. "We be 'ere."

I descended from the carriage and saw that we were, indeed, before the house, which was plunged into darkness, only the starlight reflected in the windows.

"But what is this? Is your master from home?"

"'Appen 'e's wurkin' still. Oi'll take vese up doirect, an' sh'ye whar ye boide," said Shakes. (I am having the greatest trouble rendering his speech on the page; it is both more menacing, and more sweet, with that West Country air, than I can suggest. Perhaps it is best that I leave aside any attempt to do so? He suffers also from a lack of teeth, which does not aid communication.)

"But am I not expected?"

"Y'are, but oi wager 'e's fergat." (No, I really must abandon any attempt to record Shakes verbatim. It looks like pure nonsense.)

I thought of the welcome I had in this house in the past. Blazing fires, an easy chair, hot Devon cider. And then there was Alonso himself. Bearlike and jovial, he was the warmest and most attentive of hosts. Forgotten? And by Alonso?

I stumbled on the drive. In the light of the carriage lamps, I saw its state: weeds had sprung up here and there, and bare patches had been gouged in the gravel surface. I called my host's name, but there being no reply, I followed Shakes toward the darkened house.

There was some difficulty with the door, which did not want to give. It is of the old kind: large and heavy, bound with straps and knobs of iron, like buboes. It yielded at last with a screeching that tried my patience.

"You will want to take some mutton grease to that hinge," I told Shakes. He said some or other local thing.

When we gained entry, the air was bad and cold. I followed Shakes through the darkened halls. The lamp fell on objects of a sudden, giving them a surprised and strange look, as though they had been doing something furtive in the dark and had only resumed their immobility that instant for our benefit. We went on, the fellow setting matches to lamps, fires, and tapers with his wizened hand. I must take up the matter of gas lamps with Alonso. It is surely perverse, in this day and age, to live in this antediluvian, tallow-and-wax fashion. Can gas be had in the countryside?

As we progressed farther into the house, away from the air and the friendly night, I became prey to a strange illusion: Rawblood was behind me when I looked, known and welcoming, but when I looked ahead, there lay a shadowed and alien dwelling, which I did not know.

We came to the door of my chamber. The lamp played upon the lintel and cast a little bright circle before it into the place beyond. Something fled from the edge of the light.

I stopped Shakes. "There is someone within," I said as quietly as I was able, barely breathing the words. "Oh, where is a stick, man, or any kind of weapon?"

Shakes looked at me in a blank, stupid fashion. He shrugged and seemed not to understand, for he went into the room, and I was forced to follow after. With the quick, sharp scratch of a match, the candelabra was lit. He and I regarded one another in the dubious light. We were alone.

I tutted. "Well," I said, "it must have been a rat, or some animal…" I was upset, for I cannot abide a rat. It is most unsanitary.

When we had settled my things and made the room bright and good, I turned to Shakes and said, "Take me to him now, please."

He grunted and led me out; to my surprise, we went along the servants' passage and stairs to the kitchen. And here, at last, there was warmth and some sign of occupation. Lamps were lit, though turned low, and a pot steamed on the hearth, giving out the soothing perfume of sage and gravy.

But we did not stop. On through the scullery and down the cellar stairs. We were then in the bowels of the building; the house rests, as it were, upon a warren of little corridors. These are of thick stone, which elongates and yet muffles sound in a peculiar way. I shook my head as we went, for I had a buzz in my head, due no doubt to the fatigue of the day, and to hunger.

The lamp shone on the stone walls, which were wet in places. The flags beneath our feet were very worn. I believe that the cellars here are extensive, for there are side chambers here and there, and the passages are hung throughout with iron hooks and struts, such as those that hold barrels and casks. The singing in my head grew stronger, and I motioned for Shakes to stop.

"I cannot," I said. "I believe that the air is not good. I have a ringing in my ears."

He grasped my arm then, which I found distressing. He said something that seemed to suggest that Alonso was not far off, but I was out of all patience.

"Leave go, if you please. I will await abovestairs." Then the man pulled me along. I could not credit it. He seized my arm with a tutting, as if at a recalcitrant donkey, and hauled me to the end of the corridor. I was outraged, but this scarce had room in my head, for the humming had risen to fill it.

As we rounded the corner, I saw light and a chamber ahead. I brushed Shakes from my arm and went to the entrance.

The light was dazzling, white and strange, shocking after the dark passage. It was some time before my eyes would serve me, but what met them was a welcome sight.

I guessed that this had been the largest cellar; it had vaulted ceilings and clean, lime-washed walls. The air was cool and clean. The flags were swept clear, and lamps were set at intervals in niches. The source of the humming was now apparent; a generator squatted blackly in the corner. And the room: well, I was at home of a sudden.

It was laid out according to our old schema: the laboratory. Alonso being right-handed, the shelves were on the right. The compartment that holds each bottle was packed with straw to prevent movement. A soft leather case of metal syringes sat atop a measuring glass.

On the left was my domain. For I am what was once called *sinistral*; my left hand is dominant. It was a cause for some rallying between Alonso and myself in the old days. His tools and mine lay together, two feet apart, on green baize. The kymograph, for tracing the tiny variations, the language of blood pressure. Alonso reads those delicate lines on the paper as fluently as he does English. The hemacytometer, by which I delve into the microscopic kingdom of blood, to count the cells.

There were the sheaves of gelatin for growing cultures and racks of blank slides with their wooden surrounds. In the center of the room were two scrubbed slabs, securely bolted to packing cases filled with sandbags. From the corner came gentle rustling, and the glint of eyes could be seen in the depths behind screens of wire.

It was a replica of our old workroom, needing only the tall windows and moldering velvet curtains for the illusion to be complete. For there was Alonso, head lowered, his eyes upon a pipette, the contents of which he was transferring to a screen. I waited for this delicate operation to be completed and then called to him. We went eagerly to one another.

The intervening years were nothing. We halloed and shook hands mightily. But when he turned to me in the strange light, I was forced to quick dissimulation, hard put to refrain from crying out. Many thoughts at once jostled for expression, and in this state, I told him the first that broke the surface proper.

"I am all amazement," I said. "Is it an electric light?"

It was a different world in the warm parlor, with a mug in my hand and a rug on my legs. I first demurred at the rug; he insisted. I again made to refuse, but here we each caught the other's eye and chuckled at our politeness. We are no longer twenty, and one must preserve one's health.

I thought to amuse him with my imagined intruder and told the story, I think, well, making great play of Shakes's indifference and of my own fear. The effect on him was extraordinary. The levity left him at once. He rose some way in his seat and took my forearm in a grip like iron. A shadow crossed his face, like a wave across a ragged shore. I had a conviction that, for a moment, there lay under his features the face of another man entirely…

"Did you see the eyes?" he asked between his teeth.

"Alonso!" I exclaimed, and my hand shook, spilling good drops of cider on the very good Aubusson at my feet. And then it was Alonso, with his habitual, kindly demeanor, who leaned over me.

He sighed and said, "The cellar is no place for a man to work long hours. I must keep it very brightly lit, and I think it shortens my temper. You will forgive me, Charles."

I agreed. It was foolishness, of course: the combined effect of worry, travel, and warm cider on my constitution, which is unsuited to all three.

Alonso broke in on these reflections quietly. "Of late, I have been prey to the many anxieties of a solitary man. The truth is, I am glad of you, Charles."

"You sound almost ashamed to own it! Am I the cavalry?"

He laughed and said that he was not, and that I was. And then he thought of dinner, which was laid in the adjoining parlor. I was glad of it and found as we passed through that I could detect the scent of rabbit gravy in the air.

He said, "We must wait upon ourselves. Shakes cannot help us, for he must see to the safe disposal of my equipment for the night. There are no other servants here at present."

"It is forced upon one's notice," I agreed, lifting a dusty hand from the doorframe and applying my handkerchief. "May I ask why?"

He smiled in his ruined face, and we sat. It came to me in an uncomfortable fashion that he perceived exactly my distaste at the sad alteration that had taken place in him.

I gave myself rabbit and, in a fit of distraction, took too much, which then I felt obliged to eat.

"Now," I said, aiming to recover, "have you dismissed them all in a rage? Or did you consider that the housekeeper looked tired, and you gave them all a year's leave?"

The two scenarios were equally likely, my friend being of a mercurial temper, loving and detesting in equal measures. His capacity for analysis and for feeling is larger than that of any other man of my acquaintance.

Alonso took his seat. "Neither," he said. "I found that, after my return from Siena, they no longer cared to stay."

Over the repast, we talked commonplaces. I regaled him with tales of our old acquaintance—mutual acquaintance no longer, I fear, since he had neatly severed himself from England, and from friends, for twenty years. He said little. I do not think he took much interest in my reflections and little bits of news, but they plugged the silence, and I was pleased enough with them for that.

Under cover of this light talk, I took the opportunity to observe my host. I was prey to no small unease. Why his servants should choose to depart, I could not think, and he would not be drawn on the subject. He nursed a glass of wine but did not drink. His answers regarding his scientific preoccupations were brusque. When I questioned him, he seemed to pause to listen to an inner voice and then diverted me from the subject with a bluntness that bordered on the discourteous. He is not unlike himself, but magnified, as if all the brightness and the darkness in him is refracted through a lens.

He is a large man, as I have intimated, with a great deal of that black hair that is always too long for tidiness standing upon his head at an angle. He does everything at a great pace and prefers to be occupied with two tasks at once. I have seen him scratching an equation with one hand, while with the other, he feeds a kitten with a cloth soaked in milk. He is often impatient with others of his species but tenderhearted with dumb things. When it is required that they must be sacrificed in the course of his work, he does not demur, however; beneath his sentiment, he has the level temperament required by our profession.

I was not surprised at his motley appearance; I think his shirt was torn in two places, his shoes laced with strings of different colors. In that way, he is as he ever was. Although careless of his attire—his collars are always ragged and his hats often dented—he used to be a man precise in his movements, quick and careful, and there is a great change in him in this respect. I noted how he slumped in his chair, consuming his food carelessly and, I might add, with no regard to mess. This unwonted indifference gave me pause, but there is a more disturbing change in his form.

One constant remains: his eyes. They are large, and as he is accustomed to be healthy, the whites are very pale and provide a strong contrast to the iris, whose natural color is black, or a very dark brown. They retain that peculiar illusion of being lit from within. A fine, clear eye, in summary, which incidentally has no need of spectacles.

I will cease to fuss about and bring myself to the kernel of this; I should say he *was*, not *is* a large man. Though still impressive in stature, Alonso is miserably diminished. He presents a wasted appearance; his skin in places is almost translucent, the architecture of his wrists and neck so clearly apparent that I suffered a moment of shock whenever he leaned into the candlelight... His face is as of bone. To be seated beside him... Well, it was like eating my dinner with a dead man. I know not how else to express my horror. I looked on him and was both revolted and ashamed at once. For I should offer him my understanding and place my skills at his disposal, not shrink from him as though he were a bogey that little children dream of.

Had I not encountered him in his own house, had I not been led to him and told *Here, this is Alonso*, I would not have known him.

When the plates were clear, he pushed back his chair and regarded me.

"I must wonder," I said, "what is the nature of my visit?"

"How long do you make your stay with me, Charles?"

"As long as you would have me, for my part! But I have made arrangements for one week."

He hissed between his teeth. "It is not much," he said, "not much time." He seemed to speak to himself more than to me, and I knew not what to answer. But presently, he came out of his reverie and rose. "We must use it well, then." He winced as he lifted his emaciated length from the chair.

"Why have you come back, Alonso? Truthfully?" The question burst from me. I had not known I was going to ask it.

He smiled. "Come, we will drink to one another, and to old friendship."

Cravenly, I followed his lead and did not pursue it. I thought I knew the answer to my question, and I was afraid to hear it from his lips. *I have come home to die.*

When we were settled once more in the easy chairs and with another cider safely in my hand, I went once more unto the breach, recalling to him an idea we had had, of applying mercury to alleviate Paget's disease.

"I made no progress on *that* matter," he said. He yawned. "I had quite forgotten some of the peculiar starts we used to indulge."

I said, "Please choose a topic for discussion, Alonso, since you will not be frank with me! Perhaps you think that I am some official, come with forms and regulations. Or the boot is on the other leg! You do not care to have another at your shoulder, peering at your methods. I can assure you, Alonso, that I am no thief of other men's thoughts. I will keep away from the cellar during my stay."

I had a flush in my face from the fire. I attended to my brow with a handkerchief.

He hid his eyes. I thought that perhaps he wept, but when he showed his face to me, it was one of merriment. My temper cooled somewhat. Alonso was not himself.

"Oh, I feel like myself again!" he said. "I was right—to send, as you say, for the cavalry! No, I do not fear your scrutiny, or the machinations of a rival." He turned toward the fire then, and in its warm light, I saw again how tightly the flesh clung to his bones.

"It is not that I do not wish you with me. I should be glad. I am not ashamed to say that I had hoped… For your talents fit the purpose, like a glove. You must know"—here he placed his index finger lightly on mine; for a moment, it rested like a butterfly on my knuckle—"that the English journals can be had abroad, even in Italy. Even, Charles, the journal of the Royal Microscopical Society, containing your treatise. I find that you are a coming man."

I had not thought that Alonso would read such poor things as my offerings to those minor papers. Did I blush? I sincerely hope I did not; I cannot deny that I was moved. Such a little thing it was, on the relation of Thames water to the Whitechapel cholera epidemic. Kindly received in some specialist circles, to be sure, but creating no *stir*…

He went on, "I would not wish you to leap before looking. It is lonely work, as you will recall, and it takes a strong stomach." He creased his brows. "So, we come to the crux of the matter. I should hesitate to ask this of you. And yet here it is—*I do ask*. I beg you," he said. "Do not fence about with me any longer. Do you not know why I have come back? You must know," he said.

"You are ill," I said. My heart rose bitter in my throat.

He grimaced, his white face creased like paper. "Yes. As you observe, I am. It is an old family affliction. It has dogged the Villarcas since… well, since there were Villarcas, I suppose."

"Perhaps," I said, as caustic as I could manage, "you might be a touch more specific. I am, after all, a doctor."

"I have seen all the doctors. Let it be. I am here because I had need to see Rawblood again. To touch its walls once more, warm from the sun. To feel my house breathe about me in the night. Rawblood and the Villarcas are one in ways that perhaps I cannot fully explain. If I am to die, I will do it here." There was silence for a moment, and then he said, "But that is not all, Charles. Why have I asked you here? In your heart, you know."

"I will not guess, Alonso."

"I have come back to revive the work."

It seemed to me then that in that darkened room, the shades of what we had known and done together lay in the long gabled shadows and played about the flickering edges of the fire. The past was all about us, strong as wine. I closed my eyes and spoke firmly—not to the wreck that sat so quietly in the chair opposite my own, but across the years, to the man I knew then. "It is a sad fact that a man cannot recapture his past," I said. "We cannot be as we were."

"Nor would I wish it," he answered me tranquilly.

No, I thought, *it is I who wish for it, that you, at the least, could be restored.*

I said, "I do not know that I would have the heart for such things now. I think that we were wild young men." Even in saying so, I moved myself ever closer to his mind. For we began to settle in our old parts: his to lead, and mine to caution.

Alonso made a steeple of his hands. He leaned toward me. The light moved over the young eyes, the ravaged face.

"*Une longue et affreuse cuisine,*" he said. "Do you remember?"

"Yes."

"Do you indeed?"

I did not know how to answer him.

He went on, "Your French was always execrable. A tonic, then, for your memory: the science of life is a superb and dazzlingly lighted hall, which may be reached only by passing through a long and ghastly kitchen." Alonso regarded me, turning his ring on his little finger. It is a peculiar thing for a man to wear: fine and gold, set with white and red stones. It looks made for a lady's hand, an engagement band perhaps. Most men would not wear it. Fire caught the gems. Motes of light threw themselves across the darkened walls. He did not press me; he knows better. Only the muted grumblings of the fire and cheerful trickle of cider from jug to cup intruded on our silence. I knew myself to be in Rawblood, but other places moved before my inner eye, places that were peopled by my younger selves, suffused with other desires. A tonic for my memory, indeed. I have but one Father, who art in heaven; the earthly one that was, I do not consider. But it was Alonso who taught me how to reason, to see wherein lay our purpose beyond toil, dirt, and suffering. It was Alonso who raised me from the childhood of my thought.

So I rose and took a candle. With it, I went to his kitchen. It was in darkness now and smelled of cold fat. The shadows fell thickly everywhere in the guttering light; nevertheless, I found what I sought and returned holding it before me.

Alonso smiled when he saw the knife. I may say I laughed too. I made the old pledge—pricking my finger and handing the blade to him. He did the same. We saluted with bleeding fingers and pressed the mouths of the wounds together. We sat there both, two men in our middle years, clutching our fingers and grinning like schoolboys. He sighed, as one does when pain is relieved.

"Will you swear," he asked, "not to bring any person near Rawblood? Especially into the house. We cannot have local gossip dining out on us."

"I cannot think I will have occasion—"

"Swear it, Charles."

"Very well," I said. "I swear!" There was a peculiar sensation at the base of my neck, akin to effervescence; my mind was unclear, and my thoughts moved as clouds do, quick and light, through my skull: the emptiness of the house, the shadow I had seen in my chamber. I looked on my friend, and it seemed that his face was what it had been when we were young, and then there sat before me once more a ruined stranger.

It became apparent to me at this juncture that I was drunk. I must have said something to this effect to Alonso, for I heard his voice drifting up to me from a great distance, and he seemed to be speaking of cider.

"For a West Country man, I have an unpatriotic indifference to it; I cannot stomach it. However, it is said in the village that the apples were small and bitter last year, and that may account for its strength. Is it not to your taste? I will give you port."

"No, no, it is very good..." I took another draft, which exacerbated matters, and said carefully, "I fear I do not have the head I used to."

"For the best, perhaps. I would that you slept soundly tonight."

I thought how good he was, and how careful of me. He was ever so. Moved, I drained my mug. I heard him murmur, but I could not catch it.

My head began to gradually detach itself, or so it seemed, from my body. When I made to describe this interesting sensation to Alonso, he looked at me strangely, and it became apparent to me that I had giggled, and muttered, but said nothing. I judged it time to take my leave.

As I mounted the stairs in a meandering fashion, I was troubled by a stray thought that demanded that I sit: I cannot recall it. It was a conviction of the firmest order. Thankfully, in good time, I rose and dismissed the matter.

"Men are whole," I said to myself, "only in the company of other congenial men." I was favorably impressed with this epigram and repeated it several times. It spurred me as far as my room.

There was business to be attended to there. The furniture seemed to have lost its definition, moving and dancing so as to turn up in just the right place for a man to bark his shins on it. *What a to-do,* I said to myself as I clutched my aggrieved leg. But I made shift and wrestled myself out of my clothes and into a nightgown. With a negligence that is quite unlike me, I neglected to speak my prayers. I fell, slowly and long, toward white linen and coverlets and the hot brick that warmed the whole, and passed straight through them into a fair, where a fellow with the head of a bear was attempting to persuade me to marry his sister, while I expressed my urgent desire to shave him of his fur and return him, I said, to the state of man.

4 October

The sunlight pours in through the leaden panes, giving affront to my aching head. I am once more abed, for as well as pain, I am suffering from an excess of impressions, at which I grasp, fruitlessly, through the dull fog that lies behind my eyes.

I awoke this morning to nausea, my vision uncertain. The neuralgic headache, my old enemy, was hard upon me. I have been prey to it since I was young. Headache is the symptom of numerous afflictions; in most instances, the cause of the difficulty is to be found not in the head but in various organs of the body. It is a doctor's bane, in that it is the commonest of maladies, yet debilitating, and it has as many causes as there are diseases of the body or mind. In me, it descends abruptly, like a hawk, when my nervous system is overset by excitement, or travel, or alcoholic drink. In this particular case, all three were at work, and I was not surprised.

Sometimes, air will dispel it, though the effort of getting out into it and staying there with that brass band playing within one's skull is repulsive to the sufferer...

To that end, I rose and went out of the house and into the garden, which gives on to the moor. I avoided the front of the house. I had a desire for solitude. The day is crisp, and white clouds pass busily about in a blue sky, as if to confirm that far above us is a world of intention and great moment, of which we paltry creatures know nothing.

I thought of Meg. The presence of trees, grass, and wide horizons seemed to bring her closer; when I am in the city, the odor and the hubbub come between us, and I cannot call her to mind. I cannot summon her face, for the pattern I have is one blurred with the round-ness of infancy, the character overlaid with that lisping winsome qual-ity that all little girls share. She will be sixteen next summer, and I will choose for her some bauble or ribbon and send it to her, and that will be that. I have not laid eyes on her for twelve years. She may have grown into any kind of a young woman. She is my sister, but I might pass her in the lane tomorrow and know no better. I am ashamed to say that I prefer it so. By report, she is unmanageable. It must be thought on, for she is assuredly no longer a child, and something must be done.

I will take this opportunity to describe the house, for I saw it at good advantage today from a gentle rise by the drive, warm in the sun, which played over the ancient diamond panes.

To a modern eye, the building is barbarous, having none of the cleanliness of line and purpose with which the wise builders of today fashion their work. The angles all disagree, many windows are inserted in the stone front in a dashing sort of way, and it crumbles at the edges here and there. It is very *low* Elizabethan, the roof adorned liberally with gables and that sort of thing, which gives it a peculiarly imposing silhouette.

The house is not high, stretching to three floors only, and from above, it seems to cling to the ground, lending the building an air of perma-nence and solidity. I have found it a place of comfort in the past—it lends one's thoughts wings and one's heart ease. It has stood during ages, through terrible storms and high winds. I am not as well apprised of the history of these parts as I should be, but I imagine that it has withstood battles also, those tempests that are made by man. It seems evident from the very name of the place that this is so.

The two wings extend back from the front, creating a U shape, and they form a partial courtyard behind which is a haven from the worst of the moorland bluster. I recall that Alonso ordered it cleared many years ago to make a rose garden. In doing the work, the men's hoes struck often against some ancient and curious piece of machinery, half buried in the black Dartmoor earth. There were uncovered some fragments of tile and coins, a rudimentary system of lead pipes, the remains of a fire iron and wooden shoe. These accoutrements of the quotidian become bizarre when viewed at the remove of centuries.

The garden that was put there was an agreeable arbor, forming a perfect palette of color. Pink Duchesse de Brabant roses flourished in particular, and the nodding of their pale heads against the old walls and verdant paths was a pleasant thing to see on a summer evening. Odd (I am considering many things odd today, but so it is) that a man of Alonso's character should have conceived such an idea as a rose garden. But he is full of oddities.

I am sorry to record that the garden is now turned to wilderness. Nettles and furze combat each other in a vigorous tussle for supremacy. Brush and bramble abound. The sparse patches of dry grass that remain uncovered are dwarfish and doddered. Instead of damask and blush and crimson, the place is colored with the villainous yellow of ragweed. It is a complete briar patch and a perfect breeding ground for vermin. I will mention to Alonso a ratting dog.

It has always struck me as strange that Rawblood, this little piece of England, should be the property of one who is not truly English. I have heard the account of how my friend came by his complexion, his name, and his house. The Hopewells are Alonso's maternal ancestors. A violent, hot-blooded line. Rawblood was theirs. But they lost through imprudence—a wager, I believe—and the family scattered and dwindled. Many years later, a Spanish nobleman heard a young woman, the last of the Hopewells, speak sadly of the end of her family and her lost childhood home. Greatly moved, he searched the county end to end, purchased the house, and gave her back the deeds—just to see her smile. They married later, of course, and so their son Alonso is half a Spaniard, half a Devon man. That is how Rawblood came to the Villarcas.

It is a pretty romance containing, as all good romances do, great tragedy. Alonso and I both were orphaned young.

Looking at the house in the yellow light of this autumn morning, I thought it did not seem an ill inheritance, though it was bought with pain. I traced the familiar lineaments of windows, doors, and corners, my eye resting lazily on the geometry of the casements, the furtive ivy that laid thin tendrils up the walls. The sun was higher now, and I removed my hat. The air was sweet, and the breeze blew by me, and I began to feel that the pain flew away with them little by little, and I became playful. I kicked a stone, dallied with it, passed it from foot to foot, strolling to and fro on the sward.

Standing on that rise, clutching the weathered brim of my hat, the dew creeping into my boots (badly in want of a mend), I felt at peace. I may have spread my arms wide, to take in the morning. I am sure I closed my eyes and removed my shirt collar. The air played about my face, and the call of wood pigeons rose from the coppice behind.

It seemed to me then, as I stood on that little knoll in an obscure corner of Devonshire, that I could see England spread before me, in dense, bright fields, bound by ancient hedgerows of rowan and hawthorn; in high, bare moors and cushions of heather; in little cobbled towns where the mills still turn in the old way and carts make their way to market in the morning under the early stars; in dark lakes and high peaks, where red kites circle—all the work of the Creator wrought in infinite symmetry.

"Who is like unto thee, O Lord, among the gods? Who is like thee, glorious in holiness, fearful in praises, doing wonders?"

—EXODUS 15:11

As the clouds scudded for a moment over the sun, my eye was caught by a movement at a window. I peered, and obligingly, the clouds gathered closer over the day. I saw a pale face looking at me, oddly bisected by those diamond panes. There was that peculiar illusion created by dark clothes that the head was suspended in air. My reverie was observed!

To think oneself alone and surrender to whatever vagaries of thought are presently occupying one, to perhaps scratch one's head and whistle a tune only ever heard in the imagination—only to realize that, all the while, there have been eyes to see and a mind to judge—it is not a pleasant experience. In this instance, I felt cold, as if I had one minute past swallowed a chip of ice. With a violence that is quite unlike me, I shook my fist at my audience, my anger, I am sure, writ clear upon my face. Pain renewed itself around the plates of my skull.

They were gone as soon as looked at, in a flash of pallor. No features were discernible; there had been some kind of hat, which hid them in shadow, and yet, I received a strong impression of disdain.

I counted the windows from the corner, determined to remonstrate with whatever housemaid could be so remiss as to look on me so. I counted and counted again, for it seemed impossible that my outrage could be so neatly justified. Once more, I numbered them: one, two, three, four. There could be no mistake. The intruder had gazed upon me from my own room.

My host was knocking mud from his boots as I came to the door. I found this homely and peaceful action enervating, out of reason. Alonso should control his household better; he must ensure that his servants do *not* peer at people through windows.

We went in together, he unhurried and I stalking ahead in my offense, stumbling a little in the dark hall, my eyes unprepared for the change of light.

"How did you rest?" he asked. "One of those d--ned birds has got in again." He swore again and batted with his hand at a small, dark shape that sped by him.

The swallow rose and beat itself against the roof of the hall; it hammered itself against the high glass window. There was a terrific rush of air as the bird flew past me on the stairs. Such a wind, produced by so small a thing!

I arrived at my chamber precipitously and investigated it thoroughly. As was to be expected, perhaps, it was empty. My ascent had given the intruder some minutes in which to withdraw. Nothing had been disturbed—I could trace only the signs of my own occupation. The room bore still that thick quiet of recent slumber. The bedclothes lay in the tumbled disarray in which I had left them. My shirts hung in good order in the garderobe, the door slightly ajar as I had left it. A fly buzzed urgently in the casement, punctuating the silence with its efforts to penetrate the glass. Several dark hairs were tangled still in the comb, flung carelessly on the dresser. My shaving water sat, congealing, on the washstand.

And yet, I was not satisfied. There was a quality in the air, not so definite as to be called a scent, but for me an unequivocal confirmation that I had not been misled; someone had been here. I moved to the window and looked. There, I saw the sward, rising above the drive, still sunlit, where I stood moments ago. Under the cedar tree was something...a pile of earth, something...

A crudely dug rectangle scarred the vivid green. A fresh grave, not large. Long enough to hold a small woman or an older child. The sight filled me with peculiar feeling, as if all the sadness in the world had been drawn down into that spot. Memory and longing were in me. I was on the verge of recalling some monstrous secret of existence. My insides were pulled about with sadness. There was something unpleasant about it, as if these feelings belonged to someone else, and I was but a vessel for them.

But it was impossible. I had walked on that spot beneath the cedar tree not ten minutes since. The turf was unbroken then. And yet, there it lay below, before my very eyes. I caught the scent—or thought I did—of dark earth in the morning air... I bent and peered through the imperfections in the old glass. I thought I could perceive some mist there, as though it had been closely breathed upon. I thought, *I am standing where she stood; thus, she must have watched me*. It was strongly borne upon my recollection in that moment that there were no servants in the house.

A feeling of great cold descended upon me, and I felt that the window receded, that I was being drawn back, far away from the room, from the light, and from the green world outside. I was in a tunnel, whose destination was somewhere cold and black and deep. I gasped, staggered, and fell. I wriggled blindly as a worm toward the door but was defeated and lay gutted upon the dusty boards.

Slowly, orientation returned. The physical symptoms dissipated. The walls righted themselves. I raised myself up but regretted it; my insides were being stirred with a pudding spoon. I was obliged to sit on the unmade bed to recover. Consumed by a great thirst, I drank water from the ewer, holding it as weakly as a kitten. I write this reclining against the pillows like any sickroom patient. These attacks have exhausting, tintinnabulous propensities; the pounding in my head is as of a gong.

When I had recovered sufficiently, I went to find Alonso. The windows by the front door were open, letting in sweet air but also a draft. I shut them. I looked also toward the rise, where sat the tree, spreading its great limbs over the hill. The turf was smooth, unmarked. No grave, of course.

I found Alonso still at the board; or rather, a newspaper rustled in his place at the table, the sides of which were grasped by his long hands. A spiral of cigarillo smoke rose from behind the print. Cold dishes sat on the soiled cloth.

I sat, and the paper was lowered. His aspect does not improve, viewed under the morning light. We observed one another in turn, he kindly and with his head on one side, and I through the fingers of one hand, in which rested the bulbous melon I must currently term my head. I do not doubt that I presented as sorry a spectacle as he.

"You cannot complain that the swallows accept your invitation," I said, "if you leave your windows wide open."

"I did not leave them open," he said. He peered closer at me. "You have the black dog on you, I perceive." His use of our old name for the affliction was almost too much to bear; many were the times he sat by me in darkened rooms as I lay insensible. "I have chlorodyne in the house," he said.

"No doubt. It will not surprise you that I do not touch opiates. How can I say this to you?" I raised my eyes to his. "I am deeply sorry for all that passed between us then. How can you forgive? How?"

"Ah, you mean Manning's cure," he said.

"How can you smile? How?"

"Ah, *tontería*," he said. "We took our chances. *Sólo el amor*."

Alonso is rarely Spanish. Mine is but a smattering, so I may have this wrong. But I believe he said, "It was only love."

In the days when our friendship was in its infancy and we were students, consumed with idealism and ideas, Alonso and I were bound together by our fascination with all things sanguinary. With the benefit of mature reflection, I must concede that our preoccupation amounted almost to infatuation.

We kept vials and pipettes of blood and made experiments with it in the cold nights. We infected it with bacteria (we were great admirers of Pasteur, who was then only beginning to make his mark) and observed the differing effects of infection on a host, usually a cat, which after a period of observation we then had to dispose of.

We wished to analyze blood and to study it, to penetrate its secrets in the most scientific fashion, but our feeling for the stuff had a reverence in it too that bordered on the mystical. Alonso claimed he could determine the blood of a woman of the rookeries of St. Giles from a Lord's merely by working a splash of it between his fingers and from its scent. (I tested him thoroughly, using cat's blood, chicken's blood, and that from the cadaver of a young boy found in the vicinity of Seven Dials with his arm missing. Alonso was wrong on every count, but this did not deter us one whit.)

We would be the first to read the properties of blood and divine its influence on character. We were not acolytes of Blundell; we knew why his transfusions failed. He sought to replace the blood as though he were refilling a lamp. He did not treat it as part of the essence of the creature, which we knew it was.

Though I prepared the journals of those early forays into blood and bacteria for publication—they were not contemptible as research—I always refrained, dogged by a persistent hope that the matter was not done with, that we may yet bring that Work back to life and make our names. But we never returned to each other or to that subject that consumed so many waking hours of our youth—until now.

The cellar looked inoffensive on this new day and in the light of our renewed amity. All was neat, orderly, and gleaming. I felt that excitement rise in me that precedes a day's hard work, of judgment and interpretation, of recording and analysis, of straining the boundaries of our knowledge.

When I looked to Alonso, I saw the same eagerness on his face. It is so when we work side by side—we attune ourselves to each other's thoughts and moods. He grasped my arm, our pulses quickened.

"We can control airflow, and temperature, to a fraction of a degree. If I had built this above, we could not do this. And if the temperature at which these are stored and at which we work is constant—why, then the results of our labors cannot be imputed to error or to exterior forces, such as degradation. For if the environment remains a constant, the effect of exposure and temperature on the work will be calculable."

There are six cages, each containing two rabbits, and two tanks containing four frogs each. There are blood samples too, which have been taken from their hosts and contained in flasks. They are kept in a glass cabinet with a lock, and the key hangs around my friend's neck. They stand in a rank of eight, and as we work, Alonso watches them anxiously and touches them gently, holding the dark, ruby liquid to the light.

There is a stout wooden chest, bound with iron, the key to which is thick and has many wards and joins the first around Alonso's neck. This chest contains flasks also, although we do not hold them up to the light and admire their color.

When Alonso had shown me all, I gave him the appreciation due to such an undertaking.

"It is a labor that cannot fail to impress," I remarked. "All that remains to be shown me is our purpose."

He straightened his thin frame and glared at me. "Our purpose, dearest Charles? We must drag England into the nineteenth century. On the Continent, they are readying themselves for the twentieth! Virchow, Magendie, Bernard, Pasteur, Koch, Ehrlich—these are the great men of our time! You say that this is fine"—he waved an arm at the stone walls—"but it is not! We are not in a hospital—we do not occupy a laboratory in one of the great universities. No, we are working at my private expense, in my home. The frailty of English medicine is spelt out here, where we stand, in this—this *cellar*. This is where English medical research has come to live!

"In Germany, in France, in Austria, men of science are encouraged to push back the limits of our knowledge—they are supported by the state and by private philanthropy, in practice and in principle, by which I mean financially and ethically.

"In medicine, we are a nation of amateurs. And even the most gifted of those amateurs must plough through the obstructions of an insipid morality that claims itself religion. Vivisection and the need for cadavers provokes an outrage in the English breast only equaled by its arrogance. But the outrage must be faced and overcome. We will lose every-where—in medicine, in battle, in governance of the empire itself—if we do not place the progress of science highest among our aims."

I regarded him with a little censure. It is an example of the license I allow Alonso that I do not take to heart his diatribes against God and the long disquisitions against that good and patient institution, the Church of England. It was not this that gave me pause. It is a strange thing, but I have not been accustomed to regard Alonso as English. I felt a little affront, which I tried to put down, for he has the right of birth and of half his parentage, does he not? And yet.

"We can attempt something here, certainly," I said. "But it is not true that there are no coming men among us. That new Fellow of the Royal Society, I cannot recall his name…"

"The Royal Society is a gentleman's club, a watering hole for old quacks."

"Linton? No, for it was more unfriendly to the tongue. Listen?"

As we spoke, Alonso reached into a dark cage and produced a rabbit, hanging by its scruff.

"This is Actaeon," he said. "He is the patriarch of this little family. Do you recall, Charles?"

"The predisposition of certain families," I said. "*Immunity, which travels in the blood.*"

With a syringe, Alonso took blood from Actaeon, who scuffled his white and brown feet but appeared otherwise resigned. He made a careful screen, added a drop of amber stain from a dropper. I watched the pale, long fingers, his lowered gaze. Intent, carven face. It seemed in that moment that all was right with the world again. The years fell away, and everything was in its proper channel.

Alonso said, "Six of these fellows are your run-of-the-mill rabbits. The others, however... Look." He placed the slide under the hemacytometer and motioned me forward.

I could not credit it. "Is it so with all six?"

Alonso's look was fatigued and wry both. "It was a great deal of trouble to find them," he said. "That six are of the same family, all immune to the *Pasteurella multocida.*"

"We began it..." I said. Our study all those years ago. Alonso was a man possessed. But then we parted ways, and he abandoned science. And it was over, or so I thought.

"We began it," Alonso said, "and we will finish it now. Because we are armed with new knowledge. You have read Ehrlich? He has given us the key, in that little word, at the end of his treatise...the *Antikörper...*"

I squinted for a moment. German is such an effort. "The antibody."

"The antibody. By examination of both infected and immune rabbits, I believe we can isolate the antibodies that provide the protection from *Pasteurella multocida.* We must duplicate that antibody, synthesize it, and introduce it to other rabbits that lack immunity."

"And?"

"We wait. Rabbits will do what they do and breed. The next generation will prove it. If we are correct, if we have worked the trick, their descendants will be born with immunity to *Pasteurella multocida.*"

"And if it can be done with *Pasteurella multocida,*" I said, "why not with cholera? Why not with syphilis?" We spoke quickly now, words running into each other.

"Yes, Charles, yes! The transfer of immunity! Inoculations are one thing—"

"But to inoculate a family, for generations to come? Radical! Revolutionary!" I felt a little faint. "And the implications are... Alonso, if it is possible to engineer congenital immunity..."

"It follows that it is possible to prevent congenital disease being passed down in families. Chorea, cancers, all hereditary afflictions."

"It is the first step toward eradicating disease altogether."

"Not in our lifetime. But yes, it is the first step."

"*The transfer of hereditary immunity.*" I took him by the lapels and shook him. "Can it be done?"

He grinned, and I glimpsed for a moment the young Alonso. "I do not know!" he said. "Shall we see, Charles? Shall we make our names after all?"

I laughed immoderately as he slapped my back.

I am not blind to the connection, here, between Alonso's situation and this line of scientific inquiry. He is dying of a disease passed down through the Villarca line. Perhaps there is something to be done... Foolish, no, cruel to speak of it at this juncture. The outcome is so uncertain. But I cannot deny that I have thought it. And I know it is in his mind too. Strange that hope can so resemble pain.

I will add one observation of this afternoon, which relates to the nature of my specialty. Microscopy is considered by most to be tedious work; it is a poor relation in the medical profession. The work will consist of examination of the blood and tissue of both groups of rabbits, the immune and the diseased; of counting the blood cells, red and white, one by one; and of keeping scrupulous records. And it will take months to complete. It is plain as the nose on my face that Alonso is in need of assistance, and I shall arrange to return to him next month for a longer visit.

That is all so. Microscopy is the purest of the scientific disciplines, because it deals in examination only.

None of these concerns were in my mind when I looked into that lens. How can I describe what I saw through the hemacytometer? It is a privilege, given to few, to glimpse the components of life itself. I am a God-fearing man, and I will not be ashamed to say that I feel as close to Him when I look through a microscope as I do in the church.

> *"If I have told you earthly things, and ye believe not, how shall ye believe, if I tell you of heavenly things?"*
>
> —JOHN 3:12

[pages missing]

5 October

It strikes me on rereading yesterday's entry that I have quite put aside and forgotten the fear engendered in me by the mysterious face at my window, the crude grave beneath the cedar tree. I am forced to doubt that these phenomena occurred anywhere but in my own mind.

I must ascribe more of my maunderings to the account of the neuralgia than I had thought (reading them, I am almost ashamed to own them, save that they may serve as a salutary account of the imaginative capacities of an excitable mind). It is of particular clinical interest, reading back over my *tale*, to note how the pain warps perception: my observations are careful, astute, ordered—and completely erroneous.

Arriving at the untenanted house, in the dark, after the fatigues of the journey, I was in a perfect neurotic, suggestive state: exemplar, the "rat" seen in my chamber. One could almost make a case for self-mesmerism. I had found it most chilling! I could laugh aloud. Oh, no doubt, I saw everything through a veil of suspicion! And so in the morning, the pain reflects my sensibility as through a prism, diffusing it and concentrating it—my mind reverts to the idée fixe of *something* in my room, choosing in its obsession to *place the face I conjure at my own window.* Well, this is quite an experience for a humble practitioner of medicine! A foray into the world of intrigue and apparitions, more usually to be found only between the pages of the popular novel! But I am content to depart now from the realm of the Gothic and return to the bright landscape of science.

6 October

There were trials today of both a practical and spiritual nature. We began the process of taking specimen slides from all the mucous membranes and affected organs of the immune and of the diseased rabbits. It was long and full of suffering. We have cauterized the smaller incisions against infection, and the stink got the better of me more than once. I am all but purblind. Hours of bending and looking and bending and looking. I begin to feel like an automaton.

"How long will they endure like that?" I asked as Alonso laid by me the section of bowel, glistening and pale.

"It is remarkable what the living frame can withstand," he said. He turned from me. "They will live," he said, "long enough."

The rabbits' cries were like wind whistling under a door.

"I will sever the vocal cords," Alonso said. His back heaved like a bellows. It was somewhat better once they were silent. Eyes shone in the depths of the cages.

* * *

Later, we sat on the step in the evening sun and shared a cigarillo, the oak vast at our backs. A welcome breeze played lightly with our coattails. The land was spread before us like warm toast.

"Bernard's wife left him," Alonso said, "on account of his forays into vivisection."

"Not before he spent her dowry on it," I said. I think I was doing an impression of cheer. "And we have no wives to object. We lucky fellows."

He drew on the cigarillo and held the smoke within. The day was merciless on his parchment face.

I laid my hand on his shoulder. "There is no other way," I said. "Do not feel it too deeply. It must be living tissue."

Through the linen, the bones of his shoulder were sharp beneath my hand. Their proximity seemed for a moment unwholesome, as if the skin were reflected back, exposing the muscle and beneath it the gentle connection of scapula and humerus in the glenoid cavity. The white bones shifting in perfect precision. Bile rose, and I was for some moments wholly occupied with that sensation.

I became aware at length that Alonso was speaking.

"I am disgusted with myself," he said. "I cannot adhere to my principles but am swayed by the maudlin, the easy sympathy that is the layman's privilege. It argues a want of purpose in me. If one is to undertake such things, it must be done with gravity and steadiness. Not with sensibility."

I thought of what lay in the chamber beneath our feet. "It is always the question," I said. "Can we believe that we are endowed with sufficient authority to take such actions—I will not say cruelties, for that argues an intent of which I think we are both absolved—such actions that are, by their nature, the cause of egregious suffering? But the furtherance of knowledge—I cannot think it comes cheap. We are in the *ghastly kitchen*, I acknowledge it.

"And I will not say to you think of the lives that will be improved, of the families who could be rid of congenital predispositions to disease. I will not say think of the good we will do in identifying particular immunities and isolating them. We do not *know* whether what we do will benefit any man or beast. It is the nature of medicine, of science. We proceed always through the fog of doubt, seeking the clear air that may not come."

Alonso sighed and rubbed his hand across his nape. His hair stood up in quills. "And once again, you prove your worth, Charles," he said. "For naturally, you are right. No neat answers will be vouchsafed us." He threw the cigarillo hard into a gorse bush. "Foolish to look for them."

I make no complaint here about the methods. I state fact only.

IRIS

AUTUMN 1913

I'm fourteen.

The churchyard is quiet, sunlit, the ranks of stones leprous and upright. Beech leaves litter the turning grass—red, burnt orange. The summer's been disappointing, gray and full of inconsequential showers. I saw it through window panes running with endless rain. But today, the sky is clear, the sun bright and low in the sky.

She's under a long slab of white slate in the northwest corner. It gleams in the low light. My father's hand, warm under my elbow. The pouch in his jacket pocket thumps gently against my waist as we go down the ranks toward her.

"Good day, Mama," I say.

I put the rowan branch down. The berries are bloody red on the white. I broke it from a tree on a high tor above the Dart. My hands smart from the tussle. Thin red grazes cover them. My father puts his offering beside it. Long-stemmed bearded irises, unseasonably forced in some hothouse somewhere. The delicate, overlarge petals ripple in the breeze.

My father spreads his coat on the grass, and we sit by her head. He turns the red-and-white ring on his finger, idle, absent. He has worn it as long as I can remember. It's a ladies' ring, I have come to realize in recent years. The thin gold band is absurd and elegant on his long hands.

Sometimes, we speak; he tells me about her: stories of her childhood, about her eyes or what music she liked. Today, we just sit.

There's an old mound next to her grave. It's misshapen, covered in viper's bugloss and late foxgloves. I don't know why it's there, but I like it. A small blooming hill in all seasons. Bumblebees move through the undergrowth busily. Papa told me once that it was her brother's grave. But there's no headstone. He never said more about it.

I watch the red leaves fall, tossed on the breeze. I'm protective of him at these times. I have nothing to mourn; I never knew her. Papa loved her very much, and she died, and that makes him more important than me when we come here. But today—it must be different.

I shiver in the light wind. My body is still strange, too full of edges. This is the second day on which I have ventured from Rawblood since the illness took me.

The meningitis gnawed away time. There are great holes in my memory. I am grateful for them. I was ill forever. I wish to remember less, not more. My father's hand on my head. *Papa, this is the disease... No. Hush.* January and February passed, but I didn't know. Spring is missing, a dark swathe of nothing. Summer faded back in softly, was warm light shining on glass bottles and teaspoons on windowsills, drawn curtains, my head hot and cold against the pillow.

Fever, long and deep, is like a journey. I saw things. I traveled. Sometimes, I catch the tail end of the fever dream. Dark and moonlight shifting... But it always slips through my fingers, and that's better,

I think. With autumn, I am learning to slide myself back into the waking world.

If Henry Gilmore were buried here, I would visit him. I know what I'd bring to his grave. It's blooming now in the hills. Great spiked armfuls of golden gorse. But he's buried away in the Methodist cemetery at Princetown.

I turn and face Papa squarely. I say, "I have made a decision."

"Yes?"

"I will be a nurse," I say. "That is what I will do."

"There is time and to spare to think about that."

My father's ideas have such shape, such mass—I could hold them in my hands like stones. In his presence, I become elusive. My thoughts and feelings dissipate in his strong opinion. I never speak to him as I am about to do.

"Perhaps," I say. "But there is something we must resolve between us," I say. "If we are to go on."

"Indeed?" he asks, and the slight downward turn of his mouth nearly stops me, but I mustn't; I mustn't stop. I will not be lied to any longer.

"I've had a great deal of time on my hands these last months," I say. "So I thought I should start to learn. I should prepare myself to go on to nursing. And I live in a house full to the eaves of medical books. Very convenient. But where to begin? With such a vast topic before me, where was I to start? So I thought, *I'll begin with us.* I will learn about what ails us, the Villarcas. The disease."

His dark, unreadable eyes. He says nothing.

"I read everything," I say, "that I could find on families, on congenital diseases. Which pass down, generation to generation." Long hours propping the moldering books open before me on the coverlet. My weak hands suffused with the dry scent of spoiled paper, old ink.

"And what was your conclusion?" he asks. He's quiet.

"*Horror autotoxicus,*" I say. "The term coined by Ehrlich. It is a protective mechanism. It is how the immune system distinguishes between healthy tissue and disease. *Horror autotoxicus* is a good thing. Very dangerous not to have it."

"Very," he says.

"So I would like to know," I say, despising the quiver in my voice, "why you have fed me this story. Why you have misled me since before I could speak, lied to me *all my life*."

Papa's finger is under my chin. He tips it up until we are face-to-face. "Yes," he says. "I thought, somehow, if it were a rational thing…that you would not be so afraid. I was wrong, I think."

"You are a liar," I say.

"If we are to speak of lying, I would have you explain how you broke the Rules each night and lied to me each day. I thought to wait until you are stronger, but here we are."

"I don't know what you mean," I say.

"Who roused the house in the middle of the night, Iris? Who told me to go to you, that you had fallen ill? The game is up."

I didn't know Tom had gone to Papa. "Don't punish him," I say. "It was my fault. Don't send him away."

Papa says, "Well. We cannot go on as we are. I wish to trust you, but so far, you have not been worthy of it. Duplicitous."

"I know where I learned it," I say, amazed at my daring.

"But I have reason." Papa's eyes are on my mother's grave. And that other quiet shape beside her, which crawls with scent and life. "I am protecting your life."

"Why," I ask, "should I not have a friend?"

"When I have told you this," Papa says, "you will cease to be a child. I had hoped I could give you a very few more years of innocence. But if it is not to be… It is fitting that we do this here. Where she is buried. Where they let me bury him. It was not common practice. The vicar drew the line at a headstone. Very unforgiving, the Church. But they lie together at least. Brother and sister. I gave them that."

Something caws in the bare trees behind, and I startle. "Papa..." A shadow passes over us. A rook wide and beautiful overhead, the rough voice calling.

"Look at me," Papa says. "If you are old enough to call me a liar, you are old enough to interpret the evidence. Come. Apply logic. What is it really, the disease?"

"Perhaps it is merely your fear," I say. "That I will leave you alone."

"No," he says. "If only it were so."

"Tell me, Papa."

"You must come to this yourself," he says. "You must. I will not end your childhood for you."

I take a shaking breath. "All right," I say. "I will take it that you have a good reason to keep us away from the world."

"I do."

"Because of danger to us, or...because we are dangerous?"

"Both."

"We two are the only two left of our name. So the Villarcas are indeed predisposed to die young, as if from congenital disease?"

"It is so."

"But it is not a congenital defect. Because those who marry *into* the Villarca family also die from the same cause."

"Yes."

"But it is not contagion."

"No."

"We do not die of natural causes. It follows then...that we are killed."

"Yes," he says heavily. "Good."

"How may one be killed? In battle, at sea, falling from a horse...any number of ways. But we all die of one cause?"

"Yes."

"Murdered."

"Yes."

"It argues some kind of agency. Intent. Are we being hunted, Papa? Is it some sort of feud, an old enemy of the Villarcas…"

"You are close now," he says.

"But this has plagued us for many lifetimes. Many, many years. So the feud is passed down through generations, father to son, perhaps…"

"It is one person," he says. "One."

"Not possible," I say, and the hairs on my neck are upright and cold.

"*She* is like a disease, in many ways," he says. "It was not all a lie. I believe she travels in our blood, passed down, that she is a biological inheritance, as much as a spiritual one… But *she* is like nothing on earth, really. *She* comes in the night. Sometimes, in mist or fog. A woman, or once a woman. White, starved. *She* comes with the sound of grinding stone, and despair. *She* looks into your eyes, and then…"

"A ghost." I am disappointed. I had thought, perhaps, that he might tell me the truth.

"A ghost, a curse. Words, merely. What have they to do with *her*? *She* has taken us all," he says. "One by one. Given us death. *She* took at the last your mother and by doing so nearly killed me too. We are the last, you and I. Be assured that this is not a story in *Blackwood's Magazine*. Do not make that mistake. This is no mournful lady, floating through deserted halls. *She* bears no message from beyond the grave. She has no desires save one, which is to end you, to take your life." His face is bleak. "Understand?"

I will not be taken in again. I will not.

"I was a child when I saw her," he says. "It felt as though the living marrow had been sucked from the world. I think I have spent the rest of my life recovering from the sight of her." He stops and presses his palm hard into the springy turf of the grave. There is an expression on his face that I never, ever want to see again. The sound of blood rushing in my ears.

"She has taken us all; I am determined that she will not take you, Iris. And if I am to keep you alive, keep you safe, you must obey me to the letter. For this is the heart of it: *she* comes to those of our family, comes sooner or later—when we love. Do you understand me?" He takes my face in his hands and looks, and this is more frightening than all the rest, because he is sad, so sad. "Iris, do you understand what it means?"

"That I must take the greatest of care," I say. "Not to…" I stop, because actually, I don't understand. From somewhere deep, there comes the thought: *Moonlight…* Sickness runs through me, everywhere.

"If you love," he says, "or if you marry, or if you continue the line, *she* comes. These things do not always go together—heavens, that is another conversation, for another day—but *she* will make no distinction. So you must not. Do not join anyone to our family. It is a death sentence for you and for them. Those Villarcas who live long lives and die peacefully in their beds live and die alone. And they leave no one after them. It is a risk to know others," he says. "Even to have servants in the house. To receive visitors… Living contact. For there are so many ways in which… So I have tried to seal myself up, to forbid strangers the house, to have no household…

"It does not work. People are like water; they always find the cracks. The answer lies in a harder road. You must seal *yourself* up like a bastion. You must keep everyone at a remove. Always. Control your feelings toward others, immerse yourself in matters of the mind, work yourself to the bone, so all your impulses, all your energy, is diverted from the heart. Do you think, Iris, that I do not also live by strict Rules?" He takes my hand. "It is a high price. In the past, it was too high for me; I knew of *her*, and all she could do, and still I… But never again. I have paid enough."

"How can I believe you, Papa? Is it not just another *horror autotoxicus*?" The air is full of his rich weight. I can't breathe.

"You know that she is there," he says. "Have you not felt her? Waiting in the shadowed places outside the lamplight, at the bottom of wells. Behind you, in long dark corridors… She has walked beside us, the Villarcas, for many years. She will have her eye on you already."

"Get off," I say. I push him, run from his vast shadow, toward the lych-gate. The horses back away to the full length of their ropes, dark eyes wide. The catch is slippery under my fingers. It won't budge. Inside my heart is a new little cold place, where horror lives. *Something, uncurling in the moonlight.* I press my face to the weathered wood.

Papa's hand on my shoulder is light. He doesn't speak. His sad, lined face. He gives me a handkerchief.

"You, Papa," I say. "How are you safe?"

"I cheated *her*, Iris. Again and again, I cheated her. I glimpsed her when I was a child—but she came for my mother that time. Then for my father... She came for your uncle, and many years later for your mother... They were all taken, torn from my side, and I was left alone, and I could do nothing. *Nothing.*" He points across the churchyard with a long finger. "That my Meg lies there," he says. "It is...unconscionable. Were it not for you, my Iris," he says, "I would have had no cause to remain. I would have died, and *her* purpose would have been complete—were it not for you. You are the one thing that keeps me on this earth. So you see, Iris, I have learned from my mistakes, and I will never, ever let *her* have you."

His fury takes me with it. It courses through me like shock. The world is new-made, vivid, dangerous. We stand hand in hand in the sunlight, and I feel what people must feel in church. The colors of the grass, the stone, the very sky are altered. And I am changed, forever. He was right.

I whisper, "How, Papa? How did you cheat her?"

"I have paid a certain price." His trembling hand wanders to the pouch at his waist.

"I could—"

"No. Do you hear? It is like hell itself. I will not have you go near it."

"I could leave," I say. The road winds away over the moor, lovely in the late afternoon.

"Yes," he says. "That is another choice. Leave Rawblood, leave

Dartmoor. I have tried it; others have tried it. It does not go well, in the end. We may leave for months, even years at a time. But we sicken eventually. Only returning to Rawblood heals us. Damned if we do, damned if we don't."

Papa smiles. It's thin. There's none of him in it. All about us, the rusty scent of bracken. Far off, the cold, brown Dart runs over stone. A swallow cuts across the sunlit air. My father's hand rests gently on my head. "Yes," he says. "You are a Villarca indeed. For this is also love. What we feel for this place, for Rawblood. Perhaps it will be enough."

I nod. Surely, no person could ever rouse in me this wild exultation. Could match the grandeur of the land.

"What does she want?" I ask. "From us."

"It is so strange," he says. He's thoughtful of a sudden, removed. It is at moments like this that I remember that my father was a doctor once. "So inconstant, her wishes… They are crude like the desires of a child. She wants us close—she wants us here. But she does not like us to grow, to live. It is as if she would have Rawblood and all of us in it suspended forever, unchanging…under glass, in a museum case. What for? Do we amuse her? Sometimes, I have thought, over the years, that we are merely playthings of a kind. But she kills her toys, in the end." His face is worn and folded. Something has been leached from him. The sun is in the evening corner of the sky; the yellow light is fading on the gravestones.

I understand. As I leave him, he's taking the pouch from his pocket. I don't look back, of course. I don't watch.

On the bank by the road, Nell and Soldier quarrel, snaking their heads around each other, nipping little bits of hide between yellow teeth. I stare at the mound that is my mother, the florid hump beside her, which is—my uncle? For a moment, I see them, my family, laid out in time; a series of interconnecting rock pools, glassy under the sun. The sea washing in and out of us… I should be afraid. I am afraid.

"Iris," he says. "I am not a pantomime villain. I do not *wish* to send young Gilmore away. Only tell me: Can I trust you to act in your own best interests, and in his? It is not safe to be his friend, Iris, no matter what you think. For either of you."

All those hours spent staring at the ceiling, coughing into the basin, head hot on the pillow; all that time spent thinking of what to say to Tom. No need. Diseases or ghosts, it comes to the same thing in the end.

Loneliness is not what people think it is. It is not a song. It's a little bitter thing you keep close, like an egg under a hen. What happens when the shell cracks? What comes forth?

The breeze has picked up. Before I can stop it, I shiver. Papa sees.

"It's time to leave her," he says. In the sunlit corner of the churchyard, my mother's grave is a riot of purple, red, white.

"I'll stay." I don't want walls around me yet.

"You're not a week out of bed," he says kindly, "and the air has a bite to it."

I bow my head to his will.

"If we trust to one another," Papa says, "there can be far greater freedoms. I do not wish to keep you from the world, you know, or keep the world from Rawblood. By the by, why a nurse?"

"When I saw Mr. Gilmore, and when I was so ill myself, it seemed to me that there was something worthy in healing people—it is so terrible, illness…"

"Yes," he says. "That is understood. I meant—why a nurse? A doctor, surely."

"That," I say, "is what I want above all things. I had not thought—"

"Private study. And afterward, perhaps Paris? The Sorbonne awards degrees to women. Edinburgh? I will write. But it will not be possible if you cannot do as I say, if you cannot keep people at a remove, if you cannot be trusted to protect both yourself and them…"

Keep him from me, then. Snuff out the light. "You can trust me, Papa. I will do as you say." Perhaps Papa is right: I am beginning to grow up.

"Thank you," he says, weary. "Thank you. You can be happy, Iris—and you can be *significant.*"

When will we cease to bargain with each other, my father and I? Over the wall, Soldier puffs a longing breath at Papa. He knows which one of us carries the sugar.

My father says, "I am sorry for my faults, of which there are many. As a father, as a man. But I will not fail you in this." He makes to hold me, tentative, wary of rebuff. He makes a little *oof* as I throw my arms around him. I hold tight. The world is strange. One doesn't always understand. But there's always this.

"Tell me about our family," I say. "Everything, now."

We ride slowly with the sun at our backs.

WINTER

He lies on the mahogany table. And a ghostly him below, reflected in the shining, polished wood. I'd thought he'd be white, but he's gray and yellowed at the edges.

Martin gazes at the skeleton. "Tall," he says to himself, then rouses. "Iris, do you think you can?" Martin Goodman is all warm colors. Skin like baked bread.

I am intent. The bones lie in beautiful order, each leading naturally to the next. His skull is a calcified apple. "Cranium," I say. "Mandible. Cervical vertebrae. Sternum…" I touch each yellowed bone. My fingertip sings.

This is my secret: when I touch the skeleton, I become part of the dim air of the dining room, the shining mahogany, Martin's tabby-cat hair, which hangs in a brilliantined strand over his warm forehead. I move through the granite walls of Rawblood like water. I reach out across the dark-gray sky, the moor, the hills above, where snow is beginning to fall.

"Fine," Martin says. "Good. Now do it again." He reaches out with two hands and sweeps the bones into a pile. It's shocking, terrible. It was a person, and suddenly, it's a jumble of bone. "Lay him out as he should be."

⌀

I show him the house before dinner. He peers into the galleried heights of the hall. He stares at the shining banister that snakes up and away to the upper floors. He stares at the vast marble mantel that flows down like lava around the cavernous hearth. Horses and vines and cherubs and men with horns dive and surface in the white fall of stone.

"It's from Italy," I say. "My grandpapa brought it. Carrara."

He starts. "Do you go there often?" He's polite.

"Papa will take me when I'm older," I say. A short visit. I cannot be absent long from Rawblood.

I show him the red parlor, shining and dark paneled and hung with velvet the color of fresh blood. I see the room for a moment as he sees it. Somber and rich and malevolent. It's an unpleasant feeling, like putting on someone else's still-warm shoes.

"No pictures," he says.

"There are." I point forcefully to the heavy oils that line the room. Herons, broken buildings, wild swamps. Men leading soft-colored cows through gates.

"Of people, I mean. Where are the pictures of your family? The Villarcas."

"I think they would remind Papa of Mama," I say. "It would be too sad." I am fairly proud of this prim answer. In truth, I think Papa is afraid to be surrounded by so many, many dead.

Martin touches his rare beef gently with the tip of his knife. He jumps when my father speaks to him, his sweet expression alert. My father tells him he's a promising man. He nods thirty or forty times.

The snow is heavier and heavier, falling in silence onto the steps, onto Martin as he climbs into his trap, drifting on the velvet-lined skeleton box in the back. "Golly," he says and turns up his collar. White stars settle on his eyelashes, his cheeks, his hat. He lingers.

I see his thoughts in his face. Why should he be turned out to drive for two hours in the snowy dusk when there is a great house, filled with empty rooms, to hand?

"Safe travels, Goodman," my father says.

He raises an ungloved hand, warm skin flushed against the white land. "Well," he says. "Iris, I will see you next week"—he puts out a hand, and heavy flakes fall on it—"if this allows it!"

I wave.

"He doesn't like us," I say to Papa, when we're back before the fire in the red parlor. I mean that he doesn't like Rawblood. "And he smells of lemons."

Firelight, the crack of the grate. We sit here most evenings. A gentle ritual. I look forward to this time most. The warm end of every day, Papa's vast, dark form at his desk or in the armchair opposite mine. Half-moon spectacles on the tip of his nose, his black-and-white badger hair ruffled, crazy against the firelight.

"He thinks we are immoral," my father says. "Or—no. He thinks I am immoral, and that I am raising you in the image of my turpitude."

I have only very recently discovered that my father is amusing. The light in the depths of his mahogany eyes. The slight twist of the mouth. I hadn't known. He makes me laugh.

We have achieved a new normality these last few months, which brooks no mention of white women or of death. We look forward now.

We do speak of disease and of medicine most evenings. The words run like water, beautiful. *Olecranal. Coronal. Iliac. Parietal, occipital.* I had not dared imagine a future before. I am beginning to see it.

"You could teach me," I say to Papa. "We don't need him."

"No," he says cheerfully. "I am utterly outmoded. I would not know how to begin. And it can only be a good thing—for you to be exposed to others' opinions, to bring the world, a little, into this house. You have shown yourself most sensible, Iris, since I told you how matters stand. So if you are sensible, it is good for you to be with people—however irksome they may be."

It was to be study in Paris. But next year, there will probably be a war, so, no. I may have to wait, Papa says. But we will contrive something. I believe it.

"Such a stern young man," Papa says. "So sure. He has that glassy look—of implacable certainty, implacable morality. Does he have very firm opinions on young ladies and propriety and so on? I think he must. He reminds me very much of someone I knew once." A small, private smile.

"Who?"

"Oh, it was so long ago. Before you were born." The fire catches his eyes, lights them. He looks, for a moment, quite young.

"Sounds like a pill," I say.

"Goodman's not the only one who deals in black and white. No, not at all a pill. I loved him very much."

"Pill," I say.

He shouts with laughter. "Oh, well, a little, perhaps. Anyhow. Goodman is intelligent and a good teacher. He wishes to supplement his income; we wish you to be taught. Everyone is happy. So what do we care for his opinions?"

"Nothing!"

Martin Goodman thinks we scorn him. We do make light of him, a little. But he misunderstands. Papa would never, ever permit anyone but us to sleep the night at Rawblood.

⌒

Outside my bedroom window, the roof is white, marked only with the tracks of some night bird. The window in the stable block is dark. Some nights, there's a little flickering light. Sometimes, the shape of a head. Faint halo of candlelight. Not tonight.

I sit on the satin stool before the mirror. The ivory comb drags through my mass of hair. The sensation is delicious, tortuous. My eyes half close in the rhythm of it. Behind me, in the glass, something moves.

I whirl about. Papa stands in the doorway, a vast black shadow. "Will you have a story tonight?"

When I have recovered my breath, I say, "Yes, Papa." I pad across the cold boards on bare feet. Hurl myself into the bed linen.

"Hervor?" he asks.

"No," I say. "Something else." I no longer like Hervor and *The Waking of Angantyr*. I didn't pay enough attention, when I was younger, to the end of the story.

Papa sits by me and tells me tales of us. The Villarcas. My family. I suppose other people pray before they sleep. We don't pray at Rawblood.

When he's gone, I lie waking. The lamp burns down. As a rule, sleep comes easily these days. Wraps about me like wet silk. It escapes me now. After some time, I rise and drape my petticoat over the looking glass.

Hervor becomes a queen. She has two sons, Heidrek and Hegel. Hegel is kind and good. Heidrek is murderous, jealous, cruel. Hervor is forced to banish Heidrek from her kingdom, even though she loves him. Hegel offers to go with his brother, out of love. Hervor gives Heidrek Tyrfing, the sword, to protect them both in exile. She sees herself in Heidrek and loves him, with all his flaws.

As soon as they are out of the kingdom, Heidrek draws the sword Tyrfing and murders his brother. He crosses to a neighboring kingdom. Heidrek is charming, and he is taken in by the kind king. Heidrek then kills the king and his infant son. He takes the kingdom from the kind king.

But seeing that Heidrek is not bound by fellowship or loyalty, his subjects decide that they need not be either. They kill him in the night and take the sword. Heidrek dies alone and unloved, a murderer of his own family.

Hervor was brave but wrong. She shouldn't have gone into the underworld and woken her father. She should have listened when he told her not to take Tyrfing. She should have left well enough alone.

CHARLES DANFORTH

7 October 1881

We are a true bachelor establishment at Rawblood. As I have said, aside from Shakes, there are no servants. I assume they could not stomach Alonso's pursuits. It explains his strong feeling regarding the common attitudes toward experimental medicine. We dine off an eccentric array of cheeses, jellies, and pigs' faces, whatever thing Shakes can salvage from the diminished larder, augmented by river fish and small moor rabbits, full of buckshot. This last, I find I cannot touch. I have lost my taste for rabbit.

Our beds are roughly made—last night, my foot was rudely greeted by the sharp prongs of my mustache comb, which had tucked itself into a fold in a sheet—and our linen unlaundered. Piles of unwashed crockery tower in the kitchen, and Alonso has acquired a terrier, called Punch, who is to dispatch the insalubrious invaders who have seen fit to take advantage of the state of martial law that now prevails there.

No doubt, it would be tiresome to continue in this way for long. But I cannot deny the exhilaration of it. We live unhindered, unchecked, and unobserved. I take pleasure in breakfasting, standing, on jelly eaten from the pot with a spoon, talking all the while with Alonso of what interests us most, without being obliged to think of the shudders of the maidservant or a housekeeper who bustles in and out with sugar bowls.

But I digress. I visited the village yesterday to purchase cabbages. Our charges must be fed; they consume a great deal of vegetable matter and have long since exhausted the kitchen garden at Rawblood. I was much surprised by a meeting I had there.

Dartmeet lies on both sides of the river, as its name suggests. The village is linked by two great bridges, formed by slabs of stone laid across the river—Dartmoor's famous "clapper" bridges. The people bustle back and forth across them or shoot across the water in skiffs, and the river is often full of children, swimming like fishes, shouting, and doing violence upon one another as children are wont to do, under the auspices of play.

After making my purchases, I tucked the parcel under my arm and took my ease along the river and was pleased with the effect of the sunlight on the brown water, where speckled trout rose, and, in a quiet corner upriver from the dwellings, was privileged to witness a kingfisher taking refreshment from a pool. The path was lined with banks of bracken and yellow gorse in which, to judge from the scuffling and chirpings that emerged, the many urgent businesses of a country hedgerow in autumn were being conducted. Butterflies crossed my path, flashes of blue so small and quick as to tease the eye. They assert their presence in a trembling, diffident fashion, as if conscious of the brevity of their existence; indeed, it is only the unseasonable warmth that has drawn them out, and when the weather turns, as it will soon do, it will put a period to them. In the distance, the moor rose in smooth, long furrows, marching on as far as the eye could see beneath a clear sky.

As I dawdled on with my eye occupied with Nature, my mind set to work independently, with no great urgency, on a problem of calculation we had happened upon that morning. So engaged was I in rehearsing arguments that must make Alonso see that accepting an ordinary ratio of red to white corpuscles—rather than counting within each screen— would save days and hours, that I did not hear the hoofbeats on the narrow path, the approach being hidden by a bend in the river. The consequence was that, as I rounded the turn, so did the horse, and I was under the animal before I knew it.

There was the suspension of attention that occurs in moments of crisis, when all that was apparent in the world was shining legs and iron and hooves and a great deal of sturdy bone and equine muscle bearing down upon me. I threw the cabbages one way and myself the other.

Raising myself from a tangle of brush and bracken and finding good quantities of both these estimable plants about my person and in my mouth, I was engaged for some little time in ridding myself of them. When at length I was at liberty to take notice of such things, I perceived that the horse—which had borne all the appearance of a demonic thing, with flared nostrils and fearful strength, as well as the dimensions and speed of a steam engine—was in fact a small brown mare, now cropping the grass contentedly. Of her two riders, one sat stiffly atop her—a small, plump child with white skin and coppery hair. I stared, and he stared too and put his thumb in his mouth to suck.

I presently became aware that the other rider stood beside me, offering consolations of a heartfelt and sympathetic nature. This person held in his arms the string bag of cabbages, which had burst open, and was saying, "Dear God, I had not supposed that anyone would have been on the path! For in Dartmeet, they go by the high road, and I thought, if there should chance to be a traveler, that perhaps they would hear Sadie coming…"

"You thought, in fact, that I should get out of your way," I retorted, for several bruises were making themselves felt. My assailant was a man, younger than myself, fair, with large blue eyes, dressed for riding, and who clutched his hat to him tightly, with entreaty in his face.

"Not at all! I cannot be profuse enough in my apologies. I am fond of this ride, and it being narrow, almost a sheep track, it is not used by carts or horses as a general rule. I was paying insufficient care and was thinking only of my own pleasure; you are quite right, sir…"

He went on in this fashion for some time, before I tired of the whole thing and said that it was no matter and that I had best get on. But this would not do at all for the gentleman, who hastened to introduce himself as Mr. Henry Gilmore. This was his brother, Robert—here, the small red-haired child plucked his thumb from his mouth in order to give me the full benefit of his stare—and they were of Trubb's Farm, which lay—did I know?—to the east of Princetown. I said I hoped that he would ride there *at once*, as sedately as he knew how, at which he laughed. Nothing in my manner or my evident desire to be rid of him was of any avail, save to convince him that he must at all costs aid me and seek to repair the damage he had done. I suppose he is one of those men who places all their consequence on being liked. I could not oblige him in this, but nor could I fight him, and as it was less exertion to go along with his cajoling, I named myself to him and told him that my destination was Rawblood.

"I will put this up on Sadie," he said decidedly, clutching the cabbages to him. "Rob, you will hold it there, and no nonsense from you—I do not believe they have more than one or two slugs on them, so you will not mind it—and we will go along together. If," he said, for the seventh or eighth time, "you are quite sure you are not hurt, Mr. Danforth? And are fit to walk?"

"It is Dr. Danforth. And I am not made of porcelain, I assure you." Here, my leg gave a twinge that confirmed this statement, but I elected to keep it to myself. Here followed an encomium on doctors and his assurances to me that I must be a clever fellow indeed. For he himself could not keep to his books, which was a good thing, very likely, since he was to be a farmer, and farmers would do no good with that sort of stuff in their heads.

"I will be a butler," said Robert with a plump frown. "Not a farmer. Farming is dirty."

"Is it so, mischief?" Henry Gilmore said and reached up to clip him about the ear.

Mr. Gilmore was an entertaining companion, I suppose, to those who care for such things. His talk was light and full of interest in the doings of the world and those in it; however, it was impossible to keep him to one subject for longer than a moment, and his talk flowed freely, with the idle brightness of a stream, over innumerable topics: the slight indisposition of the queen, and the price of corn, and the wisdom of enclosures. To know just a little about so many things—it cannot make for resolute character. I prefer a mind more sober, of a more uniform hue; Mr. Gilmore is a motley piece. But he asks for one's thoughts in so deferential a manner—with such an ingenuous air and such a cherubic countenance!—that I was led into feeling that my opinion held the gravest weight, and it would be churlish to refuse it in a quarter where it was esteemed so highly.

I found, as we went through Dartmeet and the outlying cottages, that he sacrificed all his acquaintance on the same altar as his unfortunate sisters: he was an incurable gossip. We could not pass one homestead set on a distant hill but he would point to it and inform me that the eldest girl was enamored of the blacksmith at Bovey Tracey, and her family did not look well on it, since he was a lad of the first kind… It was all harmless enough, and there was such a lively humor and lack of malice in his utterances that it seemed impossible to quell him. So it went on, until we passed a gate hung with late, fragrant roses, and here, he slowed to a halt.

"And here," he said, looking at the gate, "here lives Mrs. Gowan…

and Miss Charlotte Gowan." And he paused in the lane with such an expression on his face that I paused too. Finding the sudden cessation of such a copious and generous outpouring of confidence as unnerving as I had done its beginning, I asked, what of the Gowans? He shrugged. The mother... She was well enough, although...

"And Miss Gowan?"

"She is the best girl in the world," he said simply.

"Henry is soft on her," said Robert, breaking his thumb-struck silence. "Soft! Never saw anything like it."

"You settle, you," said Henry. The words were mild enough, but his face was crestfallen. When I sought to turn his mood and offer him my felicitations, he only shrugged and turned the subject. I saw a stern reserve in his face, which sat so oddly in a countenance not designed for it that I was hard put not to laugh.

"You are young yet to be thinking of such things."

"I am six and twenty," he said, turning to me quickly with the sternness abated not a bit.

I was, I own, surprised. I had thought him not yet twenty. I murmured some apology for prying in his business (although in truth, it was proffered to me on a platter).

He laughed, then, and slapped me on the back.

"You will understand, Danforth," he said, "if you do not already! Presently, or *some*day, you will understand!"

Such is the force of his good nature and open ways that I could not be affronted by this presumption but looked, I fancy, a trifle sheepish and desired him to not beat me any further, as I had taken a good drubbing today already at his hands, at which he laughed even harder.

When we reached the path that leads down to Rawblood, through the orchard, he made as if to go on, and I detained him with some word of thanks. He looked at me curiously.

"Do you stop here?" he asked.

"Why yes, my host is Alonso Villarca. Whom you may know." I waited to see what pearls would fall.

He rubbed his head and said, "I had forgotten that it is now called Rawblood. For you know it was Dempsey House before."

"But that must have been fifty years ago."

"Arr, 'tis not over long in these here parts!" He affected an accent and an air that reminded me irresistibly of Shakes. "I had not recalled... I thought you meant Two Bridges, over the way."

"Why should I not stay here?"

"You may, of course. But no one else chooses to, and Mrs. Hitchens, who was the housekeeper, whose daughter married a corn chandler in Exeter—"

"Yes, yes, very well!"

"She stayed until the last, she says. For having had employment there with Mr. Villarca's mother and father, she wished to, and because of having known Mr. Villarca since he was a baby. But she could not stomach it and left too, in the end."

I exclaimed. I felt for Alonso. It was no wonder that he cherished a strong consciousness of the small-mindedness of the English.

"If they choose to go, that is their affair. I will not presume to judge the promptings of another man's conscience. But what Alonso does is for the benefit of all, of medicine, and of England..." I heard myself going on in this fashion and was obliged to pull myself up when I realized I was repeating a large part of Alonso's speech to me in the cellar.

Mr. Gilmore looked at me in puzzlement.

"Oh, the experiments? But they did not care for that, indeed," he said. "For Mr. Villarca has had fits like *that* since he came back from the university, and they are all devilish fond of him. No, that would not have troubled them. It was the other thing that sent them off."

"What other thing?" I asked in no small exasperation, for I had expended a good deal of passion on what I perceived to be an unappreciative audience.

"It was—well!—they got the priest to the house."

"For illness? For what cause?"

Here, Robert, who had been occupied with pulling hairs out of Sadie's mane, piped up. "For the haunting of it," he said in his high voice. "For the Rawblood ghost!" He settled back to his task, cherubic face intent.

Henry Gilmore nodded and turned serious eyes on me. "Aye," he said, "it was so."

I was so taken aback by this piece of village mummery that, for a moment, I could not find a thing to say. Presently, I found my voice. "I have known Mr. Villarca these twenty years—more! Those who held household positions for my friend seemed in fact excessively happy with their lot, and with the house, and with their master. I think it very wrong, Mr. Gilmore, to put about such things. Why, Alonso cannot get another servant to wait on him! That country people believe in such things and can take a sudden whim into their heads—well, it is due to small knowledge of the world and cannot be helped. But that you, a man with pretensions to gentility, should repeat to me this piece of nonsense—it is beyond anything. I will ask you not to spread such a tale—for all the good it may do!—and avoid further damaging my friend's comfort and position here."

"He has done that himself, Dr. Danforth, if you will forgive me." He sighed and turned his face to the sun, as if to gain some strength from it. He is a remarkable sight in a Devon village, to be sure. The planes of his face, and those curls of guinea gold, shining in the afternoon light—he belongs on a frieze in the Parthenon, not standing in shabby gaiters on an English hillside. "You cannot argue with local opinion," he said.

"And what is local opinion's opinion?" I allowed the scorn to enter my voice.

"It is like this. After the Villarcas—that is, the old master and his lady—were taken in those shocking and horrible circumstances, it affected this district for some time after. You may be sure the name Rawblood was a watchword for notoriety. But as for Mr. Villarca the younger, there was great sadness for his sake in these parts. Folk were resolved to be kind to him. For he was but a lad, my father says, and a pleasant one, although full of freaks. They see him as a Devon boy, you know. As one of their own. Or rather, they did. And he came to manhood and went to the university and was set to be a doctor, and all seemed well."

"I have been here in years past," I said, moved despite myself, "and Rawblood seemed home to him indeed."

"Yes," said Henry Gilmore with an inflection I could not place. "I had heard you and he would spend a deal of time together here in those days.

"But then, of a sudden, he abandoned his study. He went off to Italy with barely a word to anyone. And was not seen or heard of for nigh on twenty years! It was a great sadness to those who had seen him grow from boy to man. All the household kept on full pay, mind, as though he were expected any minute. If folk did not know before that the Villarca purse is deep—why, they know it now.

"Then, but a few months ago, there came the word of his return. Late August, that was. You can imagine the hubbub! There was a bustle, and deliveries, and linen aired, and peculiar things in boxes carried to the cellar, and someone set to hack at the brambles on the drive. There was quite a joyful scramble. Rawblood was to be set up again! We were most glad, in Dartmeet and all around. For it is not good to let a house stand empty so long. It makes the stones and the walls strange—mad. And do not tell me that houses have no feelings, all their own.

"Then Mr. Villarca arrived himself. Well. You have seen his face, Dr. Danforth. I do not need to tell you that he is a horror. He is fearsome to look upon. As if his years numbered seventy, not barely above forty. It is not his looks alone; he is wrong. He speaks to people who are not there. He rages and curses in the night, in place of sleep. There is something amiss. The household began to have great misgivings. It is as if a different man sits in his body. Some asked, is it indeed young Mr. Villarca? Or is it an impostor, like in a story, come to take his inheritance?

"Strange things were afoot within the house. It put fright into people. As a natural consequence, they began to recall the happenings that took place all those years ago in his father's time… Mr. Villarca answered their fears with grim words, or with silence. And the priest did no good; indeed, it seemed to make matters worse. And at last, those who worked at Rawblood took their leave. He is alone again. Perhaps that is how he likes it.

"Now, no terrible things passed in that place"—Henry Gilmore waved a hand at Rawblood, which lay below us, snug in the folds of the hill—"when the Dempseys were there, and it was Dempsey House. Some say now that the Villarcas never should have been allowed to come here—although how old Ned thinks he could have prevented them, I do not know—but is there perhaps something to it? When foreigners come here, they bring their own things with them, do they not, that may be strange to us—whether it be a new way of cooking a lamb, or a language, or something else you might not want them to bring."

I was conscious of the echo of my own thoughts concerning Alonso and his rights to his nation. I replied with more heat than I should have done. "You are very mysterious and like to coax my interest with hints of *terrible things*, Mr. Gilmore, but you have so far offered me no more than suspicions unworthy of a young gentleman. You have, in short, acquitted yourself no better than a woman, gossiping of indiscretion in a tearoom. You cloak the matter in intrigue and hint at direful conclusions and tell me nothing. Perhaps you wish me to be frightened or impressed, and I can assure you that it is not so—no, no more, sir. I bid you good evening."

He shrugged and seemed to wish to speak again but thought better of it, slung my cabbages down from Sadie, and bade me a friendly good night. As they went around the hill, Robert was laughing. It sounded evil to my ear.

I went down toward Rawblood, eager, the cabbages jostling in my arms. I had received from this encounter a renewed energy and consciousness of the necessity of what we did here. There was much work awaiting me, and I went to it gladly.

Later

At dinner (pickled onions, pickled gherkins, dried apricots—not good— and a duck roasted with a ravigote sauce—very good), I told Alonso of my meeting in full, unvarnished detail. He whistled a quick indrawn breath and said, "I had not thought to trouble you with this. It presents a strange appearance, I know, and locally, my credit has suffered."

"You may confide in me with perfect confidence," I cried. "I sent the fellow about his business, you may be sure—do not fear that I will be taken with his fancies!" Alonso's pain roused in me much fellow feeling.

"Well, I will. It's quickly told: *The Mystery of the Rawblood Ghost.* Not an edifying tale, I fear. It began shortly after my return. There was some murmuring among the servants. A footman had woken in the night and found that he could not breathe, due to a hand over his mouth. Mrs. Hitchens saw something in the pantry. I know not what, but she broke a row of preserves.

"As the days went on, matters worsened—there were cries and running in the night, and the servants were heavy-eyed by day. They trembled at the approach of dark. So I took steps to nip it in the bud. I brought the reverend in from Honiton. I thought, what harm can come of it? And perhaps it will sufficiently allay their fears. He visited the place, threw water about with a fine disregard for my curtains, mumbled some cant words, declared it clean, and left.

"I was wrong. It was a great error. For it lent credence to their fear—by taking counteractive measures, I had approved the existence of it, do you see?

"That very night, one of the housemaids ran from the house, with a deal of noise. She said that a person had been in her chamber. Well, it *may* have been so; she was well looking, and I suspect that—anyhow. The household turned out, naturally, myself included—such a brouhaha! She stood on the lawn, and perhaps there was some congenital disease in her family, or something had happened to disturb her modesty, or…I know not, but there was a ghastly white in her face, and her eyes started from their sockets so that she rolled her eyes like a spaniel. We stood about her, in a circle of nightcaps and shawls, and she in the center like a sacrifice, her hair down her back and face turned toward the moon, her mouth agape, uttering that frightful noise."

My friend paused here, and I could see the movement of feeling across the hollow mask of his face. He went on, "Nothing could persuade her to come in or to stop her moaning. And yes, the night was cold, and she took ill from it. I think her wits wandered a little from the fever, for she spoke after in a child's voice—a high reedy tone that quite chilled the heart—and her mind was overthrown. All she would talk of was the… person in her room. Pale, she said, and with eyes like… Anyhow." He shook himself. "No, it was not a salubrious or pleasing occurrence, to happen in one's house! I sent her to Exeter, to Everett's house there—you understand me."

I did; it is an asylum that Everett presides over. I nodded a little without expression, to show him my faith in his judgment and that he might continue without recrimination from me.

"And," he said, "it was not taken kindly by the other servants; they would not then stay. They began to speak of the past happenings in this house, all those years ago…the 'apparition' that was seen then. The Rawblood ghost then came into being, in their minds. A white figure, a cold woman who haunts the generations of Villarcas at Rawblood and tears the life from them…

"Charles, it gave me such pain. That the tragedy that took my mother and my father was to be revived; that they were to appropriate my real loss to construct such nonsense, to feed their superstition—it was intolerable. I let them go, and gladly. That those I had counted my friends, who I had known since I was born, would make such a scandal, which they knew must cause me grief... It cut me to the quick. I was angry. I have lived all my life with that horror close behind me—"

I caught his hand in mine and said, "I know."

"I had not shared this incident with you," he said, "for it shames me to think on it, that I pandered so—there is no better word!—to their ignorance. And worse, with no result. Is it never to be done, Charles? Never?"

I put my arm about him. He shed a tear, like an ashamed child. It is most unnerving to see Alonso thus; it is like seeing a mountain or a tree cry.

"And this is why," I said, "you would have me swear not to bring any soul near the house."

"I will not give them more fodder."

"I understand," I said. "I am so sorry for your trouble, my friend. Does Shakes not subscribe to this local antipathy? Does he not fear the specter?"

"No," said Alonso, thoughtful. "He does not. It would not surprise me to find that he is immune from such things. I find it credible that Shakes defies all natural laws."

I laughed heartily and raised my glass to him. "Well. I like the way we go on here! I can almost thank the Rawblood ghost for introducing me to so delightful a style of living." I waved an apricot at him. "I only regret that I should have given Gilmore such a trimming. If he tells of it, it will lend weight to the tale..." Thinking to turn the conversation, I said, "But the history of the Villarcas and your esteemed parents—why, I confess, that does seem to me romance of the best kind, meaning it happened here, in the world, between two people, and not between the pages of some novel." As soon as the words had left my lips, I regretted them. Alonso has rarely spoken to me of his parents and only once of their deaths.

"The best, you say?" Alonso said heavily. "Do you believe that, my friend, with all that ensued? For myself, I will remain a bachelor as long as I may."

His temper has not improved over the days. When I had proposed that a housekeeper from Taunton or Exeter could be hired, who might not share the local prejudices, his decided negative was close to violence. His curses, delivered to a young woman who had come to the back door peddling her hedgerow blackberries, were something to hear. If I had not that day determined the source of my "face" at the window, I should have come to know shortly after, by his discourse and his actions, that no flesh-and-blood woman could be in the house. He is in deadly earnest: none but us three shall come near Rawblood.

Though he works as ever with the precision and constancy of an engine, this work takes everything from him. Alonso looks—if I may say so—haunted. His face, as I have said, is a Pompeii; his eyes are filmed over in recent days with some care or feeling that I cannot fathom.

And yet, and yet...despite this, it seems to me that his cheek has a hint of color, which it did not have when I arrived. And the lines of his face are carved a little less deep. Does he look somewhat improved? Somewhat...younger? I will wait to remark upon it, for I do not wish to torment him with wishful thinking.

Turning his abrupt gaze on me, Alonso said now, "Gilmore has a short memory, for my mother's family, the Hopewells, were here before the Dempseys... They lost the house, but the Villarcas got it back. Now, tell me, do you not think her a fine figure?"

Puzzled by this erratic speech, I said that I could not venture an opinion, since surely...

"Charles! Tell me! You need not spare my feelings. Do you not admire her looks?"

I began to feel alarm, observing the level of the decanter.

"I am sure she was the best of ladies," I said. "But she has passed to a better place than this, and perhaps you should reserve discussion of her for a time when the port is not on the table."

"Port be d--ned. You are unobservant. Truly, have you not noticed that she dines with us every night?" This he said with a peculiarly teasing note that I recalled from the old days; with it came the recollection of how detestable my friend could be when in this mood.

I said, "I am not here for you to make game of me. I do not care for such jokes, and I am persuaded that, after reflection, you will be sorry that you were tempted to speak thus and glad that I would not encourage it."

"I make only a *little* game of you, Charles. For I meant only to show you... There she is, you know. I had her put there, so that we may sit together." He pointed behind him.

I have never had occasion to notice this painting in particular. I doubt I could have described any painting in this house, or any work of art in any house at all, although I must have encountered them. I am not one for the Arts, and folderols, and things of that sort. Music is but an indifferent sound to my ear—I cannot for the life of me distinguish the tuneful from the discordant. The beauty of dance leaves me unmoved. But looking on it—there is something of life that has been lent to this assemblage of canvas and oil.

The background is dark, suggesting a long, bleak landscape, but there is a light in the sky, as if behind the hill, the sun was setting or a great fire burned. A cave draws the eye over her left shoulder, with a strange altar visible within and heathenish markings along its walls, which are obscured by blackening and charring. If there was a fire, the viewer knows that it happened long ago. In the foreground is the central figure, the subject of the portrait.

She is a woman entering the middle years, and no attempt has been made to hide the marks those years have placed on her. The skin is white and bears the pallor of invalidism. And yet there is a determination and vitality about her; she sits as if she had paused for one moment only in the frame, to indulge the painter. The hair is dressed in the absurd, flamboyant style of forty years ago, but it has luster and movement; a curl that lies on her shoulder looks as if it might be shaken any minute by a stray breeze. The eyes are blue and large and stare from the frame. A hand is raised, as if in admonition. A ring gleams there, red and white. It is the ring that now sits on Alonso's little finger.

How odd that a series of marks on a canvas can, seen at a distance, convey so much character and feeling! I think her a fine figure, but I would not want her for my wife: she does not look like a biddable woman. I said so, and Alonso was amused.

I left him, as I do each night, sitting before the fire with a glass by him. I wonder, when does he take his rest? For he seems to be abroad at all times—I have seen him strolling on the lawn under the stars at ungodly hours; I have seen him coming out of the dawn, from the moor, when I am only yawning and rubbing the dust from my eye.

He renewed his offer of laudanum to aid my rest, but my day of exercise had tired me sufficiently for sleep of the soundest kind. I assured him somewhat testily that I would do well enough without it and was presently gratified by drifting comfortably into slumber, thinking of Mary Villarca's pale skin.

My sleep was troubled, a little: I dreamt that Alonso leaned over me. He cradled my head and poured some liquid into my mouth—when I protested, he hushed me, fed me from the cup, and gazed on into the distance. I was swept into dark folds of cloth like swaddling and could not speak. Presently, his form receded through arches of blue light, thrown sharp and thin against the black night, and I saw, weeping, that he was gone into the cathedral without me. I was left outside, surrounded by a high and sonorous song, like the hum of tender bees.

~~In haste, late at night~~

~~There is someone here. They are behind the door. I hear them. Someone watches my sleep.~~

8 October

Nothing pleases me today. I have become a *drunkard*. I have no recollection, for instance, of that crazily scrawled line—I will not call it an entry—of last night. Who did I believe watched me? Anyhow, my mood is not aided by the communication received today via post.

The letter is short but to the point. In broad terms, it is laid out that my sister, Meg, is ungovernable and that Mr. Bantry will not keep her.

I do not understand women. How is it not borne upon this girl, my sister, that it is my sole support and the Christian spirit in these people, the Bantrys, that prevents her being indigent and thrust upon the world with nothing but what she stands up in? Mrs. Bantry suggests that I come to visit, that perhaps my influence will sway her. I am puzzled how to answer her. It is hard, she says, that the girl has no mother and no father. Her mind lacks firmness as a result. She is led easily astray. There are hints of moral turpitude. She would benefit from the guidance of a brother. I will never return to That Place save perhaps in my coffin, and I hope to avoid it even in that circumstance. Those terrible hills. Bury me anywhere, I say, but there.

My father hanged himself before Meg was born. My mother died as she came into the world—an unlucky, redheaded infant. I have said that I would keep her—and I do. I send money that she may live on eggs and cream and not trouble me. Yet trouble me she does.

In times past, Meg would write. She must have been small then. (How did she find the money for a frank? Did she steal it? I am in despair.)

It was hard to know how to answer those childish scrawls. They were disturbing, to say the least. There was always some ludicrous grievance, some allegation of mistreatment, some fantasy of persecution... Hysterical, deserving no reply, and I have enough to do, God knows. At some juncture in the passing of the years, her letters stopped. Sadly, there seems to be no improvement in her conduct.

What can be done? Am I to bring Meg to share the hospitality of Mrs. Healey? Predisposed as she seems to be to vice, am I to leave her to her own devices, with the city of London at her feet? What will she do while I work? Perhaps darn my linen or polish my boots! No, I think not.

These are not matters to be addressed in a letter to a farmer and his wife. I need only think of them bringing the letter down to the curate to be read and dictating their reply to his curious ears... I think Meg must be married. It is much the best thing. I must put it aside for now. The money has been sent this month. Mrs. Bantry will not turn the girl out of doors.

I have put so many miles and years between myself and That Place. I wish it would not dog my footsteps.

> *"He that, being often reproved, hardeneth his neck, shall*
> *suddenly be destroyed, and that without remedy."*
>
> —PROVERBS 29:1

9 *October*

The fearful noise went on without respite—*crack, crack!* Part held by the dream, and with limbs too new to serve me, I shuddered under the sounds, which, with maddening slowness, became intelligible: I was awake and in Rawblood, and there was some person or other below, at the front door.

Some dreams act upon a man like excessive exercise: his body and his mind are cudgeled about by them, and he awakes to the day more exhausted than when he lay himself down. Such was my state.

So I took too long to descend. I paused for the things that one must do in the morning. I should not have. Sometime during my mindless ablutions, the incessant beating stopped—I was glad of it.

I was shuffling my way down the stairs when a sound rent the air like a knife. The howling of a broken-legged horse? The shriek of a steam engine? I could not say. My body was as weak as an Italian noodle.

In the dim hall, the front door was a flaming arch of daylight— against it stood two black figures. They wrestled strangely, swaying to and fro in a dance. One of them was a curious shape, misshapen like a snake that has eaten. This rotund figure shrieked, and the other raised its arms against the noise in defense or in supplication. I ran toward the light.

In his arms, Henry Gilmore bore a child, whose pale face was dominated by black, dilated eyes. The face was swollen, and the tongue rolled crazily from the lips. It took me some time to recognize the plump Robert; he now bore witness to some scene invisible to us and cried out at it. The source of that piercing note became apparent, emerging unreal from the small mouth. Alonso leaned against the jamb, his arms held stiff before him, warding himself from the small bundle.

Mr. Gilmore wept, his fine countenance outraged not by grief, but by anger. He thrust his burden at Alonso, who flinched and flung his arms before him once more in a violent, dumb show.

I grasped Mr. Gilmore by the shoulder and forced myself upon his notice. "Is there a belladonna plant on your grounds?"

He could not answer me but made shapes with his mouth. I took the child from him, a great, soft weight. Gilmore released his grasp, unwilling. As I turned to enter the house, Alonso barred my way.

"It may not come in."

"You cannot be in earnest."

He said, like a man in a dream, "I am."

As I made to pass him, he thrust me back with a slow and lazy motion. It took an age to fall. I met the gravel drive, holding the child protected as best I could before me. My back and arms bore the blow. I was knocked breathless.

"Belladonna?" asked Henry Gilmore, suddenly roused to life. "It grows in the kitchen garden."

"Very well," I said to Alonso from where I lay on the drive. "He may die, as you know, without treatment. Do you still say me no?"

"I do." Alonso went inside then, and to my disbelief, I saw the front door close; I heard the rattle of the bolts shot home. I lay in the sunshine, with the poisoned child in my arms. The world had become a strange place. Henry Gilmore took him from me as I got to my feet, and he wept again—the child wept also. There was nothing to do but what I did next.

"Lay him down on the bank, upon his side," I said. "Do not let him move, or bite his tongue, or swallow it. Put your fingers in his mouth—so—but mind you do not prevent the passage of air. And have a care…"

Even as I said this, he winced, for the child had bitten his hand. I showed him how to depress the tongue, and he did as I bid him, palely.

I left them and went around to the rear of the house. The dining parlor panes yielded easily enough to a stout piece of Dartmoor granite; fortunately, they were not latticed but had been replaced in some time past with a large bay window.

The house was quiet. I listened for any sign of opposition, but hearing nothing, went to the stairs and climbed. I did not trouble with stealth. When I reached Alonso's chamber, it was empty. I went through his possessions carefully, knowing that it would be hidden but not too well. I found it wrapped in a handkerchief with his collars (which were all dirty). There was a stench in the room that teased my remembrance. I closed my eyes for an instant, but it was gone. The bottle was of cloudy green glass. It was oily, as if with the residue of much anxious handling. It bore a vaguely evil look. I hoped it would bring deliverance.

There was my bag to be fetched, and various articles from the kitchen that I thought would be of use; I moved about the house quickly. I did not hear or see a living soul.

When I reached the child once more, he was picking up objects from the grass—invisible to us—and describing them in a high, sharp voice. I took up the green vial and administered the solution of hydrochlorate of morphia: five minims, in a teaspoon, which he did not like. I did not like it either; I could not be sure how much of the drug had been ingested, the liquid collected so around his tongue and in the pockets of his cheeks. I thought he should be got out of the light but should not be taken far in his present state, and I directed Gilmore to move him under the shade of the cedar tree, where he lay, moaning, eyes rolling to the heavens.

He wore his night shift, for he had been wandering by Rawblood this morning, although perfectly lucid. There was something terrible and moving about the plump, bare legs. Gilmore, set to find him, had ridden all night. Finding Robert and taking him up in the saddle, he prepared to make his way home to relieve an anxious household, when Robert began to speak of the rats that raced up and down his body.

Some belladonna berries were clutched still in his hand, which he could not release due to the rictus and tried to eat. This we prevented, but the pulp of their flesh stained his palms as he kneaded them to liquid over the course of the afternoon.

I made my examination. A beautiful rash began to appear, vivid and red, over the surface of his body. It mottled the skin with scarlet, covering him like a creeping vine even as I watched. The pupils were fully dilated. The pulse was approaching one hundred and twenty. The tongue was thick and distended, with froth adhering to the sides. I judged it too late to evacuate the stomach. I believe he would have been asphyxiated by the procedure.

"He wandered the moor all the night through," said Mr. Gilmore, his demeanor calmer now. Though his face bore deep marks of anxiety, these were softened as he looked on the child. "He seemed...as always, when I found him. How can it be? How can the poison take so long?"

"It is often the case with the atropics—that they take up to eight hours to manifest themselves." The child's wrist was plump. I turned it about, palpating it. "I will venture a theory," I said to Gilmore gently, "that he had a substantial supper."

He laughed a little at that. "Robert has the keenest hunger in our family," he said, "as you may see." The child shook.

I laid my hand on his shoulder. "He is, what, ten years of age?" Gilmore assented, and I turned my attention to holding the child still.

"He would not allow me in, even to speak to you," he said after some time. "The nearest doctor is in Moretonhampstead—more than an hour's ride away! He knows it. I would not have believed that anyone could be so indifferent to the suffering of a child."

"My friend is no longer a practicing doctor."

"Does that mean that he may let babies die on his doorstep?"

I had no answer for him. I said Robert's name instead, but he did not know it.

"He will desire soon, I believe, to urinate and will be unable to do so. The usual remedy is a catheter, but I doubt that I possess one of a suitable gauge. You must prepare yourself for his distress."

Gilmore looked troubled. "Should we not make a push for Moretonhampstead?"

"I would not advise it."

"I do not think that he will die," Gilmore said. "Not now, for you have taken him in charge." His face showed the pure vulnerability of hope. The loneliness of his trust descended upon my shoulders. The child began to cry again. Tears streamed from the swollen black eyes.

As the day faded, the shadows lengthened along his body and played with the lineaments of his face. Fear and fatigue will play tricks; these were strange ones. For it seemed to me then that beside us, in the dappled shade of the tree, was a grave new dug. The scent of fresh-turned earth was bitter. I chided myself. But I could not quite shake the fancy.

Just after four o'clock in the afternoon, the crisis came. Robert spoke to his absent dolly and held a lengthy conversation with it, in which the dolly was forbidden to go to the fair. The fair had many mans at it, and the lights were too bright. I agreed that this was so, and without warning, he shook in my arms, and then it was a corpse I held. I regarded him carefully. The bloated face was white and still. All I could think of was Alonso and his madness. Henry Gilmore wept noisily and pressed his fists to his eyes.

I grasped Robert's cold, plump wrists and raised them above his head, then brought them down to his chest with a thump, just above the heart.

Gilmore cried out and clawed at me.

"Be still," I said. "Be still or help me. Sixteen repetitions a minute. Get your watch."

I do not think I have ever applied the Silvester method with such violence. I worked the slack arms up and down and dealt his heart such a blow at each descent that I thought at one time I heard a rib crack. It mattered not.

At length, there was a great shuddering; the child's breath whistled in with the sound of a squeaky door. The bruised eyes opened, and he vomited.

"That is well," I said. "That is very well." I think Henry Gilmore wept again, but I sank into peace and thick exhaustion. Robert and I regarded one another. His gaze still held the light of some place beyond the grave.

I went with them back to the farm. Mr. Gilmore put us all three up on Sadie—there are no more riding horses at Rawblood. We rode in the dark with the sleeping child between us. Sadie knew the way, which was as well. Henry Gilmore could not see through his relief and his weeping.

Into his shoulder, I said, "Do not tell them that Alonso would not help. I swear to you that there is nothing that he could have done and that Robert was as well cared for under that tree as he would have been indoors. I swear it. If you have any thought for me, who kept him here—do not tell them."

He said nothing—not to me then, nor to his family later.

In the candlelight, the faces of Mr. and Mrs. Gilmore were ghostly. I spoke my doctor's piece. They wept and laughed and thanked me. I cannot remember my words; theirs, I could not hear. There was a mist on me.

At the end of my duty, I walked out onto the moor again, into a night like coal. I hoped that I would be lost, but with the indifference of fate, I saw the hills I knew within an hour and Rawblood below, with every window glowing in its familiar pattern. I wondered briefly at the expense of light, but the thought and the answer exhausted me both. The house was lit to guide me home.

I found Alonso in the parlor, where the night air whistled in through the broken window. With eyes half closed, he gestured to the table where were set the glasses, and the port, and the gin, and the cider. There sat there also a profusion of those little green bottles.

If I had been in any doubt as to whether Alonso was still addicted to laudanum, the matter is clear now. It is a subject we do not broach, imbued as it is with so much past pain and so much intimacy. But I confess I had hoped he had thrown it off, these twenty years. It would seem he has done the opposite.

I sat beside him in the seat that was pulled up close to him and made ready for me. Alonso's head hung low on his chest.

"I do not believe I need even frame the question, Alonso, that is in my mind. Why?"

"It is bad," he murmured to his waistcoat, "to have others in the house."

"This is an obsession with you," I said. "Gossip, yes, should be discouraged. But to deny shelter to a dying child?"

"You do not understand the dangers, Charles."

"Explain them."

Alonso reached a hand toward me. He raised his ravaged face to mine. "I had thought you had been caught in the mist," he said. "Oh, Charles, I was afraid you had been caught in it."

"Well, I have not," I replied. "I am here." There was no sense to be had from him that night. I took him to me.

I have never seen him afraid of any natural or man-made thing, except one. He will never venture forth from the house when there is a mist. When he achieves his more acid heights, I am tempted to point out that, for someone dogged by this persistent mania, he has chosen a peculiar climate and position in which to live.

"Manning's cure," he said to me. "Eh, Charles? Eh? *Manning's cure!*"

Here is how, twenty years ago, I accidentally caused Alonso to become an opium fiend.

There is nothing I could have refused him in those days, or he me. It was a constant point with him: that the man and the work were one. It was a joy the like of which I have never known, before or since.

I think that we were drunk again. I know we sat before the fire, in the dark. The house was in dust sheets; we had no time for so petty a thing as housekeeping, and the furniture loomed pale in the firelight behind us like a choir. We settled, as was our habit, on the boards before the smoldering hearth.

"We work with animals now," he said. (We did indeed. There were at that time several cages in the cellar, their occupants in varying stages of disrepair.) "What if we were to introduce the study of Man into our efforts? Do you not see that this is the logical end to our work?"

"I understand the principle. The execution of it?" I studied him. He was suffused with a spirit I had not seen before. The gin and the giddiness that had affected us all evening began to achieve its highest pitch. The scuffle of London at night seemed now to come from a long distance, as if we had already left the paltry mortal world behind and ascended to a higher plane.

"We will choose the test," Alonso said. "Each for the other. For fifty days, you may do what you like with me. You may administer any medicament. I will take it without question. You will note the effects. And I will be unconscious of the treatment. I insist that I am given no hint of what is underway or what you are dosing me with. I cannot seek to countermand it or to avoid it."

"It is a great exercise in faith."

"But of course," he said. "I will be doing the same to you."

The distance and the knowledge that had been building in me reached a height. I laughed. He did not but looked at me kindly.

"You will not kill me. Do you see? It is our absolute trust in each other that will guide us."

We spent some time devising the methods by which we would proceed. We must be sufficiently healthful to minister to one another and for observation; the doses must be given in quantities that were moderate enough for the subject to maintain muscular control and a reasonable degree of mobility. We must always record. No matter what state of illness or fatigue we felt ourselves to be in, we must always note the results. And at the end of fifty days, we would make sure that the process began its reversal.

We made preparations for isolation. No one knew of our intention. Now, when I look back on that time, I think perhaps we should have consulted with someone or other. We arranged for other men to attend our patients. We sealed the house in certain ways and gave out that we would be away from town. We did all to ensure that we would have the leisure to conduct our research undisturbed. In our usual fashion, chaos reigned jointly with order in these preparations. We arranged an ingenious method of goods delivery through the coal chute—but I discovered at the end of our experiment that the street door had been left unlocked throughout.

We began. It was commonplace. He gave me a piece of bread every morning. I took it without reservation. And I gave him a thimble of brandy five times a day. Other than these small practicalities, we did not discuss the matter but went about our business as usual— indeed, much more pleasantly, for we had not the bother of social obligations or duty. For a month and a half, we were a contented little island.

On the last day, he handed me his book that I might see the progress of his research.

The first note in that book was an extract copied from Chambers's journal. When I read it, I laughed. I noted it:

> Lastly, let me urge upon all who adopt the Styrian sys-
> tem to make some written memorandum that they have
> done so, lest, in case of accident, some of their friends
> may be hanged in mistake.

It became a something of a settled joke between us: "Do not be hanged in mistake!"

I was most interested in the record of Alonso's work, as I had read of the Styrian system, the practice of eating arsenic to give stamina and wind for hard work. It is common among certain tribes in Europe; immunity builds progressively and cumulatively as the dosage increases.

I remained in perfect health throughout. He attributed a certain fatigue to me, but I was not conscious of it. I can in honesty say that I suffered no serious ill effects. My skin had a pallor, and my hair acquired a new sheen, but these were nothing. The treatment was a pleasant suspension of the humdrum. I spent most of it consolidating my reading on bowel disorders. When I was weaned off it, I felt the effects of poison for a day or two, but mildly, and was not incapacitated. His notes were thorough. The dosage increased in perfect increments. He was never in danger of being hanged.

And what of me? How did I use that license we had extended to one another? I chose a true poison. If I have railed against that person I saw before me today, I have no right to do so, for I made him. I gave Alonso opium. I began him on this path. It was a terrible error on my part. I had heard of Manning's new cure for opiate addiction. It consisted of a cordial of chlorate of gold every few hours, with daily hypodermic injections of strychnine and atropine. I thought that it would surely work.

It did not. When the time came to ease him off the opium, Alonso reacted most violently to the cordial; he was delirious and enraged. I believe all the injections accomplished was to give him the idea to inject the morphia intravenously. Thirty days beyond the end of our trial, his lust for the drug was greater than ever.

Alonso must have known that I was giving him laudanum. He must have. He was a doctor and not of my average talent—very gifted. But he did not turn from our purpose, for he trusted me. And then it was too late.

I must plead a certain license and draw a veil; I find, after all, that I cannot speak of those times. There ensued secrecy and pain and various other things. The other things being predictable, common to many other tales, easily imagined. I need not repeat them here. Alonso became a travesty of a man. When he retired to the country and then to Italy, to pursue opium eating in peace, when he became the shadow he is today—it was relief I felt.

Late, by night

~~By stealth or by force, I must get out of here, I must.~~

My dreaming self, my night self, is a most alarmist person. What possesses me to write these things? The hand is surely mine, and fairly neat. As it should be. I was not so very far gone last night. Sleep writing—a new phenomenon?

IRIS

SUMMER 1914

I'm fifteen.

I am half buried in straw in the depths of Nell's stall, watching the gentle shift of her elegant legs. Her tail swoops and flicks, black and yellow and steel gray. I'm not in trouble yet, but I will be when they find the broken vase in the dining room. Best to sit it out. The straw is warm and prickly. The stable is quiet. I slip in and out, treading the edge, the abyss of sleep.

My father's voice is suddenly in my ear, and it's all I can do not to leap to my feet and squeak.

He is strange, of late. My father. He looks at things that aren't there. He answers questions I have not asked. He speaks to people who I know are long, long dead. His lined face pierces my heart. His great brown eyes are soft, too soft, where they should be sharp. He sounds all right now.

Of course, he's not actually in my ear, but close enough, in Soldier's stall next door. Must have been dreaming deeper than I thought, or they've crept up on the lightest of feet. His question, Shakes's voice replies.

Papa's saying, "The poultice should set it right by next week."

Someone clicks their tongue, and Tom's voice says, "Come up, now."

They're quiet. I picture them all three bent and earnest over Soldier's hoof.

"He's doing well," says Papa.

"Yup," says Tom.

Papa says, "The horses will miss you."

Tom says, "Someone else'll come along soon enough."

"And the horses will learn to like it," says Shakes, comfortable.

"Not everyone wishes to work at Rawblood," says my father. He sounds tired. The hollow sound of Soldier knocking his bucket with a hoof. He hopes it's feed time. My father whispers to him. The good hard clap of a palm on shining hide. "I will look in on him again tomorrow," Papa says. I feel him, his dark presence behind the stall door as he goes.

From Soldier's stall, there comes the whisper of caps being put back on heads. Someone lights a pipe. The blue smoke is idle on the air. Soldier knocks his bucket.

"Well," says Shakes, "maybe it's no bad thing, you going."

"Suppose," says Tom, "you keep quiet, just for a bit? Just while we muck out the boxes. After that, why, you go on and get it all off your chest. I'll be miles away, but you'll feel better."

"Used to be such a nice little bugger, you did."

"Ah, well."

"Grown too fast, your common sense hasn't kept pace. Bad lot. Not fit to be around gentle people." Shakes's scorn rings high into the stable rafters. "Young ladies and so on."

"'Round here?"

"That's cheek, right there," says Shakes. "Yes. Drinking and chasing girls and whatnot."

"Whatnot."

"Army'll teach you what's what," says Shakes. "Mark my words. War will."

"Well," says Tom, and there's a little crack of uncertainty in his voice, "not sure I'm right for it."

"Best notion you've had in years."

"Not mine," says Tom, "as it happens. He gave me the boot." There's silence. Soldier knocks his bucket.

"How's that?" Shakes says.

"Himself. Told me I was no longer needed."

"Well. See? Drinking. Chasing girls. That's what you get." But Shakes's voice has lost its confidence.

"Gave me a hundred quid, told me to enlist. Well shy of eighteen, I am. He said they'd take me anyway. And they did."

"A hundred quid? I'll go and all." They go away down the stable, voices raised, bickering and fond.

Long after they're gone, I am pinned in place. My eye at the crack in the stall door, straw rustling, Nell breathing warm into my back.

I have abided by his rules, in recent years, so closely. I have kept my word. I have obeyed him to the letter. But Papa is sending Tom away, and that is *not* in our agreement.

When I think of Tom going to war, my heart stops, actually stops.

Before the glass, I smooth the dark fabric one last time. The stays are unfamiliar, another skeleton between cloth and skin. I am tight but brittle somehow, as if I might break. The perfume of lilies hangs in the air, which I regret. I have tried to wash it off my wrists. It is pale, lingering, persistent. I don't think it's a scent for skin. For wigs or cloth or something.

It took an hour, maybe more, to get the riding habit on. Sixty tiny jet buttons fasten me, throat-high, to the mandarin collar that brushes my chin. The jacket small, severe. Whalebone pinching me in at the waist. Swags and swathes of serge skirt; a heavy train, with a loop for the wrist. The deep, deep blue faded in patches to stormy gray. Attic dust still clinging in the folds.

I present a strange, antiquated silhouette. Tall, wasp-waisted. Armored. Anyhow, I don't look like myself, which can only help. My flesh is restless. Behind me in the glass, the window shows blue sky. That's good. I must look different, be different, now; I will no longer be told what to do and what to fear.

There's no denying things haven't come out quite right. I smell like a syrup or a sweet, sickening. The corsetry is snappy, cracking. I can't feel my lungs. The glass shows me pale and cross. I pinch my cheeks, but it makes no difference. *Part the hair over the left eye or catch it back in a low pompadour and pull out softening locks over temples and ears with your comb... Soft bandings across the hair are universally becoming.* My hair won't even stay under my hat. I lick my wrists, rub them on the skirt. Bitter, oily taste on my tongue.

I give it up. I spit into the ewer, take my whip in hand, and go.

"There you are, old chap," says my father, melting out of his darkened study into the bright hall. His spectacles are askew. His nose wrinkles at the cloud of roses. He says, "Riding? Iris, there was a vase, in the dining room—"

"To Grimspound," I say quickly.

He sees me. He stills. Even at a distance, I feel all his muscles go quiet. He says, "Where's your twill?"

"It's muddy," I say. As if this were a sufficient reason to go to the attic, find and put on my dead mother's riding dress.

"It fits well," he says at last. A quick furrow between his brows. "I'll put you up," he says, and we go.

The sun is blinding after the dim hall. On the blazing white drive, Nell stands, her pale legs in constant movement, shifting, twisting her into the glistening surface. A brown hoof lifts, strikes the marble chips, tosses them into a spray. Matilda throws herself sideways. At the horses' heads, the groom tuts, soothes each in turn.

When I come near, Nell stills, lifts her ears. I stroke her neck. Her withers curve against the sky.

My father's hand is cupped for my foot. I swing the habit up over my arm in an unfamiliar, heavy swathe, reach for the high pommel, step in. Something happens as he lifts me—beneath my foot, his hand is gone, and I'm caught, suspended in air. Then I fall. My skirt billows.

I land neatly on my feet with a crunch of gravel. Nell turns a dark, surprised eye.

When I look, there is a thin, old gray man where my father should be. His arms shake by his sides as he stands. I begin to say, "Papa, are you..." But the old man flaps his hand like the muscular wing of a bird. His lips are trembling, loose. He shuffles toward me, hand outstretched once more for my foot. His eyes are somewhere else.

"Meg," the old man says, reaches for me.

The groom brushes past him, comes silently to my side, throws me aloft in one quick movement, settles my foot in the stirrup.

My father stops, blinks. He turns, goes up the steps, goes inside. I look after him, a bent figure vanishing into the shadowed hall. Then I put Nell's nose into the breeze. She huffs, plays with the bit, wanting to go. The drive scatters around us with the sound of breaking glass. It's not till we're on earth, grass, that I hear Matilda behind. I don't look back. We pound up the hill into the copse.

We slow out of sight of the house, and Matilda comes up beside us, settles into place at my side. The breeze wanders through the trees. My heart is heavy and burning.

"Horse coming on nicely," he says, nodding at Nell.

"You'd no call to do that," I say, "to shame him like that."

His face is unreadable in the shadow of his cap. He says nothing.

"He was all right. How could you show him up?" A feeling like taut wire in my chest. And I think again of what I heard yesterday in the stable. "How dare you," I say to him and nudge Nell. She moves on, ears pricked at the rustles of the woodland. Matilda hurries to keep pace beside her.

I say, "Fall behind, Gilmore."

He starts to speak, then touches his cap, pulls Matilda up, falls a proper distance behind.

This was supposed to go so differently.

We move into untenanted country, alone but for the larks and the rabbits. He stays behind, a precise five feet. I feel him like a weight. Bees hum. Grasshoppers sing. My head aches. The stink of lilies hangs in my throat.

He comes up beside when we reach the ford. He fixes me with the side of his eye, blue and white. He pulls his cap off, rubs his head, puts it back on. The Dart runs wide and bronze before us. I've never seen it so high. Shining surface, deep water. Summer rain running to the sea.

"Iris," Tom says.

I lift my chin up and away.

He says, "You ride with Shakes. Not with me."

I'm silent, eyes on the burnished river.

"Why today?" Tom asks.

I think of what Shakes said to my father in the stable. Tom watches me and waits. He's taller than I remember. Quieter. His face used to show everything. He has shut himself away, and I'm facing a stranger. Matilda, who likes to dance and bite and fret, stands like stone under him. His hands on the reins are not boy's hands.

It's no good. We haven't spoken to one another in so long. I can't remember how to do it.

Tom gives me a long measuring look, then shrugs, sharp and furious. "All right," he says and surges past. He plunges Matilda into the ford. She moves surely through the water, climbs the far side, her wet tail a mean thin streak of bay. Tom wheels her around on the bank to face us.

Nell steps out with cautious hooves; she fusses as the river stones shift under her. She bends, breathes her disapproval at the quick brown surface. I let her make her own way. She won't fall. When the water's at her flanks, the folds of my skirt come loose from my hand, and the hem skims the water. The cloth blackens, hauled in by the running stream.

I say, "Damn," pull at it, gather it up.

"I've time to finish that book," says Tom from across the river. "Or pop over to London for the day to see the king, shall I? Take a cruise on the Nile. Still be back by the time you get here."

Matilda shifts, patient, under him. She bows a long mahogany neck, salutes us from the bank. In the river, Nell stops, plants her legs, shivers.

"Particular, aren't you?" Tom calls. Nell pays him no mind, breathes crossly at the water. Tom drops his reins, folds his arms as if for sleep, tips his cap over his nose, snores.

I push Nell on. She doesn't want to go. "You've done it a hundred times," I say and give her a hard cut across the quarters with the whip. She leaps forward. The riverbed vanishes.

We're buffeted from the stony floor, off the shelf, into deep water. Nell is lifted, taken, caught in cold brown current. She's swept, we're swept, like paper in the wind. My skirts are a heavy balloon in the insistent, downward suck. All around, little waves ripple, and cold water grasps my waist, arms, chest. The horse's neck rears like a sea monster in front of me. Nell swims. Her muscles move like pistons. I float, cling to her straining neck. My foot drifts loose from the stirrup. The heavy skirt pulls—the river wants it. Water rises, skims my chin. Knotted, cold fingers loosen; I feel them go. Cold mouthfuls. I think, *So this is what it's like.* A glimpse of Tom sliding off Matilda, face very pale, caught in an expression I don't know.

Nell strikes the sandy bottom, finds her legs. She ploughs busily through the water, up, out, onto the bank, casting walls and waves of spray in all directions. I lie forward on her, hug her as she moves, solid, suddenly earthbound.

Tom says "hell" and wipes his face with his neckcloth. His fingers have a twitch in them. The cloth won't go where he wants.

I come up beside them. Nell is iron-gray, wet. She leans in, nostrils wide, to adore Matilda. Matilda blinks; her hide shivers with pleasure under the scatter of cool drops. I throw my habit back over her quarters where it hangs, sopping.

"The bottom drops away. On the right," Tom says.

"Yes," I say, "it does."

He reaches his unsteady hand to Nell's neck. "Good girl," he says. She pays him no mind, and her nose touches Matilda's. "Check her legs," he says and makes to get down.

"She's all right," I say.

We look at one another. It's like the skin's been stripped from both of us. I don't know what to do, so I say, "Race'll dry us off. If you remember the rules."

He's gone before I say *rules*; all that's left is the pounding of hooves and trembling air between the trees. Nell shivers with longing, and I let her go.

She runs like a greyhound, flattens her Arabian ears, flattens herself over the land. The woods blur. As we come out of the copse, we pass Matilda. She's straining at the bit, held back to a canter. Tom is twisted in the saddle, looking behind him. He doesn't hear our approach on the soft woodland floor; he starts. We fly past him into open ground.

The moor, wide in the sunshine. Wind hits us like a breaker. Ahead, the tor spills out of the hill. The old wall curves toward it, cuts across the green. It's been some time, but of course, I remember: the first boulder, shaped like an egg, is the winning post. No jumping the wall. No cutting across. Tom always wins. I am vague and blind, eyes streaming. Follow the long, hectic curve. Nell elongates beneath me, opens up her stride; clods of earth scatter and fly. My habit is blown out stiff behind us, solid in the wind. Emptied. Nothing left but my heart and the drum of hooves. When Nell sees Matilda's long brown nose inching up beside her, she hoots. I've never heard a horse make this sound before. It's impossible that we could go faster, but Nell's gray neck snakes out, and she becomes a flat pattern of flying legs. Cold thrills run under my skin. A loose stone, a rabbit hole, an old nail, a dip in the ground—if she doubts for a moment, if she puts a foot wrong, we'll break our necks. The egg shivers, thrums, a hundred feet ahead. The land rushes toward us at a gallop. Matilda is nowhere to be seen; golden lichen and gray rock flash by. Past the egg.

I pull Nell up, cheeks stinging. Her breath comes in hard explosions. She slows gradually, like someone waking from a dream. I stroke her hot neck, sticky under my palm. I tell her she's wonderful. My ears ring in the sudden quiet; we're wind blind.

Behind me, Tom says, "She had me off at the wall." He's leading Matilda with one hand; the other hangs limp, strange. Fine scratches cross his cheek. Black mud covers his side. Matilda pushes Tom with her face. He pushes her back with the awkward hand. This is all wrong. Tom never falls off.

"Serves you right," I say at last. "Going over the wall's cheating. Not in the game."

"I didn't." He comes to lift me down, one hand limp, the other formal.

"No," I tell him. I slither off, wet, awkward.

Tom says, "You smell like an old woman's wig." Lilies.

We tether the horses to a small twisted rowan tree that grows from the side of the hill and go up. We find a patch of high shade in the tumble of stone and sit. I spread my skirts wide to dry, an expanse of wet serge. On the rock pile below, an adder emerges from a shaded crevice. It coils itself decidedly, silently, in the sunshine. Around us, the land is blue and green and purple. Clouds pass. Somewhere in the warm distance, sheep make complaints.

"I didn't do it to shame him," Tom says suddenly. "Dropped you. Saw you fall. He's worse, Iris. These days."

"I was all right." I am belligerent for form's sake. I try not to think of the strange gray man who took my father's place. I try not to think of how he reached for me and called me by my mother's name. "I was angry," I say. "Not because of Father. Or yes. In part… Are you going away, Tom? Are you going somewhere?"

He says, "No, are you?" The words are light, pattering.

I take the wrist lying at his side, bend it slowly back. He shouts, sits up. The adder vanishes into the dark like water poured from a pitcher. The wrist is swollen, pink beneath the brown of his arm. The bones feel too far away beneath the skin.

I fumble beneath my wet skirt.

"Knife," I tell him.

He eases it from his pocket, puts it in my hand. The crack of tearing cotton.

"You'll have a job to explain it," he says.

"Tear my things all the time."

When I have three long strips of petticoat, I take his wrist, bind it tight and smooth. He bears it, shivering. I give him back his knife, his wrist.

"You're going away," I say. "Don't lie." His eyes are on Matilda, below. She rubs her poll against the rowan bark. I say, "I heard you and Shakes yesterday."

"What's that?" he asks and turns to me. The lines of his face are strange and thoughtful. His cheekbone beaded, smeared with blood.

"That Papa gave you money." The words are fragments in my mouth.

His good fingers drum the granite. They stroke the wet, dark line of my skirt where it lies. He rubs the hem between finger and thumb. "This bugger," he says, "nearly killed you."

"It was my mother's," I say. "Are you going to the war, Tom?"

"Where," he asks, "do I go if not there? What do I do? Going to be your groom forever, am I?" He pulls his cap off. Lies back on the rock, face to the sky, eyes closed. In the bright day, his face is thin, white, absent. An old bruise the color of plum jam spreads over his forehead, disappears into the eye socket. Another, older than that, yellowing beneath it. The hand that clasps the cap to his chest is swollen, the knuckles rich purple, soft black.

"Been fighting," I say. "What have you been at, Tom? *Fighting*, drinking"—and then, inspired—"chasing girls."

His look is very blue. "What of it?" he asks. "What do you care about it?"

"You're not much good," I say. "At fighting. From the looks of you."

"No, not much," he says. "Have to get better. When I go."

"Don't, then," I say, but he goes on.

"I wanted to say, anyway." His hand quivers on the granite. "That I should've known and not taken you out that night. I should've known you were ill. So, sorry." Having discharged his duty, he nods and turns away, passing his hand across his eyes. His white wrist is linen-bound, unbearable. I think of how I made him ride behind me through Dartmeet. I recall what I said to him after the cave, years ago. My voice shrill through the fever. *Too old to play with the stable boy.* Something, some feeling, rises in me like water.

"I've treated you like a servant," I say. I find the word, which is unfamiliar, exotic. "That was unforgivable."

"No," he says. "Hardly." He puts his head in his hands. "*Chasing girls,*" he says, high-pitched. It's a fair imitation. "Shakes'd die." His eyelids are large, dark-lashed, so white they're nearly blue. Gleam of teeth through his fingers. He's still angry.

"And I'm sorry," I say. "I'm sorry that your father died. I should have told you that much sooner."

He shakes like a dog that's been told to stay. In his neck the blood courses, the tendons move delicately. Too close to the surface, too easily reached. He's flesh, bone, breath, all held together with wishful thinking. I cannot stop imagining him bloody, blown apart.

I touch his cheekbone, and beneath it, the elegant hollow that curves to his mouth. His breath is warm on my fingers.

He winces. "What are you doing?" he asks.

"It will be all right," I say. "But if you leave," I hear myself say then, "it'll not be right with me again, ever." I can't find the words to tell him how awful it would be: how my heart would lie dead in my chest like a stone…

Tom puts my hand away from his face. "Get off," he says. "You daft?" He is blank with dislike.

"Sorry," I say. "I mean—"

"Barely a word to me for a year. Now this. Last thing you said to me was to leave you alone, that time, do you remember? Alone. I suppose that's what it is—you're too much alone, d'you see? That's all. Who do you know? No one. Only me. He keeps you all alone out here, Iris. It's not right. Makes you strange. Poor kid."

It's like a rapid series of blows to the face. I feel the wind behind each one. Colors are blurred with salt.

"Oh, now," he says lightly. "Oh, come off it."

Things are happening very fast, or too slowly. I press my eyes hard into my hands. Lights bloom and contract against my lids. Sunlight smarts on my steaming cheeks.

I wait. I wait until the needling stops in my eyes and the breath doesn't hitch in my throat. I wait.

When I'm calm, I look up. Tom's back is to me. It is rigid, expressive. I slap him hard. The flesh rings through his thin shirt.

He shouts, "Owyoubugger."

"Look at me," I say. "I've something to say."

His shoulders drop. His entire being slumps. "Iris," he says to his knees.

"Go on," I say.

He looks up. Before he can speak, I feint another slap at his face, light and fast. He shouts, rocks back, eyes wide. My fingertips graze his chin.

He holds his hand to his cheek and stares. "Funny, I *don't* think," he says. But it is. He is aghast; he should be clutching pearls at his neck. After a moment, he laughs too, his high, rattling laugh.

"Do you know," I ask, "why I kept away from you?" And I tell him. About the bargain. About the Villarcas. About *her*. Tom listens intently. The air and the sun seem to cleanse the words. The world changes as I speak. The fear goes out of it.

When I'm finished, he says, "My dad told me something like it, you know, very like all that, before he died." His mouth narrows, a bitter line. "Those old men. Ghosts and curses and so on. Just an old-fashioned way of saying they didn't get on. It's all nonsense, you know that, don't you, Iris?"

"I do, really," I say.

"He must be lonely," says Tom.

I am shaking, released. I guessed right the first time, after all, on that day in the graveyard. *She* is just Papa's fear. That I will leave him alone.

We sit. We watch the warm, humming land. I look at him: the line of his nose, his jaw. Memory drifts through, in no order. Feet in shallow streams. Long days and the taste of grass. Snow, shining horsehide. The pain of the tooth I lost in that tumble, the dungy stable yard, the pink ragged gap under my tongue. His eyebrow, the line of a swallow against the sky. He held the foal's head that summer. Its dark eyes, his careful hands. How violently, how ferociously, he willed it to live. So much of my waking life has been spent in this way, being quiet with Tom.

"I meant it all," I say to him. "What I said. I'll never be all right without you." I'm not afraid. He turns a grim blue eye on me. Actually, I am afraid. A feather floats through my chest. It sidles, drifts, settles.

Tom is suddenly white and awful. "Bugger," he says. He takes two handfuls of damp serge habit and unfolds them gently. He spreads the hem wide and pulls hard.

Stone skids under me. My shoulder meets his collarbone with a thump. I say, "Watch it."

He says, "Sorry."

Close to, he's strange. His eyelashes dark feathers. The vast shifting geometry of his face, the pink cavern of his ear. Breath in my hair, wind in long grass. The tiny sounds of his skin. Baffling, disconnected glimpses. Eyes opaque like panic.

I draw a finger along the dark swell of his brow. "It's all right," I say.

His hands unfold; they make a flower in the small of my back. His breath fills my head like the ocean. We're alive. The sky's larger than it has ever been.

❧

"I'll come," Tom says.

"No," I say. "He's to hear it from me." The light's lazy on the drive. The scent of cut grass. Rawblood is long and quiet in the afternoon.

"You're a state," Tom says.

I am. My skirts are drenched again and heavy with mud. On the way back, Tom pulled me onto Matilda midriver. We let Nell make her own way. I sat before him all the way home, his heart against my back.

I put my tongue out, throw Nell's reins at him. The soaked skirt is heavy on my arm. The front door screeches, but no one comes. I creep through the sunlit rooms. Across the great hall, where the sun lies in warm bars on the flags, down the west corridor, where it falls in great diamonds across the floor and walls. At the door of my father's study, I pause.

What to say? What has been decided? Marriage, I suppose, though we haven't spoken of it. All I know is that there is no time. No time before Tom goes, so it must be now. I wait for the doubt to catch up with me. It doesn't come. I am warmed from within. The tor, the sunlight. I carry it before me in my mind's eye. I have broken our bargain, but he will forgive me. My father has wanted my happiness, always.

The study door opens with a noise like a knife in the back. The room's hot, suffocating. Stink of old sweat. The dark paneling is raked with scars as if by claws. Screws of paper litter the floor. Something small and dark scurries under a bookcase. A book flung facedown in the bare grate. Shakes doesn't clean in here. This is Papa's place.

My father is dreaming. Half propped at the desk, glazed eyes under heavy lids. Leather wallet open on the shining walnut, the hint of shining metal within. His face is absent, but his long, graceful hands are busy. The bunched-up shirtsleeve, the tourniquet. The needle, gleaming and ready.

I whirl, about to go. This is most dreadful; this is a thing I must never do: watch while Papa uses his pouch.

My wet skirts make a grand sweeping noise across the floor.

"Iris?" His voice, slow and muddy. Slack-tongued.

"I am going, Papa. I am so sorry. Very sorry—" I hear myself, high, rabbiting. A nervous child.

I stop with my hand on the doorknob. I think of the long years of solitude, the years of *the disease*. Those nights I feared I might not see the end of—that death would swoop down soft and take me up, unknowing. The long days of loneliness. The shame, the guilt, deep-rooted. *I am a pariah, infected.* The tales of ghosts, of deaths and curses… I am an ignorant oddity, riddled with freaks. Nearly a grown woman, but I can't put my hair up. And all so that Papa wouldn't be troubled with people. So that he could take his morphine in peace. Suddenly, I'm not sorry at all.

"Tell me, Papa," I say. "If I had not been interested in medicine and found out that *horror autotoxicus* was a lie, would you have ever told me any different? Though when the disease was no longer any good, you came up with *her*… Reasons that I can never leave you. Diseases, ghosts: you liar, Papa. You'd have me forever a child." His eyes, dark and steady on mine. "Do you know, I even convinced myself that I had seen *her*? I had a very high fever… I was so afraid. I have been afraid all my life. Enough."

I go to where he's slumped. I pluck the hypodermic needle from his nerveless hand. He reaches, vaguely, and I put it behind my back. "This is all you care about," I say. "I have long accepted it. I have looked up to you. I had hoped to be *like* you. Those were childish hopes. You are not to be emulated. You are a coward who'd have me shun the world as you do. You kept me here alone, under glass like a microscopic slide.

"You made Tom a groom, threatened me with diseases and ghosts, hoping to end our friendship. You nearly succeeded… And then you tried to send him away. But, Papa, there are some things you cannot control. I have come to tell you that we are to be married."

He says, in a thick, dreamy voice, "I see."

"Good," I say. "I hope that you will give me your blessing."

He sighs. "I see," he says again. "*Her.*" He looks up. Something empty and dead is using his eyes.

He stands. Is Papa so tall? A stench comes off his body.

"Papa…" I waste no more words. Because that is not my father.

The great walnut desk topples with a crash. I leap back and say *no*, but he's fast. His fingers are around my neck; they press stars up into my eyes. He squeezes my throat with one hand, with powerful ease. Pain. Whirling white. Cracking like little bones breaking… His grip's too low to break the hyoid, but I'm suffocating. Something like a rock smashes into my cheekbone; he hits me with a great, closed fist. Things burst, and then there's singing, singing in my ears, in my skull. The room blurs and fades. We're deep in a cloud. Sound is muffled, far away. Through the misty streaks, he reaches behind me, for the needle. As he does, his grip loosens, just a little.

I break his nose with the heel of my hand. A quick red crack. Blood in the air, suspended droplets. He roars, and the fingers are gone from my throat. I drag air in once like a bellows, then I'm off.

Tom's outside the study door, white and questioning.

I can't speak and I can't see for tears.

Tom looks at me for a heartbeat, then he takes my hand, and we run. The quick, heavy steps of the stranger behind us.

Running, running through Rawblood, Tom pulling me—my arm stretches like rubber about to break, he's pulling me so hard. Fingers squeak on doorknobs, panicked hands slap the corners, corridors seem to narrow as we go. The stranger just behind, breathing like a furnace.

We explode into the great sunlit hall. The riding habit falls through my treacherous fingers; I can't catch it up again, and it drags soggy behind me, catching in cracks, leaving a shining wake, slowing me. It is all the dreams I've ever had of being chased. I run from the darkness; it's close on my heels. The stranger's breath hacks and rattles, sounds like battlements, stone grinding against stone. A great shadow looms like a turret at my back.

My foot catches in my skirt. I fall. It's endless. Something heavy hits me, knocks me into the earth with a cracking of ribs. I hit out with both fists. I still hold the needle in one hand. I'd forgotten. It punctures flesh somewhere with an abrupt sound. Glass splinters. There's blood in many little streams all over my hands, running red in all directions into the dark.

Cool flags under my cheek. The hall is barred with sun. It falls everywhere in broken stripes. A messy, shining trail across the stone. Halfway across the hall, the trail becomes mingled with glutinous red. It is obscene, like the path of a great, injured worm. I sit up.

By my feet, the black shape. A pile of cloth and strange, pale flesh. The blood runs everywhere, pools, shines in little runnels between the flagstones. It runs over the shattered glass that lies everywhere in the warm light. The broken hypodermic needle protrudes from Papa's chest, moves gently with his shallow breath, shining. Air twitters through his punctured lung.

Tom's small, curled in the corner by the fireplace, back turned. His head bobs. A grinding noise comes from him.

Papa puts forth a slippery red hand. "Iris," he says. "This." He twists the ring from his slick finger. Slow.

It slides into my palm like a little stone.

"Yours now," my father says. "Dear heart."

"Papa," I say. The dark clown mouth spreads outward on the gray of his waistcoat. "Papa," I say. "I understand now. I did not believe… I am sorry, so sorry…"

My father says, "I know." Or perhaps it is "No." He starts, staring at me or something behind me.

A cold finger runs down my spine. I whip around.

There's nothing but Rawblood, warm in the afternoon.

My father reaches for me. His eyes are fixed and wide, brown pools. "I see," he says, "*her.*"

His bloodied hand is light on my head, and then he goes. Cloth and cold flesh are left. Dead.

Sounds come as if through water. Wind whistling through a window somewhere. Blood hitting the floor sounds like *tick tick tick*. I press my face to the face that was his. It's cool India rubber. The bright air turns, a carousel.

Tom stirs in the corner, white. I think about him, about what Shakes thinks of him, about what other people might think… I think of *her*, and my being goes cold. I saw nothing, nothing but Papa's dark shadow, his blood. But *she* was here. He saw her; she took his life. Where is she now?

"Tom," I say.

He raises a gray face. Something clings to the corner of his mouth.

"Take it," I say.

The ring gleams white and red in Tom's warm, trembling palm.

"Take it. From me to you," I say. "Now leave. Go now. Run." When Tom doesn't move, I shout it over his protests. I slap his hands away; he tries to hold me. *Go*, I say. *Go, go, go.* Until he goes.

When he's gone, I sit. I am small and dry inside. The tears that stream down my face are nothing to do with me. My habit, wet again, this time with blood. The scent of it is heavy in the air. It seems an age since this morning, an age since the rock, the sunshine, the air. Did it happen? It's impossible. Nothing has ever happened or will ever happen again; I have always sat here with the sticky wet red drying on me, clutching the cooling corpse.

Without doubt, this is my doing. The great, great depths of my stupidity are revealed. My arrant carelessness, my arrogance. I'd thought the Rules didn't apply to me. Papa told me; he warned, but I didn't believe. I didn't believe in *her*. I thought I could do what I wished, and the cost is beyond bearing.

I close the eyelids over his dull, staring eyes. It's not easy. They want to stay open. I sit. I move beyond feeling. Grief, loss—what do these strange, weak words have to do with the jagged tear, the rent that goes right through the heart of me? My father is dead, and I killed him. It should have been me. I should have known that it would come to this.

Perhaps I cannot see her, but I understand now what Papa was trying to say. *She* is in everything. She's all the sickness of the world. But also our own particular plague, just for us, the Villarcas.

I speak to her in my mind. I ask her to come. I beg her to take me—I plead. I, who am now the last of us.

Too late. In the distance, the keening of oak. A door. Someone is coming now.

CHARLES DANFORTH

11 October 1881

Mᵒre tissue samples today. Alonso and I take it in turns now. Why should we both suffer?

The cellar was quiet. I did not turn on that ghastly electric light but carried my own lamp.

The rabbits lie, panting and still, bound tight about their midriffs with white linen. There is the smell, not unpleasant, of basilicum powder and carbolic. With their heads on their paws, in their human bandaging, they have the appearance of a conceit, dreamt of by some satirical illustrator. (*The Field Hospital*, perhaps.)

I did what was necessary. As I moved about the room, their gazes followed me, bright, showing me back myself in each dark, nutlike eye. I did not like the sounds they produced before—much like an eagle's scream—but I am tempted to say that I like their silence less.

As I came to the end of the row, I saw that the old buck—I forget the

absurd name Alonso has bestowed upon him—had escaped his dress-
ings. The rabbit had pressed himself into the corner of his box, small
and furred and brown. At his throat, the bandage hung slack from his
neck where a neat rusty mark betrayed the tracheal incision. The mess
of white linen and cheesecloth lay in the corner of the cage, brown and
yellow-stained, much clawed as if he had attempted to bury them. I
opened the door and made to take him, forgetting in that instant.

He turned to flee, laying bare his other side, and showed me my
mistake. I saw our handiwork full well. He is an anatomy lesson. Along
his left flank, the hide and flesh are neatly reflected back and excised.
The anterior ribs are sawn away and blunt. Beyond them, there is a
warm cavity through which can be seen the pulsing, the inner work-
ings. The gentle rise and fall of the exposed lungs. Pink they are, and
pretty, looking like soft crepe for a party. The network of blue vessels
runs through his exposed landscape. As he shifted, there was a glimpse
of the spleen, protruding deep red like the tip of a tongue. The blackened areas scattered here and there show where we have taken tissue and
cauterized with the hot iron. A loose swag of purple bowel hung plump
by his hind leg.

All this, I have seen before. And I had my own part in its doing.
But in that moment... Well.

As I wrapped him, taking care not to touch with my fingers the
exposed parts, he began to make a sound, which I had not thought
possible. It was very like a tin whistle, but mournful. I soon saw that
it was merely my handling, which produced a compression of the
lungs, sending air through the puncture in his throat, his larynx. The
sound acted upon me, however. It was ineffable, and I cannot say I
am yet recovered.

Afterward, I went up to the kitchen and, after some hunting, found
an onion. I brought it down and left it inside the door of his cage. He
did not look at it or me. I do not know if he will eat it, or if it will do

him harm, or if rabbits are partial to such food. Now, I am half inclined to go and take it away again. I do not know what to do. Oh, God—I am tired.

12 October

We go on, we go on. The days are long, and the nights are wordless. Exhaustion takes us both to its bosom at dusk. There is no sound at the board but each man's private consumption. Afterward, we slump in our dusty chairs and drink, deep and long; eventually, I take myself to my rest, uncertain of my steps and with a thick head, only to rise the next morning, cursing, to begin it all over again.

Alonso's hair seems to be dark again. It is streaked now with black, creating a strangely pleasing effect, somewhat like a badger. Could he be dyeing it? I cannot summon the courage to ask. He looks perhaps fifty now, rather than seventy. Rawblood improves him. I cannot say it does the same for me.

My visit has stretched on and on… It must end now. I have said I will return here next month, in order to be present for the next stage, where we will introduce the contaminant into the healthy host. I cannot believe it will work. I begin to doubt our thesis most seriously. Truthfully, I do not think I will come back. I can concoct some excuse, when the time comes.

It will be good to return to my life, spartan as it is. I think of my cheerless little room with some relief and find myself dwelling on Mrs. Healey's unlovely physiognomy with something like longing. The doing of great things is all very well, but there is comfort in monotony and the performance of one's duty. My practice no doubt suffers in my absence—I do not like Babcock, much as I try, and I was loath to leave matters in his charge. Truthfully, I think him knuckleheaded; I believe he will inflict his antiquated notions on my patients and perhaps even *cup* them. But enough! It does not bear thinking of. Suffice to say that I will be relieved to take up the reins again. I have told Alonso of my departure. He said little but made me a brandy flask to take below.

Drink has become necessary—for us to bear one another's company and for the continued performance of duty. The cellar begins to smell quite noisome.

This unseasonable heat begins to wear on me—it is out of tune. There is still no rain. The countryside is restless—the autumn berries are full on the bramble, beside the trembling butterflies and the bumbles; the flowers hang heavy in their strange bloom, and the stale air is redolent of their perfume, and yet, the trees are bare. The birds do not know what to do. Everywhere are swallows and geese who should have departed, weeks past, for sunnier climes; they circle in the air, silent and attentive. There is a forced lushness and fruitfulness on the land, as if it waited for a blight.

13 October

We do not progress. I have an influenza at present, which gives me a thick head and a languor. Today, I attempted to work but found myself rapidly overcome. Everything begins to look like flesh and bone to me.

~~In haste~~

~~eyes like black and white wheels and a balding head. Get out get out~~

Good *God*. I shall put this diary on the other side of the room at nights.

By the by, the heat does not abate.

15 October

~~Do not look into her eyes. do not My God the eyes~~

My diary was in the drawer, which was locked. The key was in my pocket, in my coat, hanging up on the other side of the room. Yet the book was open before me, ink and pen dragging great blots across the page.

Perhaps I should tie my own hands.

18 October

I write barricaded in my room. I have understood at last the nature of my visit here. It is vengeance. My life is in peril.

I will lay out events as they happened, precisely.

Yesterday, overcome with lassitude, I strolled onto the moor—I felt in need of air. The heat is relentless. As for the work, we have not succeeded in perfectly preserving the tissue without killing the infection, and so a transfer is as far away as ever. We proceed like insatiable butchers. The cellar air is thick with rot and pain. My limbs were glad to feel their length again; my heart lifted with each stride.

When the house was well behind me, I found myself a perch behind a tumble of great stones and sat to feel the sun. It was a good thing to do. All around me was the moor, green and gray, and the little twisted rowan trees, which bend so obediently to the wind in these parts, their berries crimson darts against the dull land. It is a salutary thing, to sit and observe Nature, which cares nothing for my travails. I saw a sheep with a late lamb, newborn, I fancy, not an hour before—it made a charming picture, the lamb all disobedient legs and determined certainty and the ewe encouraging it; I watched its trials, becoming engrossed in its efforts to stand, wincing at each tumble. When it achieved uprightness and took its first unsteady steps, I found myself moved beyond reason and had to turn away.

It occurred to me that the lamb's might be an enviable lot—to possess no intellect, or curiosity, or duty to God or to mankind. To have a purpose so simple and pure—to desire to stand, to puzzle at it, to strain, and so!—achieve it, and then walk away, into a sheep's life, toward a sheep's death. Alonso would say, and I can hear his tone, that this is, in short fact, exactly the manner in which the large part of humankind passes its existence.

I was thus engaged in reflection, a frown on my face and a stick in my hand, slapping at the heather (men in idle moments, I find, will always seek a stick and something to hit), when I heard a sound like a saw drawn badly across the grain of the wood. Startled, I perceived then the crabbed figure of Shakes traversing the crest of the hill, silhouetted against the moor, making his way east. His back, turned toward me, shook, perhaps with the cough that racks his frame. He had not seen me—I was seized of a sudden with mischief. I rose from my seat and followed.

I believe Shakes was acquired from a debtors' prison somewhere. Or perhaps I invented that. He is from Devon originally, there can be no doubt—his vowels proclaim it. I cannot like the man. He hangs on Alonso. Alonso will break his pen, and before he has done more than curse at it, Shakes will be at his side with a new one or mending the old, standing very close, seeking to breathe, it seems to me, his master's breath. And the man looks at me. This may not sound like provocation, but to be regarded in silence, from under craggy narrow brows, for minutes on end, quite puts me out. I think him *overly and particularly attached* to Alonso.

I followed him across the moor, stumbling a little in my haste. He moves at a sharp clip! I kept low, behind stands of heather, and darted from the cover of boulder to gorse bush. I thought at one time he was sure to turn and threw myself to the floor, anointing myself liberally with dusty, cracked earth—but he did not, and after some time, I felt it safe to stand and walk behind. Bracken and moor rose all around. The great barrow sat, amber with autumn, on its distant hill.

We crossed a clearing in the brush, which was strewn with stones. My foot struck some object, and I stumbled and nearly brained myself on another. It struck me then that the stones were not scattered on the ground but had a semblance of order: of a sudden, I perceived, as though I had walked unawares into a funeral, that we were in the confines of one of those barbarous old Briton villages that litter the hillsides. I stood within a house, a tiny dwelling place, smaller than my bedchamber at Rawblood. The floor was grass, and heather furnished the corners. My foot was on the hearthstone.

I was quite upset. No man had lived here for a thousand years. But it was still a house. I took care to make my way out of the dwelling through the door and not by hopping over the walls.

By lucky chance, there was in my coat the flask that Alonso had filled again for me with brandy; it is a mighty remedy. My despond quite lifted; I was in a holiday humor.

Shakes was singing in a light baritone, unexpected and pleasing to the ear. I paused to note some of the words, for they caught my fancy. I attempt a transcription, below, from pencil notes:

She spake, and 'neath the moon, she took my heart away.
(And if I am a hollow man, who art thou to know?)
Broke and flung awry I was, a pale man at the break of day,
An' I'll not sing for her no more, no more for her my woe.
No more her brock bright eyes for me, no more her sateen lips,
No more with her at moonlight, a-dancin' heel-an'-toe,
[unintelligible here] *the night-tide dashin',*
Last pleasure [Something here, tasted? wasted?] *long ago.*

[something something] *Devon lass, an' all of Devon pleased,*
(And if I am, a white bone man, who art thou to know?)
Laughing tho' my death it fell, I went wi' heart at ease,
A-dreamin' arl the time o' cheeks like early snow.
"Take my bones to crossways! Hang 'em by the moor,
[nonsense, unintelligible]
Ware the white bone man, with the white bone hand,
I'll take you arl, as she took my heart, all them year ago."

There was more in this vein, many verses warning of the "white bone man" and his particular modes of vengeance, but the wind took the words quickly from his lips. Shakes moved eastward at a trot. His air of purpose drew me, irresistibly, as a child draws a wooden toy behind it on a string.

I did not pay much attention to our route, and suddenly, I found that we were in a part of the moor that I did not know; we had in fact crossed Hamel Down by some circuitous means and were coming to the old post road. This road follows in its turn the old Roman way and is therefore straight and well laid, though not often used. It is turned to turf and sand and not well trod, and by hanging back, I had no trouble concealing my footfall behind Shakes's own wandering steps. More brandy was taken by me.

Shakes came to a halt ahead, and I saw that our little way had joined a larger road. The perfume reached me before I saw what it was we had sought, although these were southern blooms and not the red campion, cuckoo flower, and wild garlic of my childhood. The sickly meadow-sweet clung to my nostrils; this at least I knew. My distress reached its summit. I made to turn, too late.

Flowers, all together in sickening banks. It is only twice in every life-time that so many are assembled. At weddings, and at death. I was young again; I walked once more toward that broken crossroads beyond the tumbled church wall. I caught once more the scent of my father's grave and heard my mother weep.

The blooms lay on parched earth; plucked strands of heather, and foxgloves, and briar flowers; eyebright, honeysuckle, gorse, yellow cinquefoil, and ox-eye daisies. A little stone lay at the head of the mound.

It is with trepidation and grave conscience that the faithful man considers a roadside grave. The soul of a suicide is an abomination rightly excluded from the consecration of the churchyard.

But this mound with its cloak of color did not rouse disgust. It bore an air of pilgrimage.

I had forgotten Shakes. He stood like the stone beyond us, with his eyes on my face, and I perceived with horror that my efforts at concealment had been for nothing; there was no surprise in his look. But all the fine gullies and wrinkles of his visage were wrought with silver, as if a jeweler had been at work on him. The tears flowed steadily, never spilling and yet forming a mask of reproach.

"You follow me, Dr. Danforth," he said. "You think yourself so mighty that even this is your concern."

I smiled and stammered.

He drew himself up, straighter and younger. He was tall and powerful, standing sentinel over the moor. "This is none of yours," he said.

"I do not know what to say," I told him. "I am—well, I am mad, to have intruded on you so. I cannot excuse it. I wanted to feel the air and then—" I stopped. It was worse to give reasons; they were thin. I did not myself know my cause.

"I look after him," Shakes said. "I looked after her too." His eyes were on the grave. "Mary Hopewell. Or she was. When I met her." His wizened face softened; it was both grotesque and fascinating, a thousand tiny folds collapsing into one another. "I have been with them through all of it," he said. "But you! You are nothing. You are like the leeches who fasten to the calf in the mire. You take blood to eat."

I thought to give the man answer, and angrily. But Shakes seemed suddenly to stand at a great distance from me. I turned and ran, making I know not what sounds, the sandy bottom of the road undulating before me, and I was fallen with a stinging blow, mouth filled with fine shale, before I realized that I too was blinded with weeping.

I saw, in that moment, the true nature of my state. I was now very heavily under the influence of an opiate, which in all likelihood had been in the flask of brandy. Drugged.

I thought to turn, to retrace my steps, but the path that had been so true beneath my feet turned into sedge that grasped at my ankles. I fell. When I opened my eyes, I could see the heather bells waving before my face, but I could no longer tell which was air or which the peaty earth. My tears ran upward along my face. Was it the springy turf that lay beneath me, or had I indeed dropped off the world… I was pressed against the cold, unyielding sky and could find no way to return to mortal ground.

Death follows me here. Every place I turn, I am confronted with his silence. All my building of little walls and the strings that I use to bind together my life are for nothing; all are mown down and cut. I am collapsed like a puppet in a cheap vaudeville. I thought I was a man, but I am wooden, forgotten. I lie in a pile in a dark corner of a hideous theater. The monsters that move behind the wings are hungry. Their fetid breath reaches me like the touch of fever. There is no light, not here, save that cast by a hideous moon; it turns its blind gaze on me like a worm, searching and indifferent. Only the hungry maw awaits. When I felt it draw me in, I rejoiced.

"Aye, let it be done with," I cried. The jaws took my feet lovingly, and the cool throat was like a haven as I slipped into it. I smelled the breath of a thousand dead men as the beast licked up my calves. *I will let you have it all*, I vowed. *Take this awkward parcel of flesh and let me return to the dark.* The stars that wheeled overhead formed shapes, lewd and grotesque. They dimmed and flared orange, dancing a dance that I knew, though I was shamed for all my knowledge. The stench of my own frailty was too much for me to bear. I kicked, to urge the swallowing on. The mouth was a vice; it threatened to crush my shins; I yearned for that deliverance. *Break and scatter this ill-assorted assemblage*, I prayed…

I sank.

The voices were old and slow. They discussed the binding of my hands. They spoke of one's daughter, who had said last week that the marsh mallow lay thick in this spot.

"It is a flag," said the other. "You pay note to it. It turns you back from this country; well it should."

"Arr."

There was a little rustling and the creak of a board. The voices tutted over me like concerned mothers. These sounds were so homely that I wept. I knew nothing after that for some time.

When next they spoke, it was through a purple light, so beautiful I could not bear it. My hands were bound above my head, and I shivered with the cold. A skin of cold water was tipped up to my lips. I was consumed with thirst. My all was directed at lapping the water from the bladder, but when it was in my mouth, it tasted of the brackish dark and of the monsters I had seen. I understood everything, in that moment— and with a cry, I let it flow from my mouth in the coming light of dawn like a child that cannot sup yet.

19 October

They brought me back to Rawblood on an old door, off its hinges. Alonso tried to put hot rum in me. I would take nothing from his hands.

Shakes looked at me from a corner, eyes bright. I paid them no mind but went unsteady to the cellar.

My shoulder was dislocated with the force of the winches used to draw me from the bog. It was my right, praise be—so the pain is not too bad to write or to wring a small neck.

The fur and blood clings to my hands, under my fingernails. I feel very like the lady in the play. It will not come off. Most were dead already. When was the last time they were tended? Those that were not dead—I broke their necks. We have all suffered enough. I think I wept as I did it. I have closed my ears to the song of mortality and refuted my vocation as a keeper of reason and fact. My hand and mind protest even as I write the words. How much better for all mankind and creation that such things never were, and that such betrayals never came to pass.

After it was done, I stood for a time. The candle guttered. The cellar walls glistened, peculiar. The corpses looked very small in the uncertain light. I went to the last cage and touched him on his stiff, thick-furred shoulder. I do not know what I thought would transpire. Absolution? From a rabbit? "Actaeon," I told the dead thing. "I recall it, now. That was your name."

Presently, standing among the hutches with the doors swinging to and fro, I became prey to a strong sensation of being watched. As I turned and turned about, I caught always something at the corner of my eye. Some gangling thing. I was caught, held as if by mortar to the ground. My feet would not obey me but kept me in place as they do in dreams. I shrieked then, and the candle shuddered, threw glimpses of unknown things against my frenzied eye; a hideous long shape…an elongated shadow that danced at my feet, following me, as shadows do, across the floor…

I turned and ran from that charnel house. How could I have thought it a place dedicated to knowledge and reason? They were rabbits only, true; that my actions were a deliverance to them, I know, so why does this act weigh so heavily upon me? Why does my conscience so protest?

From the very first, I never judged Alonso by the standards I apply to other men: he has been for me a person apart from rules and even morals, a creature of exotic charm, and instinct, and, I had thought, integrity. I did him grave wrong once. But I ask myself now if this was the greater one: to allow our friendship to proceed along such lines; to be restrained by undue deference to his mind and his character, so that we are brought to such a pass as this. He is gone; his scientific mind has gone... This has been a madman's errand. I cannot credit that I was borne along by it... Such is the power of remembrance, of fondness. For a time, it may persuade the willing mind that black is, indeed, white. But I am no longer willing.

I go now to beard the lion in his den. I do not know what will result. I will secrete the diary in a crack under the floorboards. If something happens to prevent my return, it will not be easily found.

I waited for him in the study, in the gloaming. I did not hear him come. I looked up, and he was standing before me, a great shape against the dusk.

"In the dark, Charles?"

His great presence is so striking; it is easy to overlook how deep, how musical is Alonso's voice. He lit the lamps, and their warm, homely yellow cast the illusion of cheer on the room. I watched him. Yes, I was right. He has gained flesh; he looks young now, as if his time in Italy had drained his life and Rawblood restores him... His skin has regained its old warm luster. His eyes are luminous.

"Charles," he said. "The rabbits."

"I will not let you do it any longer, Alonso."

"You do not like it," he said heavily. "Nor do I. But we could have consulted—"

"I thought that I would die in that bog, and that moment brings realization to a man. I have understood everything."

"I doubt that," he said.

"Alonso. It is finished. Though no doubt of average talent, I am still a doctor. I do not have an ague or a cold; I am not a drunkard. It is very simple. You have been sedating me with an opiate since my arrival at Rawblood."

"True enough," he said.

"The laudanum is in the wine? In the food?"

He said, "Both."

"What is my intake," I asked, "by the minim?"

He reached into his pocket, and I jumped, but it was only a pencil he sought. I shuffled for a scrap of paper—I found only a crumpled railway timetable. Alonso took it from me and scratched; he handed me the results.

"It is an estimate only," he said.

ADMINISTERED

13 minims in coffee or similar, 8 before noon

12 minims in cider or food, 2 after noon

14 minims in wine, brandy, or food, 8 after noon

17 minims via pipette early morning while sleeping

= 56 minims

"You write like a dying spider," I said, "crawling across wet sands. That is over five grains of morphia per twenty-four hours. So much…"

"It must be high at night," he said. He grimaced. "It must. Charles, you of all men know my intent—"

"Your intent… I do not know. But I do know that you have become a fearful thing."

I was abruptly disgusted beyond measure—with myself, with my persuadable nature, and with him. I wished to punish us both: for his hubris and for my acceptance of it. I found him beyond all moral sense, but I found myself despicable, and it was worse. "Sit," I said. "Please."

He did so and looked at me in surmise.

"I have solved it, you know," I said. "The mystery of the Rawblood ghost."

"Charles." He started toward me, imploring, and for a moment I was moved by the distress in his great eyes. Before I recalled myself.

"Do you recall Pinel?" I said. "A minor talent, but a solid one. He describes that particular state, *manie sans délire*... Shall I translate, or will you? It is madness without delirium. An intelligent madness, rational and by design. Moral insanity. And Koch—I cannot call psychiatry a science, but I do not despise his work—has diagnosed a state of mind he calls the *psychopatische*. The *psychopath*, I suppose you could say, in English.

"What are the hallmarks of the psychopath? One: very likely it is hereditary. Some insanity in the lineage, passed down."

Alonso's eyes were fixed on me. "Go on, Charles," he said. "I begin to follow your thinking."

"Your mother murdered your father," I said. "It was much reported. The Devon Demoness... You yourself have told me of it once. Only the once. I know that it was never proved in a court of law. And I know—we do not speak of it. But, Alonso, the time for tact and equivocation has passed. The history of the Villarca family is uniquely bloody.

"The second distinguishing characteristic of the *psychopatische* is a moral blindness, amounting to an enjoyment of others' pain. That ghostly figure that crept into your servants' rooms, attempting to suffocate them in their sleep...that violated that girl in such a way that she could no longer hold to her sanity... It was a horror. But it all belongs to human action. I see before me the Rawblood ghost. For who could it have been, Alonso, but you? Similarly, I do not believe it an accident that the Gilmore child was taken *deathly ill on your grounds*. You are responsible for his suffering—you contrived his death. You refused him treatment but let him lie outside, where you could observe..."

"I would not let any child enter this house," he said. "If I keep people from me, it is much the better for them."

"On that last point, I must concur," I said. "I do not know what happened to you, Alonso, in the years since I saw you. I do not know what evil has touched you. But you have acquired a need to inflict pain on others. Human subjects not being always readily available, you devised the experiment with the rabbits. Under cover of science, you could indulge with impunity the impulses that are necessary to your character." I paused here, for there was something rising in my gullet. I thought of Actaeon, and I tasted bile. "I am nauseated to have participated in this ghoulish theater.

"Third"—here I faltered a little, for I knew myself to be culpable in making Alonso what he was—"an early degenerate influence or way of life can set the mechanism of the mania in motion. And that is my responsibility also. For we were morally degenerate, you and I, when we were young."

"It beggars belief," he said, and his tone was acid, "that you have found a way to place this at the door of our *degeneracy*—if that is what you insist passed between us then." In the low golden lamplight, his face was wrathful. I shuddered.

I said, "I am sorry, so sorry for my part in it. I fear what passed between us in *that* fashion may have contributed to your madness. Also, I caused your opium addiction—I am immeasurably sorry. I must remind you: it was through error, not through design..."

Here, Alonso stirred. "So you have always said. Manning's cure. Is that the end?"

I thought of all the evenings we had sat exactly thus, in two armchairs, arguing, debating. That was a simpler world. "Yes," I said, exhausted.

"Charles. You cannot, cannot believe this. You are spinning wild falsehood and convincing yourself in the process." He was imploring. His face was open. I steeled myself against the feelings that rose in me. He is not the man I knew. It is but a cunning semblance, put on to keep me in check.

"I do not think you have killed yet," I said. "I think you will though. I do not, for instance, know—what was your plan for me, for your revenge? Bring me thoroughly under the influence of the drug, and then?" My throat was dry. "I also believe that behind your madness, my friend remains. So I appeal to him. I ask him to think. Think what you do, Alonso." I rose. "I go tomorrow. At first light. If you think to intrude on me in the meantime, be aware: I have my pistol handy." I turned on my heel and went to my chamber.

It is so hot. Where is the rain? I have flung open the windows to the night. There is a scent of smoke, a bonfire perhaps, which pervades the air.

I have also brought the little dog, Punch, into my room. He is accustomed to sleep in the old stable, but I think he will not mind the change of accommodation. Punch is a small, hairy terrier of the best kind, full of grumbling and sudden thoughts. He is good proof against vermin, of which I have a horror. Last night, as I was getting into bed, a mouse ran clear across my foot. A truly unsavory experience, and I think it will not happen with Punch in the room, for he has an admirable, bloodthirsty nature. The only part of his character that does not please is his firm belief that I deserve and desire his trophies to be brought to me; he will not take them away again. The dog will sleep at the foot of my bed, which will be a nice, cozy thing. I have need of another creature near me as I sleep tonight; of the presence, in the room, of another living heart that beats.

Alonso has knocked at the door. I think I jumped a foot in the air. My entire nervous system is singing and prickly with fear.

"I have my pistol trained upon the door," I said. I took up the poker from the fireplace.

His voice came muffled through the panels. "Charles, you do not understand. The laudanum. I have it here. You must take it. Or it will be the worse for you..."

I said, "Do not threaten me."

"That is not what I mean," he said. "It offers protection—"

"Enough," I said. "I have heard enough."

"Damn your eyes," he said. "I have borne patiently with your insults to me under my own roof. I have endured your crude conspiracies and aspersions on my character. I have allowed your self-deception to pass unchallenged. If you do not take it, Charles, you will regret it."

"You are a monster," I said. "I do not know you."

There was only silence then, so I suppose he went away.

I turned the key in the lock twice. Punch and I will sleep in princely state tonight, behind good solid oak. I will keep some vestige of my damned pride. I know that it will be a testing night. I am prepared for the worst. Narcotic withdrawal is not a pretty thing.

To look into Alonso's eyes, which I have loved, and see the malice that sits therein—I will never forget it. I am swept through with sadness, as if by a wind. What will happen to him? Assuredly, he must be dealt with. He cannot be allowed to go free.

I see in Alonso a man who has allowed his past to rule him. He carries his parents' demise with him always, as some carry a miniature of their beloved in a locket. He is in love with his tragedy. I will not become him. Alonso may be ruined. I need not be. I have been trying to forget, to obliterate; how foolish. Did I think perhaps that the Lord did not know of my mistakes? Assuredly, He does. I must face Him with an open heart. My secrets are manifold and sinful; I have kept them in a box in the depths of my soul. Now, I will try another way; I will acknowledge my wrongdoings. I will atone.

Strangely, I am full of hope. I am resolved that this sad chapter shall not be without result.

Upon my return to London, I shall take new lodgings. Farewell, Mrs. Healey! I only bear with her, after all, because she does not mind, too much, my nocturnal pursuits. Of course, by Koch's definition, I, with my "moral aberrations and behaviors," also fall into the category of *psychopatische*… But I will give all that up. That sordid toil is exhausting, in the end. I shall inquire for a country practice. I will tell Mrs. Bantry to prepare Meg to join me in a few months. I had not thought I should ever have her with me. I thought myself unfit for the young. But I believe…some form of peace is not beyond my grasp. Perhaps, perhaps I will go to Grimstock to fetch Meg myself. Perhaps I will look once more on those cold, gray hills where I was born. And perhaps it will not be as terrible as all that.

Redemption… I am testing the word on my tongue. By the longest of paths, by trials of fire and long endurance—I have come closer to God.

So, strange as it may seem, I owe Alonso thanks, in the end.

> *"For whosoever exalteth himself shall be abased; and he that humbleth himself shall be exalted."*
>
> —PROVERBS 14:2

O, O God, preserve m[ ]eliver us from t[ ] evil y hand shakes so I fe r I canno wr te it O O I hav een such a thing.

Still my limbs o still my beating heart. What to fix on, what to think, or be, my God, my dear God… And prayer is of no use, for did I not cry out the Lord's prayer? And it went unanswered.

I thought Alonso was the fearful thing. I was wrong. Oh, God, her eyes,

her eyes

What deep hole in th[ ]orld did that white thing crawl[ ]rom. The slender tips of ten white fingers reaching for my hear t

She ha[   ]ite cur g rms. How c[   ] was put there. Wh[   ]ould be
capable of su[   ]eed? And how could I not see? My merciful Lor[
and the eyes

Dawn

Praise God. Praise God for the light, and for the day.

I am on the hill in my nightshirt and overcoat. I am chilled to the bone—
but I could not spend a moment more within the house. I would have
fled from my room in the night, but the thought of encountering that
monstrous thing in a dark corridor, seeing the guttering light fall upon
that white form—it could not be borne. I did not sleep again but lit the
candle and counted the hours until dawn.

When blessed day became perceptible through the quarries, I rose
from the bed. All was strange—shadows fell too short or too long, and
the pale, gray light abused my aching eyes. I could not feel relief. It was
gone, yes, but it had heard my feeble cry and responded. It had a mind
and a will. I shiver now with dread, for it is filled with overwhelming and
alien intent. I strenuously avoid naming it.

But I am an observer and a man of science; let me not forget it. All
must yield to reason. I will diagnose.

Postulation the first:
*The severity of the situation can be assessed, to some degree,
by establishing: What was the fate of the dog?*

The resolution that was needed to screw myself to the sticking place
was almost beyond my power. I sat on the grass, stroking it as if it were
alive, feeling its texture, and breathing in the air, my ears filled with the
hilarity of an early-morning cuckoo. This did my heart good. What do

the grass or the birds know of the treachery of man or the foulness of that thing within? I should have obeyed those notes from my drugged self. I told me to flee; that is what I should have done.

When I was calm, I went in to that place quickly. It did not take long to find what I sought, and I came out again within a few minutes. Nothing occurred. But the very walls are loathsome to me now.

Punch was curled still under the window seat. He was quite cold and dead. I have brought him outside, not wishing to leave him in that place. He was a good little dog; he did well what dogs are meant to do. I became occupied at this juncture with the cramps, the dizziness, and the tremors that shook my frame.

We were sitting thus when I heard the sound of someone approaching from the copse. I was not frightened; I think that I may never feel fear again, for something has been taken from me that will not be given back.

I noted presently that Alonso was seated beside me.

"You have seen *her*," he said.

I nodded my head.

"You had locked your door, and I could not get in to you." He spoke gently, as I have heard him do—oh, an age ago—to children and horses. "You are not well." He slid his hand under my overcoat and laid it on my back, which was wet, as though I had been exposed to a sudden spring rain.

He went to his pocket and brought forth the vial. I made to take it, but he produced a syringe case from his pocket and fitted the vial in; I saw it was an ampoule.

"Do you want it?" he said.

The itch on my flesh was too much to be believed. My very fingers curled with wanting it.

He nodded and said, "Better this way." He took my arm and found a vein, his fingers gentle, and it was in.

I think he attended to himself after me. I do not recall, for the world was turned to butter. Presently, I felt that he lay along my side, both of us turned upward like daisies in the vertical sunlight, under the puzzling sky.

"What is it? What manner of thing… What I saw in the night. My soul is riven by it. It is impossible that God and that thing both exist. One or the other is a fairy tale."

"Tell me what it is you saw," he said.

I told. I was mildly irritated to find that I trembled as I spoke. "Her wounds. She—it—bleeds. Her shoulder was dripping. She had a shorn head, and scars, like, I know not what. It was like the land, under the moon. There was a sound," I said, "like creaking. Or of stone, rubbed upon stone. Very old machines, which ground together like death. There was smoke, which filled the air like brimstone. The room seemed… ablaze, though there was no heat. Flame licked up the walls as though we were trapped in some prison, in the depths of hell." I felt once more the horror on me. "Is *she* a phantasmagoria couched in withdrawal from the morphia?"

"Do you think it is?"

"No," I said. "*She* stood there, white and rotten…" Once again, the weakness came on me, and I was convulsed with fear. I grasped his arm. "And the dog," I said. "*It died of fear.* How do you live? Knowing that such horror is in the house? Do you not see…"

His hand trailed along the line of the collar of my nightshirt, leaving soft runnels in my flesh. "Strange to say," Alonso said, "she does not trouble me; the fact being so plain, perhaps, that I am already damned. Other things haunt my dreams. A small blessing, given to a fiend. No, as you may have guessed, it is the laudanum that keeps her away. I always know when she is near… But it is as if a veil separates us, and she cannot get through."

Postulation the second:

Opiates offer a degree of protection. The apparition can have no effect if the subject's mind is so dulled. The residual laudanum in my system saved me from her.

"It was *her*," I said. "That you wished to study. Not congenital disease. We have no sway over that thing. Did you expect that we would shake a microscope at it, and it would go away? Why did you think that she travels in the blood?"

"Why is it so impossible that an intelligence, an agency such as *her*, should use a lineage, procreation, as a vehicle? Sometimes, Charles, I feel *her*. I feel her here." He tapped a blue vein, bulging in his pale wrist. "Within. Coursing in my blood." He shook himself. "You had no right to kill the rabbits. Once more, Charles, you have ruined me."

"You have used me abominably," I said, abruptly furious. "You play the victim, but you have kept me here under the claim of friendship, lied to me, and imperiled my life." I pointed toward Punch. "You have used me worse than that dog."

"I do not deny it."

I rose to go.

Alonso reached up a long arm and grasped the collars of my night-shirt, pulling me to earth. He put his lips to my ear. "I do not understand God," he said. "But believe me, I begin to understand hell. And if I am to go there, I will do something first, and that is *finish the work*! Give me your notes."

"Alonso," I said. "To speak plainly: you are addled with opiates. Once, you were a clinician, a diagnostician of the first water and a man of medicine. But I was a fool to follow you in this. *It will not work*. We have tried. *It will not!* And as for the methods: nothing right or good would cost our souls so. I have been wrong about a great deal. I grant it. But I am right in this." My eyes were clouded a little with tears. "For the opium has dulled the fine razor of your mind. If you cannot see this, then it is as I had suspected. In truth, you are no longer a doctor."

I removed his hand from me and went into my book. I tore the pages of our records from the spine—our tallies, our notes, our whole work. It was a cancer, I see it now. Remarkable that so much pain can be told in numerals, in India ink. I set a match to the sad scraps before me; they burned without a sound, blue and gray and orange. He cried out and reached for them. I believe he would have buried his hands in the fire. But a breeze came off the moor then. The pages went with it easily, out of reach, whirling into the sky. We watched the tiny points of flame rise in the early morning air.

I said to him, "We must find our way to that *lighted hall* by other means than the *kitchen*."

His empty fingers trembled, held before him like a begging bowl. When he spoke, it was savage. "Two decades, I have wandered in the wasteland. My sole comfort was that you were ruined also."

"You may be assured on that point," I said. "My life, since we parted, has been nothing but a long mourning." I put an arm over his shoulder, which heaved and shook. The shape of him was familiar to my arms. I held for a moment the young Alonso. I did not know where I was; this time was overlaid by that, like magic lantern slides.

I said, "In the end, I have protected you, though I did not mean to do it. *She* would have taken you all those years ago, had you not been addicted to laudanum."

"Does that comfort you?" he asked. His face shone with contempt. "It should not. Do not spout such drivel at me. This was thrust upon me, and I am a servant—no!—a slave to it. How it offends the mind!" His hand was tight on my jaw. "How my senses and my reason are revolted! Order, logic, science. These are the systems to which I was devoted. You took them from me, like a thief. You are in the right of it. I am no longer a doctor. For you took my profession. You owe me *at the least* your life! I am unhinged. I will suffer this until I die. I do not sleep; I do not eat. I am beset all around by this. There was no Manning's cure, Charles, was there? It was no error of judgment. I know you better than any man alive. You were afraid of your God. You made me a slave to opium, to punish me for what you desired."

To give Alonso opium. A terrible lapse of judgment on my part, but a forgivable one. *Sólo el amor*. Etc. Etc. All this is acknowledged. It was an accident.

Well. Here is the thing that I have never told, not to a soul. Our endeavor of fifty days was tainted from the start. He was everything that was bright, blinding, to my eyes. I have said we were degenerate together, and it is so, but it was more than that. Degeneracy alone would have been bearable. I had lived with my shame all my life. I think they might have put me in the pillory in Grimstock had I not left. I am hardened to the fact of my degeneracy.

But love, I did not know. It is a terrible, terrible thing. I was unprepared for the great fall. I did not know, before Alonso, how it strikes you down like sickness, like madness. I was unprepared for the fear. I feared Alonso was not the true moral deviant that I was. I feared that he could not forever be satisfied with such a poor thing as me. I lay by him, wakeful in the night, thinking of the time when he would go from me. I thought God would take him to punish me.

When Alonso said to me, that first night before the fire, "Do you know what it will be, that you intend to administer?" I said that I did not. It was a lie. I saw that the time had come to act, to bind him to me. I took his life as sure as a knife in the heart. And in the end, he went from me anyway, so I destroyed the thing I love, and all to no purpose.

"You are right," I said. "There was no Manning's cure."

"Very well," Alonso said. A tremor shook him. He sighed. "And I in turn will allow that I brought you here, willing to destroy *you*… I needed your eye for the work. And for you to be safe from *her* and fit to work, you needed opiates. I thought I did not care what happened to you. I thought it was justice. Your debt to me, as it were. But you came, and it did not feel like revenge. Strange to say, it was a great pleasure to be in your company." He passed a hand across his brow and grimaced. "I have deceived myself, Charles. I brought you to Rawblood not for any purpose, save the simple one that I wished for you. I missed you. It was selfish and wrong."

"No," I said. "It was not."

We looked at each other, and it was the bleakest of things.

Alonso said, "Once, you had my trust and my love. But you thought God did not like it. Foolish, foolish. Why could you not make peace with it, your heart? Such utter waste," he said. "Of our two lives."

"I know," I said. "It is my fault. All mine. And I have seen today...*her*. I have seen that God is a farce. I have lived my life always half in shadow. And for what? To appease whom?"

He soothed me with a strong white hand. His black hair fell across his brow.

"You look so well now," I said. "You are better, Alonso. Younger. I do not know how it is so, but..."

"Yes," he said, grim. "I think that is *her* doing. I think she likes us close. So what am I to do now, Charles? Trapped here at Rawblood, in this dim half death... What is my life to be?"

"That, I do not know." The world spun, liquid.

Postulation the third:

She *is bound to the Villarcas, to Rawblood. And they to* her: *the Villarcas sicken when away from Rawblood.*

"We are a fine pair," I said. "The sodomite opium-eaters."

He said wearily, "You wear and wear away at things, Charles, but never really face them."

"You have the right to use me any way you choose," I said. "And I deserve to die."

"No," he said. "That is precisely it. You do not. We must abandon grudges, revenge. Cease to quarrel over who wronged whom first and try to live. Let us try," he said, "to live in the morning light."

I laughed a little. "I was recently thinking…something similar. You make it sound an easy thing." I took him quickly to me; to feel the shape of his back, the line of his fierce head. I kissed him. Then I stood and went down the hill. I did not look back.

"Come to the house," I said without turning, "when you have buried the dog."

Conclusion:
There can be none.

I recall…oh, so many things. But in particular, one afternoon. We stood beside the river, drinking. We had been at the Inns with some legal fellow or other, who liked us, and then in rooms at the Temple. Deep drinking in those deep stone arches—it gives a young man a sense of grandeur. The Thames was quiet in the afternoon. There seemed to be no living soul on this stretch. Everything was scented deeply with wisteria. We leaned over the river in the sunshine and saw ourselves in the swift brown water. Light played over Alonso's face. He was lit through willow trees, golden, young. His cheek was full of the flush of pleasure. His eyes were wide, and the sun lay in them. He offered his hand to me. I took it. In the water, our reflections followed suit.

"This is a state of grace," he said.

Nothing had yet occurred; none of those actions had yet been thought of that would bring us by slow degrees to this parlous state.

I can see him now in my mind's eye: he will bury Punch on the moor, and he will take trouble to find a place that is seemly, and high, and fit. He will handle the corpse gently and bury it deep. He will cover the earth with stones. The foxes will not get it. I know all this, because I know him as well as my own desires. Perhaps he will pray over the dog, as if it had a soul. He is utterly heathen.

He will come soon, for all that. A dog takes but a little hole. Make haste.

Forgive me, God, in whose existence I can no longer trust. Forgive me, Meg, whom I did not tend as I should have. Most of all, I ask forgiveness of you, Alonso, my friend. I did not understand then the quality of action, which is not like thought. It is final.

I do not seek redemption, not for myself at least. I hope that you may find your way out of the tunnel I led you down all those years ago. Perhaps contrition, freely offered and without condition, has a merit of its own. I truly hope so. I hope that it can turn the course of events in ways we cannot fathom. Perhaps it will aid you.

This poor book. The cover is marked with tiny burns and with sprays of rabbit blood. The pages hang drunken from the binding. There are great ragged edges where others were torn away. A poor legacy. But it is all I have to leave to you, Alonso. It is my full and last confession. I make one request only. That my sister, Meg, should not be left to starve. I have nothing to bequeath. I throw myself on your mercy, utterly.

I am glad that I spoke the truth to you at last. I said those things that I could never have said, had I not known that this was my last day. Perhaps it was the only honest day of my life.

Please know, it is not for our long and sad history that I do this. Our sins seem as nothing in the face of the evil I have seen in the night. You do not comprehend what it is to look on *her*. You cannot. I have known, since before I heard your footsteps this morning on the hill, that this was my fate. Perhaps you will say that it is a cowardly choice. But there is no longer any choice for me. To see *her* is to know the vast terror that lies outside the circle of firelight, beyond man's ideas. The curtain has been torn back, to reveal the gaping chasm in the world. Nothing endures. All is blackness. Horror. We are falling through the dark. We never cease. We never land. We drift in the endless void, suffering. *There is no morning light.*

As I made my preparations, the day darkened. One minute past, the room shone dim as if a hand had been clapped over the face of the sun. I was not surprised; it seemed right that the days and hours be out of joint. But then there came the sweetest sound that I have heard. I have gone to see. I could not deny myself. Through the window, the grass is slick and gleaming; a gray sheet lies over the far horizon. Diamonds cover everything; they cling to the old glass and run down the panes—all things shiver and dance through their prisms. Even through the dry dust and sour smells of this house, I can catch that other scent. There is such kindness in it—the earth without, beneath the rain.

I have it by me and ready: the rope. I have owed this for many years. I hereby discharge my debt freely, and in hope.

IRIS

1915
Earlswood Asylum

I'm sixteen.

Weak sun across the floor. Mouth like cotton. Dust motes. The others are waking too. They stir gently in their beds like yellow chicks. Their movements are small and tentative as if they're already weary. Groans of aching joints. Somewhere, someone sobbing. Morning, I suppose? They mostly keep me under; I'm not so good with times and days. The battered tin clock high on the wall. The yellow square clipped to the end of my bed that means dangerous. No visitors. No letters.

The large blond woman next to me stares, her eyes blue orbs. "What time's the train?" she asks. It's one of the many things I don't know. I stare back. She is fascinating in her trembling whiteness, like a milk pudding. "What time?"

"Hello, Julia," I say. "Lovely day."

She turns away with a sniff, leans as far away from me as her restraints will allow.

I watch the second hand of the dented clock. I allow myself to think about him for one minute exactly. One minute, each time I wake. No more, in case they see his name in my eyes.

Lottie releases us from our night jackets. Everyone shakes their arms for a moment after, to check they're still there.

"What time's the train?"

"Not for hours yet, my love." I don't mind Lottie so much. The other, Doris, always tells Julia it left an hour ago.

Out in the garden, I shuffle. I hug the fence, the wall, grimly. Once around the perimeter, twice. Sweat beads, drips from my nose. I shuffle on my weak, stiff legs until they loosen, until I can approximate a walk. It is better to be under the sky. At least there's that. At some point, Julia joins me. She walks beside me in silence. Her jowls shake.

"Did you kill your daddy?" she asks. "That's the word."

"No," I say. "It was *her*."

She nods. We walk.

"I killed the baby," she says. "Didn't mean to."

"Right," I say. "Sorry."

"I know," she says. "Me too. We're all sorry."

I say, "We're not alike, you and I." I hurry away on trembling legs.

Most of my waking hours are spent fighting the fear that I'll die in here.

∽

There's nothing, nothing to break the gray days. Might as well have chucked me down a well. It comes to the same thing. Sometimes, I feel myself falling. Falling in the long dark. I think of Hervor, journeying through the black land of death to wake her father. If only it could be done.

⌒⌒

Food. I've been out for a while, not sure which one this is. Lunch or dinner though—breakfast is bread, and this is broth.

A shiver, white wobbling flesh in the corner of my eye.

"Hello," Julia says. I don't.

"You're sad, I bet," she says.

There's a bone in the heart of my broth. I trap it between the spoon and the bowl. Bone. Dull metal. Whose head should this be? I press with the spoon. A little crack, a good sound.

"We're all sad," she says. "I know, I know. You're different. But you're not, actually, so pipe down."

Seems unjust. "Go away."

"Bollocks to you," she says fairly cheerfully, and when the bone is broken in little bits at the bottom of my bowl, I look up again, but she's gone.

After soup, we're marched back into the ward. We lie flat, each on our cot. Lottie, Doris, Annie go around. They draw the canvas over us, fasten the buckles. Chinking dull metal, leather. All around the ward, the sounds of fastening up. They're quick. There are three of them, thirty or so of us. And sometimes, just sometimes, through the phenobarbital, someone remembers this. Not tonight, apparently.

The sting of the needle. Annie moves off down the row. Don't have long, be quick. What? The moor. It's a blustery day…

Don't make it too good. Don't make it so that you can't bear it when you wake up here.

…Dusk is coming, but it's still low, golden light. It's clear from here to the sea. Faint blue line. Invisible sun sinking, an eerie glow in the white west. The clouds in that corner of the sky have golden rims. I say, *Look*... No. Forget that part. I'm alone. I'm walking up the path to Hay Tor. Toes plant in the turf, breath comes good, hard, the good squeak of damp grass under my boot soles. The land falls away, and the wind rises. The strange metallic scent of gorse. It's blazing, yellow. Must be spring.

Something bounds across the path. Small, bright, long-legged. The color of warmth, blood, sunsets. It pauses, throws a stretched and spiny shadow.

The fox stands, perfect and poised. One slender black forepaw raised. Red rusty fur, ears wide petals on the narrow head. Young, not a cub, but only just. Great wild golden eyes hold mine.

We look at each other, the fox and I. We're still. Caught by the land, each other, the sky. The delicate muzzle curls. The fox snarls, silent and white. Tiny perfect teeth. It's so fierce and so small. I grin at it, and it's gone like smoke. Glimpse of a brushy tail.

Why didn't I ask more questions? *Papa.* Why didn't I ask you everything about *her*? About yourself. About everything. I suppose I didn't believe, in those days, that people actually died. Not really. I've only ever loved two people. You can only begin to believe in death when it cuts you where you love.

The muffling, the black. It closes over.

∾

Morning. Julia's wailing. It's clear why almost immediately. The stink is everywhere.

Julia struggles in her night jacket. She wriggles. Her face is shiny with tears; her blue eyes are perfect circles. Doris watches.

"Oh, that's dirty," she says. "That's shameful."

She takes a cloth from her waist and unbuckles Julia gingerly with fingertips. It's all over. The bed is slick with it.

"Revolting," Doris says. "No use thinking you'll get a change. Linens is Tuesdays. You know that."

"Couldn't," Julia says. Her voice is thick. "Couldn't, couldn't stop." She cries, a long, high, cracked note. It goes on and on. Around the ward, other voices take it up. Cracked, keening.

"She's set them off," Doris calls to Annie. To Julia, "You've set them off." She tuts, hands on hips. "Nasty, nasty," she says. "You think about what you've done, when you're sleeping in it tonight." The stench rises. All around, women shrieking.

Julia doesn't argue. She quietens. Shame moves up her, through her face, until it enters her eyes. They become little glassy pebbles. She goes somewhere else entirely.

We line up on the bench. Gray morning. Thin cloud. Wind flaps in our white shifts. We're straggling sheep. Eyes blue and black with sleep. I sit next to Julia. She stinks. She's shaking.

Doris starts at the top of the line, moves down. She opens mouths. She pokes in them with a fine metal implement. She runs a finger around yellowing teeth, taps them with a fingernail, checking for looseness. Papery tongues, cracked mouths. We're a puzzled, shaky lot.

"Look," I say to Julia, "sorry about before."

Julia stares. A shining line of saliva drawn across the center of her chin like a wire. "Sorry," I say. But she doesn't reply.

When Doris comes to me, I let her come in close. I wait until her pink hand hovers blurry and huge by my nose. I close my jaws neatly, fast. I bear down until I taste blood.

It's only as I'm sinking, sinking, the needle sweet in my arm, urgent hands battering me about the head, the blood all red and tinny between my teeth, that I see it—Julia's smile.

Nothing, after that, for quite some time.

~

Morning. Again. Which? No matter. When Lottie comes to me, she doesn't take off the night jacket. She loosens the buckles at the back, sits me up. Too late, I see she has the needle in her hand, and I want to weep. I can't bear it—going back down into the black cellar so soon.

"Soother," Lottie says. "No, no, keep still. Just a soother this time—because you've someone to see you." It doesn't seem likely. The phenobarbital washes up and down, cleans all the feelings away.

A man comes down the ward. Flat, shining hair. A strand escapes as he sits down beside me, hangs, heavy with brilliantine, over one eye. The firm line of his cheek like the curve of a tunnel. He strokes his lapel in slow, small movements, as if the suit were a house-trained animal. His smile is shy. He smells of pipe smoke, of lemons, clean skin. His brow amazes with its smoothness, the color of warm bread.

Martin smiles. "You're awake," he says. "That's fine."

I smile back. My tongue is thick, disobedient, inert. But inside, I am singing. I want to tell him how his face brings the taste of heather, the sound of swallows in the eaves, the clear brown river. He has brought Rawblood into the long, dirty room. I ache with my happiness. I should have trusted that someone would come. Martin seems an odd choice, but I should have known that *someone* would... Of course, this couldn't go on forever. It wouldn't make sense if life were so cruel.

Martin smiles, I smile, and I have a thousand questions—I want to ask him... But no. At Earlswood, the walls have ears and hands and eyes and needles. Everyone knows that. All that in good time.

I whisper, so light it's barely a breath on the air, "Martin, thank you. Home."

Martin smiles into my eyes and says, "I'm Dr. Goodman. Do you remember me? It's a pleasure. May I call you Iris? Yes."

I try to say *Martin, of course, I remember. Cranium, mandible...*

He takes a tongue depressor from his breast pocket. My jaws are gently parted, and the depressor pokes like a dry stick. He watches. His eyes kind.

"I was never permitted to be a guest at Rawblood," he says. "But I am quite happy to have you stay in *my* house!" He smiles at his joke. "As long as you like!"

He waits until my breathing has steadied a little. Fastidious, he takes his handkerchief from a breast pocket. The cloth looms. It's rough on my slippery face. His fingers are scented with lemon.

He says, "That's quite enough of that. You don't know it, but you're in luck. Real luck. You can be passed over to me for treatment without reservation. Do you realize? The 1913 Act was your salvation. And you did so well. There was no trouble obtaining the certificates. It will all be different now, Iris."

I stare at the yellow square at the bottom of my bed. Of course. No visitors. This is no reprieve. Rawblood is gone. Father is gone. Tom is gone. There is only this room. There will only ever be this room. The air dirty and laden with sorrow.

I turn my head and snap at his hand, but it's gone. The empty click of my teeth.

He says equably, "Yes, you're fond of that, I hear. The biter." The world shifts. He's lifting me gently. "*Swimming* in phenobarbital," he says, pained. "Barbaric. And bedsores. I am very sorry... But we can begin to treat this rationally, with modern techniques. I know your history, I know your case—I have an excellent impression of your mental state, before, which will inform your treatment. It—is—a—piece—of—luck." He spits each word delicately into the air. "I wish you to understand that this is none of your doing. How to begin? The behavior of the brain. We are only so far removed from the savage. When a leopard tears apart a bull, it is obeying the promptings of its mammalian brain, which has a similar structure to our own. We cannot expect, simply because we have put on linen and eat off china, that this urge will never manifest in ourselves. We wish to tear flesh and also to be moral human beings. This struggle can lead to a disintegration of the personality, particularly in women. The violent animal is at war, eternally, with the natural impulse of a gently reared young lady. For let us not forget—the leopard is also natural. And he is strong. In some, very strong indeed. In you, I think. It is a congenital defect. There is a long history of it in your family. Again—it's so important to stress this—it's not of your making. You yourself have said that your father warned you of it…"

"No," I say. The rage rises, welcome. "He warned me of *her*."

"Her. Well. I would have done the same. I would have told the story in a way that would not appall or frighten a child. Believe me, Iris, I find no fault with your father. He did what he could. But *she* did not kill him. Did she?"

She was there. "I can see how it looks," I say. "But it was *her*." She brushed me with her cold fingers. My father's gaze on my face. The cold space at my back. The thrill that ran through me. *I see…her.* Pheno can't quite stop the tide that rises, rises, threatening.

"There is no *her*; there is only you." Goodman is curt.

I want to say *you've got it wrong—you parasite, you llama-faced nobody, you…* But I can't. Because, of course, whatever part *she* played, I did it really. Because Papa warned me. But I would not listen.

"Tell me, Iris," he says, "how long can a mind be torn between two divergent impulses without fracturing? I do not know. But in due course, that is what takes place. A fracture. A young woman raised in relative isolation. Few pastimes. The masculine impulse encouraged by masculine pursuits—anatomy and so forth. Then the catalyst—what was it? Something. Some form of sexual incontinence, perhaps. That would be usual. And the leopard is free." He mimes a paw swiping across the air. "You say that you do not recall your crime. I think you cannot acknowledge the actions of your savage other self. Your distress and your grief are not acknowledged by you, because you have shut them up. They are locked in the cage. They are the property of the leopard.

"I can help you with this. I can tame the leopard. I can make him safe. And you can live, contented, in the gentle state that was meant for you.

"I will speak to you man to man, Iris," he says. "I will be blunt. The world is being torn apart outside." His hand holds mine, warm and firm. "We are engaged in the war to end all wars. All over Europe, the hungry leopards are loose." He sighs, and for a moment, his voice forgets about the lecture. "It is unconscionable, what is happening. But it will end, and God willing, there will be a world to live in after it ends. You may partake of it. You have a real chance for rehabilitation. No more drugs. Exercise. Responsibility. Restitution. Now, will you help me?"

Reprieve here, after all, perhaps. A hidden chance.

"I should add," he says, smoothing his lapel, "that you have received some letters. I have these safe. I have read them, of course. I deem them not too inflaming or exciting. So you may have them if we can agree."

I prepare my tongue, my mind carefully. Must get this right. "Thank you, Dr. Goodman," I say, "for your care and attention. And I will help you."

Martin sits and licks the tip of his pencil. His gray eyes shine.

There is only one person who would write.

✑

Clouds boil overhead. The light in the garden's like the depths of an aquarium. We move along the wall, away from the others. Annie and Lottie sit on the steps, hands idle in their laps. They speak low to each other. No one's paying us mind.

We hug the wall and sidle. Dirty brick the color and odor of congealing blood. In this wing, the office wing, the windows are unbarred, and the one I want swings very slightly open.

"Come on," I say, but Julia's forgotten what we're doing.

She shakes her head, says, "Naughty," pulls at the hem of her gown, bares her mottled shoulder. My heart sinks. It would be one of her days. She smiles, shy and slow.

"Just a leg up," I say, quick and fierce. "Not naughty. Come on, you. It's this one here. I must have them. He will never give them to me." I don't know if she understands, but she nods and takes my foot in her hand. I pull myself up and wriggle, half in. The window frame indents my stomach. I smell paper and inkblots and metal. The walls are the familiar olive green, but there are comforts here. A blue-and-white china teacup stands in a saucer on the desk. The leather blotter is rich and dark. On it lies a soiled handkerchief. I imagine Goodman sitting in the chair, writing at the desk, using the handkerchief… Where are my letters? This seemed a simple idea, but the reality is different. The room is redolent of lemons. It will resist me. Something of him lingers here, not just a scent. Dread pulls at my heart. I struggle to pull myself farther over the sill, and just then, hands wrap about my ankle.

"Come on," says Doris's grim voice. I seize the worn curtains in fists, hold on to the frame, kick out hard. It's some comfort that I feel my heel crunch on bone. But there's shouting, feet pound the turf, and in a moment, there are many more hands. The curtains give from the rings with a rending sound. I writhe and scrabble for grip. I hear a sound like a dog growling, and it's coming from me. The weight is terrible; they all hang on me like lead. My fingers cling, then slip, and I fall toward the sorry earth. My head hits it hard, and sparks fly out.

Warm hands, cool metal. Somewhere, heavy snoring. So.

Voices far above.

"Do take care, Doris. It's the biter."

"Proper rats in the attic, this one."

I am seized, delighted by how exactly right she is. I know all about the rats. Pleasure, pure and piercing, occupies all my attention for some time.

"...weren't there above a fortnight," Doris is saying. "They were quite amused by all the cleaning and washing the English nurses insisted on."

"Dirty blighters."

"Oh, I know." She's suddenly in my ear, and I startle, though I should know better by now. The flowering, exquisite slide of the needle.

"You've stuffed it up, Lottie."

"It's not my blame. Stop shifting about, you."

"Give over. Behave yourself."

This to me, I think. I'm doing something to earn these rebukes; I can't tell what. Limbs and eyes and fingers are fantastic, indistinguishable.

I will wait. I will bide my time. I will not die here.

The needle once more. This time, it slides true.

"There, now. You won't be worrying us for a while."

Something spreads through my veins like coral growing.

"What was I saying?"

"The French."

"They're terrible ungrateful."

The voices fade into the far dark, go elsewhere.

A new hand on my brow. Lemons. "Oh, Iris." His voice brims with sorrow.

I float. The pool is black; I breathe the water in.

1916

I'm seventeen.

My lids part to gray light. Drifts, flurries. I am moving in spirals, in drifts of snow.

A whoosh of rich, mossy smoke. A pipe. The click of teeth on the stem. The scent of lemons, his careful, diffident tenor, like water running over rock. The sound of a thumb quickly licked.

I feel the pressure of his attention. Tiny sounds of coins, cloth, paper. He's standing over me, hands thrust into pockets, tinkering beneath the cloth.

"Hello, Martin," I say. "The defective is awake."

"Ah," he says. A hand on my eyelid, pulling it upward. Flash of white light, pink thumb. "We can do better for you," he says. He sounds very sad. "I think we must try." Money rattles in his fingers. A hand on my head. I hold still.

"Dr. Goodman," I say. "Please don't make me sleep. No more. Please."

He takes my hand. "Only a little more, perhaps," he says. "Listen."

I ask, "How long have I?" I try to sit. My limbs are wet string.

"It is Monday, September the seventeenth."

"No," I say. "It's June." I taste the air. It has mold and swallows and bonfires in it.

His hand light on my head. Papa waves at me from the lavender garden. I cough. My throat is coarsely chopped wood.

"Tube feeding," he says kindly, "can be rough on one. Here."

The water is cold shards of iron in my throat.

I'm not in the ward. I'm in some green place I don't know, with metal studs binding metal walls together. A basin in the corner. Drips from somewhere.

"I need to go outside," I say. "Let me go to the garden."

He sighs. "May I speak frankly? I have tried, with you. I have instituted an intensive regime of healthful exercise, of improving pastimes, of electric therapy, of water therapy, of talking cure. In the course of these, you have injured four nurses, two with fairly serious bites. You have repeatedly attempted to enter my office and remove property. Letters, which as your behavior shows, you are not in a fit state to receive. You have attempted to leave the hospital on three separate occasions. This has resulted in you receiving"—he ticks them off on his fingers—"a punctured trachea from a pencil, serious avulsions on your fingers and shoulders from a blunt knife, and various lacerations about the neck from objects such as drinking mugs, the unscrewed leg of a bed, and the toe of a hobnail boot—and these wounds heal slowly and badly because you are malnourished through tube feeding while sedated."

"I'm sure you're right," I say. "I don't recall."

"Precisely—this is the familiar refrain. You do not recall. You do not remember your actions, and more specifically, you say you do not remember the act that brought you here. You insist that you are wrongly incarcerated. Your behavior toward me and my staff remains violent, troubling. As I am sure you must see, it is impossible to leave you in the general population at Earlswood. I cannot allow this to continue. But I have removed all privileges, all possible sources of comforts… There is no means of reprimand now that is left untried. *I have failed you.* So what else is to be done?"

The green walls are sweating. They look unsafe, like a sand castle. They will fall in softly, bury us deep.

"I have a proposal for you, Iris. Now. You refuse to accept your crime. And in a sense, you are right not to do so. For you are at the mercy of your congenital condition, do you understand? It is *not* your fault. But nothing will change for you, do you see, if you do not have courage. You may stay here forever, and bite Doris's fingers, and be sedated for much of the time, your waking life narrowed to hours a week, the dosage of the pheno increasing as your resistance to the drug increases, which will exacerbate the accompanying memory loss. You will experience nothing and recall less. Eventually, one day when they wake you, your hair will be gray, and you won't know the old woman in the mirror."

I very slowly put out my desiccated tongue. I stretch it out to its dry length through dry lips. I stare at him, eyes wide. I open the shutters. Just for a moment, I let him see in. "You won't let me go," I say. "Just as you'll never give me my letters." I have long since schooled myself to believe them a fiction.

He goes white and blank, licked pencil suspended in air. Then he nods as if I have a good point. His eyes are Persian cats. "I will not coerce or persuade. I state facts, merely. I have a high opinion of your intelligence. I will trust it now." He places a manila folder, the color of clotted cream, on the bed by my knee. "Here are the studies—I will not insult you by suggesting you will not understand them. You will not be sedated for the next two days. You will be in isolation here. I'm afraid some of it will be unpleasant. Withdrawal, you know. At the end of that time, you will inform me whether you will return to sleep." He pauses and stands. The coins tinkle in his pockets. "I could do it without your permission," he says. "But I don't think that's the answer. I believe, I believe that you wish to be better. I wish for you to decide—which is the only way it will begin. So think."

Through the dark, the cold sound of his exit. Metal, bolts, shining keys. Through the thick wall, someone snoring. The walls are bending, pulsing, concave. The ceiling is low, very low. My lungs don't seem to be working. The rats make little scuffles in the attic. Something breathes hot and gentle on the back of my neck. The scent of lemons is light in the air. Under it, the heavy stink of a big cat. I pick up the file. The words *Prefrontal Leucotomy* are written on it.

> Dogs are given large lesions of the occipital lobe by means of lobotomy. They become sweet and harmless even when they bit and fought before...

⁂

When I surface, Goodman's in faded gray, collar sharp white against his vulnerable throat as he swallows. He raises a questioning hand, waits for my permission. I nod. He lifts the gauze. Gentle fingers brush my forehead. The light, inadvertent touch of his hand on the tip of my ear. Warm skin. Lemons.

Did it go well? I try to ask. I'm not sure what comes out, but he seems to understand.

"Beautiful," he says. "Perfect trephine openings, closed over nicely."

Relief leaks through me, a slow, good drip.

He says, "Oh, you clever thing." He may mean me or not. He replaces the bandage, settles it with infinite care around my shaved skull, sits back in the chair. "May I show you some pictures?" His face open, eyes soft. "Tell me what you see."

I look at a photograph of a cat. I say cat. I look at a photograph of a hat. I say hat. House. Bird. Gate. Flower. But sometimes, those words don't come when I say them. Sometimes, what comes out is *handle* or *ee* or *owls*.

He touches the back of my hand with a finger. "It will come, Iris," he says. "It will."

We smile. Then there's a picture of something delightful made of curls and waves, which jumps off the card into the space between us. I feel hilarity growing. One moment, it's in me; the next, it's out, and I'm laughing. He smiles, holds his arm out, brings the picture closer, which sends me further into happiness.

"Hm?" he asks, and this completes it. I am collapsed.

I ask, "What is it?" What comes out is *heartburn*. I try again. *Meat man*. The words struggle through hoots and caws of laughter.

Dr. Goodman turns the card, looks at it. His wide gray eyes widen farther, rise to meet mine. The smile spreads sweetly across his face; he's grinning properly like a boy with a fishing line. His laugh is unexpected, quick, low. We laugh together, almost weeping with it.

The name comes on a wave of feeling. *Rawblood*. How did he come by a picture of my house? It brings me back to myself somewhat.

"Am I better now?" I ask, and that works all right. "I can go…" Where? I've lost the word again. But I hold tight to a few certainties: that yesterday, I read the file, that I said yes. That he promised that after, I could.

"Iris," he says—a moment of confusion before I recall that's me—"I am committed to it, Iris. We will entirely reduce your capacity and desire to harm others."

"You did the…thing." The word, which tastes of tin. "So now I am better," I say. But there's that strange slippage of the tongue. What actually comes out of my mouth is *burn it*.

"I must go," he says with real regret. "It's a pleasure to see you so well." He stands, peels his thumb absently across the stack of cards. They snap, they rattle, *tick tick tick*.

I put my hand to my head. He moves to stop me, but the bandage falls to the floor with a *shhh*. My hand explores the bare surface of my skull. So strange and soft, no hair. The stapling, the stitches, cover me, tiny railways. And the ridges of older scars that are healed.

"There are six holes, not two," I say. *Isn't it. Arc with sage myth* is what I hear. "There should be two apertures only." *Circus time, embolism, hearty making.*

I take my time. I fix him with my eye. I scent the air for traces of the season. Nothing but carbolic and lemons. I ask, "How many times? How long, when are we?" *Suffused, umbrage, arbitrary. Sibilant.* His eyes shine.

"Iris, you must have patience," he says. "We are learning so much. You are a pioneer."

Something hurts, not my head. I test everything gently.

My midriff is swaddled in dressing. Something raw under there. Incision between my hip bones. I'm not an idiot, can imagine what they took. But I stare the question anyway.

"You will understand the necessity for that," he says. "Your defect could only produce defective… Well." The slow swell, the curve of his lip, is fascinating.

I'm quick. The cards scatter with a whir. His fingers taste of lemon. There's a spurt of salt and tin. *Should have taken my teeth while you were at it.* Pillowy flesh and within it the bone. Whirling, whistling, whistling voices, a cacophony. The door flung open, and things and women's hands hold me down, and white starched shirt fronts press the breath from me, and, of course, the needle.

The door swings shut; the bolts go home. Broad silence. His blood in my mouth. I spit onto the stiff pillow. Through a wall, someone snores, far off thunder. I explore. My trembling fingers confirm it. Wasn't yesterday I saw that file. Not by far. How many times have I seen those cards? Will I see them again tomorrow—for the first time? Have to snap that thought off as it comes or I'll lose it.

How long, how long, how long?

I was wrong. I'll die here. I should have known. My eyes won't make tears but dart about the room without my say-so. The world is made of slippery angles, crazy, gleaming. Actually, I am losing it; here I go.

Iris, my father says in my ear. *Burn it.*

I'm nineteen.

TOM GILMORE

2 january 1918
Somewhere in france

Iris

sorry for the silence. Not been myself. Got back
from leave a week ago. Moved again yesterday.
can't say where. the rats always seem to find us
all right. No secrets safe from rats.

Red sky this morning. Crates came with the new
boots but only left feet so we've cut the toes off.
We were doing the barbed wire last night by full
moon. Two men shot. one by them and one by us in
error. in the head. Not clean shots. I won't go on
about all that.

Sorry for the jumble. all my thoughts.

a few weeks ago I thought I saw you. We were in a town. Everyone blind drunk and looking for women. I couldn't quite take it. Took a bottle to the fountain in the square. moonlight. Sound of water. Everything very still and muffled up in sandbags.

Scent of lilies. Didn't see her till she was at my shoulder. came up quiet as smoke. I jumped a mile. But it was a worse shock when I looked at her. I said sorry for gawping you look so like someone I knew. would have sworn it was you but she was different colors. Red hair. For a moment there was rot or decay in the air like something was dead nearby. but no. just lilies. Anyway I said sorry again. but she just smiled so I thought perhaps her English not very good. then she said in a very English voice, *you must go to dig the grave.* for some reason it was the most frightening thing anyone's ever said. I said what do you mean but she was gone. And the smell of.

I wasn't right for days after. think perhaps everyone is mad now. and there's always something dead nearby. You and I. would we know one another? Am not what I was. Expect you're also changed.

Anyhow then came leave. Not a moment too soon you might say. Home was awful. Farm knee-deep in dust. weeds high in the yard. In the house floorboards rotted through. Windows broken. Dead pigeon in the chimney. Well the stink. Wasn't so bad last time I was down. Or maybe I didn't notice. it looks a place where only sad things have happened. Is that true? But I did what I came to do.

Your ring. Kept it with me all this while. Not in a pocket or with my things. On a string around my neck. Was afraid I'd lose it in the mud. Or it'd be stolen. There's as much of that about as you'd expect. thought I might give it back to you one day. that won't happen.

Left it for you. in the cave. on the stone. The water in the walls sounds like death. That's where it is if you want it. Do you remember? *That the ones you love may never die.* people used to believe that sort of thing. What a joke.

Never thought I'd be glad to see the trenches but I am. Even very flooded, which they are. came back here to the mud, bad bread and weevils and found things were solid again. The relief. And the company. Men are easier. These buggers know how it is. you don't start thinking.

There's a song that goes 'round. "we're here because we're here. We're here because we're here. We're here because we're here…" Just goes on like that. Always thought it maddening but not now. it's the only true thing left to say.

We were always the greatest of friends you and I. friends might sound weak I suppose. To those who don't know. It's not weak. Every memory and all the years.

I send these letters to Rawblood. Old man Shakes still there I hear. Think of him old and alone in the empty rooms. Hope he stays in the stable. I was only in the house once. that day. It was Enough. That house. You don't reply so either you're gone or you can't forgive or these never reach you at all.

Hope you understand. Why I must let it all go now. this is the last time I'll write. I can't keep doing it.

I should have done something. I know. You told me to run. shouldn't have run. Shouldn't have left you… Are you getting these? this is the last. can't keep seeing you everywhere.

Think am at the very end of what a person can be or stand.

Anyhow this is good-bye.

Yours,

T

MEG DANFORTH

NOVEMBER 1881

Near Grimstock, Lancashire

B lood bonds can't be broken altogether. More's the pity. I feel it
when Charles dies.

In general, I try not to think of him. I have a letter on my
birthday, and a letter at Christmas. That is that. I have not seen him
since I was a baby. When I was but little, I wrote him pleading notes. My
older brother. He did not answer, and I told myself that I must have the
direction wrong somehow, or that he was on a long voyage, and when
he returned home, he would read my letters, come to Bantry Farm post-
haste, kill Samuel Bantry, give me cake, take me to London, give me
dresses, and so on. He did not.

Later, Mrs. Bantry told me that cock tail feathers were for summon-
ing. So I burned them each night. *Come and save me.* Cocks on all the
nearby farms were bare that summer. But still, he did not come, and I

learned not to hope for it. It was a slow learning. Later still, I tried to see him with the Eye. Many, many times. But never did I, not once. His mind must close me out powerfully. He must bury me deep. My Eye is very strong—if I cannot see him, it means he keeps no memory or love of me in his heart.

∽

I'm in the hayloft with the ladder pulled up. Samuel Bantry is below, wandering the farmyard, calling for me. He doesn't know I'm up here— he's just chancing it, idling away his time. It's easing into midmorning, and he'll be into the village for Friday drinking soon. All I must do is hold tight.

"Meg," he says, "come out. If you do not, you shall have the strap. You do not want the strap, do you?"

I keep my scorn silent. Does he think I will answer? Chancing it or no, he's got that slinking, black tone in his voice.

"Copperknob," he says. "When I find you, you'll pay." The leather hits his palm with a thwack. As insults go, it is weak. I've had worse all my life. Red hair means witches around these parts, and there's nothing more to be said about it.

Below, a bucket rings with Samuel's kick. A hen flaps across the yard in a rattle of clucks.

His pace slows. He's thinking. His footfalls are quiet. I move behind a tower of hay. I dig in and down into the musty warm. The loft feels unsafe, of a sudden. But I can see the rickety pine of the ladder against the wall. It is here, so how would he get to me? And what would he do if he did? Slaps. The strap. My ears would be soundly boxed. And that would be that. Bruises, a few welts, and tears are nothing new, to be sure.

But I am not sure. There is another look that sits deep in his eye these days. I am lately fifteen. Women are punished differently from children.

Scuffling below. Something is dragged across the muddy cobbles. It bodes ill for me. I make myself a mouse and burrow deeper into the hay. It is difficult, because something is happening.

The loft blinks about me like a great eye. Planks creak, and there is hay in my nose. Below, the sound of metal ringing on cobbles... But behind that, through that, I see...a purple sky over a far moor. Dawn over warm land. Dew on the velvet grass. Two men on a hill, crouched by a dead dog. I cannot hear. But their anger, their despair comes from them in waves.

The hay is hot; the seed trickles into my ear. Something clangs as it comes to rest on the edge of the trapdoor. I must move, but I am slipping in the sky over a house with many gables and chimneys and... Samuel's eyes and ears rear up into the loft like a sea monster surfacing. An old sheep hurdle makes a handy ladder after all.

Mrs. Bantry's eyes are round and owlish. She fills my vision like a landscape. Behind her, a corner of blue sky. I start to say—she puts a finger to her lips. I hush.

The earthy stench and gluey mud cover me. In my mouth, under my nails, in my ears. My hair is rattails of brown. An acceptable color at last. Under the mud, there is blood in various places. I'm on the midden, where I fell, I suppose. When pushed. Above in the loft, Samuel is whistling. He is off to Friday drinking, having shown me what's what.

We scrub me in the horse trough by the lane. I climb in, sit down. The water rears, a high and glassy cliff, then crashes. Mrs. Bantry pours the cold cupfuls over. I wince under her hands, but we do not discuss it. What would be the use? The bruises are dark feathers on my wrists, my neck, my back, my legs.

I am splintered. The outside of me is weeping and holds Mrs. B, for her comfort and for mine. Another part of me is thinking, how long, then, until, until... Because Samuel has never strapped me on my thighs before.

A little of me, the clearest, deepest part of me, is thinking of my brother.

Mrs. Bantry counsels me, as always, not to cross him, not to cross Samuel. We both know, from long experience, that it will serve no purpose. However closely I obey, he will find cause. Today was not too bad. I have been bed-bound for weeks in the past. Each one of my ribs or fingers has been cracked or broken over the years. My collarbone was broken twice.

The truth is that were I not first in line, the black eyes, the loose teeth, the ringing ears would be for Mrs. Bantry. Still, she wants me to be spared, as if it would not mean her pain. She is behaving as if there were justice and some kind of reason in the world, which is admirable. She is a good woman.

Mrs. Bantry taught me the first steps. She taught me that the witches' ladder is made with yarn of certain colors. She taught me the feathers and the flowers, their sakes when whole, when burnt.

She never really believed. I saw that the first time that they sang in my hands—the feathers, the blood. The first time I had the Eye. They were little games for Mrs. Bantry. Women's games, passed down through her family, thrilling and secret. Ritual, habit. Without consequence. It must have been a great shock when they leaped for me, with bright fire and with power.

She was afraid then. She never taught me more. But it was too late. By that time, the roots and the earth and the blood spoke to me themselves and told me their uses. Mrs. Bantry has always cared for me in her way, though she did not understand me. But in some things, she cannot defy her husband.

I know something that they do not, not yet. My brother will die. Is perhaps dead already. Who will send the letter? I have a day, three at most, before they know that there is no more money. I breathe and banish fear. I scold myself. All is not lost. There is always something to be done. I will discover my course.

೦ಐ

It's a clear dawn, pale moon still suspended. The heather is springy and good under my feet. I run, my bruises singing; there is not much time for this. The vale beneath Bow Peak is soft in shadow. The brook is a crooked silver seam on the valley floor. I follow it up along the thin slice of bank, against the current, morning dew creeping through the soles of my boots. At the head of the valley, the spring leaps like an eel from mossy stone.

I take from beneath my shawl the stoppered phial of vinegar and oil and the tin plate. Copper is good. Silver is better. But this is what I have. I put the tin plate under the spring. Water rushes over, good, hard sound. The light is coming; the valley glows. The moon thin, bitten silver.

When the moment is right, I take the dish of spring water and put it on the grass. I pour in the oil and vinegar and wait. The water goes still as glass. The moon and the dawn are in it. I breathe deep. I say what I need to say. Then I ask. *Show me the answer.*

Nothing. A tiny midge lands in the dish. The surface of the water shivers in concentric circles. I wait. Nothing happens. Perhaps it is the wrong question. *Who will help me?* I ask. I wait. Nothing.

When the Bantrys find that I can no longer be kept, they will turn me out. I understand it. There is so little to go around. Samuel will do what he will before they put me out though. I would stake my life on it. Money has been the thin invisible line that kept me from disaster, and now it is removed. I will be a hedge beggar, and sooner or later, I will die—of cold, of hunger, raped and beaten to death in a ditch. That is what becomes of hedge beggars.

What is to be done? It is borne upon me that my situation is hopeless. I look at the blank moon in the pale water; I laugh a little. It reflects the truth: there is no one who will help. He never gave me cause to love him, Charles. But I think of him dying, and my eyes burn. Tears strike the still water; it whorls and shivers. Tears for him and for myself.

The moon scatters and rearranges itself. It's all about me in silver shards. A terrible white face with madness in the eyes. Horror binds my heart... The water shivers, a sound like cards shuffling, and it's gone. I am somewhere else entirely.

Around me, warm stone walls. A house. Passages and rooms open out as I go; in the center is a hall, like the chamber of a heart. Faint, without, the sound of rain. The scents are everywhere: rain and stone. A room now, a library perhaps, a study. Leather and panels of burnished wood. Through the leaded panes, wild gray hills.

Below me, a chair, kicked hastily aside. I swing in space.

The pain is immediate and savage. I cannot pay much mind to anything but the great crushing sorrow wrapped tight about my heart and the rope, coarse and bristling even tighter about my throat. These are not my hands; it is not my throat. I look through the hanging man's eyes. This man... His flesh holds things in common with my flesh. It remembers. We have seen the same mysterious things in the warm nothing dark that comes before birth. As I feel the shape of our noses, which are the same, and the pond-green of our eyes, which is the same, I understand with a lurch of sorrow. Here is my brother, at last.

We sway, creaking, from the beam. We choke in agony. Our legs kick uselessly in space. Our air-starved body gives up, bit by bit. I am to know him only for a heartbeat, as he dies.

A face is in my brother's mind. This is his dying thought: a man. Dark, vast, and still as if carven. Black hair streaked with white, long elegant hands. The light in his eyes that is like the sun on brown river water. Deep. The love Charles feels moves into me like a blow. I am stunned. I am weeping with it. Who is he? I will never know. A most torturous gift, no sooner given than torn away.

But there is this.

As my brother's brain becomes a bonfire, as it fires thousands, millions, of stars into the endless night, as his flesh changes from living pink to dead, I hear it. My name. As his throat is crushed and blood bursts in his eyes, he feels me.

Meg? he asks. *Whatever, how? Oh God, I am afraid...*

Hush, I say. *I'll be your guide.*

He is glad. He lets me touch his heart with mine. At the last.

When it's done, I am very weak. I sit and clutch the turf with my fists. I weep. I claw the ground. He has left me again, and this time for good.

MARY HOPEWELL AND HEPHZIBAH BRIGSTOCKE

1839

Mary Hopewell was endowed with the kind of beauty that seems not long for this world, so composed is it of the symptoms of sickness: pallor, delicacy, languor, a low voice, and a cheek painted pink with the hectic flush. Though much admired, she had never married, it being pronounced by physicians that her health could not endure it. This would not have troubled her, having attained the ripe age of thirty without encountering anyone whom she wished to marry. But she was of a generation of women whose brothers, father, uncles, and cousins had all been lost to soldiery, to that small French tyrant who terrorized the world so for many years. The Hopewells were an old family, hailing from Devon, but Mary was not long to have the benefit of them. Having lost all her menfolk to Bonaparte when she was a child, most of her female relations perished, as the years passed, from the same complaint that plagued her. The consumption took each in quick succession, and then Mary was alone.

Miss Hopewell sold her cottage at Brighton and went to live with her one remaining cousin, a Mrs. Anstruther, who was married to a legal gentleman with a promising career at the Inns and had a young family, which showed a marked tendency to enlarge itself at every opportunity. Miss Hopewell asserted that she considered it her duty to contribute her monthly portion to the household, but this was considered parsimonious, the fault that Mrs. Anstruther deplored more than any other, and could not be permitted. They preferred that Miss Hopewell should lean upon them. Were they not, after all, perfectly beforehand with the world? It was nonsense. Cousin Mary must put all such thoughts from her head. No, she should enjoy what she could of London and be quite peaceful.

But perhaps…if she wished to take the children for a drive now and again…that would relieve Mrs. Anstruther when she had one of her heads, which she often did in the mornings; the little angels would love it so! And Mary's skills on the pianoforte were quite superior—perhaps Alice could be set to practice with her a little in the afternoons, for the girl would never do in a drawing room as it was. The cook too could be taught by Miss Hopewell to make that béchamel that Mr. Anstruther had so enjoyed at Brighton; it had been her sister's recipe, had it not—dear Anne, God rest her soul!—some trick with the scalded milk, perhaps? And were Mary not too wearied in the evenings, it would be so kind in her to help with the darning, for Mrs. Anstruther was *not* nacky with a needle, one of her many failings, she was sure, and there was always *mountains* of the stuff… Some little favors such as these, and Mr. and Mrs. Anstruther would consider themselves richly repaid. Yes, it was positively distressing for Mary to speak of money so!

Miss Hopewell supposed London was well enough; she did not become very well acquainted with it. She mended and darned and scrubbed and nursed and taught French and Italian and the piano. She found herself often obliged to retire to her room in the evenings and, in the colder months, could not leave it. She was attended at these times with all possible solicitude: when Mrs. Anstruther brought up to her the handkerchiefs to hem, she brought also syrup of poppies and a basin to cough in.

"It's little enough I can do for the poor soul," she said comfortably to her husband. "She will not likely be with us for long."

Miss Hopewell remained with the Anstruthers for three years, during which two additions were delivered into the family. One winter morning at the beginning of the fourth year, during the bitterest season in living memory, Mrs. Anstruther visited Miss Hopewell's chamber for a cose. Mrs. Anstruther confided to her cousin that she was expecting, this summer, yet another happy event! So blessed were they. Although, it did put one to great shifts, five children and soon another who must in its turn be schooled and fed and shod... And Mr. Anstruther's prospects, though ultimately magnificent, had run aground here and there recently: some occurrence in the labyrinthine bowels of that great masculine entity, the Royal Exchange, which she could not fathom... At any rate, they must draw back on the reins for a time; a little, only a little.

Mrs. Anstruther's household economy had ever been perfection; she was a devoted adherent of the dictum of Bishop Hall: "He is a good wagoner that can turn in a little room." Mrs. Anstruther's rooms now became little indeed. The medicaments and nourishment that were prescribed for Miss Hopewell began to be doled out precisely onto the kitchen scales.

That winter brought about Mary's worst bout of illness yet. Days passed when she seemed to drift above herself. From her pillows, Miss Hopewell heard Mr. Anstruther murmur to his wife, as they strolled down to dine, "And yet she shows no sign of a *permanent* decline."

Miss Hopewell was not surprised when, in the spring, it was

decreed by the solicitous Anstruthers that she must try a change of air and a warmer climate. As Mr. Anstruther observed, she did not seem able to die.

Mr. and Mrs. Anstruther had thought the matter through with conscientious thoroughness. As much as they would miss their dear cousin, it behooved her, for the sake of her constitution, to repair to Italy with a companion, hired for the purpose. A suitable lady was found by means of advertisement, interviewed, and engaged, all by Mr. Anstruther, who, as her only male connection, had Miss Hopewell effectively in his charge until he could find a way to get her out of it.

Miss Hopewell had a small capital, which was administered by her cousin-in-law; this would pay for a tolerable standard of living and the wages of the companion. In fact, as Mr. Anstruther observed, since this capital had remained almost untouched for several years, she might be expected to go on in a *capital* way! Miss Hopewell fixed him with a thoughtful eye and acquiesced. She was tired of her life being measured; it emphasized its probable brevity.

Miss Hopewell met Miss Brigstocke for the first time at Dover, on the eve of their departure. Miss Hopewell was borne there by Mrs. Anstruther, who made much of her throughout the journey and petted her, pressing her hand and uttering protestations of attachment, mourning their imminent separation. In the carriage, Miss Hopewell gave much thought to the woman who was to be her intimate companion. Miss Brigstocke would be more familiar to her than Mrs. Anstruther to her husband, perhaps, for that pair had various and diverging interests, as married couples do—domestic, legal, sartorial, familial—and many weeks went by when they saw one another for but a few minutes during the course of it. Not so would be the connection between herself and this woman—in a foreign place, with no acquaintance and scant resources, they would be deeply necessary to one another.

The day was a bright, English one; a sharp March breeze made its way through the crevices of the carriage and under Miss Hopewell's pelisse. As they entered Dover, Mrs. Anstruther leaned forward, the better to observe the crush of people around her; Miss Hopewell leaned back—she did not want to see sunlight on the silk of dresses or the gold of officers' braid. The world was busy and awake, she thought, but she should not have any part in it. Miss Hopewell looked at the sea instead, which tossed, burdened with the black stick silhouettes of ships.

"Rough," murmured Mrs. Anstruther to herself. "Very rough today. I do hope it will not…" Mrs. Anstruther's hand tightened with true urgency; Miss Hopewell caught her cousin's thought and smiled. Mrs. Anstruther would push the packet out of harbor herself if she could.

It seemed to Miss Hopewell but a moment before Mrs. Anstruther was standing on the flagstones, calling for her to "Come down from the carriage, Mary, *do!*" and then depositing her in the coffee room of the Cinque Ports Inn with a small, gray woman. This was Miss Brigstocke, who was to share the remainder of her days.

Now that she sat before her, Miss Hopewell could see little in Miss Brigstocke to alarm her but little to give her confidence either. The other woman wore a dress of gray merino, darned neatly and abundantly. Her hair was determinedly frizzed in the fashion of one who last took note of such things at the turn of the century. Her face was small, much crossed by coarse lines, and her eyes shone black. Mary Hopewell felt a tilt of despair, regarding her; Miss Brigstocke looked emptied of life, dried, wrung out.

Mrs. Anstruther thought to order a supper and left the room with the heavy, jovial tact of one who has no interest at stake. The women regarded each other a moment.

"It is like an arranged marriage," said Miss Brigstocke at length. "How quaint of us! If we do not like one another, I assure you it will be quite proper for you to express your reservations to Mrs. Anstruther, you know, in a low voice, at which I shall look suitably devious, or perhaps drunk, and she will see that I am not fit to accompany you at all. There can be no reason for us going along with it unless we wish; I imagine another advertisement can be placed, and as for me, there is a very eligible position at Hove, which I have been considering, so you mustn't trouble yourself with that." Miss Brigstocke paused and then said in a quite different tone, "But, I confess, I have longed to see Italy."

As she said this, a great change came over Miss Brigstocke. The light fell on her in the same watery way through the panes of the coffee room. Her face bore the same scores, and the eyes remained the same obstinate, berry size. But to Miss Hopewell, a door was opened. There was a crack in the edifice of the spinster, through which strange things could be glimpsed.

"*Nel mezzo del cammin di nostra vita*," said Miss Brigstocke precisely, "*mi ritrovai per una selva oscura, ché la diritta via era smarrita*."[1]

This alone would not have bound Mary to Miss Brigstocke; it is not uncommon, after all, to have a little of the *Inferno* by heart. It was the face that spoke the words that moved her. Another woman had risen from the depths and was using Miss Brigstocke's conventional visage quite monstrously.

"I hope that we will be friends," said Miss Hopewell and found that she could smile. Miss Brigstocke smiled also and released her tight organs with relief, for there was no engagement at Hove.

The journey passed, as long journeys do, in alternating fits of interest and lethargy. Miss Hopewell kept to her berth. Their arrival at Siena was a relief to both travelers.

Miss Hopewell and Miss Brigstocke contrived to live well, as one may do on very little in those parts. They lived as genteel English ladies do when constrained by means: quietly. At Miss Brigstocke's insistence,

---

[1]   "Midway upon the journey of our life/I found myself within a forest dark/For the straightforward pathway had been lost." Dante Alighieri, *Inferno*, Canto I.

they did not settle in the town; the apartments, she was persuaded, would be cramped and vermin-ridden. For herself—well, she was nothing—but she could not be comfortable there, for the sake of Miss Hopewell's health. Miss Hopewell did not demur; it seemed to matter so little. Instead, they took a small house in the outlying district, which the agent called a villa, with cracked red walls and pink tile on the roof, over-hung with fir trees that attracted many swarms of insects. Here, Miss Hopewell proposed to end her days, leaving her remaining capital to Miss Brigstocke.

Constrained by the sense of their enforced intimacy, Miss Hopewell and Miss Brigstocke at first strove to encounter one another only when necessary. For the first month of their householding, each hovered in her room, listening for the street or garden door; only when one was absent did the other venture forth. Both lived in fear of being subjected to (or inflicting on the other) the terrible ordeal of commonplaces.

Gradually, as Miss Hopewell and Miss Brigstocke met at meal times or by surprise in the parlor, they found common ground. A chance refer-ence to painting revealed a shared taste in watercolors, which provided matter for desultory but sustained conversation. From there, they proceeded to such topics as art, music, and the benefit of foreign travel. When in early June Miss Brigstocke invited Miss Hopewell to address her as Hephzibah, Mary begged Miss Brigstocke to make similarly free with her own name.

Hephzibah took to visiting Mary's room of an evening, where she regaled her with the accomplishments and disappointments of her day. Mary sat in bed, her head cocked with polite attention, some piece of mending in her hand; Hephzibah sat in an armchair with her legs tucked under her like a girl, her long skein of hair spilling gray over her face.

"The jam at breakfast! I daresay it will sound strange to you, my dear Mary, but these foreign apricots make quite a different type of preserve, I find. Now, I would not be so featherbrained as to say that I miss *pips in the jam*, but bramble jelly does have a feel of autumn about it, does it not, of hedgerows and sunshine and cool days, and, well, *England*..."

Miss Hopewell had enough sensibility to perceive that these remarks were offerings, and she did not scorn them. When Miss Brigstocke made so bold as to admire a paisley shawl or a pair of ear bobs ("Oh, do keep them out of sight, dearest; Gabriela is a good girl, but *every* servant has light fingers, you know..."), Miss Hopewell urged her to borrow whatever took her fancy. Miss Brigstocke was always persuaded, at last, to accept these kindnesses; she made a careful show, upon return of the article, of its perfect condition. There was no mention in these courteous transactions of the truth that was apparent to both: that all Miss Hopewell's property would devolve, one not too distant day, upon Miss Brigstocke—for Mary's health did not improve.

⁓

There was a compact between the women: that they would carve a life for themselves from the rock face. They marketed and painted. In the evenings, they read aloud to each other, sewed, and spoke their prayers, leavening these worthy pastimes with indulgences, strictly rationed: a glass of ratafia, a book from the English library, cribbage.

There existed in the district, unfashionable as it was, a little English enclave and some through passage of travelers, touring parties, and commercial traffic (for *unfashionable* carries with it the benefit of *inexpensive*). But two unattached women without wealth or privilege to recommend them—who are forced to entertain in a small parlor that smells distinctly of the kitchen—are not in danger of being inundated with callers. It was, Miss Brigstocke asserted one evening to Miss Hopewell, a great relief to hold aloof from the hubbub—what liberation, to be beholden only to themselves, no longer subjects in that petty fiefdom, Society!

"Certainly," agreed Miss Hopewell.

Miss Brigstocke paused. Her face was unusually flushed. "Society!" she said again, with venom.

Miss Hopewell looked up from the pages of her novel. She put it aside and leaned back upon her pillows in order to better observe her companion. In the light of the lamp, Miss Brigstocke trembled. She had her lip between her teeth a little.

"Hephzibah," said Mary, "you are exercised."

Miss Brigstocke nodded. Of a sudden, she placed her head in her hands. She spoke through her fingers, as if they were to blame. "You know that my life has not been a happy one. That I was born in a work-house, you also know. I make no secret of it. But I have not told you something, which I fear will gravely affect your view of me.

"The workhouse gave me the name Sarah. Hephzibah, I chose for myself. It seemed fit. It is in the Bible. The name my mother gave me at birth was... *Talaitha*. My parentage, I regret to say, is not respectable. Do you know that my mother and father were of the Romany people? No, for I have not told you of it. Though I reprimand myself, I think my reticence can be easily comprehended. I have not been welcomed in polite households. Whenever I obtain a position, the matter comes out. I know not how—it happens. Perhaps a friend of my father's will see me at market in a town, and see his face in mine, and greet me. Or I will betray myself: one morning, I told my last employer that it was raining, in Romany. My mother would say that I have pushed my fate away, my people away... that that fate is now pushing me back. *Prikaza*.

"When the truth is known of my parentage, my departure is wished for by all concerned and soon follows. I think there is a great deal of native mistrust for those of my tribe—but it is not that which forces me on.

"When I see myself anew in their eyes... it is awful. *The gypsy. Gadže Gadžensa, Rom Romensa*, they say. Like with like. It is the only way they know. I thought myself so bold for running from my people... I scorned them. And what have I gained? I think I expected to discover my own nature by shedding my past. But it transpires that I have not a very discernible character, underneath it all. I am not much of anything. I left the Rom, and the *Gadže* won't have me.

"But I have said all this and omitted the one important matter: my apology. *I did not tell you at Dover.* Now, I know—by God, by long experience—that it is a thing that people wish to know. Or at any rate, they resent its concealment most deeply. Allowing you to take me, ignorant of that significant thing—it was shameful. No, please, I must get it all done or not at all. Were we antipathetic, you and I, unalike, were there no fellow feeling between us, I believe I would have confessed it straight. But I wished to come with you, and so I sinned by omission. And as I came to know you better, I came to esteem your friendship most highly, as I hope you have mine, and each day, it was harder to surrender it—the ease, the accord between us. I could not bear to be strange in your eyes. But it was not right. So if you wish me to leave, then I will do so."

Mary pushed the covers aside and rose. She came to where her friend sat and placed a hand on the bent shoulder. Through the cotton, she felt the thinness of Miss Brigstocke's rigid frame.

"It is most trying," Mary said, "to be obliged to conceal things about oneself, as you say. It is a source of constant anxiety and exhaustion. It must have been a great unhappiness to you, to always be keeping this secret—always steeling yourself for confession or discovery. I will not say, 'We will say no more about it,' for I am very interested and would like to ask you questions, if you would not find it too distressing."

Miss Brigstocke looked long into Mary's face. She nodded. She briskly blew her nose and began to push strands of gray rag hair back into her cap. "I can never repay your kindness," she said to Mary. "But I will endeavor to deserve it. Now, get back into your bed, for mercy's sake. Ask me anything you will. What would you know? All the rather dull book of my life is open to you."

Mary laughed. "Oh," she said, "anything! Tell me a tale your mother told you, at her knee. Tell me of the history of your people."

"That," said Miss Brigstocke, "would take a very long time. And I do not know enough of the old ways to do it justice." She was so woebegone at being unable to oblige that Mary was assailed by the desire to laugh. She repressed it.

A sudden light shone in Miss Brigstocke's eyes. She regarded Miss Hopewell steadily and with growing purpose. "There is one talent, peculiar to my family," she said. "I have some sight. I cannot claim more than that. My mother was a great *chovihani*. My skill is small at best—but I am able, on occasion, to tell both the character and the future of a person in the lines of their palm.

"I would look for you. What better use will there ever be for it? Dear Mary. If you have no moral objection to such things, perhaps…if you will show me your hand." Here, she took Mary's fingers in hers, cold and resistless. "Our clients prefer that we take it, being the expected thing, but truthfully, it can be enough to hold an intimate item, something belonging to the hand: a glove, a ring. Now, let us see something of your fortune." Miss Brigstocke bared the soft palm to the light. She peered, small black eyes intent, her thumb pressed to Mary's wrist.

The hand was torn from Miss Brigstocke's with vicious speed.

"Not necessary, Hephzibah." Mary's voice was cool. "I see my future plain. It is *nasty, brutish, and short*."

♋

As May passed into June, the days grew longer, and the sun beat mercilessly on the pink tile of the villa. There came into Siena at this time a certain Reverend Comer, who was touring the churches. The reverend saw Miss Hopewell in the *panetteria*, where he was partaking of sweet rolls and she was purchasing the household loaf. He soon discovered their direction. As he explained to Miss Hopewell and Miss Brigstocke, men of the cloth are not at the mercy of convention. Their calling grants them passage everywhere. They move in an elevated sphere and scorn such things as introductions.

The ladies acknowledged the truth of this somewhat dazedly, for Mr. Comer had caught them on laundering day, elbow-deep in suds. This did not deter him but inspired him to call again and often, for the reverend had a most delicate understanding and was profoundly moved by their situation: he pitied the ladies *sincerely*. He begged them to believe that he did not regard the kitchen smell in the parlor. An aroma of onions was nothing to a man of God.

In a villa consisting of four rooms, it was impossible to deny themselves when Mr. Comer called, as Miss Brigstocke said to Miss Hopewell, without actually hiding under their beds. Why should they wish to deny themselves? asked Miss Hopewell. Only benefit could result from intercourse with a person so brimming with compassion as the reverend. He had too, Miss Hopewell added inconsequentially, a pony and trap at his command.

Hephzibah could not see how this signified; perhaps dear Mary had sat too long in the sun that morning.

When it became apparent to Reverend Comer during the course of a morning visit that Miss Hopewell desired to see the olive groves at Argiano, he was much struck. To give a poor soul some pleasure—it was the least that any man of feeling or of Christian spirit could do. They should all three go there, that very day!

The expedition was a success, and when the following day, Miss Hopewell expressed an interest in the church at Fiesole, the words had barely left her lips when a sortie to that place was proposed.

Miss Hopewell acquiesced to these schemes with equanimity. If the reverend did snuffle air loudly through his nose, well, it was a small price to pay for exploring the abandoned monastery of Pontignano. If he did apostrophize Miss Hopewell in a mournful tone, as a "poor soul" or at other times as a "fragile bloom, upon a tender stalk," why, this too could be borne if he did so as they drove through the vineyards of Chianti.

Miss Brigstocke had qualms: she did not like to indulge the reverend's generosity so far. It looked perhaps somewhat...*pushing*. Miss Hopewell soothed her; in due course, the reverend would leave the district. In the interim, biddable escorts with ponies and traps did not grow on trees. One could not live always at the rock face.

On a particularly hot day, the three were taking tea in the *campagna* under a white umbrella, in the fashion of that time. Of a sudden, Reverend Comer began to gasp; his face became an even deeper shade of puce and acquired an uncertain sheen. Miss Hopewell and Miss Brigstocke rapidly concluded that they must seek relief for him.

It was the "fragile bloom" who proposed that they should walk together to the road where they had left their trap and hail a passing vehicle, perhaps the diligence, which traveled this road, and so summon help. This they did and waited some time on the hot wayside. The diligence was not in evidence; the road, which was peopled—in Miss Brigstocke's mind—with bandits, was yet empty of vehicles. Presently, however, hoofbeats announced the approach of a man in rich livery, who came on a sweating horse, returning from the discharge of some duty.

Miss Brigstocke stepped into the path of the animal, calling piteously, "*Aiuto, per piacere! Vi preghiamo di portarci a Siena!*"[2]

Mary seized Hephzibah's collar and pulled her from the road, as the man attempted to wrestle his horse to a halt in a cloud of dust. At length, when all was still, he addressed Miss Brigstocke. "I pray you, madam, do not throw yourself in the path of galloping horses."

At which Miss Hopewell said sharply, "You are a Devon man. I would

---

2   "Help, please! We beg you to take us to Siena!"

know it anywhere." Her heart hurt with half-recalled things. To hear it in this place, after so long…

"Aye," he said quietly. "William Shakes, madam, of Peter Tavy, on the Tavy River." He swept the tricorn from his head, pulling at his forelock, which revealed a pleasant face of forty years or thereabouts, topped with sandy hair, without powder or wig.

"I know Peter Tavy," Mary said. "A good place for fishing. Well met, fellow countryman. But I could wish for better circumstances! You find us in straits. One of our party is indisposed. Help should be sought with all possible speed. Is your establishment nearby? Will your master admit us? Is there a doctor in the neighborhood?"

He nodded briefly after each inquiry. Mary thought he seemed an effective, restful sort of person.

"It will be done," he said. "A carriage to fetch you. Look for it."

The horse leaped forward. Miss Hopewell and Miss Brigstocke were left with dusty faces in the empty road.

"Well!" Miss Brigstocke said in distress. "To go to some strange gentleman's house, to beg help? Mary, you have put us in a predicament. It cannot be right."

"Your solution was folly," said Miss Hopewell and settled on a stone to wait.

"It is what I would wish to avoid!" said Miss Brigstocke. "To take such aid from a stranger, and a foreign gentleman too…"

Presently, a large, dark carriage in the Italian style came rumbling along the way, and Mr. Shakes riding at its side. Two footmen, directed by the women, got the ailing clergyman into it, and Mary and Hephzibah climbed in after.

They presently arrived at a wall whose gate, being opened, revealed a formal garden of the type not often seen in that country. Even in their fatigue and concern for their companion (whose color had grown alarmingly high), Miss Hopewell and Miss Brigstocke's spirits were lifted by the perfume of flowers in the air, the rolling lawns before them, which lay lush and verdant in defiance of the white sun. The coach made its way between spreading oak trees, leaves dappling the drive in longed-for, familiar patterns of light and shade. Miss Hopewell looked about and found herself confronted by a roe deer; it regarded her briefly with a walnut eye and fled into the trees like smoke. The drive curved to reveal a lake hemmed with rushes, upon which swans sailed; on the far side of the water lay a tall white house, encompassed by rose gardens and fruit trees. The sound of the cicadas in the distance fell strangely on their ears. The ladies felt they had stumbled into a pocket of England.

The reverend was whisked away into the depths of the house, protesting that he felt—if not well—quite better, and that he forbade a fuss to be made… His querulous voice faded up the long staircase, and a deferential majordomo motioned the ladies to follow him down the marbled hall to a cool parlor overlooking an orange grove, where they were given tea.

At first, Miss Hopewell and Miss Brigstocke sat with their eyes lowered. They were still and upright as effigies, as if observed by some unseen governess; they knew themselves for intruders. But after the tea had been removed by a white-starched maid and a long interval had passed and still no one came—why, they began to exhibit the natural curiosity of any persons so placed in an interesting and unfamiliar setting and to look about themselves.

The ceiling was high and cunningly decorated to resemble a verdant canopy; here and there, brightly painted hummingbirds darted among the glossy foliage. The hides of beasts—lion, antelope, bear, zebra—lay at intervals across a shining floor of black-and-white Carrara marble. The heads were left intact; many pairs of glass eyes peered crazily at the ladies. A light breeze moved always through the room, bringing with it the faint perfume of orange flowers. Through tall, open windows could be seen the tops of trees, rustling in convocation, bearing a few pale stars of late blossom. In the distance, golden hills rose to meet the bright and blinding sky. From some place beyond their sight, there came the sound of water falling on stone and, once, the bark of a dog. The women spoke in hushed tones as they looked about them, remarking on certain little peculiarities of their surroundings. Miss Hopewell directed Miss Brigstocke's attention to a curious box of teak that sat on a bureau. It had children's heads carved on it, she whispered to Miss Brigstocke; the heads of little children with flowing hair...

They started as the door behind them was opened. A round, cheerful doctor entered and opined in flawless English that the reverend was suffering from no more than the heat; a day of rest with cool cloths on his brow would do all that was necessary to restore him. The ladies thanked him and asked who their host might be and, indeed, where? That they may thank him also and discuss conveyance back to their villa, for it would be dusk in a few short hours, and they must collect their trap from the roadside and convey the reverend to Siena and then themselves to home... The doctor smiled and said that he believed that a carriage was being made ready for these purposes. As for their host, it was Don Villarca who resided here, but as to where he might be—the man shrugged. He had been instructed by the majordomo to see to the Englishman, and he had done this—it was good enough for him.

"Perhaps," ventured Miss Brigstocke, "the lady of the house might permit us one moment of her time, in order to *properly* express our obligation?"

The doctor shook his head and gave his broadest smile yet, for (*chiaro!*) there was no Donna Villarca. It was plain, as he made his bow, that he had already dismissed the ladies from his thoughts; he bustled out to other business, leaving them still puzzled as to where to bestow their gratitude.

Miss Hopewell was overcome with restlessness, suddenly ill at ease; she thought there was perhaps a flea in one of those old hides. She expressed an intention to take a turn in the grove while they waited. Miss Brigstocke caviled at this. It would not do to make free with the gentleman's property. She would sit where she was put and wait. There arose a polite difference of opinion between them, Miss Hopewell asserting that the air in the room was torpid and bad and that she could not bear it, Miss Brigstocke asserting that she would never for her life be so remiss as to tell dear Mary how to behave but it *did* seem to her that it would not look well or be seemly to be found alone in a garden in a single gentleman's house. Miss Hopewell stood in a window, returning that if this was no transgression in Hephzibah's eyes, she would stay here and take what air she could—if it would not *offend*? If Miss Brigstocke thought it was not *wrong*? As Mary said these words, she heard rustling in the grove below.

Looking down, Miss Hopewell perceived that they were not alone; a man stood in the trees of the grove. The stranger's eyes were fixed upon Miss Hopewell. They were shadowed, narrow, deep, like arrow slits.

A slim, dark person, his face was still as varnished wood. He held a young spaniel in his arms; the dog gazed up at him, trembling and mewing with love. His velvet waistcoat, soft as the blackest night, was embroidered with bright gold. Silk shirtsleeves billowed like poured cream. A vast emerald pin nestled in the folds at the base of his throat.

The man watched her, unmoving. Mary made to stir, to break the deadly gaze upon her. She could not. He thrust the dog from him. It yelped and fell and ran. Still, she looked; she was caught in the dark tunnel of his gaze, she could not get out... There came into Mary's mind the picture of a harp string, wound tight around the peg by an inexperienced hand. The clumsy, unknowing fingers turned the wood, and the wire sang higher—and higher—Miss Hopewell felt something break within her with a terrible sound... The man bared white teeth at her, whether in a smile or a grimace, she could not say, but it was wholly terrible, and she gasped and drew back into the room; it convulsed, squares of shining black-and-white tile rippling at her feet.

"Oh," Mary said. She sank to her knees. Her heart beat like a captured dove. She kneaded the place above it hard, as though to grasp the organ—to hold it in her fist. For days after, there were dark finger marks across her breast. Miss Brigstocke questioned her, laid frantic hands upon her. Miss Hopewell was white and still. "I am well," she said. "But the window, look, the window…"

Miss Brigstocke ran on nimble feet. She peered this way and that in the warm air.

"But, Mary, what?" she asked. "I see nothing. Well, there is a little dog playing beneath the trees… I wish you could come to see. It would do you a great deal of good, for it is too sweet!"

⤬

Mr. Shakes awaited them on the gravel drive in the fading light. He handed the ladies into the carriage and touched his hat.

"I will drive your trap behind you," he said. "Never fear."

His warm tones acted once more on Mary, stirring memories of childhood and the taste of cream, of sunlit days when all was well, days that she had thought long forgotten. "Will you not ride with us?" she asked impulsively, reaching a hand as though to grasp his, to help him into the carriage.

"Not this time, Miss Hopewell." He went quietly behind to the trap and the fat pony. Miss Hopewell was left blushing foolishly under the stares of her companions.

"Mary," said Miss Brigstocke with unusual directness, "have you lost your wits?"

So the party was escorted with all celerity back to town. As they went along the road, dusk came gently. Through the open carriage windows, there came balmy evening air and the wild perfumes of thyme and sage.

Reverend Comer lay against the squabs and said nothing, consumed by indisposition and mortified, perhaps, by having been the source of such inconvenience.

In the half-light, with the rocking of the carriage providing a soothing rhythm, the women had leisure to reflect upon their day. Miss Brigstocke kept her dry palm firmly atop Mary's and squeezed every now and again. Mary did not speak. She turned her face to the coming night, to the dim, scented land.

Miss Brigstocke professed herself invigorated by their adventure but could not altogether like it. "I believe Villarca to be a Spanish name," she said. "To be sure, what can a Spanish gentleman have to do in Italy? Although of the two countries, I myself find Italy much the superior. But perhaps it is one of many residences, and he summers here only. To keep such a garden; it must require much precious labor, water, and expense!"

Something had wormed its way deep into Miss Hopewell. It sat sullen with knowledge in the depths of her. It wrapped leaden, parasitic arms about her heart.

∽

In the following days, they went about their quiet business. The reverend called on them to make his farewells; he was for Florence. Mr. Comer looked on Miss Hopewell meaningfully. Perhaps he might beg a moment in private with her? Miss Brigstocke then discerned a noise from the kitchen that announced some catastrophe—she was certain of it: foreign servants did not know how to go on, and they were positively *hostaged* to that Gabriela, who could only be termed a maid in the loosest possible sense—Mr. Comer would excuse them? The man looked at Miss Hopewell. He had heard nothing—surely, it was but a little domestic thing—but Mary sat with her eyes lowered. Another sound—a crash, an unmistakable crash! Miss Brigstocke was driven to distraction—what could the girl have done! Reverend Comer was left with no choice but to take his leave, taking an age to find his hat but presently shuffling out, enjoining them not to forget him.

When his pony's hooves had safely retreated, Miss Hopewell addressed Miss Brigstocke thus. "Not kind in you, Hephzibah, to deny the man his moment!"

"Perhaps I am not kind," said Miss Brigstocke, "but you'll allow that I am *deft*."

∽

The next morning, Miss Brigstocke joined her companion at table to find her in a state of distress. A ring, which had belonged to Miss Hopewell's mother, and before that her grandmother, and so on, was found to be absent. They embarked on the fatiguing rigmarole of remembrance that must always accompany a mislaid possession—it had been on her finger on Wednesday, did she remember? Miss Brigstocke had noted it particularly, since it did not look well with the lavender muslin she wore that day.

At length, Miss Hopewell exclaimed, she had it on the day of the ill-fated expedition—it was certain. She had removed it and placed it in her reticule as she walked to the road in order to deter unwanted interest—and had not taken it out again—but it was not in the reticule now, nor anywhere to be seen. It was then recalled that Miss Hopewell had taken her handkerchief from said reticule, to catch crumbs from the biscuits that they took with their tea, in that room by the orangery—could the ring have been caught in the folds of it and so fallen? It could have done, they concluded—most decidedly, it could have.

Miss Brigstocke was at a stand—how to effect the return of the ring or to make inquiry, when they had no acquaintance with the man, who anyway seemed to be a person of quirks? Miss Hopewell had no such qualms. A letter must be written, to ask the man to call upon them, to inquire about the ring, and to thank him—although, as Miss Hopewell observed, he had not personally involved himself in their rescue and had kept all the distance he could between the ladies and himself. Miss Brigstocke suggested that this was perhaps propriety on his part—he had a sense of their inevitable obligation and wished to spare them embarrassment? Miss Hopewell recalled to herself the countenance of the man in the garden and thought not. She was conscious of some dark and broken place within her, a gap in the row of perfectly taut harp strings.

The letter was sent, but as they received no response, the matter soon faded from Miss Brigstocke's mind. Mary Hopewell, however, thought of their carefully crafted phrases, the pains that had gone into it. Inwardly, she poured scorn on the man who plainly considered himself so much above them that he could not frame a polite reply.

⁂

One afternoon when the sun was at its zenith and the thought of movement or the thought of thought itself was so fatiguing that Mary thought she might cry with it, the two women were shelling peas in the dark parlor. The shutters were closed against the heat. Outside, the street was quiet; it was the hour of the siesta.

The green odor of the peas, their small shapes, the sound they made as they fell into the bowl, were pleasing. Mary shook her palm. The peas rattled, cool within it. It might be no bad thing, she thought idly, to be a pea on a day like this. She collected herself and gave herself a little scold. She was becoming strange. It would not do to let their solitude and the mindless tedium of the days take effect.

"I must open the shutters," she told Miss Brigstocke. "No, never mind the dust. I am sorry for it, but I cannot sit in both the dark *and* the heat a moment longer."

She moved through the dim room, exclaiming as she tripped on a stool, "I will never accustom myself to this climate. I cannot think it healthy." Wrestling with the catches, she went on, "We must take a lesson from the Italians, Hephzibah, and learn to sleep in the afternoons. The only way I can conceive of bearing these hot hours with fortitude is to be utterly unconscious throughout them!"

As she flung the shutters crossly wide, she heard a cry and found that one of the wooden doors had met with an obstacle in the form of the dark head of a person who had, to all appearances, been listening at the window.

This person raised his head, hand clasped to his brow, which was marked with blood. Under it, his dark eyes were narrowed against the sun.

"I have come to tea," said Don Villarca.

He was all courtesy; with a handkerchief stemming the flow of blood from his brow, he apologized for his conduct. He had returned from a visit to friends to find their letter and was stricken with remorse. Nothing would do for him but to set out immediately, and without his stick or hat, to repair the damage. The difficulties had not occurred to him until he stood without their villa; he did not know whether they were at home or willing to receive him. The shutters were closed… He had not wished to intrude—he was not polite.

"So," he asked, "what do I do, in these circumstances? Announce myself, like any proper caller? Go away and come back again another day, when I have answered your letter? No! I skulk in the street with my ear to your window, like a dishonest parlor maid. Until Miss Hopewell"—he bowed to her—"rewards me as I deserve and brings me to my senses with a brisk blow to the head."

Mary Hopewell was bemused by this rapid stream of confidence. A friendly, somewhat dandyish gentleman he seemed. Could he be the same man who had looked upon her so murderously? Yet the room shivered around her. The blood was scattered like rust across the purple velvet of his coat. His hand stroked the handle of his teacup. He was too vivid in the small room, his legs too long for the chair, his gaze too direct, too inquiring. It was not that he was tall, Mary thought, but that he occupied his space without apology. His voice was melodious, considered. His English was perfect and elegant. Only the faintest trace of Spanish lingered about his consonants. It hinted of another man beneath. He seemed at once both too easy and too menacing, and she did not know what to think.

"We have met, of course, Don Villarca," Mary said. "Although no introductions were performed."

Don Villarca tipped his head to her, polite. "Indeed?" he asked. "In London? I am mortified, Miss Hopewell. I cannot think."

"In your garden," Mary said. "I saw you in the garden, amid the orange trees."

"Miss Hopewell, I would never contradict so lovely a woman—"

"You looked at me," Mary said, "as I stood at the window..."

"—except to remark that had I the great fortune to meet you before this, it would be graven on my memory."

Miss Brigstocke patted Mary's hand soothingly.

"It was so very hot, my love," she said.

"I am not mistaken," Mary persisted. "And I was perfectly well enough to trust my senses..." Don Villarca was silent, and Miss Brigstocke looked at her kindly.

It was a small humiliation, expertly dealt. Mary's face grew hot. The room spun. Don Villarca sipped his tea demurely. He raised his eyes; they met Miss Hopewell's dazed ones, and she saw the cold fire that gleamed in their depths.

Don Villarca filled the air with soothing nothings. He was so gratified to have made their acquaintance, although so tardily! If his dear Mama—*vaya con Dios*, God rest her soul, departed one year past—had she known that he had not even *inquired* after them, after their upsetting time... Well, he would spare them the details. Suffice it to say that Mama was from Seville, they must understand, and Sevillan women are terrible when they are angry... On and on it went, an easy stream. All the while, his cold eyes were on Miss Hopewell. The words of old tales flew through her mind, half remembered: of bargains and pomegranate seeds. By agreeing to take their lukewarm tea and stale cake (the much abused Gabriela having chosen today—of all days!—to take an unexpected afternoon off) in their stuffy room with midges darting in the corners, he meant something else...

"Tell me, Don Villarca," said Miss Hopewell, alarmed by the pitch of her voice, "how precisely would she—excuse me, your esteemed mother—have punished you? For I am terribly stupid; it seems to me that you are a man full grown. Your mother still had nursery privileges over you? To give you a sound whipping? Is this your meaning?"

Don Villarca turned smoothly to her. There was no trace now of the savage face that Miss Hopewell had glimpsed in the garden. Yet she looked on him and trembled, as the puppy had, under his eye. It seemed to her that the dim room winked black; it was filled with the scent of the warm night land.

"But no, Miss Hopewell," said Don Villarca. "Indeed, she would never have done such a thing. That would not be fitting for me, or for her. No. She would have done far, far worse. She would, very publicly, have *cut* me! But she cannot do it now." He smiled kindly. "Perhaps you did not mean to speak so, of the dead."

Fear touched Mary then, gentle and cold.

The ring—alas!—was not to be found, but Don Villarca would have them search the carriage too. And may he offer the ladies such a carriage when they wished to drive? He kept one in Siena, which was not put to any use at all—a scandal in fact, and he would be obliged to them for justifying this woeful extravagance on his part. It was not right that they had no carriage, when the surrounding country was beautiful.

Miss Hopewell meant to rebuff his offers. She knew that they must not take these seeming alms, offered to the poor. But when her look met his, her tongue became as a stone. The quality of his gaze, it reminded her of something, an animal... She mocked herself for her nervous fancy. He was merely overbearing—it was common in vain men—and she had borne worse. Mary felt herself recovered, and then she was drawn again toward the long, dark tunnel of his eye.

Miss Brigstocke was speaking of Bristol, which she liked. "I cannot call it home," she said. "I do not believe I have the right to name any place such. No indeed. One must shift, as a governess, you know!" Here, she grew flustered. "Or rather, *you*, sir, would not know, and there is no earthly reason why you should. But there are places that speak to one, are there not?"

Mary thought of their mutual dream of Dante, of the imagined calm and sunny warmth of Italy, suffused with verse. She smiled a little. She and Hephzibah had indeed asked much of their new home. It was no wonder they were so sadly disappointed both by the place and by themselves in it.

Mary looked up to find herself observed by Don Villarca. He tipped his head toward her. The light slid on the graceful planes of his face.

"And you, Miss Hopewell? Do you miss your native shores?" His inquiry was so close to her current thought that she stopped a moment to gather herself; she seemed to be scattering further and further apart as the conversation proceeded.

"No," she said. "England itself I do not miss. You speak of places, Hephzibah, which call to one's nature—I have been visited by such feeling only once. It was my childhood home. We were compelled to leave it when I was very young, and so my memories of it are few, but they carry with them a potency. The house was under a hill and surrounded by wild moor, which covers much of that part of Devon. It was itself a wild place, with a name to fit it: Rawblood. But it was lost to us some years ago and has been rechristened, I think. There was some family lore that if we stayed too long from Rawblood, we sickened and died… Nonsense, of course, but…the heart yearns for reason in tragedy. For we left, we Hopewells. And, save me, we are all dead.

"It was a peculiar house, of granite and slate. Misshapen, and all the rooms the wrong shape, even to my young eye. But the scent of the air and the curve of the banister…" She was surprised at her own eloquence. Rawblood seemed to rise in dark shapes about her, its walls built on the air like mist… "Certainly," she said, "I have seen and lived in other, perhaps finer houses. But none have elicited in me the very particular sensation of being *home*. Even now, when I read a description of a view from a window in a novel, it is the view from my nursery in *that* house that comes to me. When I dream of a garden, it is always *that* garden, which was enclosed between the two wings of the house, as if held by two protecting arms…" Mary started. The room settled about her again. She had slipped, for a moment, across a border.

"It does not matter," she said. "That was very long ago." She stared at Don Villarca. Something precious had been pried from her without her will.

Don Villarca, for his part, was uncharacteristically silent, and it fell to Miss Brigstocke to ask him a question concerning the condition of the roads surrounding Siena.

He stayed perhaps an hour and left behind him a void. It was at the moment of his departure that his effect on the women was most clearly felt. As the front door closed noisily behind Don Villarca (who was clearly unaccustomed to manipulating such things as latches by his own hand), Miss Brigstocke and Miss Hopewell looked at each other over the remains of the meager tea and then quickly away. They no longer knew themselves. Everything was twisted out of its proper form.

"And he to lend us his carriage!" said Miss Hopewell, sweeping cake crumbs from the table. "I wish you had told him no, Hephzibah. All those favors, conferred on us, *de haut en bas*; it is most improper."

Miss Brigstocke stared at her, astonished.

"So unsettling a countenance," said Miss Hopewell crossly, blowing a strand of hair from her face. She stilled and went a little pale. "I have it," she said. "It is a snake. His gaze is that of a snake."

℘

He called often, twice a week or more. He brought them small jars of honey, paints, and a songbird in a cage. He drove them out to see fields of wildflowers and the churches, which he thought would interest them. Very well; these were no greater liberties than they had extended to Reverend Comer. But Don Villarca would not be content: he inundated them with proposals for their entertainment, always touched with the slightest hue of the improper. It was never quite possible to discern *where* the impropriety lay, but they felt it most strongly.

He vowed to obtain a balcony for the Palio that August that they might watch that delightful and violent spectacle together. The shining hides of the horses, the hard clamor of hooves as they raced in the streets…it was most stirring. And some years, no one died at all! If that was not agreeable, perhaps he might be permitted to escort them to Rome for Holy Week? Or he would engage a new bathing machine at the beach. Or he himself would hold a dance for them, perhaps for twenty couples, with them as hostesses!

Each time, they gainsaid him, flustered. Still, Don Villarca importuned. At Miss Hopewell, still, he smiled with white teeth. He could not be in her presence without falling victim to amusement. As for

Miss Hopewell, she felt a great pressure within her, a hand tight about her heart. She lived those weeks as if in a fever, her judgment and her wits disordered. She felt that she behaved like a zany. And yet, she followed still as if drawn by a string. Miss Brigstocke inquired of Mary, did she not like the man? This reserve, which then gave way to bursts of impropriety, of temper, this immoderate behavior—it was so unlike her.

"It is like one of those old tales," Miss Hopewell replied. "One has conjured the djinn; one now must accept the consequences." With this gnomic utterance, Miss Brigstocke had to be content, for Miss Hopewell would say no more.

༄

The three sat in a row on a balcony at the Palazzo Chigi-Saracini in Siena. Don Villarca's midnight-blue satin arm was flung carelessly across the balustrade. His diamond-studded cuffs sent particles of light across the hall. The night was warm. In the crowd below, fans waved gently like the white caps of the rolling sea.

The interval had not come a moment too soon for Miss Hopewell. The brightness of the lamps and the movement of bodies seemed dazzling. She shivered in her cheap cambric. The singers were shrill and out of tune, the story incomprehensible and crudely told. She feared she had the migraine. Don Villarca asked her if she were well.

"Quite well," she answered, then could not help but add, "All of this town has the odor of hot dust. The place is so dry. It makes its way in at the casements, into the clothes, and the food… You cannot exclude it. I feel it in my eyes and in my throat."

"It is a particular thing about Siena, this dust," said Don Villarca in his pleasant voice. "But dust is not dust, is it? Not in truth. It is the earth, which is composed of many things, caught up by the wind. For instance: Senio and Ascanio, sons of Remus, who founded the city; the

Medici popes; and Signore Pisano who built the duomo—they do not perish, but remain. All are buried here in the earth, and that earth has in time grown dry and lifted into the air, moving from place to place, settling and rising, whirling around us and under our feet! Do you see? This"—he sniffed the air—"is that painter who lived with his mistress and died disappointed at Fiesole! And this"—he wiped his finger down the curtain that fell beside them and showed it to Miss Hopewell, where it bore a dusty mark—"is a little girl who sees visions and was burnt at the stake in the square. This is the plague that killed two thirds of the city in 1348. This is a loyal hound who dragged his master from a burning building during the battle of Montaperti, and this—"

Miss Brigstocke, who had followed this exchange with interest, broke in with a laugh. "But how gruesome, Mr. Villarca! You speak of breathing in old bones!" She patted Mary's hand and turned to the stage. "Ah, I believe that we are going to begin again. See how that lady appears! Large people are so fond of red satin. It is mysterious…"

Don Villarca turned to Mary, his eyes narrow, lit windows in the night. He held her gaze as he licked the dust from the tip of his finger.

She rose from her seat, her handkerchief pressed to her mouth. Don Villarca rose also. He drew Miss Hopewell farther into the shadows and regarded her. She thought that, in this light, his skin had a fine sheen, which was like the surface of water, silken. Miss Hopewell looked away and coughed, hard and long, into her handkerchief. He waited beside her, quiet as a cat. When it was done, she looked up with weeping eyes.

"I cannot bear that you should look at me and speak to me so," Mary said. She lifted the handkerchief from her mouth. "As a man who knows nothing at all of suffering, you speak of it like a game. As one to whom everything has been gifted, never earned, never valued. You do not fear to be turned to dust, because you love *nothing*. You seem an empty man, a man made of paper. *Pouf!*" Mary made a fluid gesture, showing the paper man rising, like the dust, in the wind, but then she blanched and swayed, her handkerchief at her mouth. "Silliness," she said.

He reached forward and grasped her elbow. With his other hand, he touched her handkerchief with the tip of a nail. "My character gives offense," he said. "It is not the first time."

Mary's eyes were great in her face as she looked on him. "No, that would not make you offensive to me," she said. "Despicable, perhaps. A rich fool. But it is not so. You are guarded all about by luxury, true. Yes, you are armored by money. The silk, the jewels… You parrot the lines of a spoiled man. It is adept silliness. It is a guise. You care nothing about it. No, sir—do not protest. For I see you for what you are. I glimpse what lies beneath all your seemings. It is ruthless. You cannot deceive me as you do others. I saw you truly in the garden that day. *I have seen your heart, and it is cold.*"

They looked on one another. Music cut through the air about them. Lights moved in the depths of his shadowed eyes.

"What have you done, I wonder?" said Mary Hopewell. Dark, the scent of sage and night earth filled her senses. "What is it? I am not deceived."

Don Villarca gazed at her. "What a great pleasure," he said, "lies in the condemnation of others."

"You are wrong, sir. I take no pleasure in it."

"You are lying, Miss Hopewell, and not well. It will be your undoing."

She stared. Her heart was a drum. "Slander," she said. "Despicable, ineffectual—and mere slander. If you are to do evil here, you must try harder than that."

"If you are at home tomorrow, in the afternoon," said Don Villarca, "I will come and do evil by appointment."

"There is nothing to be said between us two," she said.

His finger rested on the linen in her hand, a hair's breadth from her own. He stroked the cloth gently, as one may stroke a small, soft animal. On the white could be glimpsed small flecks of blood.

"I will come," he said. "You cannot prevent it."

Miss Hopewell shrugged. She hid her fear. "It makes no odds to me," she said, making her voice bright with dislike.

They turned as one and went to their places on either side of Miss Brigstocke; they resumed their seats. Mary Hopewell placed all her attention on the play. Don Villarca lounged back on his seat and chewed at his thumbnail in a truly uncouth fashion, his eyes lidded. Miss Brigstocke soon felt that the opera was not good, that the evening was late. There was no demur from the rest of the party, and the carriage was so summoned.

❦

When the sun rose the next morning, it showed Miss Hopewell's pillow to be touched once more with crimson. She looked at it for some time and then summoned Miss Brigstocke to her chamber.

"I must rest," she said. "I will rise at noon. Will you give me the camphor basin and ensure that my straw-colored silk is pressed?" It was not a habit with Miss Hopewell to ask for concessions in this fashion. She did it awkwardly.

Miss Brigstocke embraced her. She would do all that was necessary. For Mr. Villarca was coming to call that afternoon, was it not so? (Mary suppressed her habitual spurt of irritation at the incorrect address—Hephzibah refused to use Don Villarca's title, which she thought unnecessarily foreign and full of airs.) Well, they all enjoyed his visits! Such quaint things he said. Miss Brigstocke would fetch her the moment he arrived. She could be comfortable and rest until then.

With that, Miss Brigstocke bustled off, her eyes bright with purpose. She brought Mary a tonic, the basin, and ribbons for her hair. And she would be back to rouse her upon their caller's arrival. Miss Hopewell took the tonic and sank gratefully into her pillows.

❧

She woke to the singing of crickets at dusk. A dream, half recalled; a hand pressing on the back of her neck like the heavy, slow passage of a snake. The straw-colored silk lay on the chair, gray in the evening light. The scents of the kitchen rose through the boards. Gabriela was singing below in a tuneless voice. Miss Hopewell threw back the covers and ran on bare feet down to the parlor where Miss Brigstocke sat with a candle, her cross-stitch in her lap. They regarded one another.

"He did not come," said Miss Hopewell. It was not a question.

Miss Brigstocke shook her head.

"I dreamt that I heard his voice," said Miss Hopewell, "and then yours, speaking together." She looked at Miss Brigstocke in mute appeal.

Miss Brigstocke shook her head once more, her eyes soft, and bit her lower lip. "My love," she said. "I have often thought that perhaps he is not entirely kind, Mr. Villarca. He does give one the shivers, does he not? I have ever had a distrust of men who manicure. Perhaps it is no bad thing to draw back from his acquaintance."

"Hephzibah, I am a fool," said Mary Hopewell. "But I have been spared." She gave a little watery laugh, turned on her heel, and went from the room.

❧

Miss Hopewell awaited Miss Brigstocke by the *panetteria*, as arranged between them. Hephzibah's needs had taken her to the seamstress, but she had assured Mary it would be but a moment. The scent of bread was welcome, elevating to the spirits. It was a gray day; the sky above lowered, presaging rain.

Miss Hopewell saw presently that William Shakes leaned upon a wall opposite. He stuffed a pipe with sure fingers, face intent. When he perceived Miss Hopewell, he cocked a friendly eyebrow in her direction and crossed the road to join her.

Mary said, "Well, you are the picture of ease!"

"Mostly am," he agreed. He smiled around the stem of his pipe. "I am pleased by this chance," he said, "for I wished very much to tell you: I have been lately home. Don Villarca and I have been to Dartmoor."

"Why?" Miss Hopewell asked sharply. "What should he be doing there?" She was greatly disturbed. Once more, Don Villarca trespassed on what was most precious to her. "It is quite your own business, Mr. Shakes," she said. "I wonder, however, what loyalty binds you to him? To such a—" Miss Hopewell bit her tongue, but her eyes were speaking.

"I fought beside him at Albuera, you know," said Mr. Shakes comfortably. Strong tobacco smoke curled in the air. "'Tis how we came by one another. That is why it is quite informal between us. War does not distinguish gentlemen and mere men."

"Albuera… But Don Villarca is surely not so old as that?" said Mary. And then, mortified, "I beg your pardon."

Mr. Shakes showed her his slow smile. "No," he said. "Do not trouble yourself. Men wear their age in two ways, out or in. I wear mine in my face, but my heart is easy. He's pretty enough, but his years lie heavy within.

"When we met, all those years ago, he was young outside and in. So was I, for that matter. War put paid to that, in the end. Albuera, eh," said Mr. Shakes. "We waded in blood that day. Those who wrote the dispatches called it a victory. We knew better. What the French did in the towns… No one should see such things. The stench of corpse smoke. I will recall it all my days… Forgive me. I forget myself."

"You will find no reproof here," said Mary. "All the men in my family are military men. Each one. *Were* military men, I should say. My father was killed in the Peninsula in '07, the year I was born."

"There were many left fatherless by those times," said Mr. Shakes.

"I do not recall him; I cannot pretend to a tragedy I do not feel. But my brothers... Major William Hopewell, 16th Light Dragoons. Major Henry Hopewell, 7th Queen's Own Hussars."

He asked, "Waterloo?"

Miss Hopewell nodded. Tears rose in her throat. Old grief. "That," she said, "I do recall."

"Cavalry are very bold," said William Shakes. Nothing else was spoken between the two of them for a time. Each was wrapped in their own thoughts.

At last, Shakes said, "Miss Hopewell." The Devon was strong in his voice. "Soldiers are the only men I understand. And in his heart, Don Villarca is a soldier still. He is as a brother to me. So I understand what has been taken from him, by life and by war. And I think that perhaps you also understand these things. I hope that you would know a suffering heart, however disguised."

Into Miss Hopewell's mind, there leaped unbidden an image of a young Don Villarca, whose face was open and untouched by the dark. "I had not known," she said, "that he was in that war, or in any war at all."

"Ah," said Mr. Shakes. "I thought you might not know, perhaps. Well, good day, Miss Hopewell." He went, trailing pipe smoke behind him.

"Dear Mary," said Miss Brigstocke, "do you intend to stand outside the bakery or to go in it? For I believe the rain is upon us." She clutched to her a little parcel, the contents of which she proceeded to describe. A paper of needles, merely, and some silk. For they had not the kind of worsted she wanted for stockings. "Goodness," said Miss Brigstocke, "someone has been smoking here. It is positively *pungent*."

Miss Hopewell allowed her arm to be taken. She allowed herself to be drawn under the awning of the *panetteria* as the first heavy drops of rain fell. She felt strange and deeply fretful. She did not wish to be asked to reconsider her ideas.

That evening, the two women sat as usual in Mary's chamber. Miss

Brigstocke began, as was her habit, to offer up the thoughts and actions of her day for Mary's delectation. From the unreliable character of Italian servants, to the wide cracks in the floorboards, which plagued the women greatly (imagine, dear Mary, if we were to take them up; what things we might discover! Perhaps your ring also fell in there!), Miss Brigstocke's mind roved widely. She contemplated the problem of removing the red Italian dust from the hems of her gowns, the elegance of those dogs (the little greyhounds that one could carry), and the slovenliness of the local butcher, and thence moved on to shopping in general. Idly, she began to describe a piece of lace that she had glimpsed that morning. She had been much taken with it. So pale, so intricate, the way it fell in folds like running water, and when light shone through it, the pattern was revealed: endless arabesques of blossom and curlicues, repeating themselves, over and over...

Miss Brigstocke's reverie was interrupted by a strangled noise; when she looked up, Miss Hopewell was weeping. Tears ran down her face and dripped through her fingers, shining in the candlelight. Her shoulders shook with violent paroxysms.

"Mary!" cried Miss Brigstocke in real alarm. "Why, whatever can be the matter?"

Miss Hopewell raised her head. Her eyes streamed, and her face was pink and seamed with effort.

"It is so stupid," she gasped. "It is...unconscionable to be roused to such passion by a piece of cloth. I cannot bear it! Do not *talk* to me anymore! Get out! It is bad enough that I must bear your presence, which was foisted upon me, and that you must call me your 'dear girl' and 'sweet Mary'! Do not also bombard me with this...this trifling, *womanish* stuff! Get out, get out, get *out!*" She fell to her pillow, racked with sobs. She felt the dark worm within. It stirred; she reviled herself.

Miss Brigstocke contemplated her a moment. She rose from her chair and approached the bed slowly, then sat down upon it. Giving Mary much time to retreat, she took her in her arms. She then began rocking her, uttering meaningless sounds, and stroking her head. "There, there," Miss Brigstocke said. "I have tired you. Yes, indeed. I talk too much, I do; it has ever been a fault of mine. But please, do not let my nonsense perturb you. All will seem different tomorrow, I promise it."

"Tomorrow!" raved Mary into Miss Brigstocke's chemise. "Tomorrow! Yes, we must endure that, and the one after, and the one after! Of course. The endless series of tomorrows. I abhor it! *Damn* tomorrow! To—to *hell* with tomorrow!"

Miss Brigstocke closed her arms tight and her eyes tighter.

"If you like," she agreed in gentle tones.

The following evening, a small package lay beside Miss Brigstocke's plate at the table, inscribed *Hephzibah* in Miss Hopewell's elegant hand. Having been informed in Gabriela's rough Tuscan that the other signorina was *malata* and would dine in her room, Miss Brigstocke set to her solitary supper. She eyed the package as she ate, birdlike, a cutlet and a little salad.

At last, her repast concluded, the maid rung for, and the table cleared, she reached for the parcel. Her fingers unfolded the brown paper neatly. She put the handy length of string aside for further use. When the wrappings had yielded and the tissue beneath was lifted apart, there tumbled into Miss Brigstocke's lap a creamy length of Sicilian lace.

⁓

Summer dwindled into autumn, and in the business of making the house ready for the winter, the two women found some occupation. Miss Brigstocke spoke of Don Villarca often and told tales of him to the limited society that fell in their way. She spoke of his whims and his oddities in small, hot rooms where English people took their tea, so that he seemed to hover like a miasma over the tea urn, and some semblance of him clung to the scones. As for Miss Hopewell, she did not speak of him. She preserved a reticence on the subject. But something was still wrapped tight about her heart.

Mary grew quieter with each day that passed. She was for a time much occupied with correspondence, largely directed to a Signor Fratelli, *avvocato*, Siena. One day, a legal clerk came to call, bristling with pens and red tape. He spent the afternoon closeted in the parlor with Miss Hopewell. This posed a very *minor* inconvenience to Miss Brigstocke, since she would not *presume* to intrude on Mary—particularly when she feared to disrupt the administration of business, something of importance? And thus she could not get to her tambour frame that was in the parlor. And therefore had fallen sadly behind with her stitches. Of course, she would not dream of mentioning such a trifle to her dear friend; she could not now recollect why she had brought it up.

Mary Hopewell did not reply.

"Oh, Mary," said Miss Brigstocke. "What will become of us?"

"Of you," said Miss Hopewell, irritable, "I know not. But I will die."

Miss Brigstocke's eyes filled with sympathy and tears. "You must not fear," she said. "You are the best of us, dearest. You shall be the first to be taken to the bosom of our Lord."

Miss Hopewell was silent. "I am not afraid," she said at last. "Do you know, I wish I were? It is just...so torturously dull, the prospect." She rose stiffly from her chair and went away. She was not seen belowstairs for some days.

❧

One overcast morning when autumn was far advanced, there was a great pounding on the door of the villa, so that the two women leaped from their seats where they had been mending a tablecloth, and Miss

Hopewell pricked her finger, and Gabriela went to answer the summons with much complaining.

Through the door poured Don Villarca, filling the air and the corners of the room. "I have apologies to offer, which I hope will not be spurned," he said, proffering two nosegays of vivid color. Their rich scent perfumed the apartment, dizzying. The hearts of the flowers were golden as egg yolk. The petals were the same deep red as the silk of his coat.

It is said that there is nothing so elevating as the reunion of friends. Don Villarca launched into narration of his months away from them. It had been hard! Miss Hopewell and Miss Brigstocke would forgive him, for they were so estimable and everything that was kind.

Miss Hopewell drew a deep breath. She wished to show Don Villarca a strange flower she had found. It was by a well, in a field, and peculiar— she believed she had it in her reticule. Mary said, "Perhaps you would be so good as to fetch it for me, Hephzibah?"

Miss Brigstocke stared at Miss Hopewell. "If you are tired, dear Mary, it would be well for you to retire. Conversation, I find"—this addressed to Don Villarca—"can be as exhausting as a brisk walk!"

He made no reply to this. Mary looked long at her friend. "I should think it such a kindness in you, Hephzibah," she said gently, "to go to find that flower."

Miss Brigstocke went, and Miss Hopewell was alone with Don Villarca.

Neither spoke. Miss Hopewell could not meet his bright, narrow eyes. So Don Villarca took her hand and asked her to be his wife.

A small sound was heard in the hall—a board squeaked. They stared at the door.

"Not here," Mary said. "Come."

They went to the villa's garden, a small patch of dry earth adorned by lank spider plants. Above them, the gray November sky.

Mary said without preamble, "Now, as to your question, sir, you do me great honor. I am *devastated* to be obliged to refuse. I view you in the light of a dangerous man; I do not desire any more intimate acquaintance. I could not reasonably expect happiness from a union with such an...individual. I am not persuaded that you are steady in your intentions," she said. "You cannot keep even an appointment."

Don Villarca kicked at a lump of dry earth, which broke and covered his shining black boot in red dust. "Miss Hopewell," he began, "I understand you. But I will not have that set against me. *I did come that day.*"

Mary Hopewell raised her eyes to his. She regarded him with fascination. "You understand me?" she asked. "Most kind. I cannot make a similar claim. For, sir, you did not come."

"Yes," he replied. "I did. And I was told by...the person who received me that you could not marry. I was told that it would mean your death. Then I knew that I must stay away. I resolved never to see you more."

"What a very indelicate conversation," she said. "By whom... Who told you this?"

"I thought you had made her messenger," he said, then shook his head. "I thought... But it does not matter."

"Who," persisted Miss Hopewell, her cheeks pale, "would dare presume so? Who would be so cruel?"

He made no answer, and she stared. The blush rose slowly in her face.

"Well," she said, "who are *you*, then, to go away on *this person's* authority, with no word to me, as if I were a naughty child?"

"I have sent many, many men to their graves in my time," said Don Villarca. "It is too much, the death I have dealt. So, to be the means by which yet another were to perish..."

Miss Hopewell, who had long lived with mortality at her heels, said, "Do not speak of your guilt, of these deaths upon the battlefield and then of my death, *mine*... Do not speak of them as if they are the same. They are not. It is not for you to tell me what my end might be, to blame your-self for causing it, or to praise yourself for preventing it."

"To end another life," persisted Don Villarca, "and that, your life—it could not be borne. It seemed neither of us was free to act. It was good and neat."

"What fecklessness, what presumption!"

"Yes," he said, "I see that now."

"I know my own case," said Miss Hopewell. "The obstacles that stand between myself and marriage. You will in time consider this a lucky escape—for I would be giving you a sad bargain if I said yes. Your situation, however, is not apparent to me. You say you are not free. Explain."

His lips tightened, and the furious light shone once again in his face. "This is an old truth: that when we, the Villarcas, marry, we invite the bad luck in. Foolish, it may seem to you. But it is not so.

"My grandfather left his wife—after terrible travails—and went to Vienna, could find no peace, lost his mind, and died in a hospital there. My father married, as was arranged for him, his cousin. Thinking to live in a healthful climate, they went to Switzerland, but he died in a brawl shortly after I was born. She stopped eating altogether, until she too died. My uncle wed his laundress; he murdered her while walking in the Pyrenees during the *lune de miel*, and then threw himself from a cliff. I could go on. Shall I? My family... We eschew our own country. Rightly so. It carries ill memories for those of my name. We have done great wrong there. I have chosen Italy to spend my days.

"The Villarca blood is dark and strong. The Villarca temper is furi-ous, sublime, full of poetry and madness. We seek the light, ever...but we never find it. We should not share ourselves with others. It is not a good thing. They call it in my tongue, the *luz oscura*, which means the *dark light*. Some call it a curse. I do not know. Certainly our past, the history of the house of Villarca, has shameful passages. Shameful.

Our lineage is steeped in blood. There is no family more deserving of a curse.

"But I have considered it carefully, you may believe me. The *luz oscura*… It is more likely to be madness. An inherited weakness. Such things not infrequently afflict highborn, well-bred families. We have been so jealous of the bloodline, you see. So very, very fond of marrying our children to one another. You would not breed dogs in that way—but yes, it will do for the Villarcas. Anyhow. Superstition or madness, there remains this: that when we marry, we do it badly. We drink, we lose our minds, we rage, we wound—and always, always, we die young. It is the way. I was afraid for myself. And, perhaps, of myself. You speak of a sad bargain—on my side, I fear it is so. I like to do things well; this matter, I felt, was beyond my skill.

"It was wonderful when you were so cross with me, when you looked at me with—hate. For when it was only I who felt this, nothing could result." His brows darkened; he said, baleful, "I fostered your distaste. I encouraged it. I was a boor. I do not like to think of how I behaved. For that, I am sorry. But when I came to suspect that, despite all my seemings, you did not *entirely* dislike me… Ah. Then it was frightful."

Something stirred within Miss Hopewell, like the beginning of inspiration. She said, "*Luz oscura*, you call it. Yes. It is a good name. Madness? Perhaps. But not that alone. I saw the darkness in your soul the moment I saw you."

A great stillness came over him. "We come now to it," he said.

She said, "Go on, sir."

"You tell me that I am cold," said Don Villarca. "You say that I am cloaked in despair. All this is true. I have led what people call a sinful life. I think that all my virtue is dried up, withered away. Sometimes, I walk through it in my dreams—the interior of my heart. It is like a black land, where black flags hang in tatters and venomous plants grow in sickly clumps and serpents writhe… A deadly night garden, my heart."

"I know it," she said. Her breath came a little faster.

"But," said Don Villarca. "I have seen your heart too, Miss Hopewell, *and it is just like mine.*"

His words smote Mary like a blow. She burned within.

"All your beauty cannot hide it," he said. "Downcast eyes, meticulous correctness; a decorous manner cannot hide it—the great black hole where hope should be, where life should be. You say that you see the darkness in me. I see it mirrored in you. I know your emptiness."

"I will not be spoken to thus," she said, "by a man who—"

"What? What, Miss Hopewell, have I done? Nothing that you know of! But you feel it—the great cavern within me. Because like calls to like, always. Will you deny it?" he asked, his hand urgent on her arm. The light in his arrow-slit eyes. "Will you deny that we are the same?"

"You are a villain," she said.

He nodded. "We are both villains."

Mary could not move, for the world had tilted forever on its axis.

"I have no one," Don Villarca said. "All of my family is dead. Their deaths were terrible, each one. *Madre de Dios.* I am alone and rotten with memory. You too are alone, Miss Hopewell. We are wasted, both; we are sickened by loss. Perhaps sorrow has taken the virtue out of us forever, has corrupted us utterly. Perhaps it cannot be recovered… Will you refute me again? Will you—"

"No, I will not deny it," said Mary Hopewell, exhausted. Tears rose, burning, to her eyes—she let them fall. A great opprobrious weight had been lifted. "We are the same. I felt it. I feel it." The power, the strange peril of the moment swept through her—the enormity of being known. His hand was cool on the back of her neck.

"You have never known freedom," said Don Villarca. "Ladies are meant to be cut from different cloth. They are not supposed to want, to know certain things. And I—I have never known peace or affection. Perhaps we are not villains at all. There has been no opportunity to

discover what we might be." His voice sounded a note of infinite longing. Mary's hand found his. Their fingers intertwined lightly, and in that
slight touch, she felt it—the aching tug of the possible. Years, a life…

Mary tore from his grasp. "It is not settled," she said. "Villain I may be,
but I will not do what you ask. The bargain is too bad. I must warn you
off it. If only you knew! Your family is lost to violence and madness—
but the Hopewells die young also. Like the Villarcas, we murdered each
other merrily, we fought duels, and we died; yes, we died plentifully…
Then, when we lost our home, we were scattered. One by one, we fell
victim to disease… You speak of the blood, the curse of the Villarcas,
but in truth, the Hopewells are no less damned… It is a sad history,
best ended. I am the last of my name, and I am not long for this world.
For these reasons and—oh!—a hundred more, I will not give you the
answer you seek, sir."

He said, "We will agree on this, in the end. I have conceived such a
passion for you, and I am very clever at getting what I want. Perhaps this
will be my most monstrous act—to take from you your life."

"Odd," she said. "I care not for that." She shook her head. Her eyes
held a resolve that was his answer: No.

He seized Mary's hand in a light grip and leaned into her ear, so that
his words filled those spaces with his breath. "*Nel ciel che più de la sua
luce prende*," said Don Villarca, "*fu' io, e vidi cose che ridire, né sa né può
chi di là sù discende…*[3] If you marry me, you shall do precisely what
you will. There is nothing that I would not understand. Whatever you
wish—whatever you desire—it shall be yours before you have finished
the thought. I will make it my life's work. Do you understand me?"

"*Paradiso*," Mary said lightly. "A paradoxical freedom; one that is
permitted, granted by another… I must go."

---

3   "Within that heaven which most his light receives/Was I, and things beheld which to
repeat/Nor knows, nor can, who from above descends." Dante Alighieri, *Paradiso*, Canto I.

"Stop," said Don Villarca, agonized. "I know, I know, I have done it so very badly. I should have begun like this." He drew from the white silken lining of his coat a sheaf of papers.

Miss Hopewell smiled. "Sir—"

"Please," he said, "read."

She scanned the first lines, the next page and the next, lifting the leaves with unsteady fingers. Her lips moved silently. Her heart beat against her ribs like a child with a stick on the railings.

"It took me some time to find it," said Don Villarca. "It was traveling in disguise, as Dempsey House. Who are these Dempseys? It will not do. So if you will have it, I will take you home to Rawblood. I do not hold *everything* cheap," he said. "I can discern what is infinitely rare and must be grasped. Say what you choose; give me what answer you will; send me away. But do not," said Don Villarca, "ever again think that I do not see to the heart of you." His face, habitually so watchful and elegant, now brimmed with feeling and with anxiety.

"You do not know what you have done," said Mary, "and I *will* have it—" She passed one hand across her brow, which was hot. The other clutched to her chest the deeds to the house. "As soon as may be. I care not for..." She left the thought unfinished; her face bore the inattentive look of one who listens to a sound far away. "You should take William Shakes home to Devon," she said. "He misses it."

Don Villarca smiled. "Yes," he said. "He does. And you?"

Mary did not speak at once but seized his face in her pale hands and looked. She looked truly and long. He looked back without artifice, without pride. She saw the tired soldier within.

"To agree," said Mary, "only to abandon you in, what? One year? Two? It is merciless of me, and cruel. What is your name?"

"Leopoldo," he said, squeezing his bright almond eyes closed with distaste. "Is it not dreadful?"

"Dreadful," she said. "I am Mary." She stopped, puzzled. "I had thought, oh, so many things…" She had a growing hilarity in her; she looked at him, and it rose and thrust against the dam. "All along, I thought you truly a villain—as if we were caught in the plot of some play…" Her mirth reached its peak like a stream in spate, and she laughed. "I mistook it for horror, but it was merely love, in the end."

"It is, perhaps, quite an easy mistake," said Don Villarca. "Your answer?"

What was there left to say? For the first time, circumstance marched together with the dictates of her heart.

⁓

He left in the twilight. Mary rose and went to the house. She found Miss Brigstocke standing by the garden door to the parlor. She did not seem to note Miss Hopewell; she was pale and trembling, and her eyes were wet currants. In one hand, she held a withered red bloom. In the other, she held, betwixt her fingers, a thin band of old gold adorned with rubies and diamonds.

Miss Brigstocke was whispering. "*Lav hi azar, yak, alazas, b'or, amria. Ai! Ai ai, johai,*" she said on a low breath. Her eyes were blank. "*Beng tasser tute! Detlene. Ladzav, ladzav, ladzav! Jekh dilo kerel dile hai but dile keren dilimata.*"[4]

Miss Hopewell looked on her with a cautious eye. Hephzibah was a stranger to her now. She made to pass the other woman into the house. As she did, Miss Brigstocke seized her arm in an iron grip.

"You see? I have it, the flower," said Miss Brigstocke. "I have also your ring, which was in your reticule. It was not lost. You have practiced a low deception upon me. You lured him to us, like a common…a common…"

---

4   Her name is a flower, an eye, a flame, the woman, the curse… I see the ghost's vomit. The devil strangle you! The souls of dead children. Shame, shame, shame! Madmen make more madmen, which makes madness.

Miss Hopewell regarded Miss Brigstocke. "Yes," she said. "I suppose that I did."

"But you despise him," said Miss Brigstocke. "You fear him."

"I thought so," said Mary. "But I have been so very wrong." She smiled a little to herself.

"But we made a compact, you and I," Miss Brigstocke said. "We are to face it out together...Mary." She began to weep, great, broken sobs. "I thought you constant. I thought us friends."

Mary breathed deep, her eyes as bright as children's marbles. "Such pity for yourself, Hephzibah," she said. "And yet, I heard something most strange. That day, as I slept, I dreamt I heard you below, with Don Villarca; two voices were raised at each other—you spoke of me. A dream, I thought! When I asked you of it, you told me as much. I called myself a madwoman and chastised myself for it after. But let us be frank. He came, and you sent him away, told him I would not survive marriage or children. Is this not so?"

Miss Brigstocke wept bitterly and openly. "Yes, yes," she said. "It is so."

"Did you wish for my small capital," asked Mary, "so *very* much?" They looked at one another. Miss Hopewell shrugged and turned to go.

Miss Brigstocke drew breath. She dashed the tears from her eyes. "Stop, Mary. There is something... For the sake of what we were, I must tell you. As I held your ring, moments ago, between my fingers, the sight came upon me. I have never felt such living evil. This marriage will bring sickness and death. It will lay waste to generations. It will grow black flowers in the black land... You will not live. I beg you—I implore you— do *not* do what you intend..."

Miss Hopewell stilled her with a hand. "No more, madam," she said, "of your cant and your stratagems. You may be right; those words that you uttered in duplicity may easily be true. Perhaps I will not live.

"But no matter what might come, I am resolved that I will forge my own existence. No longer will I be pushed, and pulled, and cosseted, and lied to. Damn you.

"In short, Miss Brigstocke, I find that you have been speaking for me, where you had not the shadow of a right to do it. You pretend to protect my interests, but it is only to further your own advantage." Here, Mary Hopewell drew a long breath, and when she spoke next, her voice was weighted with unshed tears. "You speak of deception," she said, "but it is I who have been the most deceived; that is, in you. But there it is, and no longer of consequence."

She plucked the ring from Miss Brigstocke's cold fingers and went past her into the dark house.

"*Lashav!*" called Miss Brigstocke as she went. "Your future is dark, and long. Longer than you suppose. *Lashav, lashav, lashav!* "[5]

Miss Hopewell did not look back.

"Curse you, then," called Miss Brigstocke after her. Then, to the empty air, "I have tried to turn it aside."

❧

The following morning, Mary awoke to a sense of something reordered, of a vacancy in the pattern of things. She lay, still half in the grip of her dream, which had been bright and violently colored, involving long swathes of flowing cloth that stretched like roads into the distance... She turned her head upon the pillow and felt how pleasant it was. Her hair, unbound, was smooth beneath her shoulders; she rolled gently to and fro upon it, thinking of nothing much. But what was it?

In the street beyond, doors were opening for the business of the day. Horses passed by, and hooves rang on the beaten earth. Birds made shrill

---

5   Shame!...Shame, shame, shame!

retorts. From the kitchen below, there came the familiar singing of the dented kettle, the drag of Gabriela's slippers along the boards, her quiet, murderous muttering.

No sound came from the room adjoining Mary's. There was none of Miss Brigstocke's high and tuneless humming or the creaking of her ancient and torturous stays. Through the wall was a silent space. Hephzibah had gone from the house. When? In the night? It would be quite gothic, to flee in the dark. But gone she was; Mary felt it. The very air was changed; the quality of the light that came through the shutters, the shafts of winter sun laid straight along the floor. Mary looked around her little room with its dusty corners, the dark beams that seeped an astringent, resinous scent, the worn rag carpet, once green, now washed pale gray. Somewhere, a mouse made a drowsy, scratching sound. The scene had an irresolute quality, as of something imperfectly remembered. She could not feel anything about it.

The pillow beneath her head was white, unsullied. Mary looked at it for a time, wondering. Suddenly, she drew a deep, sharp breath, filling her lungs. The air flowed in a clean, cool stream. *I am very well*, she thought. It was too big a thing for so small a feeling as surprise. Her life's companion had left her. It seemed right and inevitable that it be so. *It is true. We are healed by Rawblood.* This thought was followed in that instant by others that traveled through her like fatigue, like warmth: *He will come again today. And I am going home...* The feeling that pierced her then was like light.

⁂

Mary stands before the window, upright as a wand, the floor cool and solid beneath the soles of her feet. She throws the shutters open to the blinding day, raises her arms above her head, and stretches herself wide and high, lifting onto the tips of her toes as dancers do. She throws her arms out, broadening, lengthening, into a star. She tips her head back and yawns wide.

1850

Far Deeping, Lincolnshire

The woman who grasped his sleeve in Church Street was near starving. Her bones turned up in her face like the edges of saucers.

"Reverend," she said. She regarded him with berry-black eyes that were sunken and dull. She gathered her voluminous garment about her. It was of gray flannel, stained all about and frayed sadly. The morning wind licked at the holes.

Reverend Comer sighed inwardly and prepared himself for exposition.

"Madam," he said, "I am, as you see, in somewhat of a hurry. If there is something of a spiritual nature that you require from me, let's have it. Otherwise, I must refer you to the Magdalene House on Union Street, where you will find assistance of the kind you seek."

At this, the woman bristled. She drew herself up and stared, and in that moment, he recognized her. It was, of course, too late to recall his words.

"Reverend Comer," said Miss Brigstocke, "I do not quite understand." Her tone said that she understood perfectly.

"My dear Miss Brigstocke! My word. What a charming surprise! I was thinking of something else entirely—and—and speaking quite at random, you know. Er, forgive me. The cares laid upon the shoulders of the clergy… And I was not expecting to see an old friend! But what were we saying?"

"We had not yet begun to say anything, sir." A strand of gray hair whipped across her face. She pushed it aside, seeming close to tears.

"Which will not do!" he said, desperate. "Will you not take some tea with me for the sake of old times? It would give me great pleasure."

"Well," Miss Brigstocke said delicately, "let us see. What is the clock? Yes, oh, I see. Well, I need not call before eleven, so…" He stood patiently through the performance. At last, she said, "And of course, it would be a shame to miss the opportunity of hearing all that you have been about. It has been ten years?"

He judged then that pride had been satisfied and ushered her across the cobbles.

Once inside the Rose, Miss Brigstocke's color improved. She laid her gray flannel sack gently on the chair beside her, revealing a dress, perhaps once black, now the murky green of deep water. It was patched here and there with cambric of various colors and red-striped linen that gave her the appearance of a molding deck chair on a promenade. She had no hat. Her hair waved about her like a shock of dried grass. The Rose was half full, and he could see at a far table Mrs. Munn, who had the haberdashery shop, and her daughter. They stared with round eyes, mouths busy behind their teacups. He waved, and they raised slow, wondering hands in return. It would be all over Far Deeping by the afternoon.

He ordered tea, cake, and sandwiches. Looking at Miss Brigstocke's thin lips, which struggled over pointed brown teeth, he called after the girl, "Also macaroons!"

Miss Brigstocke sat quietly with her hands folded in her lap as this part of the business was done. A scent came from her, not quite of the gutter, but strong and fermented. The reverend wished once again that she had not chanced to see him. He liked things to be comfortable; Miss Brigstocke and her state were so uncomfortable. He waited but saw that she would not begin.

"Well!" he said. "I am sure there is much to say. I am surprised, I own, to find you in England."

"Oh," she said, "I have been back in the country for some while. I left Italy, you know, that very same year that we met there."

"Indeed! It seems a pity. You and Miss Hopewell had made such a cozy life together!"

She smiled, but her eyes were on the tray of cakes, which arrived that moment.

He took three immediately onto his plate, in order that she should feel she could do the same. "Home shores are best, Miss Brigstocke! But I expect you do not regret your adventure, for travel is so enlarging."

"Yes," she said. "Most pleasant and enlarging."

"And what brings you to Far Deeping? Are you placed in the area?" He sincerely hoped not. He thought of the inevitable obligation. She was neither a respectable person nor a charity case. It was so awkward. Would Mrs. Comer be expected to invite her to dine? And that odor... It was something like a cat, or a stoat.

Miss Brigstocke smiled kindly at him, as though she could see his thoughts and wished him to know that she understood. "My plans are not yet settled, Reverend," she said. "I have been visiting a cousin not far from here and thought to see the village, which is said to be a charming place. And I find it to be so. Who could not be drawn to it? The little lanes and such cheerful awnings and everyone going about their right business under thatch and steeples. Now, do tell me, is the church, yes, with that rather imposing spire over there, is that Norman?"

He laughed and told her no, no, she had it quite wrong... Conversation went on in this fashion, rather pleasantly, he thought, for some minutes, as the merits of the country were extolled and the decline in English architecture mourned. Her manner was, after all, perfectly pretty; she had not too many firm opinions and showed a charming deference to his views. As they spoke, he observed her and was increasingly distressed by what he saw.

"Miss Brigstocke," he said after all the sandwiches had been consumed, "I hope you will not mind me presuming a little, but it seems to me that you are not in the best of circumstances. How does this come about? I am sorry to speak so bluntly…"

She blushed a little, turned away. She said nothing. A tooth worried her lower lip.

He was determined not to retreat. "Please," he said. "We are old friends, are we not?"

Miss Brigstocke nodded, eyes lowered, and said, "I am afraid that my departure from Italy was somewhat precipitous, and I did not have the luxury of looking about me for a good appointment. I took the first one offered, and as perhaps you will know, Mr. Comer, if you fall on hard times, hard times follow, for people look only as far as your last post."

"I know," he said with some warmth, "what can befall someone who has no recourse or friends. And Miss Hopewell and yourself… I hope that you and she did not part on bad terms?"

She raised her eyes to his and said quietly, "I will not discuss that, for I do not believe in speaking ill of the dead."

"Dead?" There was a rush in him, of some feeling, some old feeling; it was like seeing again, after many years, a place where you once played as a child.

"Yes," said Miss Brigstocke, "quite recently. She and her husband both… But of course, you may not have known. She married in '40."

"I did not. I am glad, although," he said with another strong current of sympathy, "I think it placed you in a difficult position."

"Yes," she said. "Mary returned to England as a bride. While I… Well, sad tales are not for happy occasions, are they?"

"She was never strong," the reverend said, thinking of the dark and shadowed cast of Mary Hopewell's eyes, set deep in her lily-pale face.

"No, I fear not. I thought…" said Miss Brigstocke delicately. "Forgive me, but I thought that at one time, you and she…" Her eyes filled with soft meaning.

The reverend thought of that Italian idyll, of the sound of his pony's hooves, and the sun-drenched hills, and dishes of olives beneath the trees. He recalled the scent of wild herbs and women hanging white sheets to dry in the hedges on warm, starlit evenings. That was before he had met Theresa and married her, and she gave him two strapping sons, whose lusty cries filled his house day and night... He would not change it for anything, of course. But it was good to have the memory of Miss Hopewell's elegant hand on his and of the sunshine. What had he called her? Only to himself, of course, never aloud, but it had been rather poetic in him—*a fragile bloom*.

"Oh, yes," said the reverend. "Perhaps there was something of that, once." His voice sounded unfamiliar to him: deep, rich, and full of feeling. It had a slight tremolo, like an actor speaking. "No," he went on. "She was never strong." He thought, *Oh, Mary...*

"Of course, Mary's death was violent, and so very gruesome," said Miss Brigstocke. "One cannot blame her health for that."

Reverend Comer felt as if she had doused him in water. To be considering something rather pleasurable and melancholy, and then to be so abruptly shocked... There was an uneasy turning in his insides. There was something uncouth in her after all.

"Perhaps you had better tell me," he said. He sounded shrill and cold now, he knew.

"I only know what I have been told," Miss Brigstocke said, "but I will repeat it. Talking is such a thirsty business, don't you find?" She took a macaroon and nibbled it, watching him.

"Yes, indeed," he said, starting. He called for more tea.

Around them, the room was emptying—the morning was yielding to luncheon, and there were many market-day engagements. The rain had begun. It struck the windows in spiteful pellets. He thought, *She will not want to go out in this, with only that gray thing for protection*, and saw then that she lent her tale mystery and interest in order to prolong it. He softened. Christian charity settled into him again. He would not oppose her.

"I understand that Mary was very happy," said Miss Brigstocke. The steam from the teapot drifted about her face. "They had settled in a house in Devon, where her family was from, you know. I have been in the vicinity quite recently, and it is a place of rolling hills and, though quite lonely, quite lovely too. The house is a madman's dream, of course, old stone and large doors and quite impossible to heat. But the situation is pleasing, in a shallow valley behind a hill, and looking out in all directions on the vista.

"Mary occupied herself quite pleasurably by all accounts with the house and with a school she had begun in the village and other things. They had brought a manservant from Italy who seemed to rule them with a rod of iron and ordered their household. A peculiar name... Rattles? Quivers? Shakes?

"Some small discords, I think, with neighbors, which is always the case in the country. A man by the name of Gilmore would refuse to keep his cattle off the land, or would not let theirs on his, or something of that sort. I am not very well acquainted with farming practices. And of course, presently, there was a child, a son, which was given some outlandish name. I do not recall it. This added to their contentment.

"She was in the habit, as the boy grew older, of taking him up onto the moor and staying there for long hours, playing games with him and telling him the names of the plants and so on. Sometimes, her husband accompanied her. On many other occasions, it was the manservant. I will call him Quivers—I cannot continue to refer to him as merely *the manservant*, and I cannot for the life of me recall... Everyone thought it odd of Mary to spend so much time with only a child and Quivers for company. But as you may recall, Mary was ever one to please only Mary. She would not have cared what appearance it presented. And some days, she and the child went out with no escort at all. Her husband showed no inclination to interfere, which is of course quite typical of... But I forget. You did not know him.

"One of these days, she went with the child alone to the moors. And she did not come back for lunch, and then not for tea. At around four in the afternoon, the day, which had been fine and bright, was abruptly covered with the fog that, as you may know, in that part of the country, descends with no warning. It is like being swaddled in wool. It descended on the house, on the valley, crept in at the doorframes, and filled the windows with moving cloud." Here, Miss Brigstocke paused. "This holds some particular horror for me," she said. "I am afraid of the fog. Being in it…is very much how I imagine death—nothing in the world but thick white and the sound of one's own footsteps. But this, I suppose, is by the by.

"As the mist rose about the house and there still was no sign of them, concern was changed to fear. Mr. Villarca was quite beside himself. It is understandable. Dusk approached, and all the household was assembled with lanterns and torches and turned out to find her. They marched in a long line across the moor, calling her name and holding the lights high. But the air was so dense, the late afternoon almost dark as night. The lamps dimmed and winked on either side as they drifted farther and farther apart. It would have been very easy to step on a loose stone and fall, to tread unwary into a bog and sink and never be seen again. Or even to wander too far and be lost on the endless heath until you perished in the cold and the black. The searchers had begun by fearing for her, you see, but now, they began to fear for themselves. They trod carefully and shivered and called to one another that perhaps they should return to the house. All except Mr. Villarca, who ran ahead, heedless, calling his wife's name in the lowering air. Voices travel so strangely in the mist, have you noticed?

"At length, there was heard a great screech from ahead, like stone breaking. Sometimes, when razing buildings, a great metal ball is used. You know the thing I refer to? It hits the brick and the girders and the glass in the windows with a sound that is not like a crash, not at all. It is a shriek, a grinding shriek. That is what this sound was like. The searchers waved their torches and stumbled toward the terrible noise, calling all the while. As they crested the rise of Bell Tor, they saw below, through the ribboning mist, what looked like a broken spider splayed upon the grass. It was Mr. Villarca, holding his wife and his son in his arms. She was insensible, wet through, her cambric dress streaked with mud. The boy was crying and speaking to his father. Whatever was said, it made Mr. Villarca give another of those terrible howls. The servants tried to pry him from Mary, for it was plain her arm was broken. At first, he only wept and held her, but he had to let her go, because the child was clinging to him, still talking very quickly in Spanish. Alonso, that is his name. At least they had the good sense not to name him after his father. Alonso. Poor little boy.

"They put her in a blanket and carried her as best they could. But as they were approaching the house, Mary woke, and the sight of her eyes was enough to freeze the blood. She stared sightless under the flickering lamplight and would only say, 'I have seen her.' Which made little sense, but she had of course received a great shock. Each time she spoke, her husband wept. But they all got inside, and the doctor was fetched, and the arm splinted, the child calmed and bathed, and that should have been the end of it."

"Villarca," said the reverend. "Peculiar. Where have I heard—?"

Miss Brigstocke looked sharply at him but went on. "After that, Mary was confined to her bed for some time. She had taken a chill on the moor. But other ailments, less explicable, plagued her also. Her eyes troubled her a great deal. They became very sensitive. She complained that the world was very dim. A veil was over everything. She could not abide daylight—her eyes streamed, she shrank from the gentlest sunshine— but nor could she bear darkness, for then, she saw things that were not there. The maids were woken in the early hours of the morning by her weeping and lamenting—that there was mist in the room. She could not see, for all the mist. Once, she threw a pitcher at a figure who, she said, stood in the middle of the room, bald and like a worm. She howled for it to take its gaze off her. Its great white face hung over her at night.

"She had a great conviction that a grave had been dug outside her window. She would spend hours looking at the particular spot with her clouded eyes. It was pretty: on a rise, beneath an ancient cedar tree. She said a murdered girl was buried there. It became such a mournful and incessant refrain that her husband had the hill dug up one day. They turned up yards and yards of earth, probed down into the ground, made an absolute mess of it. There was nothing to be found, of course. No unmarked grave, no girl. But still, Mary stared at the ravaged hill. Sometimes, she said, she heard the spade turning the earth, heard the corpse fall into the deep hole.

"She began to shun her husband and her child. There were no more days in the sunshine on the moor. She lay in state with the curtains drawn. Mr. Villarca would have taken her away, to some continental rest cure, but Mary would not go. She blamed him in some measure for what had befallen her, for marrying her at all. 'Why did you give this to me, not telling me the price?' Her voice was always very carrying.

"And as her sight went, so did her reason. She flew into rages, running through the house, white-eyed and blind, breaking china. She wounded herself, hurling herself into walls, and bloodied her head with beating it on doors. She said the child was never to be brought to her, for she might hurt him. Those were the words—*she might hurt him*. Did Mary mean herself, or…? Anyhow, it seemed a wise prohibition, in the circumstances.

"When one day, Leopoldo Villarca was not to be found, it was thought by some that he had reached his limits. Men, you know, have their limits, all. It is something I always bear in mind. He was there one evening at the supper table, and he kissed his son good night… The next morning, he was gone, and so was a horse from the stable. One may draw one's own conclusions. And people did, mind you.

"His absence seemed a relief to Mary. She became more docile, in fact, and submitted to seeing a doctor who was very good with eyes, though he said there was little to be done. The cataracts that had formed on them were well advanced, and permanent. She even admitted her son to her room for half an hour some days. She ate and strengthened somewhat, and her nights were quiet.

"The bog threw up Mr. Villarca's corpse two miles from the house, in open country. It was a shepherd who saw it. Boots, just boots sticking out of the ground. I daresay he thought he'd found a fine pair of hessians for nothing, until he saw what they were attached to. They are strange, bogs. They will take things down and hold them, preserving them in the dark for oh so long. But something shifts, and up it comes, good as new. And so it did. There was no telling how it had happened, but there was one thing... Well.

"They were loath to tell Mary, I think. But she took it well. She shed a tear. Her eyes were like mistletoe berries now, smooth and white. She hoped he was at peace. She told them to take the child out of the house, into the village to his old nurse. He needed to be with other children, she said. And she would be in mourning, which might upset him.

"That night, Quivers woke to the scent of smoke drifting through the high halls. When he broke down Mary's door, it was too late—all was done. She was dead on the floor. Flame flickered about in her hair and had begun to creep up the curtains. They put it out. The room was filled with the haze of smoke; they could scarce see—it was like walking through mist. The poker was in her hand; the tip still glowed red. She had taken her eyes.

"I know that after events such as those I have recounted, it is a common thing for people to say, *Well, I always thought her queer* or *He was a bad lot*—as if one could have seen it coming. So I do not wish to do that. But there was always something strange about them both. They were not people who would live long, grow old, and die... I saw it in their faces, during that brief time in Italy. They were both too feeling, too impassioned. They did not understand that one must... Anyhow.

"I am not one for repeating gossip, but it was said too that Mary was overly fond of Quivers. That he had detected smoke and reached her chamber very quickly on that fateful night...that he was often in the vicinity of her room.

"And of course, Mr. Villarca, when he was found in the bog—I think I did not say—his eyes were gone, as if something had clawed at them until... It might have been anything. Who knows how long he lay in that mire? But yes, it gave people cause to think more, and they thought of Mary. It seemed too much coincidence. *Had she taken his eyes too?*"

Reverend Comer rested his back carefully against the chair. "Horrible," he said. "Horrible!" He felt weak. Such nastiness. It did not belong in this warm room, with the sound of clinking spoons. At length, he said, "You know a great deal about it, Miss Brigstocke."

"Why, yes. I have only recently come from near Rawblood. The house, you know, that they lived in."

The reverend felt an uneasy stirring in his brain. Some headline he had seen in the newspaper, two weeks past...

"I thought it best to gain a thorough picture of what had happened," Miss Brigstocke went on. "I chanced to be in the area, and in Dartmeet village, I fell into conversation quite naturally with the woman who had been the Rawblood cook. And of course, there were many others locally who had been a part of it, who had known the Villarcas. I was fortunate enough to come across some of them. The event was so sensational, you know, and so widely talked about; the press cannot be relied upon. But I think I have established the facts."

The stirring in Reverend Comer's brain had become a thunder—a terrible feeling was upon him. He said, "Villarca. Mrs. Villarca, who was called the Devon Demoness in the *Post*... Do you mean to say, Miss Brigstocke, that it was Miss Hopewell..."

"Yes, Reverend Comer. That is the vulgar name they gave the case."

"I had not connected it," said the reverend. "How could I? How could I know? Her married name…" His forehead was covered in a light, cold sweat. Both cup and lip trembled as he sipped his tea. Hot drops fell on his waistcoat.

Miss Brigstocke regarded him. Her black eyes seemed to him to have grown into two deep and dangerous pools.

"How could you indeed?" asked Miss Brigstocke. "I quite see the difficulties." She paused for a moment and went on. "Yes, I thought perhaps you had not heard the fate of your old friend Mary. So I came to tell you. You would of course wish to know what had become of her."

"Friend?" he asked. "We were barely acquainted…"

"Well, yes, you were! You were there when she first met Don Leopoldo Villarca, that day in Italy," said Miss Brigstocke. "You have visited his home, in fact! You spent a great deal of time with her and perhaps even made an offer! I would even go so far as to term it an intimate connection."

"Dear God," said the reverend. His eyes darted from place to place, over the mercifully empty tea shop.

"I doubt," said Miss Brigstocke comfortingly, "that any person in this charming village would infer it on their own. Why, you yourself did not. Were it to be pointed out, however, I think you would inevitably become the object of much local interest. She being supposed a murderess…

"It is not always comfortable to have old acquaintances from a different time of one's life constantly about one. Meeting them in the street, passing them in the butcher shop… Sometimes, one prefers to let the dog sleep out his night, to let him lie."

He saw then, quite coolly, how men were driven to kill. He felt her neck in his hands, as though he were wringing it like a hen's. He said, "What is it that you want?"

Miss Brigstocke's tone was light and brisk. "What do any of us want? I wish to be secure; I wish to be content, to be allowed to descend into old age with what dignity I can muster, with four walls around me *of my own* and no threat of the bailiffs. But I cannot see my way to it.

"I wish I could settle somewhere far from here. There is a cottage in Scotland that I have very much admired. But alas, my state does not admit the buying of property. And my cousin, who as I said lives close by, has offered me lodging with her, and so I think I will come to live near Far Deeping after all…"

He obeyed her cue like a man in a dream. "I believe," he said, "that I can see my way to such a charitable enterprise as to…assist you to purchase that cottage. I have by me a draft on my bank…" With the logic of a nightmare, he realized it was true. He saw his hand remove it from his pocket. "For I was on my way to pay the accounts."

"I thought," said Miss Brigstocke, "it being a quarter day, that that might be the case. How fortuitous."

The pen scratched on paper. She did not watch him write but turned her gaze to the window—when he offered her the draft, she took it with a little sniff, as if he had done something improper. Reverend Comer watched as all his capital, everything he had in the bank (bar thirty pounds) disappeared into a fold in the ragged gray mantle. "I think," he said, "that I will not see you again, Miss Brigstocke."

"It is most unlikely," she replied.

He felt an ache deep in his belly, as though he had been pierced there. "How long did you watch me," he asked, "and wait your filthy chance? No. No matter. I will say adieu." He heard her stand, the damp fall of her cloak. But she did not go. She stood beside him. Her scent was heavy in his nostrils.

"He stank of richness and bloody, buried deeds," Miss Brigstocke said. "I thought *he* was to kill her. When I saw her end, I was sure it would be he who did it."

A sound came from her, a growl. Reverend Comer was put in mind of the sound of tearing flesh; he knew her heavy stench then for what it was. It was the lion cage, which he had seen in Padua. Hungry lions, beset with sores, pacing with their mad, yellow eyes.

"They buried her at the roadside," said Miss Brigstocke. "Like a pauper. I went to see. And there must have been some who loved her, because the mound was covered in flowers."

"It is too late to weep," the reverend said. He felt the tinny bite of anger within. "You have everything. Your tears are not needed here— the goose is plucked."

Miss Brigstocke whimpered and cried out. "Would you believe," she asked, "that my heart is broken? I have had to shift, all my life. I have been forced to it. But Mary… Would you believe that I loved her, in spite of all?"

The reverend regarded her. "No," he said. "I do not believe it."

Her entire being drooped. She pulled her terrible coat around her. She swiped at her wet, black eyes. "Good-bye," Miss Brigstocke said, turned her old creased face from him, and went. The door of the tea shop creaked, and the bell rang a silver chime.

When Reverend Comer emerged some minutes later, having settled his considerable tea bill, she was gone. The street was deserted save for a few souls hurrying through the rain, late for luncheon.

THE UNKNOWN SOLDIER

1919

I'm all right so far. All I must do is avoid notice. Keep it simple.

At Reading, there are shouts, a hold up. But they don't concern me. Outside, a gray day, and everyone has loathing carved deep on their countenances. Rain shatters on the glass. The empty compartment smells of old dog.

Two girls come in; I stiffen up a bit. They'll have things to say. They fuss in the seat opposite, turning like cats and settling their things. Their heads bend together, brown ringlets meeting a shining cap of tortured marcel wave. Their hands discuss me, pointing, fluttering. Sure enough, the yellow-haired one asks me what time we get to Paignton. All nice girls love a soldier and all that. Or is it sailor?

I fold my arms, close my eyes. Sleeping people don't answer questions, are not compelling.

There is a shade of red that is urgently debated. Won't do for a skirt, which would be *fast*. Line an opera jacket with it. Smart. The girls speak to each other slightly too loudly, as though there is some effect being strained at that they are just failing to achieve.

Their voices scatter through the darkness behind my eyelids, knit themselves through the rhythm of the wheels on the narrow gauge. Four hours of this. Avoid notice, then home. I don't know what I'll find. I don't know what's left. And the other question, which wears at me. Is he alive? The letter is dated a year ago. I touch it where it sits in my pocket. It's almost coming apart at the folds.

It's unlikely he's alive. As I understand it, almost no one who was alive five years ago is alive now. Could go and see. It's on the way... Something stirs, painful, in the depths. No. Keep it simple. Get to Rawblood.

The uniform's awkward on me. Too big. My wounded shoulder sings. The man's face after I hit him. Pale, innocent. Gentle, closed eyes. Limbs heavy as sandbags as I stripped him. Exhausting, being in my head. Thoughts run off like rabbits. I'm sure I could think once.

In pretending to sleep, one lays oneself wide open to the real thing. Soon, I am suspended on the edge of a crevasse where all things are about to be known and my whole being is formed of meaning...

...when the world shudders and jars like a blow to the head. Some broad unknown thing whistles past, slaps something else. We rattle; we are dice shaken in a cup. There are shrieks and cracks. My heart tittups, a startled colt. Unseen machinery squeals, *ha ha ha*, like nasty laughter. The illusion that we're on solid ground is rudely, terribly, interrupted; the carriage is a wooden box designed to stave in and crush our flesh. The ragged ends of timber and shards of glass will pierce us; burning metal will twist into evil curves and pen us in as we burn.

Abruptly, everything stills, and sound is neatly sliced off. A light scent of burnt oil. In the silence, the carriage glides to a halt.

We have left the rain and come out into the light. The compartment is drenched in sunshine. The air is animated with shining spirals of dust. The chips and scratches on the wood panel are as raw as scars. Each shiny patch on the yellow-and-red moquette upholstery is thrown into relief.

My jacket is on the floor. Delicately, the girls withdraw their legs from it, as if it were dirty. I put it back on the rack. Actually, it is quite dirty. Again, I check that the letter's in my pocket. His writing. So strange to see it, after all these years. *I must let it all go now... Anyhow, this is good-bye.* I had never thought of such a thing as a *good-bye* between us.

The girls shield their eyes and murmur. They're stilled, gentled by the light. Their lips are dry, skin pale and fragile in the glare. Each thought moves through their faces; they're transparent in the sun. Dangerous clarity. I put my hat on.

We have stopped by the sea. Behind the glass, tall grass waves, golden, dead. It almost tickles the dirty panes. Through stiff sedge and nodding mare's tail can be seen a thin rim of beach like a broken biscuit. I swallow, sea grit mingling uneasily with sweet crumbs in the imagination of my tongue; everything is in disorder. The sharp dun crescent gives way to wet olive sand beyond, a blinding sheen, a net of glassy pools. The sun falls upon the bay, is hurled back in serried points of light. The sea is cast across the skyline, beaten steel. A gull bawls, high, distant. The world is dangerous. But it is also beautiful. I had forgotten.

We wait. I practice a normal face. I can tell it's not very good. The girls look at me over their hands. Peeps and chirps of laughter. One wears a dress of dark blue, the color the sea should be, the color it is in pictures but isn't, at least not out there. She's all shades of fawn and cream like an old photograph. The yellow-haired one has the face of a lascivious Roman emperor. Her wide blue eyes sit in her face like two miniatures painted on ivory. The girl in blue is whispering. "And he takes her up to his lodgings and nurses her better, and dresses her up, in these silks, see, in foreign dress. She's quite smart and nice for the first time ever. And she says, *Why are you so nice to me, chinky?* It's the first time anyone's been nice to her."

A curlew walks across the narrow bar of sand, raising each slow leg like an ancient thing. It does not deign to notice the train, silent and stopped. Through the walls come other voices from other compartments, occasionally intelligible. *Is he still!* a woman calls hilariously through a low conversation, and then there's laughter. Everyone seems all right.

"Oh, she's fifteen, I daresay," says the girl in blue.

"You oughtn't go to these smutty things," says the yellow helmet.

"Smutty yourself. So she stays with him, and they get keen on each other all right, but when he goes out one day, her dad comes and finds her in his lodgings and murders her because she's been with a yellow man."

The curlew halts in the middle of the landscape, gazes sternly at the sea.

"The chinky comes back and sees her dead. So he dresses himself up in silky clothes too—"

"Lordy."

"—and murders himself with a knife. It was ever so good."

"Waste of nice Chinese silk."

"You've no soul."

"Have a fag. Calm you down."

"Cheek. Well, I will. Ta."

The girls smoke. The one in blue is just beginning to show: a soft curve to her below the sash of her dress. She touches the curve now and again, not knowing she does it.

She sees me looking. She nudges her friend, and they retreat primly into silence, hands concertinaed together in their laps.

I wish they would go on talking. Such relief not to think. I lean my face against the glass, which is burning with cold. The curlew is gone. The sea dazzles. My shoulder aches.

The train lurches forward with a grunt and a clatter. My nose gets a pretty good bang on the window. The girls make small sounds of appreciation. As we gain speed, the track turns inland, and the sea leaves us, shuffling and then staggering past the dirty glass panes and out of sight. The sudden twilight of the carriage is shot with arcs and bolts of pink and yellow and gray, endless waves breaking. My heavy eyes. *Burn it*, whispers someone in my ear. *Burn it.*

⁓

I am myself, but not myself. I am unbounded, limitless. This is how the dreams go.

I'm at Rawblood, in my old room. I've wished myself here many times. But things are not as they should be. The wood paneling is draped with dark-red velvet. An old shaving set stands at the basin. A comical nightdress of antique design lies across the unmade bed. The folds of the sheets still hold warmth. The scent of someone else's sleep lies heavy in the air. The ghost of a big, musty body.

I go to the window and pull at the catches to bring the fresh breeze in, to take the tainted air away. They won't give. My fingers slip on them like mercury.

On the hill below, a man comes into view. He walks as though he owns the land, the sky. Officious little movements. His hat brim covers his eyes in shadow. A dented but serviceable homburg. His suit is brown, quaint, worn. Shining boots. The cold gleam of a watch chain as it swings from his pocket. Clean-shaven, except for his mustache; face open and serious. Strange eyes. Green.

He should not be here.

He strokes his mustache gently. He kicks at a stone. It bounds from him, exuberant. He dallies with it, passes it from foot to foot, strolling to and fro on the sward. He stands, breathes, smiles as if there's sunlight, turns his face upward, questing, removes his hat.

As he sees me, I stop breathing. We are suspended, arrested, caught each in the other's eye. I hiss, and my lips nearly kiss the glass. He shakes his fist as if in answer, comes down the slope toward me, toward the house.

I go quickly down the stairs. Hands are damp and squeaking on banisters, handles, wood, as I run.

A small, resolute shape speeds high above in the empty hall. The swallow circles, swoops. Wings like daggers telling the shape of air. It carves up the hall, soft rushes of sound.

Through the window in the far blue, white clouds hang still. No one is there. The sunlit rise is empty, a long, green curve. He's gone, which is not possible.

My hands itch for action.

The catch yields stiffly, and the window swings outward, slow and graceful. The swallow dives past, its passage on my cheek like a detonation. Gone into the blue, vanished. I stare at the place in the sky where it was. I breathe. The air is full of warmth.

He's gone. I'll find him in the night. I'll go into him like sickness.

⁂

Burn it, whispers someone in my ear. *Burn it.* I'm awake, shaking. Nausea rises. The first time it happened, I woke screaming. *She's* sending me *her* dreams.

Through the train window, it's a cold dusk. We're in a maze of little tracks and tiny stations. The girls are gone. Instead, there's a little boy with bloody green knees in the corner opposite, bouncing on the seat and singing, and a woman with cherries in her hat. She regards me with disapproval. Beside her, a thin woman in black eats peppermints from a paper bag. The lamps throw out buzzing amber light. The darkened window shows us back ourselves, yellow and monstrous against infinite space. On the seat next to me is a newspaper, left by some stealthy, unseen traveler. Smell of acrid wet print.

The disapproving woman puts her hand on the boy's back and shushes. Her teeth are large and brown, her legs planted wide in stout shoes. She sits encased in swathes of worn gray serge. Two of her buttons are broken. The boy bounces. She closes her heavy-lidded eyes. The hand stays on the boy's back like a passenger.

"I had a little bird," he singsongs. "Its name was Enza. I opened the window, and in flew Enza!"

"Stop that." A large, maroon voice.

"In flew *Enza!*" He widens his eyes at her, full of joy.

I slept awkwardly. My shoulder aches like memory. I pick up the paper with my good arm and read about tobacco... *Women and girls, having put on men's clothes, are adopting men's habits in the matter of smoking.* Quite.

The boy takes four marbles from his pocket and shakes them, lips pursed. The gunfire of the marbles goes *click click click*.

"If you put 'em away," says the woman, opening her eyes, "you shall have an apple."

"Psssshhhhsss," he says. "We are exploded." He rattles the marbles at me. "You're dead."

"You'll have to eat the core and the pips, mind," says the woman. "Can't be wandering all over finding you bins."

He gnaws the apple like a squirrel, clenching it to his face with dirty hands, peering over it with profound concern.

We're in a maze of little tracks and tiny stations now, and tired people shuffle on and off.

A sudden give in my shoulder, a feeling of dangerous looseness. A slick brown patch has appeared on the sleeve of my shirt. Blood.

In the lavatory, there are varnished pine boards on the wall (*Betty Tasker is a hore*), some pink soap, an overhead lamp hanging a little too low, casting a surgical light over the whole affair. What there isn't is anything to tie this up with. The loose feeling becomes a pulse, and it's no good; I'm covered in blood. It stinks.

I take the shirt off. In the dirty cracked mirror that hangs over the basin, someone regards me. Shorn head, pale skin.

Looking at one's own shoulder is nigh on impossible. A broad smudge of tacky gore. Blood runs down the arm in little rivulets, pooling in the creased places around the elbow. New wet threads busily cover the drying rusty patches. I am mapped with blood.

The light stutters. There's a *tick tick*, the one bulbs make before they blow. Oh, please. Not now. I am flickering; the mirror shows my blood, arm, gooseflesh, gaunt face, slippery skin, delivers them weird and partial in spasms as if I am electrified. The light is gone. Black.

The dark is hot. This should be respite—I have been bone-cold all day—but no. It's hot like breath. I stand. Often, I have found, being motionless will bring one out of crisis. The blood tickles on, down my arm. It feels like a finger. In fact, it feels so much, so very much like a finger… I recoil, hit the wall, swallowed in pain. All the while, fingertips that should not be there stroke up and down, and cold breath, very light, on my face. Blood, but there's another scent that I know, by God, I know all too well. I open my mouth to call out and—here's the thing—a finger reaches into my mouth and strokes it, lightly. It's a pretty ordinary finger. The snag of a hangnail. There's a callus on the inside of the knuckle like a writing callus. At certain points, the smoothness of metal brushes me: a ring. The finger strokes the insides of my cheeks and my tongue and the backs of my teeth. Someone breathes, breathes gently in my ear, and more fingers stroke themselves slowly across my soft palate, brushing the back of my tongue, moving toward the uvula and into my throat, and when I can't breathe anymore, I go down.

Light, muttering to itself and flickering. I'm splayed across the whole tiny room. One of my feet, sort of debonair, in the sink. A pool of blood on the gritty floor. The wound's properly burst. Like a little mouth.

By very slow degrees, I stand. The light steadies. In the mirror, I am wet, bloody, really unappealing. Don't want to think about how long I lay there, with the wound pressed against that floor. Can almost feel contamination climbing gaily into the cut like a day out. It hurts, really. That's the main thing. Could think straight if it didn't hurt so. I rinse what I can. Doesn't look good.

The train beats on like a drum. Cherries and peppermints look up for an instant when I reenter and then away. What's it like, to be them? They must have friends and families and lives and eat supper and so on. My family is dead. I had a friend, but he let me go. Perhaps he's dead too now.

I peel apart the pages of the newspaper, soft under my fingers like damp, inscribed skin. Only an hour or so to go. Breathe.

At Tiverton, the door opens. A shiver goes through the compartment; we're ruffled like a cage of soft brown hens. I keep my head down. Boots enter; I can smell him. Pipe tobacco and hair oil. His uniform: metal polish, sailcloth, and soap. Now I'm in trouble (I think I'm a corporal, but I'm just not sure).

"Cigarette."

He offers the box only to me; I have to take one. I nod. He nods. It won't be the end of it. This is something I've already learned: the relentless "we" of war will not allow us to part as strangers.

We smoke. I can smell my blood.

The woman with the peppermints says something to him about the weather. I feel him shift in the seat beside me. When he speaks, it is so exciting that I am betrayed for an instant into looking. A flash of collar and jaw and windburned neck.

"Somehow, a whole year's homesickness seems to catch up with me at once," he says. "Makes me feel like jumping in a lake."

The cherries and the peppermint laugh. They feel for him. I think.

"I've never met an American before," says one.

There comes the shift of him on the seat. "Better than sunny France though," he says to me, friendly. "Isn't it? *Sunny France* indeed!"

Bleeding in a stolen uniform was terrible. Bleeding and sweating profusely in a stolen uniform is much worse. Stings to buggery. Can he smell it? I give what I hope is a knowing smile, no teeth. His neck, in my peripheral vision, is prickly.

"France is just a whole lot sunnier than Germany, you see. That's all it is, I reckon."

I nod, training my eyes on the paper. If I don't chuck now, it could be all right. This is important to remember. The smell… Perhaps it's a comparative matter. Perhaps there's been so much blood for him that my little shoulder nick doesn't even touch the sides, as it were.

He says, "It isn't the things that happen that scare you. It's the things that might."

There's a curious thrum in the seat. He's shaking. I take the half-smoked cigarette from my mouth and give it to him, keeping my head down.

He can smell the blood all right. He might not know it, but he can. Time rolls back in that peculiar way it has of late, and for a moment, it's another boy who's warm at my side.

I know then. I will go to see if he's alive. I hope I remember the way. I hope he hasn't forgotten me.

Must keep it simple.

The woman in black produces another paper bag. Lemon drops. She offers the bag to him. Small white shapes. He says *no* with a palm. It's all up for me; an astringent scent of lemon comes off them, joins the cigarettes. It's not going to be all right. I'm finished. Heat stings my throat. The tide rises.

"Hey," the soldier says. "You're bleeding." He leans in and looks at me with level eyes, and I see myself in them: thin, dripping, hunted. The train is slowing, easing into stillness. A dented tin sign. It's a stop too early, but I'm off. Doors, knees, shuffles, apologies. I go, fast.

Solid ground. Voices like horns call for urgent things; whistles hurtle thinly through the night. I'd thought it was cold on the train, but I was a fool. This is cold that freezes your lungs. I move crabwise across the platform toward the footbridge. The dark has a humming, violent texture through which shapes move too suddenly.

Two guards unpack a crate; long, slim oblongs of wood. Stack the coffins on the platform, gently. They puff white breath into the air. The conductor collects the coffin tickets, face solemn. Corpses, pauper fare. Two shillings and sixpence.

"All right, mate?" says a guard to the conductor. He's bulging out of his uniform. He has large, field-mouse eyes and a thick column of a neck. He is solid enough to spare concern. "It's all a bit much now and then, isn't it?"

The conductor nods, weary.

"I was at Ypres," the guard says. "The second one. Lost two toes. Two toes! Bloody hell. Lucky. Still, shook for months. Still. Lucky." The conductor nods and makes to go. "Two toes," the guard says again and sticks his hands in his pockets. He whistles into the night. He wants something from the exchange that can't be given. Some hope, some assurance of the meaning of things. His eyes are suddenly on me. He calls, "All right, bombardier?" Bombardier, then, not a corporal.

The white lattice of the footbridge, the very height of it, its temerity in simply existing. A tricky moment on the way down, where gravity nearly takes me with it. Then there's a nice dark corner by a shed where I'm safe with some weeds and a bit of gravel. Alone. The relief. I make myself as small as possible and vomit, empty myself onto the ground.

Eventually, the whole thing's finished. Doubled over, I breathe. I feel light enough to float away.

I scratch gravel over the mess I've made. The uniform. I'd rather get rid of it, but I need it. There are miles between me and Rawblood. I am keen to end it. And *she* goads me on. Bile rises; confusion rises. Keep it simple. Remember what to do. I touch his letter in my pocket like a talisman. *Burn it*, Papa whispers like a secret.

I know it's not Papa, not really. The words are meaningless. My broken head. Like a record, stuck. I know all this. But here, alone in the cold, I'm glad of his voice.

I go quickly across the dark land.

☙

The mist is heavy. A woman is calling, somewhere. "Please," she says, and then, "I am sorry." I go through the white blank, toward her voice. When I come upon her, it is sudden, but expected. I am meant to find her here. She lies turned and twisted on the broken ground. The cambric of her dress is a wet sheen. Mud is thick along the hem; it reaches slick fingers up her skirt. Ribbons of cold cloud move through the uncertain light, touch her cheek, wet with tears, which mix with the blood on her face. Her hair lies down her back, gold.

I see the child beside her then. He's small and dark and serious. He pulls with small hands, trying to raise her. He looks at me with brown, deep eyes.

Think you've broken something, I try to say, and she turns and sees me. She cries out. It's a shuddering, ragged sound, so full of fear. *Don't move*, I say, but she's already crawling, pulling herself along the ground away from me. One of her arms scrabbles on the turf. The other drags behind, wasted and limp. She turns, her small face distorted. As I make toward her, she opens her mouth and moans. Cracked, high. It pulls at my guts. The child begins to cry. She pulls him to her with her good arm. *Alonso, come.* She shields him, her lip curling in contempt. *My papa was afraid of mist too*, I say as I approach. *And his name was…* Their mouths widen into round O's, and mother and child begin to scream. And just like that, they're gone. Hidden in the shifting white.

I cast about, calling for her. Here and there, the mist is pierced by late afternoon light. Sometimes, ahead, I hear her breath, heavy in the wet air.

Stop, I call. *Y—*

I'm awake, cold and sudden. The sting of winter air on my cheek.

The wind is high in the vast sky. Around me, the moor is white, scalded under the moon. No mist, no afternoon, no wet cambric. A scent of rot and phlegm. When I look down, I see I'm at the very, very edge. Not in it, but nearly. Gummy, dark bog squeezes up around the tips of my boots. The sound of a cleaver, rapidly striking the block. It's the sound of my heart.

I stand very still. The bog sighs gently underfoot. I wait as the chopping grows slowly fainter. And then I shuffle back, inch by inch. The soles of my boots shiver and slip on patches of sphagnum, glossy and cold. Beneath the moss, there is a frozen crust of peat. Beneath that is the slow liquid, sucking dark.

When the grit of the path is well underfoot, I stop. Slip a hand beneath my jacket, beneath the mess of bloody wool. I feel my way across the shoulder to the bitter, pulsing edges of the wound. I shove my thumb hard in. The air sings sharp. I do it again, harder, and now it all goes black and thick and sweet. I don't know how long for. Red stars collide. *I've gone too far*, I think, vaguely, through the din.

The pain washes away in small tides. It leaves behind a broken hole. The hole runs through my core and up to the insides of my eyelids. I won't sleep again. The moon blazes on the path ahead.

The dreams are coming thick and fast. *She's* impatient for me now. There are no words to express it—the terrible freedom, the malice and rage. To look through *her* eyes is to know the dark center of the world. I dread it, and it is thrilling.

Hard brushy land gives way to straw scent and dung. When the first outbuildings are in sight, I move among them for cover, making my way sideways, crossways. The heat of beasts in the sheds, their quiet exhales like tiny waterfalls in the fields beyond. Beneath my feet, the seamless frost becomes corrugated. Hard ridges. Cart tracks, wheel tracks, a bicycle, an automobile, fossilized into the surface of the earth. Close now.

My toe catches in the hard edge of a hoofprint, and I fall. My face meets the iron-hard earth. Slender licks of hot blood course freely from my nose to my chin. They trickle down inside my collar. Damn, and all that. I blow a hard breath out, heave myself up, and move on. When I look back across the white land, black blood spatter and footsteps trace my progress in the moonlight. So much for stealth.

A building, low and irregular. An unrisen loaf, flush against the land. Little black trees are twisted around it. The mirrored gaze of windows, the unlit dark interior. Well, why would it be lit at this hour? The walls move gently, undulating.

My shoulder is missing. It has simply floated off. I search the ground for stones and gather them, freezing, into my hand. I throw them in clattering handfuls at the window, then at other windows above me. Dark, shining glass. No one comes.

I swarm up the ivy on the old stone walls. *I used to climb like this*, I think, *over the roof...* Pieces of fractured memory overlay each other uneasily. Not sure of a sudden where or rather when I am. Just climb.

By the window, I tap lightly on the pane. I knock. I whisper his name. After that, I knock once more. My next knock breaks the glass. I call quietly through the hole. This is not sufficient, because he does not come. No one does. "Come out!" I am hissing, spitting like a kettle, shouting through the broken glass. The dark places within are silent.

Of a sudden, I see that everyone is dead. How could I forget this? It becomes apparent how ridiculous was my thought: that this rule might not apply for some. That a person might not be dead simply because I hope that they are not dead.

Everyone is dead. There is no longer a name to shout. He is a haze, a miasma of blood over Passchendaele. Verdun. Arras. Cambrai. La Marne. Gone. The house is dark, like other houses.

Pieces of the day collide in my mind like driftwood. The man's face after I struck him, pale and innocent, his closed eyes. Shards of glass. Girls and trains and vomit in the back of my throat. The vast sky and the bog beneath my feet. All shot through with moonlight and blood, always blood. Terrible place, my head.

My hands cannot find their grip. Cold branches slip through my fingers. I fall. Wide, cold air rushes past. He's dead. I hit the ground.

∽

She sits in the chair before the fire in my room. She looks peaceful now, in silhouette against the flames. Her golden hair lies in a thick twist at the nape of her neck. She looks into the fire, one finger stroking the brocade of the chair. Can't see her face. The light plays about the edge of her jaw. What is she thinking of? She's in my room, but I don't mind it. Where's the child? Longing fills me like a cup; I can't explain it. Where is he?

Oh, I scared you, I say. She turns, and her eyes are white mistletoe berries. She takes the poker from the embers. "Do not you go near him," she says. The tip is a hot orange shard. I approach her with light cat feet.

∽

Clatters, flurry, voices. I come to. A beam moves across the yard like a searchlight. An engine coughs. I force my aching limbs up. I flatten myself against the wall of the farmhouse.

Light pours across the yard from the barn. Figures move across it, intent. Someone calls to someone else. Three men, some large vehicle.

He stands in the barn door, a straight silhouette against the light. A familiar voice, raised, taut like cord. "No," he says. "Can't be right," and then something else.

The barn. Didn't think to look there.

"Have a look-see, then," says one of the men. Slow voice. Warm tones, kindness. They unload something long and heavy, carry it into the barn with *oofs* and *thunks*.

I edge closer. The dark night quivers. The scent of lemons is everywhere. If they find me, I'll bite them till the blood runs down like a pierced peach.

Three, four voices slide over one another. His familiar one raised high in argument.

Agreement is struck. A rift of sound. Wood rings against wood; an engine grinds into life. Slams, and someone calls, "All right. Ho!" They roll away into the distance.

I don't move for a long time. I watch the barn where it looms high in the purple air.

A long bar of yellow falls into the night like a path. I follow it. The cobbles are sleek underfoot. The scent of early morning fills the dark.

The barn door stands a little ajar. A lamp hangs on a beam, throws a rough, yellow circle. The scent of straw. He sits by the long pine box. It's stained with travel, rimed and wet. The coffin lid's askew, hastily pushed aside. He looks into the depths. His face is strange and shining.

He's different. The hands are brown, quick. That's right. But scars run across his cheek, cross his eye like the tributaries of a river. New, white seams. His hair's the same dark mess it was when we were children. My palm remembers it. His eyes blue, white, but there are dents under them, purple shadows that I don't remember.

Tom Gilmore. Different, but not dead after all. I watch them: Tom, the coffin, caught as they are in the warm, rustling light.

I could go in. I could sit beside him. I could place my hands on his. I could slide my hand into the open neck of his shirt, feel his warm thudding heart under my palm, turn his face to mine, and ask him, *Who's in the coffin? Who're you crying over?* Whatever his answer, I would put an arm around his shoulders, feel the warmth of him along my side. *We'll go*, I'd say. *Let's leave it. Go and live by the sea, where there aren't people, only gulls and the sun.*

A warm hairy head brushes my palm. I leap in shock. A tail waves in the dark like a sword. The dog smiles at me, white teeth framing the pink tongue. Hot breath, the rough drag as it licks my hand. The dog makes a friendly, high-pitched greeting.

Tom is looking at me. Our eyes meet through the dark. He recoils and then shouts. He scrambles up in the hay. Hostile, blank gaze. He doesn't know me.

I stumble across the frozen farmyard, bloody, shaking. I run for the dark, southwest hills, for home. I was wrong to come. I don't know what I thought would happen. He meant what he said in the letter. It was good-bye after all. He has let go.

Behind, I think I hear his voice. *Iris.* But I don't stop, don't turn. I run.

∽

In the dawn, I crest the final hill, see it to the southwest. I am climbing the steep incline, mindless, reckless, almost parallel to the ground. I am filled with singing, a joyful rage. *I'm coming*, I tell her. *You've taunted me enough. Come and get me.* My blood is high. One hand anchors me, clutching at icy tussocks. I haul myself up, arm over arm. My breath is good and hot in my throat. And the little stubborn thought surfaces: that perhaps, just perhaps, *she* won't get me… Earlswood did not kill me,

Goodman did not kill me... Maybe I'll get *her*. Doesn't matter, really. Either way, it will end.

I pitch forward, aching fingers desperate, as if gravity has been recalibrated. Actually, I have reached the top.

The valley laid out like a pewter plate. The branches of the cedar of Lebanon below, stretched wide. Shards of grass retreat brilliant into the distance like reverberations.

Rawblood reaches fantastic shapes against the sky. Chimneys are raised like signals in the coming light. A roof wide and white-lit under the dawn. The windows of the hall ascend, disorderly, in gleaming leaded panes. The great studded door is half in curving shadow. Something moves between me and the house, a tensing of ligaments and memory, a scent, desire. It is futile, redundant to describe a homecoming.

MEG VILLARCA

1899
Rawblood

I come into the kitchen, and he's there, cleaning the knives. Pink ointment and the long cloth flickering to and fro, the gray light touching his face, making it solemn and beautiful. The red velvet box with its serried ranks; gleaming metal, ivory handles the color of butter. The shape of his legs in the rough, stained apron, the grime caught under the nail of his forefinger, a swag of chestnut hair fallen across one lowered lid.

"Robert," I say, and he turns. The knife flashes bright and flies to earth like a diving fish. The ring of it on the stone floor.

"Ma'am," he says, cool, swooping low. "How may I be of service to you?" He pincers the knife between two disdainful fingers. He is but a few years younger than me.

"I would like some treacle," I say.

He nods and goes to the larder. I eat it with a spoon from the tin, standing at the scrubbed table. He turns his back once more, and the cloth flicks, the knives *chink* gently against one another. We say nothing for a time. I watch his hair where it lies on his bent neck, where it curls over his collar. The treacle turns, warm and slow, on the spoon. It smooths itself sweetly across my tongue.

"Once, when I was young," I say, "I ate a piece of shoe leather. I chewed at it for hours, until it stained my mouth brown. It was not a good thing to do. I had pains and saw stars for days after. It was the dye, or something used in the curing—I was quite ill. I did not regret it but only wished for more. Also, I would sometimes lick the wool of the sheep—for the grease, you see. I would do anything, I was so hungry. There was never enough to eat."

His back is upright, but I feel him soften, feel the warmth come into him. I ache. The air is full of the waxy scent of knife polish.

"It is all I can remember," I say. "Hunger, pain. I felt nothing else until I came here. Where are they, Robert? The others?"

He half turns to me, and I see him bite his lip for a moment, just a moment. "Picking," he says. "I daresay."

"Gooseberries," I say. "In late summer, they would be picking gooseberries, I expect."

He shrugs a little. "Not that you would know it for summer." He pauses and says, "Rain'll be coming. They will be in presently." *Chink* goes a knife, slotting into its velvet prison.

"Not just yet," I say.

I go to him then and touch the nape of his neck with the tip of my finger. For a moment, he bends like a willow, as if I might push him over with only this touch. Then he turns and looks and—well, there we are.

His mouth is sweet and clings to me like the treacle. Time goes sideways in a curve. It is like sunlight, like clutching fistfuls of mud,

like a ball of string dropped from a high cliff, bouncing, unrolling. His
fingers stroke across the swell of my belly. I lock my fingers about his
neck. I take a sprig of his copper hair between my fingers and pluck.
He grunts with the pain. I slip the bright pinch of hair into the pocket
of my dress.

When it is over, he kisses me and kisses the taut barrel I carry
beforehand. "You are like a plum," he says. "We belong together." He
warms her with his palm; his hand lingers. "I wish it was mine," he says.
"I wish you were both mine. Not his." He casts an amber eye toward the
kitchen ceiling.

I say, "Oh, me too, my darling." Robert likes to be romantic after.

"Tonight," he says. "You'll come." His collar is torn loose; his neck is
cream. I nod. Outside, the rain begins to pelt the ground.

I wash in the gray light of the scullery. The cold gushes of the pump,
icy water. My mind is clean. My shrill heart is silent as it is silent only in
the wake, in the lee of the act.

My skirts have that moment brushed the floor when Chloe bustles
in loudly. She holds her apron carefully before her. The folds of starchy
linen are filled with green globes, pale and luminous. They nestle and
bounce with her step. I give her a nod, and she stares around the quiet
kitchen, at Robert and at me. I hold her large blue eyes. I hold her there
like a snake until she shudders all through her frame. She drops her gaze
and bobs; the gooseberries quiver in the apron. She says, "Ma'am."

"Mind yourself, Chloe," I say. I sweep past her, nearly colliding with
Shakes, who does not lift his blinded eyes. His movements are as soft
and careful as a cat's paws. His stick taps. From within the kitchen comes
the sawing of the bread knife. His gums mumble.

I say nothing. I give him a wide berth; my face twists into a silent
snarl as I pass, lips pulled back from my teeth. He half turns his head, as
if to catch an elusive perfume. He does not need his cankered eyes; he
knows things about me.

In the passage, I lean against the wall, cool and clayey under my hands, against my back. I tip my face skyward. I am miserable.

The cold breath when it comes is a bare touch on my throat. A freezing graze, then gone. In the corner of my eye is something white and monstrous, sliding, sliding. I whirl around. My wet skirts slap the wall.

All is quiet. I am alone save for my breath. But my flesh remembers where *she* has been. It burns with the familiar cold kiss.

"Come," I wheedle. "You know *I* am not afraid." But *she's* gone, or I imagined it.

In the quiet bedroom, I take from my pocket the hair I plucked from Robert's head. Bold red it is, very like my own. I chose well. I unlock the drawer with the little key about my neck. I put the necessary things in the necessary order on the marble dressing table. I touch them each with the word of power.

The red strands are bright in the black dish, which is really a black stone with a hollow place in it. I add blood from my thumb and earth from the graveyard. I add a raven's feather and a scrap of cloth that is stained with older blood. Mine. The saddest blood. Birth-blood, with no child. That last one, I bled a great deal.

It all goes up with a quick sizzle, leaving a touch of gummy ash in the saucer.

I say the words I need to say and then lick the stone dish clean. The blood and ash are cold in my mouth. I am tired and full of doubt.

I go to find my bear.

I open the study door very quietly. My sad bear, my looming beast. He sits at the desk like a monument, his face bent to the page. A silver paper knife catches the light, gleams like a stiletto. His leather pouch lies on the desk, close to hand as always. The pen is a lovely sound, mice scratching in the skirting boards. It's a fierce feeling, to watch him so—to catch the moment when he starts and turns, when his eyes fill with the sight of me, two pitchers filling with wine. I go to him, and he touches us. The sleeper within rouses herself and touches him back through the wall of flesh. She has been much petted today. I feel her darting pleasure.

"Each time," Alonso says. "Each time, it is miraculous. That is why there is nothing new to say about such things." His hand warm on me. The scent of worn leather. I do not want to think about *each time*.

"Always reading," I say. I am light, and I keep the sabre sheathed, for now. "What?" But of course, I see it—the diary on the desk. That man. My brother—in name. Never gone, always lingering, a fly stuck in the corner of the eye. We touched one another in death. It is not enough to set against all the years he left me alone. Venom fills the back of my throat. Alonso sees my look.

"It is the only reason I knew to come for you," he says. "To that farm. Because he wrote it. He asks it of me. So do not despise it too much."

"Oh, I know!" I say. "You are very constant in your duty. And even to make me your wife! Painful devotion indeed." I mean to hurt. How have we come to this? Spite is in me like a blade. We were happy once.

When first I came to Rawblood, I was a child of fifteen. Alonso came to the Bantrys' like a great hawk, lifted me from my old life into the new: it was a savage and sudden immersion. Rawblood was a dream; I had never before seen anything larger than the hovels of Grimstock. Its very existence was miraculous. All these high ceilings, room after room, running on and on from one another, seemingly in perpetuity. Profusions of passages and little doors. I was a slip of a thing, too slender, often lost. I slipped through the cracks in things. Now, the house fits around me like a glove. I sit flush against this stone, this mortar. Rawblood, my house, my blood. My life began here. What came before cannot be called living.

My brother died here. But what I felt when I first looked down on the house from the crest of the hill, saw it gray and golden in the low light, was envy that he saw it before I.

I drew the servants back. I could not bear to think of Alonso all alone while I was sent away to school. And to a hungry hedge snipe from Grimstock it seemed a fine thing to have servants. A little chalk, a feather, a toad buried in the garden. Easy enough. People will forget bad things if you ask in the right way. They long to forget.

School—a horror I had not dreamt of. I ran away from them all. Alonso pretended to mind, but he did not. He missed me. I was always asking him to marry me. It was many years before he would listen. It was on the night of the irises that he said yes.

We were happy for a time. Then there came the other times: pain like knives, loss, and the white walls of a sickroom. All those sad, small things. Lost before they drew breath. Grief is a strange beast. It lives in one like a worm, curls and uncurls at will. I take it everywhere I go. At the heart of it are my memories of those three small forms wrapped in linen. Each time, I thought they were strong; each time, they would not stay long enough within me. Small, pale faces like wax, too perfect to live. Unnamed graves, all. Somewhere. We were happy once, but now all I see in Alonso's face are my dead children.

Three times over, Alonso held me through the days and nights after, plaited my hair when I could not, fed me broth spoonful by painful spoonful. I fought him and bit him, and sometimes, I wept. I will never tell him how much I needed the great trees of his arms around me then and his rough face against mine. I will never let him see that everything between us now is colored by those times—a drop of black ink spiraling in clear water. If he knew this, I would be a beached fish, belly up on the alien shore.

Now, I rest my hand on the great cartwheel of his shoulder, a peace offering. He plays with my little finger, the lamps of his eyes lidded.

He says, "Your skirts are wet, my love."

"I have been walking on the grass," I say, "in the rain." It is something I would do. I keep two secrets from my husband. Robert, and then of course there's the other, which is *her*.

I never know what Alonso knows or does not know.

"Do you remember," I say quickly and touch him with my lips, "that night? I had run away, once again, from that school …"

"Yes," he says, dry. "I tried to do right. You would have none of it."

"I came to your club in St. Martin's Lane. I walked from Kent into London."

"I saw you from the window. It was very foggy," he says, and an old feeling passes across his features, wind in an oak tree. Alonso is afraid of mist and fog. "The porter would not let you in. I could have killed him. To leave you so."

"But I waited."

"You did. Barefoot under the gaslight."

"I brought you flowers. 'The irises are blooming in Kent,' I said." We are dancing, now, to a familiar refrain. In this story, we are lit by theatrical lights. The dark is held at bay.

"They were no more than wet stalks," he says, prompting.

"The blossoms wilted off," I say. "I walked all night and part of a day."

"I had never laid eyes on anything as lovely as those bare stems," Alonso says. "I thought I might die then. It was beyond anything I had known, the sight of you." His long, beautiful hand is light on my face like a moth. I breathe his palm.

"If I were allowed a choice of how I am to die," I say, sliding onto his knee, "I would wish for you to do it."

"Would you now?"

"I would. Think: what perfect union."

He says, "I would do it quickly. It would be like this." The pen barks and splinters in his hands. The sound travels through me like shock.

"But looking at me," I say. "Always into my eyes. It would be so mournful and classical, just like a Waterhouse painting."

There comes the rough cough of his laugh. "My Meg," he says. "You could not look like anything so vulgar."

"How could you?" I say. "Waterhouse is risqué. It will be vulgar *next* year." I smile and slip my arms about his neck, and now we are contained within one another again.

This is the choreography of our love. It is and is not the truth. But I never know what Alonso knows or does not know.

He breathes my neck. "Lilies," he says. "Everywhere you go, the scent of lilies lingers after like a ghost."

What would he do, could he see my thoughts and my plan? Would he fix me with his stare and say something that would cleave to me all my days—before showing me the door? Would he seize the letter opener on the table and slide it clinically, kindly, past my sternum, into my heart? Would he shrug and turn again to his book? The last would be the worst.

࿊

It is past midnight when I leave Alonso sleeping, a peaceful dune in the dark bed. There's a wind up. Outside, things shudder and whisper. In here, it is still. The only sound is my bare feet on the great stairs, the stone flags. As I go, I think, *I'll see her now.* I look for her shocking white face in the shadows and behind doors. I stop for a moment as I cross the echoing hall. I stand, waiting for her kiss. But the house is quiet. The air is just night air. I am alone.

The red parlor is warm, the coals low and bright in the grate. Robert is crouched by it, feeding pinches of dry moss, twigs, and kindling into the heart of the fire. He looks up and smiles, then returns intent to his task.

I sit on the ottoman and watch. The fire lends him a glowing halo. Gradually, the greenish, brackish flame licks up; there comes spitting and the scent of apple logs.

His arm steals around my shoulders. The fire sings and cracks.

He says, "I meant it, Meg. You'll wither away here." He hasn't called me ma'am, which is a blessing.

I say, "I won't." Rawblood doesn't wither me. But Robert is earnest, pleading, alabaster in the firelight. "Think of this one," I say. I rest my hand on the taut mound of my belly. "Only think, what would we do?"

"I would take care of you," he says. His gaze falters. "I would. Not like this, of course. Is it all these nice things that keep you here, maybe?" He waves an angry arm at the room, where somewhere in the dark lurk marble velvet, Aubusson carpets, gilt clocks. "Is it that you do not want to be a butler's wife?"

I cannot help but laugh. It has not been so very long since I ate shoe leather. "A butler's mistress, perhaps," I say. "I am married; it's done these sixteen years. And talk by night is very bold. The day brings other cares."

"I will say this only, then," he says. "If you think the rest of your life is to be spent here, then go up to your bed. I will not speak of it again. I will go elsewhere for work. I am a valuable man." He stares at me, then shakes his head and makes a small sound like a click, looking sad.

"Come," I say. I kneel and pull his stockings from his feet. I stroke his fine-boned instep, his heel. I warm him with my palm. I nibble a toe, playful. When he's not looking, I slip the thin crescent of toenail from my mouth to my pocket.

"You should not be with him," Robert says. "He tried to kill me when I was a child."

I regard him. I am wary.

"He refused to treat me," he says, "when I was poisoned. My brother Henry came and begged him. He turned us away. It was luck and *your* brother that saved me."

"We will not speak of Alonso so," I say.

"You know that they were unnatural," Robert says. "The two of them."

I turn my witch-eye on him. *You are not fit to lick his boots.* He drops his gaze, stares at his lap like a frightened child.

"Forgive me," I say quickly. "I am so frightened…" I talk on in a useless, pretty way. I cannot lose him now. He recovers soon enough.

He thinks he holds the advantage. He is very handsome. I have been careful to seem mad for him.

When Robert leaves, I burn the toenail with my blood and a sprig of rosemary that scents the air. I eat the ash. I sit in the lengthening shadows.

I no sooner laid eyes on Alonso and on Rawblood than I loved them; both cavernous animals, grumbling, all their sounds and peculiarities, their good, thick skins of stone. They were wreckage when I found them, and I was wreckage too. I made us all three whole and good.

We lost one another somewhere along the way. But I can do it again. I will heal us: Alonso, Rawblood, and myself.

It is some time before I notice the sound beyond the red parlor door. Soft, heavy, with a scratching in it. The image leaps easily to mind. Some weight, heavy skirts, perhaps, are being dragged through the great hall, catching on the rough flags. A murmur comes, like stone grating on stone but very far away. A moment of quiet, and then the approach. A creak, almost inaudible. *She* stops outside the parlor. I watch the door. On the other side, something brushes the panels lightly; there is a clicking, as of fingernails tapping the brass doorknob. The murmur comes again, suddenly loud and elongated, whistling into the room where I sit. She has her mouth at the keyhole. *Come*, I tell her silently. Her breath fills the room, light and cold. The sound of stone rubbing on stone. I feel her waiting, white and dead, on the other side of the oak. *Come.*

The blow to the door is like thunder. The hinges rattle, and the wood screeches with the force of it. Her voice fills my ear, vast and anguished, words spoken in the language of broken buildings, shattered bone, sorrow, and loss. All her grief rolls through the air like mist, rolls over me, into my flesh. I am wild with it and shaking.

Thick silence follows.

"Come, please," I say. The tears course, salt, down my cheeks. "You need not bear it alone." But she is gone. The red parlor settles back into shape, the fire dead and black in the grate. The wind taps the windows and roars in the chimney. I am bereft, shivering. I will never be warm again. My sleeper kicks. Her tiny fists and feet hammer me from within.

"Hush," I say to her. I stroke her lightly. "Hush, Iris. I will never leave Rawblood. Grow, rest. All will be well." Somehow, it will.

Somewhere in the dark beyond, *she* is walking.

She likes fire, though she cannot get warm. Fire draws the solitary traveler. I saw her first in the dead winter. I had heard the tales. The truth was beyond all imagining.

I was alone before the great hearth, large enough to drive a carriage through. The flames leaped high. The hall towered above me. Alonso was abed.

I knew that it had come about again. It was the fourth time. I did not know if I could bear it—the hope, the crisis, and then months lived in the great black pit. I knew it was a girl. They are all girls. I read terrible things in the red fire. I was alone, alone.

When I raised my eyes, the ghosts of the flames danced in them. Behind them was a white, dead face, inches from my own. The sensation that ran through me was so far beyond anything I had known—it does not fit to call it fear. It was falling through air, braced for the smash on the rocks. It was a wind stirring the deep roots of the soul, which must never, ever be touched. Her black corpse eyes held me, holes in the world. Her flesh was old, white cheese. The scars on her head stood out, gray valley rims in the flickering light. I have never beheld anything so terrible. *I saw you in the water*, I tried to say. *All those years ago...*

The black eyes widened, and in them, I saw eons. The maw began to open, the raw, white lips parted like a rent in a piece of paper. Between them was the black ache of nothing, nothing, long years of nothing. There was the sound of stone grinding on stone. The sorrow was so thick it had a taste; it filled my mouth like bitter wool. She yawned wider and reached toward me; a hand unfurled like wizened driftwood and reached toward my heart, toward my belly, that gentle rise at the center of myself. I cried out then; I was to be carried into it, carried into her, the expanse of empty grief. The claw came on, the fingers brittle sticks; it hovered a hand's breadth away and stopped. The white fingers fluttered, odd and delicate. Then withdrew. She sat, impassive, her dead eyes dark and unreadable.

I felt something stir within me. I placed my hand upon the mound. There was no mistake. The gentle push came again—a long and sleepy motion, content. A small hand reached, as if to touch the white husk before me. My sleeper moved for the first time.

We stared at one another, the living and the dead. I will remember it all my days. What is that phrase? *Like calls to like.* I have seen the marks of cruelty on her. I know not what she is or where she came from. But she has been brutally used beyond what a person can stand and live.

I can well believe that those who see her are destroyed. To see her is to know emptiness. But I saw that emptiness when I was very young. They called me a witch in Grimstock, and Samuel Bantry took what he thought was his due from a witch. The hand heavy on the back of my neck, the straw pressed to my face. The sound of the belt sliding out of the buckle. He called me a witch. He made me one.

There was, in that look between *she* and I, both knowledge and acceptance. Something was exchanged. Something of mine is carried by her. In that look, she took into herself my pain, my fear. I took hers.

And that is when I had the idea. I saw what I must do, and how we would be saved.

All those years ago, in that valley by the spring, I asked, *Who will help me?* And I saw *her*. The water told me true. It is because *she* walks, dreadful and suffering, that Iris will come into the world. So I look for her in deserted passages. I turn my cheek upward on stormy nights, waiting for her touch. I listen always for her dead voice, which is like stone crushing stone. My ghastly savior, my whipping boy.

I went to Robert that night for the first time.

⌀

Chloe is brushing my hair. In the glass, my face is milky and thin. Silks rustle gently, out of view. Eliza is laying out clothes, vast balloons of fabric to be draped around my bulbous self.

Chloe is cross, but tenderness is in her; it moves through her fingertips, through my hair. It is not meant for me, this tenderness, but it comes to me anyhow, and I am grateful: for the smooth motion of the brush; for Chloe's slender form, reflected solid behind me; for her blue, black, and cream beauty—for she is very beautiful and it is comforting—for the touch of her clever fingers.

"Don't fidget so." Chloe tosses her shining head, from which dark strands are escaping. Chloe can never keep her hair tidy. "Ma'am," she adds.

"Less pert," I tell her, "or I'll pull *your* hair."

In the mirror, Chloe blanches and bites her lip. She fears me. Wise of her. The Eye comes on strong and sudden as it does in these late days, and I see that Chloe is in the same state as me. I do not think she knows it yet.

When I feel it, I send them away. "I will rest," I say. They go.

I take the cloth from the drawer. It is dark with Robert's blood. His ear bitten, as if in play… He cried out. Don't think of that now.

It will be today. Everything will be decided now. It is not right to be within walls, even Rawblood's. I know where I belong for this, and it is not here. So when Chloe and Eliza's steps have died quiet in the hall, I ease my swollen frame from the stool. My shift is wet through. So is the stool. They will see that, I suppose, but by then, I will be well away. Through the window, the world is gray and lowering. I feel the coming dusk. It lies on my skin like love.

Down the stairs, through the narrow back passages. From below, the sound of the servants' dinner. A voice raised in one line of song, ending in laughter. Past the study that hums with Alonso's presence within and into the yellow parlor, where the fire isn't laid yet for evening, which has the window with the loose catch. I worm my way out into the late afternoon, into the air. The grass is a cool carpet. I take my shoes off. Across the top of the hill, rowan berries are a red shout against the brown. I am pricked with sweat, chafed by cotton. The air is hot and awful. But the cave will be cool. I am so heavy. I carry a small world before me, filled with flesh and movement. Yes, she is coming. The cave is so far off. The pain begins, an orchestra tuning.

∽

By the time I reach the foot of Sheeps Tor, my whole being is singing, loud and lusty. Colors are interchangeable. I stop and retch under the wide umber sky. *Just a while*, I tell her, *a little while longer*. Rain begins to fall in cool, plump drops. Thunder grumbles far away. The light will be gone soon. I climb. Of a sudden, it is dark as the inside of a coal scuttle—I blink, but it makes no difference. I'm blind. The old, familiar dark. But this time, it will be different. I walk, listening to the tumult inside me. My feet are sure. I feel *her* breath on me, that other one. Even in this cold, it is colder.

I cannot account for time; how long have I walked? The ground beneath me is no longer tussocky, rough. It is dry, sandy. From somewhere comes a sweet scent, a dark scent. I realize with some relief that I am not where I had thought—not on the moor, not heavy-bellied with pain. It is all gone—the rain, the cutting wind.

I open my eyes, and the way is straight before me. The night is soft, and I am light and young, walking the long Kent lanes to London. My feet and the black road. The eglantine is out in the banks, and the night is furry with the stench. (Of course, I called it sweet briar then. What did I know?) All I think of is Alonso's face. It hangs in my eye in the dark. When coaches or horses come with hooves and winking lamps, I hide in the ditch. I am not a fool. Somewhere, I have lost my shoes, but it makes no matter. My feet are hard, and I am strong.

The walk does not seem long. Time moves in a series of stutters until I am standing barefooted before the Chandos Club. But I must be tired— there is a fine film over all things. The walls and sky of London glow, unearthly. I speak to the porter, whose fleshy jowls hold secrets in their folds. He bars me. I stand on the flags and look at the lit window where he is, and my body seems to melt; each minute passes like a torment. I think I cannot endure it, but then Alonso is there, his vast shape filling the doorframe, blocking out the dirty lamplight. He hurries across the street. We stand straight before one another like opponents.

"What is that school about?" he asks. "They cannot seem to keep you there more than a week."

"I wanted to show you," I say. "Look. The irises are blooming in Kent." I offer him the dead flowers. I take his hand tightly. We are silent in the hazy, greenish street. My feet curl against the cold flags, and my white-knuckled hand grips the grimy stalks. "Let me stay with you forever," I say.

Alonso takes me by the shoulders and says in the saddest way, "Yes, I will give you everything." He talks, and through the wispy night, I understand his words—he means to adopt me or some such.

I laugh hard enough to snap my stays. The world steadies a little. I say, "I do not want you for a father or a brother."

"You cannot want me," he says. "I am good for nothing." He is pleading, unlike himself.

I say, "I'll judge that for myself, thank you very much." His pale hand lights on my shoulder. Every inch of the miserable street is alive with feeling.

⤳

The deluge blows lateral and sharp across the tor. The rain is blinding. Black skies are massed heavy above. Inside me is a furnace that leaks torrents of pain. The air is vibrant and darkening. Spikes of grass rise icy between my toes. For a moment, there are dead flowers in my outstretched hands. Where is the lamplight? Where is my bear? Time is fitting into itself like a Russian doll. I do not recall where I am or where I was going. It is not important. I stand in the blast of the storm and clutch my roiling belly. Dead flowers and the cloying fumes of the lamps. I am there, I am here…both, neither. *She* is all about me; her coldness is everywhere: in the storm, in the cloud, the rock; somewhere under my feet on a far-off London street.

I know the ways and means that nature has, in bargaining. So I know that I am being offered a last chance to change my mind. I will not.

I wish Alonso were here. Everything is happening now.

⤳

When I come to, my face is pressed hard to the ground. "Here," a voice says. "Here." My arm grasped by a pale mottled hand, dripping with rain. I grasp the hand, which lifts me gently to my feet. Rain washes grass and earth from my face.

I say, "I can walk." I am released immediately. Shakes stands before me, a small, blasted shape.

"Of course," I say, "it would be you who found me."

We stare, bitter.

"I suppose you must come, then," I say.

He says something incomprehensible. I lead into the pelting torrent.

The pain ploughs deep; it leaves deep furrows. It's possible I may die of this. It's something I have never before considered. Everything is hectic and spangled. Shakes's dim shape is lit with stars. Each raindrop to strike my flesh is an explosion, a galaxy. I am weak with relief when I see the treacherous narrow path, the rock walls. Not far now.

The crevice appears in the rock, black against the wet granite. Shakes pulls me toward it, our hands slippery with rain.

In the cave, everything is pale and green with some kind of moss. It glows, filled with a nimbus. I waddle across the sandy floor. On the low stone altar has been placed a child's hoop earring, an egg…other indistinguishable things, rusted, rotten. I sweep them all off. The egg breaks with a soft sound.

Shakes places his lantern on an outcrop and stares at me with his clouded blue eyes.

"It is called eclampsia," I say while I still may. "Do you understand? There is nothing to be done. If you wish to be of help," I tell him, "be still. Be quiet." It killed the others. It will not take Iris.

I take the scrap of cloth from my pocket. It is dark with Robert's blood. I put it on the altar and say the necessary thing. Then I eat it. The linen is like sawdust in my mouth. I am swallowing, dry; I think it'll never go down, but at last, it does. The pain rises; everything goes red and orange. I don't know much else after that.

✑

My eyes have gone again, but I know the scent of Alonso's skin. His hand is on my brow.

"She is well?" I ask. "I cannot see." I am glad of my blindness. I could not bear to read his face.

"She is," he says.

A great shout goes up within me, and I am at the same time abruptly bone-tired. As if each part of me were stitched to the cave floor. But there is no time for rest.

I say, "Give her to me."

Something settles in my arms, a decided weight. I take my time; it is not to be believed just yet. I trace soft little legs, arms, touch fingers and toes the size of sultanas. Outside me, in the air, she is both awesome and tiny. A small mouth seizes the tip of my finger, and a chasm opens in me through which I perceive a world larger than the one I have known.

Nothing can ever be the same now.

"She is looking at me," I say. "I feel it." I am afire.

"She is," Alonso says, then goes on, very fast, "Her eyes are dark, soft and dark. Like sun on deep water. She looks at everything. She is quite red and small, but I think she will have very white skin, like you. She will be very, very beautiful, like you."

"Iris," I say. "Iris. Hello."

"The first gift you ever gave me," Alonso says. "Irises."

I smile to myself. Iris and I have talked of this many times over the months. But the name is new to him.

"Are we alone?" I ask. I mean, is that little stump of an old man lurking in a corner, watching me?

Alonso says, "We are alone."

For a time, there are only small sounds. I acquaint myself with my daughter's form: her soft head, her ears like rosebuds.

"You should not dislike him," Alonso says. "He brought me here to you. He has always cared for me, since I was small."

I recall, for a moment, Shakes's old face, running with rain. Then Iris's hand finds my finger like a starfish, and I am seized by a joy that is so deep it resembles pain.

At length, I say, "My eyes. I am afraid, Alonso. It feels different, unlike the other times. The dark is different. It is as if something has been cut... Do you think," I ask, and I keep my tone even, "that I will ever see her?"

"You may, Meg. It often returns. Very often." Alonso cradles my head with a hand. His other hand rests on her, protective. Iris talks to him. She talks shrill and clear like a brook in spate.

"Loud!" he says. His voice has strings, golden apples, bellows in it.

I feed Iris. It is like nothing I have known. The world has been pried apart. The kingdom unrolls before me. Blindness is a small price to pay for it.

I say to Alonso, "Each time, you saved me, instead of them."

The bloody horror of it. The little limbs. Three linen-clad bundles. Their lives taken to save mine. My hand tightens as I think it, and Iris bleats, outraged.

"I know," Alonso says. "I am sorry for it. But there was never a choice… Not for me."

"I thought I could never forgive you."

"And now?" In his voice, I hear shaking and hope.

All these years, I have chosen not to see. He is not a bear. He is not a tree to lean on. He is a man and an imperfect one. He is arrogant and frequently ill-humored. He is childish, held in thrall to his past and chronically addicted to morphine. His heart is restless, quick, and deep.

"I can," I say. "I can forgive."

On the hill, *she* showed me the long walk from Kent to London. The walk ends here.

The shaking in him grows. I think I hear him weep. That seems right. I weep too, into his shirt cuff. I lie back, Iris a plump little pillow on my breast. Two hands are playing with my hair: one very large, one indescribably tiny. There is the dim sound of rain in the distance. Almost immediately, I am asleep.

❦

I smell Shakes before I hear him. He is moldy against the clean scents of blood and sand and rock. (I had not thought sand and rock had scents, but I live in a new world now.) And there are other men with him, and Alonso. Iris stirs, makes bird sounds in my arms.

"Try to bear it." Alonso's voice is in my ear.

I am lifted onto something. My every fiber protests—I am torn up like carded cotton.

The men grasp the canvas. I hear their oily fingernails. They heave, and they strain. I feel their suspicion, their dislike. It comes through the touch of their hands on the canvas. They think I belong in a cave.

The litter lifts, and the ground veers away. I am carried, swaying. As we leave the dark and come into sunshine, the warmth and light are like an endearment. There is a strong scent, which is acrid and despairing.

"Alonso," I say to the great expanse of dark. I know he will be there.

"Yes." He is beside me.

"I smell burning here."

There is the tramp of feet. Somewhere, a blackbird gurgles, high and long. Iris stirs against me. How can I know what is happening in Alonso's face?

"Shakes made a fire of all the trees along the path," he says at length. "He set them alight with kerosene. They burned...so brightly, even in the dark, the rain. I saw them from Bell Tor." He says, "I can never repay him." His voice is taut with colors; it has a shape. Perhaps in time, I will learn to parse these shapes and colors, learn the language of voices.

"We will have to change many things," I say. "Alonso! Where will she sleep? We need a nursery." We had settled on a bare box room for the nursery. It has large windows; the light floods in. How beautiful, we said, it will be when painted white and blue. That was ten years ago. We have not touched it. How paltry was our hope.

"She will sleep with us," Alonso says, "and in time, we will contrive."

"And," I say, "I want more women around me."

"It seemed to me," Alonso says, "that you were not overly fond of Eliza or of Chloe."

"I am," I say. "But there are some of the household I do not like. I would have you let that butler go, for instance. He stares. It is unnerving." I hold my breath. If it did not work, then I will never sleep soundly.

"Gilmore?" Alonso is quiet a moment. "I fear he was not well, my Meg. They found him in his bed this morning. Heart, perhaps. I do not know..."

"Dead?"

"Yes," he says.

My own heart performs a peculiar stutter—there is relief, and then the great, black weight descends. I test it, the darkness. I let my guilt wrap about me. I settle it firmly on my shoulders. I must do so, for I will carry it to the end of my days.

Alonso is saying, "I will go to tell his brother, who has Trubb's Farm over the way. He was a Devon man, for all his citified ways."

I recall dimly a Henry Gilmore and a Charlotte Gilmore, seen and spoken to outside church. She cannot bear children. One of those shameful snippets you come by, if you are neighbors in the country. Did Robert come here to be near his family? I never asked why he took this remote post on Dartmoor. All these things I did not know. The dark weight hangs a little heavier. I am laden with sorrow and sudden fear. What have I become?

There is always a high cost for strong witchery; I will pay for Robert's life in ways I cannot fathom. It has begun already; I am blind. But Iris is hot and small on my neck. No, I would not change the bargain.

I sway, suspended in air. The breeze combs through my hair. We go across the moor, and all the way, I have the image in my mind of a great summer tree, wreathed in flame.

❧

"Iris," I say. "Oh small person, oh light in the dark, oh little baby, will you not hush?"

She cries. Her screams go through my head like bolts slammed home. She is feverishly dull and fretful. She is perfection. Three weeks since we brought her home, and each day, she grows in beauty. I feel it in her flesh. She is strong and growing and mine.

The red drawing room is filled with the August sun. I walk through the beams, straight paths of heady warmth. Iris weeps. Her face is tiny and wet on my shoulder. Sometimes, I cannot accept that she lives outside me now. Her every breath draws my heart after it. Each one of her tears is like a blade.

I speak to her, and she quiets. She speaks back to me in her strange, wailing voice. I tell her stories of myself. I tell her about the Bantrys' farm—the animals, not the people. I will not tell her tales of sorrow or of fear. I tell her about Peter the donkey and his patient eyes and pot belly. I tell her about the golden hens and the dirty, spiny-backed pigs.

We talk like this for some time. "They were my friends," I tell her. "Although I have had other friends, and good ones, since. I had a friend at Rawblood who is gone now. A woman, pale and sorrowful..."

I knew the moment I was carried across the threshold with Iris in my arms. *She* is gone. She was the cold core buried deep at the heart of the house. No longer. The very air in the halls and rooms is changed. Everything moves faster and rings brighter now. How weighty and thunderous it was—her presence. Now, going on through the days is just that—going on. Her terrible, dark glamour has been lifted from us, and we are merely people. Irritable people, kind people, everyday people who darn shirt fronts and make jam and spill inkpots and tread mud into the house. And this is as it should be.

Ours shall be all new beginnings, I promise Iris as her cries become shorter and sweeter.

"There was also a man called Robert," I say. "He was not handsome, but beautiful—as beautiful as a woman—and determined."

Iris answers me in a descant of bubbles and trills.

"He had coppery hair, though darker than mine. We looked somewhat alike, perhaps like brother and sister. I had a brother, but he left me to a dark farm with Mr. Bantry and belts and whips and other things… No, hush, hush. We will not speak of it. Robert's face was like…it was like music." Iris breathes deep. She's going. I tell her softly, "He gave his life for us. Or—I took it from him, that you and I might live." I am shocked to find that I am weeping. I have grown soft indeed.

The house creaks a little, and an eddy of air shivers through the room. I lift my head from her forehead where it has been resting gently. Iris breathes like factory machinery. She always sleeps as though it were hard work.

I tip my face in the direction of the parlor door and say, "Come—sit with us, Alonso."

He comes without a word and sits with a great creak. The shape of him is mountainous, the ottoman suddenly a silly, fiddly thing. His hand lies on mine, and his finger strokes Iris's cheek.

"You should not have survived," Alonso says. His breath on my face. The faintest trace of Spanish in his words. "Nor should you, little one. But you did. Your lives are rare gifts, and I will always remember it." His caress.

I want to ask *And how long did you stand there in the doorway, my love—what did you hear?* But what good would it do—to know? We sit, Iris sleeps, and I think how alike they are: the sensations of danger and of love.

The bark of the cedar tree beneath my fingers. Sun warmed. He says nothing, but he's here. He's always here, in the summer, in the evening. Light on old bones. I feel his attention, where he sits, back against the vast cedar trunk. His skin. The scent is everywhere. Parchment, malice. Why must it have been he who helped me? Impossible to owe such a debt.

"Come," I say.

Still, he says nothing. But he comes. I hear the creaks of his passage. I hear the summer grass beneath his uncertain steps. The knife slips across my fingertip like silk. I reach through the warm air. I put my blood on him where he stands before me. Trace the deep sockets of his eyes. I say the words, and the tree and the earth shiver.

"Have them, then," I say. "Have your sight, and my thanks."

His surprisingly long lashes are viscous with my blood. And tears, because Shakes weeps then. Color and light creep into him. I feel it. I yearn. His wonder fills the air. Silent, heavy.

I may do this magic once only. So Shakes will see, and I will be the blind one now.

⟡

There is the soft sound of cloth on glass and the reassuring bustle of a broom. Chloe and Eliza talk quietly as they clean. I have found that if I lie still, they think that I am asleep and speak very freely—as if my bandaged eyes had stopped up all my senses, not just one. I have heard the talk of the autumn fair. I have heard of Chloe's little brother, Tom, whom she loved but who died as a child. Their lives are tantalizing and bright, their likes and dislikes strong and fully formed. They have been masquerading as scenery, but they are full of action.

They are silent today, quick with intent. The air seethes with thought.

Eliza murmurs, "Did you go to the brother?"

Chloe does not speak. She makes a sound both sharp and wet.

"Did you ask at Trubb's Farm?" asks Eliza. I picture her—brackish eyes narrowed, eyebrows acrobatic with conviction. Cloth squeaks on the fire brasses.

"Went yesterday." When Chloe speaks at last, her scornful tones are unrecognizable. She is hesitant, as though each word were a step through a bog. The Devon is strong in her voice. I had not noticed it before. "He called me a whore and sent me off."

"You have a month before I can't lace you up," says Eliza. "No more. You hear me? Go again. You make him hear."

"He won't help. Not that one," says Chloe. "I am for the workhouse or the Home. They're the same in the end. You go in those places, you don't come out. And all I can think is that I hope it looks like *him*." There is a gentle thump, rustling. A seagull cries somewhere in the distance. I think, *How like these strange times, a gull on Dartmoor.* But the gull is Chloe, who is crying.

"Come here," I say. There is a silence like death.

"Ma'am," says Eliza, suddenly close. "Please." The red thread of panic in her voice.

"The two of you," I say. "Come here."

The scent of Chloe's tears. Salt, rain, clean skin.

"It is Robert—Gilmore—the butler, who did this?" I ask. I recall the day Iris was born, when Chloe brushed my hair and I saw her secret. I knew it even before that, I think. I saw it in her sullen eyes that day in the kitchen.

They say nothing. There are movements in the air. They are shivering like puppies.

"And he is dead," I say.

"Yes," says Chloe. Her voice is puzzled, as if she can't quite recall. The many, various hidden costs of my deed. "It is not Eliza's fault, ma'am. She warned me of the error of my ways, and none of the blame for my sins should rest on her."

"Can you write?" I ask. "Either of you?" There is silence. "Speak up."

"I can write," says Chloe.

"Bring paper. Fetch a pen. Then sit down by me."

I think the instructions are obeyed. At any rate, there is bustling and the dry scratch of paper, and then there is quiet.

"Write what I say," I tell her. There are some false starts. I speak too quickly. Chloe falls behind, and I cannot then recall the rest of the sentence.

I am as brief as may be in the letter. If Mr. Gilmore will be so good… There are considerations… I rely on his charity, his Christian feeling. I trust he will not blame the innocent for the sins of the fathers. It being his own brother who has transgressed, he will feel a responsibility… Perhaps he also will recall my brother Charles, who did him a kindness once, when his brother was sick with a poison… Herewith enclosed is something toward…

Then I dictate a reference for Chloe. It is firm and favorable and fairly honest.

"I am not quite happy about it," I say. "It is in your own hand …"

"I made the writing different." She is curt.

At my direction, Eliza goes to the escritoire. "Ma'am," she says delicately, "where…?"

I have to laugh. "The key on the lavender ribbon," I say, "hanging from the back of the mirror. As you very likely know."

Eliza brings the money in a dirty, copper-scented bundle. We are flustered by the great amounts of it. We divide it up and begin to count, but how am I to know what is there? It's no matter anyway.

"Take it," I say. "Go now to Henry Gilmore. Take him the letter and half the money. I will send him more in due course. The other half you take with you. Go to Exeter—or no, too close—to Bath. Take rooms. You are a widow. It may be they won't like it, but you can pay, which means everything. Stay within doors. Eat well. Engage a physician. When the baby is born, you must come back. You must give it to them. To Mr. Gilmore and his wife."

"Do I have to?" Chloe asks. It sounds like her old insouciance, but the timbre is wrong and brittle. "May I not take the child…"

I think about this for a time. "I don't think you can," I say.

She says nothing, but the money is lifted in its greasy leaves from my lap.

"Will he take care of it?" she asks.

"His wife cannot have children. He'll be kind for that. He's a farmer and not a successful one. He'll be kind for the money. I will give him enough to be very kind. I'll make sure of it." I wonder what I am promising. "You must," I say.

Eliza, who has been very quiet, bursts out, sudden and shrill. "Must this, must that. Why should she? It's a terrible thing you're telling her to do."

I find her by her voice. The slap lands flush on her cheek with a crack.

"I was left and raised by others for money," I say. "I know well what it is I'm advising. It is better than the alternative. You may believe me." I think of the workhouse babies I have seen. I think of Iris's tiny toenails, of her treble voice and her cheeks.

I will watch Chloe's child. I will cling to Charlotte Gilmore like a best friend. I will give Alonso's money out like water.

"It will be hard," Chloe says.

The gray despair in her voice raises hairs on the back of my neck. I see her sunk, underwater, weeds waving by her face. I see her blue eyes fixed and staring. Hidden cost.

I will not let it happen. I will ensure they do what I say. I will ensure that she can bear it.

I reach. "Show me," I say.

She takes my hand with her small rough one and guides it. The gentle, fragile swell.

"It is a boy," I say. "You'll name him after your brother. Young Tom. He will be strong and handsome and very kind. Women will like him. These gifts are his already. Now give me an eyelash from your eye and a hair from your head."

She puts the hairs on my open palm. Her thin fingers are cold. I close my fist about them. I say what I need to, quiet into our locked hands. Then I open up and blow them away. "Now you have given him your black hair. You have given him your blue eyes. So he will always be marked as yours. Wherever he goes in life and whatever he does, your son will always be using the gifts you gave him."

Later that evening, Alonso holds me, enclosing me in the scents of bay and leather. My blind eyes are stinging with tears. He murmurs and asks me things.

"I find I have spent all the householding," I say. "Everything in the drawer. And Chloe was pert, so I turned her off. I am ill-tempered, and blind, and worthless."

"Nothing of the kind," he says into my hair and asks nothing further.

So I tell him what has passed with Chloe. "It is foolish," I say. "Is it atonement?"

"For what?" Alonso asks, and the edge of his voice is delicate and sharp. I can hear him thinking.

"For everything," I say. "For the woman I am, for the things I have done... For *them*. For my three lost ones." And for Robert. I have drawn too much blood. I have taken a man's life. It weighs and weighs like darkness and will do all my days. Robert's death will cover me always like sickness.

And Iris's little dead sisters... I recall them each day. Each day, I must realize anew that what I have done will not bring them back. "I have been a fighting hedge snipe all my life," I say. "'I wish a different fate for my daughter. But she will be tried too... Oh, it is all connected, Alonso, do not you forget it...'" My voice deepens, takes on the rough edge that means the Eye is on me.

His hand on my back. "Meg?"

"You look after him," I hear myself say. "Do you promise to do it? Take care of Tom Gilmore."

"We will," he says, frightened. "Together, we will make sure the Gilmores do right."

"Promise," I say in the terrible voice. "He must dig the grave."

"I promise," he says.

The Eye lifts, floats away as if it never was, and we're alone.

I kiss his hand. I am swept with feeling. Alonso's touch, the warmth of sunlight on my face, the scent of fresh-washed cotton—everything cuts deeply now, as it never did before. Love has finally settled into me. It has turned me belly up on the shore, just as I always feared it would.

∞

The air is filled with autumn. Dry leaves and the scent of dark berries and mold and hay. The morning air is wine. I make to rise quietly. Alonso's cuff links are chinking from the corner of the room, where his dressing table stands. The quiet harrumph as he clears his throat. I feel his attention, but I have urgent business. Iris will be awake—no doubt she is talking to the dawn. Before my feet meet the cold boards, there is a flash of white deep in the center of my skull.

"Draw the curtains," I cry. "It hurts; it burns." There is a whirlpool of movement beside me, and Alonso's hands are on my lids, pulling them gently apart. I shriek and tell him no, no. It is an ax blade to my head, the light. My tears are hot. His fingers shake, and he asks, what is it, what is it? My words are unwieldy. I cannot make him understand for some time. Through the lightning flashes are perceptible knots of oak on the boards, my pale toes, the rippling hem of my nightgown.

I can see.

∞

There follows a time of anxious rest, of cold compresses bound across my eyes. Of smarting headaches. But the world bleeds in, day by day. The veils lift, one by one. Objects take on shape and form, resolve themselves into distances.

Bright light still causes me pain. I must cover my eyes until they are strong enough. Each day, Alonso removes my blindfold for an hour—then two, then three. He oversees me with the exactitude of an experiment. He is impersonal, gentle. There is something unsettling in it. I long for his temper.

Colors are blank and strange—for a time, I see reds and pinks as blue and vice versa. I lie cushioned in my downy bed and watch the window. Swallows cross the sky, which is the veined red of freshly butchered meat. Alonso brings me late summer poppies, a flower that I have loved always for its overblown fragility, its deep orange-red hues. But these are the blue of a drowned face. I cannot tell Alonso how sad they make me. They sit in the vase at my bedside. They lurk in the corner of my eye like unease.

Most days, there is some activity down the hall, sounds of heavy things moving and the scent of fresh paint. I ask Alonso, what is it? His answer is short and vague.

Iris plays in my lap. She is heavy now. Her desires are becoming sophisticated. Her understanding, her knowledge, grow daily. She likes certain songs and cannot bear others. She has taken to punching me heavily when displeased. Hair covers her silken skull. Soon, I tell her. But when? I keep my eyes covered when she is with me. I am afraid to behold her for the first time. I fear my skewed sight.

We go on quite well. October comes. As she tucks the bedclothes around me, Eliza says in hushed tones that Charlotte Gilmore has been blessed with a child—a boy. They have named him Tom. So that at any rate has been well managed. I give Eliza money for the Gilmores. For the little boy.

The next day when I take off the compresses, there it is—through the window, the gray sky, the precise hue of dirty silver.

I inch farther along the road to recovery. Alonso writes letters to men in big towns, who claim to know things about eyes. They make promises to visit. I don't need them, I tell him—I am healing. He does it anyhow.

One day, Eliza leans in and whispers, although we are alone: Chloe is to be married. A gentleman from London, no less. "So, ma'am, she is shortly to be Mrs. Coulson, and it has all ended happily." If marrying were a guarantee of happiness... But I say nothing.

❧

I lift the stinking camphor-soaked cotton. My eyes are red-rimmed and new. Alonso is not beside me. Where? The room is as it was, as it has always been. Brown and shining in the dawn, the beams above. The sounds of Rawblood are muted. Full day will come soon enough.

I think of Iris. Longing is in me like an arrow. Today is the day that I will look upon my daughter.

Someone has been digging beneath the cedar tree. Why should that make me sad?

❧

The door is ajar. It is painted white. Painted blue ducks, blue umbrellas, and blue seashells climb it in a riot, curling around the door handle. I picture Alonso's face, puzzling over what Iris should have, what she will like. The door swings open, silent, well-oiled. No one will be woken by it. The care, the thought.

Morning sun falls on fresh white walls, varnished boards. Curtains flutter at the windows, the color of a kingfisher's back. A white-and-black mottled rocking horse gallops, legs thrown out, nostrils red and panic-wide. On the bright walls are flowers, tigers, horses. A white dresser is ranged with an audience of china animals: deer, dogs, cats, mice; they stare with cold, clever eyes. A white cradle, fine as spun silk, stands shiny-new in the corner. Above it hangs a mirror, and knots of blue ribbons, and seashells, and a silver locket. They turn gently in the light.

Alonso stands over the cradle with Iris in his arms. They look at one another, my husband and my daughter, in fierce concentration. They have not seen me. His hair sticks up in white-and-black whorls on the back of his neck, the pouched lines of his face sewn up with sleep. She is a translucent glimpse between her new dark silken hair, dark lashes, and the pale blue blanket. The flowers of her fists open and close gently in the air. My heart is full.

I go to them. At the slight sound of my feet on the boards, Alonso looks up. I smile, but he nods, serious.

"It was finished yesterday," he says. His voice is a bare whisper. "I am pleased you came today." As if he had expected me for some time.

"It is wonderful," I say, and I mean it.

He offers me the pale-blue blanket, the dark scrub of hair just visible. "Here," he says. "She has gone back to sleep, I think."

I take her. I look at my daughter. I look at her for some time.

I had thought her plump, but her face has a symmetry to it that is startlingly adult. Her eyelids are large and white. Dark lashes rest on snowy cheeks. She is different. She is different from the picture I had of her in my mind and from anything I have ever seen...

That is not so. She is very like someone I have seen. There is a stirring within me, hot. I hold my daughter, and I try to understand. "I feel—" I say. "Alonso, I am not sure that I am well."

"Sit," he says, and I do, upon a white wicker bucket chair, piled high with cream-and-blue cushions. "Give her to me," he says.

"No," I tell him. I hold her; I keep the perfect small face before me.

Iris's lids flutter, open. I look into her eyes, *her* black, black eyes, and I see.

Dimly, I hear Alonso say, "Blood, Meg, you are bleeding." I had thought I was healed, but some treacherous fragile part of me has given way. It is impossible, but I feel the orange tautness, the familiar pain. Eclampsia again? It shouldn't be, can't be, but the lights are flashing, pulsing in my skull. The blood comes frightening and fast.

It seems less important than the other unutterable, terrible thing. I have understood.

I had thought *her* gone, but it is not so. I look at my daughter, and *she* looks back at me, pink-and-white skin glowing, dark eyes clear and wide and young. *She* puts a corner of blue blanket in her mouth and gives me a secret smile.

"Alonso," I say. It doesn't sound right. A rough and wet sound, like a great bird cawing.

He does not hear. He is pressing a great wad of linen against me, against the blood. The red bubbles up around his hands.

There are tears on my cheeks. I hear a scratched and broken shrieking. It is mine. The tinny scent of blood is strong. Everything is darkening, turning burnt orange. The shrieking grows. Beneath it, a smaller, thinner child's cry. Iris and I weep. I look into her eyes and imagine them bereft of sense, filled with the darkness of eons. I imagine her face older, corpse white, unwitting, mouth thin with suffering. I imagine shearing off the silky dark hair to the tender skull beneath; I picture it cruelly wounded, again and again, until it is covered with scars, like valley rims under awful moonlight. It will come to pass.

I must tell Alonso. I must tell him, and we will prevent it—someone must prevent it—but my mouth has gone soft like wool and cannot be used. A long, rusty, useless noise emerges. "It is her," I say. "*Her.*"

The sound that comes from him is worse. He peers at the corners of the room, his eyes crazy. He looks everywhere but at Iris, wailing in my arms. He collapses at my feet, and his head slumps on his arm. His white-and-black head, striped like a badger. His long hands slick with my blood.

Was there anything I could have done to turn it aside, anything? Had I not been so busy, so in love with all my secrets. I do not know. I do not understand.

"This is a beautiful room," I say to him, though it doesn't sound like words. "You have made it so beautiful for her." The white wicker chair, the cream-and-blue cushions—all are dark, syrup red. A glossy pool covers the boards by my feet. As I watch, it spreads gently, silently.

Charles, my pompous brother, is in my mind. I touched him in his death. Perhaps he will come to find me in mine… All the while, I had thought I was forging my own path. It seems to me now that I have wandered blindly, tangled in old, old events, as if in brambles. Caught on their piercing thorns.

Time is short. I will Alonso to look at me. His shoulders shake, and he presses his face into his sleeve. *Please*, I tell him with all my being, *look up, look into my eyes. Look.* His head is lowered. He does not look. In my lap, Iris weeps, her hands reaching toward my face. I can no longer move my limbs—they are bound with iron and dead. I cannot comfort her. This is the first, little one. The first of those awful sorrows that will befall you. I would do anything to make it otherwise.

With a great crack, everything goes quiet and radiant orange. The silence is shocking. Before me is an orange silken ribbon, rippling, stretching into the distance, which will lead me—where? For a moment, tiny in my ear, is Alonso's voice. He is weeping, calling for me. He is far away. I try to cling to the sound, to him. But the way ahead is smooth and easy and delightful. He fades. I flow. I follow the orange ribbon like a road. I go on and on, and it is cool to my bare feet.

WAYS OF ESCAPE

1919

F rank is the only one to wake.

He starts up into soft light. The pre-op tent is amber, shadowed, the air sad and sulfurous. Breath and flesh. No one stirs. They lie in rows, neatly bandaged. For once, they are all asleep. Through the canvas wall, the nauseous grinding of the generator.

Between the rows of cots drifts a shape like a black candle flame. The figure stops by each sleeping man and bends, as if to kiss or drink. His fingers come away gleaming: cigarette cases, coins. Frank watches. The thief comes toward him, organized and graceful.

When the man touches him, Frank does nothing. He looks into the thief's face, what he can see of it. A gray scarf covers the mouth and nose. Brown eyes hold his own. They narrow, creasing at the edges, warm. It's as if the thief is smiling beneath his mask. But it could be disapproval.

The fingers move like anemones inside Frank's jacket. They light on Frank's father's watch, his tobacco. They curl around the solitary coins in his pockets, the bundle of letters near his heart. They linger on the handwritten label that is sewn to his breast pocket, listing his injuries. The fingers stroke it.

"I need it," Frank says.

The thief hums tunefully. The label slips its moorings, vanishes into his hand.

"Leave it," Frank says, but there's no one there. The tent flap stirs in the breeze, lets in the night.

Far out in the dark French fields, there comes a long, high note. It's most likely a dog, but for a moment, it sounds like music.

✑

Sister wakes him. "Time," she says. "Come, you." Her hands are hard and careful. She's a farmer's daughter.

The man lying next to Frank shudders. A broken silver chain dangles in his bandaged hands. Eyes the color of fire peep through gummed-up lids. He wails. He makes inexplicable sounds like water going through a cistern.

"Private Trevor," says Sister. "That's not a song. As far as I know, songs have words. Goodness."

Private Trevor's ululations come higher and higher until they fade. Then he says in a strong Welsh voice, "Took my wedding ring, the shit." The chain swings.

Sister says, "Everyone was had. Such a thing. Who would do it to the wounded?" She is cool, offended—by the language, by the theft, or both.

"My label's gone," Frank says. He should say, now, that he saw the thief. But he doesn't. All his attention is taken up with what's shortly going to happen to him. He's shaking.

Sister's lip twitches, her eye flickers toward his leg, and Frank is ashamed of his stinking flesh.

"You're from London, Private Coulson," Sister says.

"London," Frank says.

"There you are then," she says. "Just think. Such a quick thing, and then you're home. Back to London. With a nice girl waiting, most likely." Frank thinks of Madge. Her letters resting somewhere near the thief's heart.

They come with stretchers. Frank is carried, swaying. He stares up into the blue morning. When canvas closes once more over his head, he thinks he'll die.

This tent is not like the other tent. This tent has many flat surfaces and edges. It smells of hot metal and sawing and blood.

The doctor says to Frank, "Be over before you know it, bombardier."

The doctor's eyes are black underneath them, as if he's been in a punch-up. He wears a mask over his mouth.

Flat on the table, Frank breathes ether and swims. The doctor looms over him, a tired pink and yellow, eyes narrow. It looks like he's smiling behind his mask. Or it's exhaustion.

As the dark closes over, Frank realizes that someone is beside him. It's someone he knew long ago, or maybe someone he doesn't know yet. He feels the warm track of their fingers as they trail across his cheek. When he licks his lips, he can taste their tears.

✐

In England, Frank is taken to a madhouse. Earlswood Asylum was built for lunatic women, a nurse tells him. They are sealed tight in the west part of the building. They shan't bother him. The nurse's name is Lottie. She has smooth brown hair and a surprised expression. When she leans over to tuck in the sheets, her white bosom rests gently on his arm. The doctors and nurses work on both sides of Earlswood. These are the times. Everyone must do their part. "It's a pain," Lottie says as she tucks, binding him tight to the uneven mattress. Frank is left alone in a room of iron beds and men. Days go by.

⁂

They wheel him out into the garden. He blinks in the light. The grass is green and young. When he reaches down, the silky blades rise to his hand, to his caress. The garden has flower beds. There are marigolds. Geraniums. Young trees are planted across the sward in hopeful, shivering groves.

A long chain-link fence cuts the garden in half. Beyond the fence, the earth is bare in patches, as if the grass has been torn up by its roots. The ground is gray and naked. One tree remains in the corner, its lower branches broken, twisted. A scar cuts across its trunk, deep and troubling. A discarded shoe lies in a puddle. This is where the lunatic women go.

Frank sits in his bath chair in the sunshine amid the flower beds. Presently, the women come out. They are clothed in tubes of gray fabric. They stand, trembling. They stare. They are like underground things released into the light.

Frank sees Lottie through the fence. She is stern, unlike herself.

A breathless blond woman ambles over. She looks at Frank long and hard through the wire. Breath squeezes through her lungs. Then she throws her shift over her head. She hops and shuffles her feet, her headless body long and pale. She presses herself against the fence and then recoils from it elegantly, twirling.

"Julia," someone calls.

Julia dances faster. She dances and throws herself against the wire until they take her away.

For the most part of most days, Frank lies in a cot in the long room with the other men in the other cots. There's some talk and the wireless sometimes. Sometimes, there are card games. Frank doesn't talk or play cards. People are too detailed. He prefers the vast white ceiling. His phantom leg sends him frantic. It sings with phantom pain. There is not enough morphia anywhere, for anyone. Sometimes, Lottie sits by him and knits. He's quiet, she says, so she doesn't drop stitches.

On Wednesdays, the women visit. Sometimes, old men come and little boys, not many. The sisters, wives, mothers, cousins come with stockings drawn on their legs and bright lips. Then the men sit up, and everyone smokes and plays cards. They laugh. No one peels back the bedclothes to see what has been lost.

One Wednesday, Madge comes. She tells Frank she can't marry him after all. He won't expect it. There's silence between them for a time. From other beds, other people's talk. The summer air is thick with it.

"I do feel it," Madge says. "I feel for you, Frank." Her large eyes are rimmed with wet.

"Not at my best," Frank says. Words are worn down to nubs. He says, "Well then."

"Your leg?" she asks.

"No." It is though. Tendrils of pain curl around his shins. Both of them.

Madge pats her eyes with a scrap of linen. Her eyelids large, blue-veined, powdered.

"Daisy's marrying," she says. "Fancy."

Madge's sister. Small, thin, with a chin made for digging.

"Fancy her getting married before me," says Madge.

The pain stirs again in Frank's missing toes, brushes through his knee, up into his groin where it nests, feathery. "Well," he says, "needn't be like that."

He first kissed Madge outside Mayrick's Music Hall. He thinks of slicked-back hair and feet moving, slowly, one two, one two, hands meeting, grainy light, her face. Music and beer in his blood. Her hair. The scent of dusty evening streets. Breathing into each other's mouths, not daring to move.

These things are there, but removed, as if seen through gauze.

"I thought it best to bring them," Madge says. She means to put it down carefully, but it slips. It lands on the bed with a soft *shhh* in the blank place where his right leg should be. The paper is thin, curling at the edges. His letters.

"I don't have yours," Frank says. "We were robbed. At Dieppe." He thinks to tell her about the thief: the gentle hands, the dark eyes, his veiled mouth. Madge folds her handkerchief into neat squares. Her mouth narrows to a fine, dark line. He doesn't tell her.

Frank makes to take his letters. Perhaps there's something of him in them that he can recover. The twine comes apart in his hands. The letters spew over the bed. Over his lap, his leg, and the not-leg. Words. Madge reaches for them with a cross *tsk*, and her hand grazes the cotton sheet, gentle, as if touching flesh.

Pain furls and unfurls, floats on surfaces, reaches deep.

"You'll come again," Frank says to Madge. "To see me."

Madge doesn't say yes or no. She narrows her gaze as if affronted. He hopes she'll come. Once, twice more, if only to prove herself kind.

❧

The sun is hot wax, pouring down his face, his neck, rolling and dripping over his hands, his knee, his absent foot. It seems to Frank that he can hear the blades of grass stroking one another, the deep movement of beetles in the earth. He can smell the wicker of the chair he sits in, the hot tar of the road beyond the high wall, softening in the

July heat. A bird whirs and scuffles in the tree behind him. The red of his eyelids.

Something ploughs through the air by his face, pounds the earth by his ear. Frank starts up. Sun floods his vision.

Behind the fence, the breathless woman is running. Up the garden, down, up. Her feet tattoo the bare earth. She falls, hitting the ground with a grunt. Her blue eyes are limpid with shock.

"Julia," the voice calls, not unkind.

Julia shakes herself, leaps up, and runs. A silver cord of saliva dangles, flies from her mouth as she goes. Need shines in her face.

Frank closes his eyes. The warm earth turns.

He does not immediately recall where or when he is. The air is scented. The lawn stretches empty and living into the dusk. Shadows cluster under the spreading trees. The garden is garlanded, dark. Distant, from the house, comes clanging metal, far voices. He catches the vague scent of suet, which means cooking. White moths flicker in the fading light. The thin twist of a crescent moon.

Behind the fence, there stands a figure. It is white against the dusk. The skin, the hair seem white, all white. It stares with white eyes. It is as still as though painted on the air.

Frank's insides lurch. Fear comes like a bullet past his cheek. He makes to turn, to run, before he remembers: he is in a chair and in a hospital, the fence is not ringed with barbed wire, and he won't run anywhere, not ever again. The ground heaves up, and he is falling.

He's caught by a thin, strong arm. Lottie puffs, comforting in her crisp white. She pushes and maneuvers him back into his safe, enclosing wicker cage where he collapses, full of gratitude. Lottie and he breathe heavily like cattle resting. In the last of the light, her small features are strange, still beneath her cap. Her skin smells clean with Pears soap.

"Pay her no mind," Lottie says.

Behind the fence, the girl is a pale spear. Her white arms hang straight. Her shift flutters about her white ankles. Her face is peaceful beneath the turban of white bandage. Her eyes are not, after all, white, but lashless and closed as if graven on her face.

Lottie watches the girl, hands tucked into her elbows, knuckles tight.

"Who?" asks Frank.

"That's the biter," Lottie says.

The white girl stares inside herself.

"Her head," Frank says.

"She doesn't bite anymore," says Lottie. "Supper."

❧

The next day, Frank watches. Behind the fence, Julia runs. Her feet hammer the earth. She blows like a racehorse and runs, drawn by the invisible, desirable thing. The hot day wears on.

As the afternoon sinks into evening, the girl is suddenly there behind the wire, a white pillar on the summer green. Frank wheels himself close to the fence. The lines of her face are deep, intent. Ripples pass over soft, closed lids. Something urgent passes within. She's smaller than expected.

"All right," Frank says to her. It's as good as talking to salt.

He puts two fingers through the chain-link.

The white lids shiver. They part. Her eyes are black scrawls on white. As the girl leans in, Frank knows with delicious certainty that she'll have his fingers off. He feels as if it has already happened, the clamp of her teeth, her mouth closing like a trap on him. He doesn't move.

Slowly, she rests her cheek against the wire, against his hand, like an exhausted child.

Frank turns his face to the sun, and they stay like that for a time.

* largo*

In the hot days that follow, Frank makes for the fence and sits by it. Sometimes she comes, and sometimes she doesn't. Frank feels she recognizes him, that there's friendliness between them somehow. Her eyes are rarely opened. She does not acknowledge him after that first time.

"I never see her come or go," he tells Lottie.

"Well," Lottie says, "she walks and falls like the rest of us, I assure you."

largo

The prosthesis is stiff and smells richly of leather. It makes Frank think of harness rooms and shining hide, horses' eyes, and the scent of the blacksmith. Longing curls up deep in his midriff, sudden and brutal. He is surprised. It is a long time since he has thought of home, of anything but the present moment. The long room grows slippery, won't stay still. The metal and leather are ungainly, hopeless in his hands.

"It's the strap," says Lottie. "It's like so." Her hands are cool, light. They move on him, birds walking on sand. "It's awkward. You'll grow accustomed."

As they rise, the floor skids and bucks. The leather is tight about his knee, his shin, binding him like steel. He wonders if it should be that tight, but only for a moment, because then he is walking, with Lottie under his shoulder, grim and solid.

"It's like being on the sea," Frank says. He is exhilarated. The windows, the walls, everything sways at an unexpected level. He is man-height once more.

Lottie hums. "Is it?" she asks.

"I don't know," Frank says to the top of her head. His smile is painful, like a crack in the ground. "Better."

❧

The sun falls through the beech tree, dapples the ground. Bark against Frank's back, warm with the late day. Lottie sits at his feet, eyes on the daisies in her hands. She works steadily, piercing the juicy stalks with the pin. The white-and-yellow heads hang lightly from one another, impaled. Her white cap nestles in the grass. Without it, her head is small and beautiful like a nut. Lottie throws her eyes up at him, then down. Frank feels her attention, her alertness on him like an embrace.

"My brother went to sea," Lottie says at last. "He was killed. Sounds so silly, doesn't it, when everyone was killed, so many. It was well before all this. He drowned off the coast of Gibraltar. In '06."

Frank says nothing. Sometimes, the story is sufficient unto itself. Sometimes, silence is what's called for.

"Stan," she says. "He brought me oranges from Seville. You see, when Stan came back, the first time, I thought he was my dad. Because that's who I had been waiting for. My dad. Not a brother. I was four. Met him at the gate."

She talks, and Frank leans against the tree. Her words fall around them in the warm air. It's a short story in some ways. In others, it's still going on. Lottie is ashamed, and loving, and puzzled by turns. The words she doesn't say are there too, running through like ribbons. Her smooth brown hair looks warm in the sun, warm like the tree at his back. It seems to Frank then that it's all part of the same thing: the sun, the tree, her hair, her voice.

When she has told him what she needed to tell, they are quiet for a time. At last, quite naturally, he lays a hand on the shining wing of her hair. She smiles. "Families," she says. She holds her hands high. The daisy chain forms a ragged O against the sky.

Frank feels she has given him something. He'd like to give it back. He tells her about his mother. The aching blue of her eyes, her coal-black hair shot with gray, like veins through ore. Her name, lilting and foreign. Chloe. She tied knots in her handkerchief to remind herself of things. When her mind went, she kept the habit, though she no longer knew what the knots were for. When she died, her drawers were full of lengths of knotted linen. Blue, red, white, yellow. Silk, cotton. A long record, a litany of undone tasks.

She had been in service when it happened, in a bad, lonely place with a name like murdered flesh. She ran away. She had the child. Frank's hidden brother.

Afterward, she went to London. She met Dad. He and his little boy, Stephen. He was grieving his dead wife. They married, and Frank was born. The four of them made a family.

Dad would plait straw men for Frank and Stephen, both his sons. The warm light of the stable, the red, large hands moving with intricate precision, the shape of a person slowly emerging from twists of disparate strands.

Stephen, his half brother. Frank loved him with a younger brother's passion. The tooth Stephen lost in a fight about a girl in a pub, long before the war. It made him more handsome, not less. Stephen, who, being older, always remembered to tell Frank about the things he had learned through four years' advantage (about girls, mainly, that was that).

They made a family, but a ghost was always in their midst. The other, hidden brother, never seen, not spoken of. Somewhere, a strange boy with Chloe's eyes—which are also Frank's eyes—with the same coal-black hair. It's like theft, somehow. Or like a knotted handkerchief, a thing undone.

Lottie asks, "You ever wonder where he is?"

Sometimes in dreams, Frank runs after his hidden brother, arms outstretched for capture. They dart and duck, identical faces colored high with exertion, with pleasure. At the end, Frank seizes him, and they melt into one another like toffee: black hair, white limbs, blue eyes.

"No," Frank says. "Stephen was my brother." Stephen, whose skull was shattered by a bullet at Cambrai. "Anyhow." The hidden brother is most likely cold in the ground. Lottie looks away. She knows. Everyone is dead.

In the distance, over the green summer lawn, through the wire, something stands white and still. Lottie looks at the girl, says, "D'you know why she's like that?"

"Well, she's..." Frank shies, curious and coy, from the word.

Lottie shakes her head. "They cut out little bits at a time. Did it too often."

The white girl stands apart, patient, black eyes hooded. Her face is brief, a slip of paper beneath the heavily bandaged head. Something travels through Frank's nethers, light and cold.

"Bits of," says Frank.

Lottie bites her knuckle. She looks at him with sympathy and taps her head once, lightly. "Through the skull, or the nose. The biter. She was a handful, in the beginning. I think that's why they went at her so many times. But it won't be long now. She can't eat. She breathes and all that. But she's gone. We don't even use her name anymore. We don't, when they go like that. Sounds bad, doesn't it? But, I don't know... It'd be like pretending they didn't do it. Making out like she's alive. You don't want to know what it's like over there. I declare, I could spit." Lottie rubs her glowing face with a small hand. "Sometimes," she says, "I think, well, *she's* all right. She doesn't know anything about it anymore. And there are so many things to feel awful about. D'you know, it's me I'm sorry for. I want to dance in nightclubs. I want to eat grapes on a lido and wear proper stockings and I don't know." Lottie stops abruptly and stares at Frank. "I'm a proper monster, I'm sure." She breathes quickly, hands folded together as if for church. Her eyelashes are thick and lustrous in the yellow light.

He touches Lottie's cheek. They look at one another, intent, as if examining for flaws.

"I've a good mind to," says Frank.

"Go on then," she says.

∾

Later, when the sun is cooling on the grass, Lottie says, "That girl who came to see you."

"Madge," Frank says. "She told me it was no good."

"Do you mind?"

Frank is not sure. He doesn't ask himself this sort of question. He fears he would never stop.

Lottie yawns and says, "What'll you do? Now."

After a while, he says, as if practicing, "My dad was a cabby. I know horses. I can run a motorcar. I suppose there are still motorcars and horses."

"I suppose." Lottie touches his hand where it rests on her shoulder. As she does, the light goes. Pain, which visits him so rarely now, lunges through his leg. It races across his flesh with wicked appetite. It rolls into his bones and swills around.

He presses an arm into his wet eyes. The afternoon is gone as if it had never been. What he speaks aloud then, he doesn't know, but he must have said something, because when he surfaces again, Lottie is saying, "It doesn't matter. Everything's broken up and in bits. All the old ways. So you can take those bits and do what you want with them. Do you see?"

Her voice runs over him, and her hands rest light and urgent on his chest. Everything about her, her scent, clings to him like perspiration. He feels everything. He wanted to give her something, but it's too much.

Frank says, "I shan't be driving motor cars or riding horses, shall I?" He puts her from him. "Don't," he says.

"Suit yourself," Lottie says. He feels her leave his side, feels the slight movement of air.

Annie brings him a pillow. She proffers it vaguely. "Leaving us tomorrow," she suggests.

"Yes," Frank says. On the other side of the ward, Lottie is laughing at something. Her hand covers her mouth. She's far away, low lit. Her eyes move over him easily. They haven't spoken since that day. Annie brings him things now and tends his new, healed flesh. Her touch is always tentative, as if she can't quite credit his existence.

"Where will you be going, then?" asks Annie. She holds the covered bedpan with absent grace.

"Bromley," Frank says. "To my uncle. He has a garage." As he speaks, Annie's eyes wander. She's tired. Her question was a courtesy that she cannot now sustain. Or perhaps nurses just know lies when they hear them.

The golden lamps are dimmed one by one, and the shuffling of men recedes into sleep. There is the usual crying out, of those whose fear catches them unawares before they settle. Every evening, they are surprised. Their memories of mud and blood and bared teeth, which the day has held at bay. Frank stares at the ceiling, willing everything to be white. Where will he go, when he leaves Earlswood? He thinks of ditches and newspaper and mossy bones. The night moves on.

At length, Frank sits up. He leans from the bed and takes his leg from where it rests on the cabinet. Buckles, the now familiar melding of flesh and leather. He takes his uniform from its neatly folded place in the drawer. There's almost nothing else; everything was taken at Dieppe. He dresses with care and ceremony, slow with the buttons. He smooths his shirt under his jacket, draws the trousers over his stiff, unfeeling leg. He looks at his few things that are left. Not much of a life.

The final thing sits cold and heavy at the back of the cabinet, wrapped in oilcloth. Frank puts it in his pocket. He makes his way between the beds, out of the ward, and down the bilious green corridor. No one is there. Shouldn't there be someone?

The door to the garden is locked and bolted, of course, but only on the inside. No one is guarding against those who wish to get out. The night is warm, still, scented with smoke. A bonfire smolders somewhere.

The tree spreads darker shadows across the dark. Under its branches, the grass is damp and riddled with roots, lumpy like objections. Frank tries to sit. His stiff, unreal leg skids, frightening. He leans against the trunk and shakes. Memory comes in sharp bursts, unbidden.

Frank thinks of the boy he saw caught in the propeller at Verdun. He can't recall his name. The boy turned to Frank, grinned, showed the gap in his teeth, and shouted, *Look at that. Thunder later, I shouldn't wonder.* The sky behind him was like steel. And then his arm was gone, then half his head.

There was a man who came out of the dark, one night, to give him a cup of tea. Frank couldn't take it for the shaking. The man took his hand in his. They stood, rifles slung over shoulders, hands clasped in the quiet dark. Until the man closed Frank's fist about the cooling tin mug and went.

Frank thinks of Stephen, who before that had been the last boy to hold Frank's hand and give him comfort. The weight of his arm about Frank's shoulder. His rough tobacco scent. And the other. Perhaps in the gray waste of death, Frank will find both his brothers.

The sliding on Frank's face is hot. His hands dig into themselves. Moonlight shivers through the tree. Night flowers, honeysuckle, old earth. Burning leaves. Frank thinks of all the old things in the ground, dead and long-ago buried and forgotten. He thinks of all the new things that uncurl, green and hopeful, each day. He thinks of rocky islands, where there are only birds and the sea. He imagines a great hole at the center of the earth, which spews things out for a moment—houses and lives and string and lit windows and beer and red dresses and words from books—and then sucks them back in again like a whirlpool, like a drain. Everything, he thinks, will go back down that hole. And what's at the bottom? There used to be reasons for things.

He takes the revolver from his pocket and opens his mouth. It tastes of oil and shot. The click is shocking, rattles his skull. Frank screws his eyes tightly closed. Little lights dance against his eyelids.

The blow comes through the dark like the wing of a bird. It glances off Frank's brow, and he staggers. The sky and the tree and the grass revolve.

A white hand, white fluttering linen. The length of fence post shines in her hand, furry with earth where it was pulled from the ground. Her teeth are yellow like the smile of the moon. Her head is free of bandages, and without them, she is suddenly sharp, alive, the shape of her skull tender beneath fine new hair. The scars stand up like valley rims in the moonlight. The raw wound where her shoulder bleeds, syrup dark on her white skin. Her face is a mask. Her blank eyes have no center. The eyes expand, grow, and take up her face. They swell, spread into the air, take in everything until the world is made of one mad eye. How did you get over, he tries to ask, get out?

The girl swings the post high above her head.

Frank has time to think a few things before the second blow falls. One of them is *Not ready at all, am I, actually? Not yet.*

The eye glistens. Something whistles. Everything droops and cants, is melting pitch.

❧

Lottie finds Frank in the garden, sprawled facedown. He's naked as a baby. His service revolver rests under his loose palm, silvered with rain.

When Lottie turns him over, he wakes, spits, coughs. The hummock on his head sends out pulses of delicate purple, of black. Blood trickles down his face, a line drawn by a hot pin. He feels rotten.

He holds Lottie close. She lets him. The shape of her is fleshly. "Shhh," Lottie says, her gaze wide and dark as a deer's. "Thought you'd done it," she says. "Thought it was all up with you. We've been looking... I was beside myself. Such a commotion. The storm—"

"Storm?" asks Frank.

"Look," says Lottie.

The tree above them is stripped of most of its leaves. Branches hang raw and broken. Around, the grass is littered with the debris like the aftermath of a battle. The lawn is laced with pools of rainwater, gleaming. The ground beneath Frank's shivering body is sodden, mired.

"And," says Lottie, "the biter—"

"She took my clothes," says Frank. Rage drops over him like a hot cloth.

Lottie looks at him, careful. "She was gone this morning," she says. "Room locked, bed empty, windows barred. She'd vanished, like in a penny dreadful."

Frank says, "I know. With my uniform. Clocked me over the head."

"Well," says Lottie, uncertain, "no, she'd died."

Frank stares. "No," he says. "Let me..."

"We couldn't see her anywhere. Or see how she'd got out. Gave us all the chills. But then I looked under the bed," Lottie says, quickly now, "and she was there. With her head all bare. It was pretty bad. Her skull through her hair. All those scars." Lottie starts to cry. "Crawled under her bed, curled up like a cat, and died. Perhaps she was afraid of the thunder. I think I was fond of her after all. And oh, those beds are bolted to the wall, you know. It was a business getting her out from under. And then—" Lottie stops, draws breath. Overhead, the clouds are breaking up, pierced by blue. Weak sun on her face. "When you weren't in your bed either, I was that upset, I had the oddest thoughts. I thought"— she pauses as laughter struggles out of her, high—"they've only gone and run away together. I knew she was dead. I'd seen her, dead as anything. But my first thought—both of you gone from your beds, like an elopement..."

Frank grips Lottie's arms through the sleeves. He squints up at her, a vast blunt shape against the brightening sky. He wants to tell, to make her see the great mad eye, the yellow moon grin, the biter. He starts to say how it happened. But the words lollop and scatter before they meet his tongue. His head sings with canaries. And he isn't sure, any longer, what has passed. There seems to have been a bargain made, somewhere, in which he's come out best.

Lottie blows her nose and grasps Frank's hand, intent. "They wanted to bury her in the yard around the back," she says. "Where they put the ones with no people. But I wouldn't have it. I was sorry I stood by all those years. D'you hear? That I let them do it. She was no more than a baby. All she talked about was home. When she could still speak.

"We were quick. Didn't know when they'd come for her... We packed her up. Me and some of the other girls. Those who minded, like I did. It's little enough we could do, goodness knows. We were in a state. Where to send her? There's a man who wrote to her. They would never give her the letters.

"Corpse, pauper fare, is two shillings and sixpence. Us girls paid it between us. I hope we did right. Ever packed a coffin tight for the train? It's a business. I put the last letter in with her. So she has one at least." Lottie weeps.

Everything is too near, pressing on Frank's skin. The wreckage of the garden, mournful. The battered crimson heads of poppies, scattering the ground. The crack of a broken branch swinging in the wind. How did things get so sharp? The scent of wet earth, of green, is overpowering. The ringing of glass from somewhere, which is the milk cart arriving; late, strident, unnecessary. Most of all, the itch of his leg where the thigh fits into the smooth prosthesis. The bluish, clumsy handwriting of the scarring, then leather and steel. He's a man, and then he becomes something else entirely at the knee. For the first time, it occurs to Frank that this might, eventually, become something he rarely thinks of. In the same moment, it comes to him that the war is really over.

Frank asks, "What was her name?"

"Iris," Lottie says. "Iris and something foreign. Enough for you?"

Frank breathes. The milk cart moves down the road with a clatter. It's enough. "Let's go in," Frank says. Then, "I'm not decent."

"Seen a deal worse," says Lottie. She pulls, and he pushes and wavers to his feet. As they go, the wire fence gleams in the coming sun. It will be hot again this afternoon. At one end, the mesh sags, slack and shining. A ragged hole gapes in the ground where a fence post is missing.

IRIS

1919

Burn it, Papa whispers. My dreams are peopled with the dead.

Coughing, awake. Smoke billows, acrid and bad. Before the fire in the hall. Rawblood's like a shell around me. Outside, the moor is quiet. Upstairs, everywhere, wind whistles down the halls, through the passages, raising dust sheets, rattling the swollen doors. Rawblood has its own internal weather now.

Must keep the fire going. I am cold, very cold. I break old packing cases open and snap the legs off white-veiled furniture. This was the only hearth whose chimney was not hopelessly blocked. The flames dance, pirouette with the wind. They have a greenish tinge. Something to do with the peat. This affected me more than the rest. I knew when I saw the pale green flames leaping in the deep hearth that I was home.

She won't show herself. I have raged through the house. I have torn boards from their moorings. I have clawed holes in the plaster. I have

crawled through the cellars like a grub. I climbed into the velvety, suffocating chimney—it spat me out, guffawing soot. Maybe she's gone.
Maybe she's dead like so many others these last years. Can ghosts die?

The dreams are very bad now. I dread sleep. I cannot bear to look
through her eyes. What she does. The things she feels. They are bleeding
into everything, spilling into my wakeful hours. She's here all right. I feel
her. I taste her in the air. She lies all over like a skin. She lingers in the air
like perfume. Rawblood breathes her like a lung. This house. My house.
It is a part of me, like a limb or an eye. But something has poisoned it. It
is suffering and sick.

I cannot go into some rooms. In the study, there is a hanged man.
He sways, creaking, from the beam. His blackened face, his toes pointed
gracefully at the floor.

∽

Fire. Black. Fire. I start awake. Mustn't sleep.

The image that swims in my mind's eye is the skeleton. The bones
laid out on the mahogany table. The ivoried yellow of them, the perfect
order, so quickly reduced to piles of nameless bone. All those years ago.

I feel a bit like that skeleton these days. All of me spread out and
unreal, spiraling on the eddies of dust up into the distant heights and
reaches of the house. It is so cold. Mustn't sleep.

∽

I'm in the hall outside my old room. The narrow doorway before me,
black, framed with moonlight. In the shadow, there stands something
thin and angular and white against the dark.

So this is where you are, I say. I'm disappointed, somehow. It's too
simple. The face is hidden in shadow, but the pale skull gleams through

the shorn hair. *She* turns her head a little. A glimpse of bone-white planes and dark sockets. Something moves for a moment, in the pits of her eyes.

I've seen you before, I say. *You were in the cave all those years ago. You did not get me then, and you will not do it now.*

She shudders. Her balding, scabbed head dips and bobs. Moonlight crawls across it, and somewhere in the shadows, her mouth moves like worms in the earth. No words come. Desire rolls through the air, cold on her breath. It is old wanting, implacable as stone. Her will like the depths of a cave. The skin on my face and arms puckers and contracts. My flesh slides softly on me, gathers in chilly pools at my neck and wrists.

Between us flows a tide. Years and my family's blood. The twin weights of fear and guilt, carried always. My father's fingers fumbling on the needle, seeking the vein. And all the others whom I did not know. My mother's love. Treading through the generations, wading through our lives, devouring us as easily as knocking the heads off dandelions. It has all been this. *You*. The reek of *her* rises in my nostrils. It's rot and hurt and burnt rope.

What is it that you want? I ask. *Take me, by all means. Where will you go, now that you've driven us all into the earth, one by one… What will you do when you have no one to torment? Too bad. I'll not give satisfaction. What can you take from me that has not already been taken? Nothing. I am bereft, without limits.*

She shivers as if with pleasure. Dark blots and shadows chase across her thin, enfolded form. It's moonlight and cloud playing through the window, perhaps, or perhaps not. I'm uneasy, of a sudden. What exactly is this? And I can't quite recall how I got here.

Something unfurls toward me. It lies between us like a deep cut. It's an arm, scabrous and wasted. The bone-white hand opens. I am already reaching for her, eager. The tips of our fingers meet. The sensation is surprising, smooth, familiar. She and I stand so, arms outstretched, fingers stiff and spread in formal refutation.

Then I hurl myself at her, teeth bared, fists clenched. I smash into her, and she's hard as glass. But I go on. I rain down with crashing blows. I scrabble deeper, seeking the heart of her. The world is full of shining and blood and inhuman sound.

I claw her smooth surface, beat her with my fists, elbows, skull. A cracking sound like the world opening. The truth comes slowly, as if through water. As Papa used to say, *There is always an answer.* It's simpler than I thought and worse than I could have imagined.

Pieces of the mirror come loose from the great gilt frame. They fall, blade-bright, to the floor, ringing, breaking. Each silver piece shows me back myself. Scattered, disassembled. My scabbed head, an evil moon, crossed with the many lines of old scars. My pale, wizened frame. The black eyes crawling like beetles—they are my eyes. I see *her* now for what she is. *She* isn't sending me dreams.

I thought I was haunted. It's the other way around.

My hands are bruised, bloody, shaking. But I don't stop. The thuds I hear are the deep thuds of my fists as they beat upon the floor, on the bright ruins of the mirror. I roar and smash. I smash until there is no treacherous surface to show me myself, to show me *her*, who are, after all, one and the same.

I was wrong. There was something left to take from me after all. What have I become? Martin's voice, Goodman's voice in my mind, now of all times. "*There is no her. There is only you.*" I am roaring again, my voice so hoarse, it sounds like stone grinding against stone. So he won in the end, because I died in there after all.

⁓

I go through the ways and halls of Rawblood. As I pass each room, I hear the voices within. My uncle Charles, playing with a little dog. Mary Villarca reading to her husband and laughing. I could reach out and touch them. I could do worse than that. I have done it.

In every fiber, I feel the hurt. What was done to me was unfair, *unfair*. Long years, I was taken bit by bit. Flesh, bone, organs, and brain. For what? For sport. To prove or disprove some thin, half-formed thought.

My rage grows, a warming flame. I am lit from within. The house opens up as I go. Rawblood reveals itself. The corridors grow long and strange to me. Doors lead off. There are many more rooms than I knew. Some doors stand ajar.

A white, many-paneled door chased with gold. Through it, an empty ballroom. The strains of distant music. Evening sun pours through tall bay windows. A gentleman stands in the center, in a great powdered wig. Sapphires wink at his neck. He stares at his severed wrists and weeps. Blood splashes onto the parquet, falls in gouts on his blue satin shoes, drips down his elegant heels, pools in his sapphire buckles. His eyes are dark and longing. He looks at me. He raises an elegant hand and points. His accusation like a knife. I turn away in haste. I don't know him. I've never met him. But I remember him. I recall the dark flower of rage that budded, that opened in me. Then he died.

Farther on, a rough stone arch set into the wall. Through it is a high wooden hall with a minstrel's gallery. Two men sit at table in brown hessian robes. They dine off silver plates. Some meat, dark and rich. Their soft chins shake, and juice runs down. Candlelight plays on the silver and on their tonsured pates. Behind them, on the rushes that cover the floor, are the bloody corpses of two young girls. I both know and do not know what they did here. And what I did. The rage stirs; *she* stirs. I hurry on. Behind, the crunch of teeth on bone.

There's a gap in the wall. Door-shaped perhaps, but not a door. Rawblood simply stops. It is dizzying. The place beyond bounded only by the night sky. Three small dark men sit on hides spread across the grass. Firelight plays about their tattooed faces. Their features are achingly, instantly familiar. I can trace my father's lineaments in theirs. Long-ago Villarcas, Hopewells, whatever name it was we first bore…

But no, they are of a time before names, long before Rawblood was. The tips of their spears gleam. One of them weeps. The others raise burning brands above their heads and peer into the night. Their eyes meet mine. Their mouths open, long, impossibly wide, great black holes. They shriek. They run. Their torches trail through the night air.

I let *her* in. I run after them over the hills in the dark, beneath the stars. The hunt. I catch them, in the end. I turn their faces to me, show them *her* eyes. In them, vastness. Rage, and nothing. I did it long ago. I remember.

The corridor undulates and hums with time. For it is not Rawblood alone. There are doors to cities, high mountains, wherever my family are. The walls cannot be trusted. They flicker like reflections on water. They are brick then granite then aching blue sky then cellar walls... All the places laid over one another. So many. I had not known there were so many. There is no end to it. Dark paths, trapdoors, corridors. Rawblood creeps outward like ivy, stretches ever back and back in time.

Everywhere, there are doors and walls and forests and pavilions and voices. Everywhere peopled with my family. All the generations that led to me. I touch them all. I am in them like a drop of ink spiraling in water. They bring me into being, and I end them... It's an endless, hellish circle. *She* is a wheel.

I have tied us here. My family pine for Rawblood; they love it with a fervor. They sicken when away from it. All because I cannot bear to be parted from my home. Those who live before the house is built: they see it in their dreams and yearn for it, always. Aching desire that cannot be fulfilled.

All the doors are singing. Dark and strong. I am called by them, deliciously. I've heard this song before, of course. But that was years ago. It sounded like water then, behind cave walls. The ones that stand ajar... They are inviting, and their song is very loud.

There is a certain door. I know it's here. I remember it. This is what happens. I go through to a blue-and-white nursery. I am tight-gripped in a blue blanket, looking up into my mother's face. Her arms are loving about me. For the first and the last time. But her face changes as she looks at me. Horror spreads slowly across it. The scent of blood and lilies all about us. My mother dies. I am left squalling in her arms with my grieving father, and it all begins again… My life. My death. *Her.* This happens. Has happened. I remember.

She stretches herself with pleasure at the thought. *She* loves to go around and around. Describing circles through time.

No. I won't. Keep it simple. I am Iris. And Rawblood is my home. I place my palms on the shuddering walls. I close my eyes and feel for the rough walls of my childhood. I seek them with my fingertips and all my being. Where Papa and I were everything to one another. My house. If I am very still, I can feel the familiar granite. I keep my eyes closed and follow the wall. My fingers trace my old ways. I go on, down toward the great hall. I go by the ways I know. I keep my eyes closed, and I don't turn or stop for the voices that call through the years.

In the hall, the fire glows red. I crouch by it. Papa always said there was no heaven, no hell. But there is. I'm in it. In the dark beating heart of it all.

I feel him before I see him. Something vast and dark, lying in the shadow of the hearth just outside the firelight. No, anything but this.

"Papa," I say. My heart is cold.

The black pile stirs, heaving. Something runs shining in the runnels between the flags. It touches the toes of my boots, and the scent of it rises, hot iron cooling.

His face is pale and streaked with blood by the light of the dying fire. But of course, I would know it anywhere. Years collide and memory. My father, the first person I killed. Or the last, depending on how you look at it. He's here, and I will not let it happen, I will not.

He turns his head with a groan. His breath whistles in and out. The syringe gleams, buried in his chest.

I throw myself to the floor beside him. I try to take his head in my hands. I cannot grip; my fingers slip on the blood. But he sees me. I smile. "Papa," I say. "It is I, Iris. Hush, I will help."

He convulses at my touch. He is white with fear.

"I see," he says and coughs. "*Her.*"

My father's last words: I hear them with new meaning, now. *I see*, he was saying to me. *You* are *her.* In his eyes, I am reflected; the monstrous ruin of me. My fingers are not slipping on the blood after all but slide through him, insubstantial. He claws at me in terror, but we cannot reach each other, to hurt or to comfort, and this is worst of all. My father dies once more, long ago, beyond my reach, here, before me, the blood pooling warm on the flags.

And then he's gone. The flags are clean and bare, and I'm alone, in the crackle of the dying fire. For how long? Some acts have such power that they never really end. Rawblood's not a house, any more than I am who I was. We are changed. Here, my father is always dying.

I run for the front door, unbar it with a crash, heave on the great iron latch. I kick. It won't open. I beat at it. It holds. I try the window. It's welded shut. I take up the cast-iron doorstop, arms trembling. I hurl it at the panes. It bounces off and hits the floor with an ear-splitting crash. I am sealed tight in my tomb.

I look at the high, quiet hall of Rawblood. The fire cracks quiet in the grate, plays warm on the flags. The great marble mantelpiece, white as snow, a riot of griffins, falcons, archers. The staircase curves elegantly up into the dark. These are sights I have longed for. Now, I would do anything to get out. But I don't get out, of course. I remember. I've done all this before. Around and around we go.

There is always an answer. There must be something I haven't tried. I dash the tears from my face and think. I search the long and terrible depths of my memories. There is something, something… Years and colors and thoughts dance before me, intermingling, the threads of all I've done.

And I have it. It's very simple. It's sad. I can't bear it. I have never been able to go through with it. Each time around, I have neglected this necessary thing. No more of that. I am Iris, and I must get out. I can govern my fate. *Burn it*, Papa murmurs.

"All right," I say.

The house shifts about me, a growing thing. Can Rawblood hear my thoughts? Does it know what I intend? I collect chairs, tables, hatstands, whatever is left. I bring them to the shadowed, flickering hall where the fire burns. I crack them over my knee with numb hands, pile the timber in. The flames tower into airy heights and spit hot. Old curtains, oil paintings obscured by the grime of years, anything. I crush the remains of a wicker chair. It all goes on. Dust and sparks fill the burning air. All the while, I weep. Rawblood. My bones, my heart.

In the study, I find old bottles of spirits under cobwebs. They shatter in the fire, and it roars, explodes its confines, licks up, blackening the white marble mantelpiece with hot tongues. Once more, I sift through memory... There's nothing. We are in uncharted territory now. What will happen?

I thrust two chair legs into the flames. They catch like torches, and I run up, along the snaking staircase, touching flame to everything as I go. Rawblood burns behind. Heat at my back. I am blackened and breathless. When the torches are burnt down, I let them fall. I race ahead of the fire.

Through my old room. Someone is in the bed. A man, pale behind his mustache, shaking. A little dog growls and leaps for me, teeth gleaming. I hurl it from me. It disappears, snarling, into the thick smoky haze. I reach the window, gasping. Out into the cool night air. I crawl along the ridge of the roof toward the stable until I can no longer feel the heat.

I turn.

The house is afire, a great candelabra. The windows are white with flame; it licks out and up. Spears of fire pierce the night. The doors are singing, high…all ablaze, all burning. My home, my prison.

Grief pulls at me. Rawblood burning to its bones, a dark skeleton against the tower of flame. Everything I have left in the world, all that I am.

A great crack as something vital gives. The house screams. The roof caves gently in. Slates fall from the roof in showers, hot into the molten center. Smoke boils out, great acrid clouds. I roll away, and the black follows, billows, filled with sparks, a multitude of tiny red eyes. The fire reaches up. It blossoms into the sky, towering over me. The air's too hot to breathe, and my lungs are bursting. Good. It's right to die with Rawblood. Neither of us has a place in this world anymore.

I fall through walls and waves of black. Red stars everywhere.

∾

I come to slowly. Warm light on my face. I sit upright, heart hammering. Rawblood rises quiet around me. I'm in the hall. Flames dance neatly in the hearth. Everything is as it was. It didn't work.

I could burn it again. I could throw myself into the fire. It will make no difference. I will never get out. I am trapped. My howl rings through the rafters and shatters the air. My terrible face reflected in the windowpanes, repeated darkly, over and over. A skull, mouth agape. A reflection on water.

Where would I go, if I could? Where do monsters find refuge? I look long at myself. I trace the white ghastly lines of my face. Papa was right, at the end. I'm not Iris. Iris died. They made holes in her head, and she died. I am all that's left. It's too hard to cling to memories, to life. The void is all there is. You gleam for a moment as you fall. You wink out in the black.

My hand holds an ornate silver doorknob. All about me, the song. The door itself is mahogany, prettily carved. Through it, I hear weeping. A woman. Her cries mingle with the music. Delightful. Why should I not go in? It all happened, long ago. Surrender need not be a gentle act. *She's* in me like a pulse.

The knob gives a pleasurable little squeak. I open the door.

A dark room heavy with the scent of disturbed sleep, still-warm wax, a candle recently extinguished. I move quietly to the bed. Two white bundled shapes. A man, a woman. There has been an argument. She weeps quietly, turned away. Piles of golden hair. My business isn't with her anyhow. Her turn comes later. A glowing poker, flame.

The man sits up. Watchful, elegant face. *You*, he says. He is leaden, pale, and sweating.

Come, I say. *I'll show you my eyes.*

I don't touch him. I don't need to. I show him. The pick on my skull, the bone dust. A half-life in the underworlds of the mind. Days and years. I spread my knowledge through him like sickness, spoiling everything I touch. I rot his heart.

He cries out like a child and runs from the warm room, from his weeping wife. I cling to him like smoke. She cries after us, *Leopoldo!* In the stables, he flings saddle and bridle on a startled horse. The horse shows the white of its eye. It shies and curvets and tries to throw him. It knows that death is near. He beats its quarters with the whip until it leaps forward, sweating. I curl about his shoulders as he rides. Faster and faster under the moon, as though he could outrun the thing that sits all about him. Me. When the ground begins to soften, the horse knows and slides to a halt in a tangle of legs and hooves. He flies over its head and into the mire. He's waist-deep, struggling.

It wasn't the holes in my head alone, I say. In the end. *Malnourishment. Infection. Strokes. Abscesses in the brain. It was slow. I'll show you what it was like to die my death.*

The bog takes its time. He goes under after some hours. Before that, he claws his eyes out, rather than see what's in mine.

When it's done, I am alone and cold on the desolate land. Despair drops like a hawk from the sky. The rotten bog fills the air. I am sick and shaking. What have I done? How do I get out? How do I stop? I clutch at the tussocks of sedge. I look to the horizon, a line of pink where the day's pushing in. If I go now... How can I escape *her*, who travels with me always? But I must try. I must.

The little thing stirs inside me, the dark flower. It grows, unfurls. Too late to think of flight. *She* strokes me, comforting. She seeps through my organs, my limbs and eyes. She spreads like a hundred little fingers, little tongues. The dawn, the land, my memories all fading, receding into nothing. The black rises once more. It fills me, gentle. She comes.

I will take them all. Then I will never have been. Door after door and high hills and cities open before me. I show them my eyes. Some rave, some plead. Take others' lives as they go. Many trembling hands grimed with blood. In the end, it's the same. Their soft hearts stop beating. And I am at peace. I tumble through nothing, full of dark and song. How long have I fallen? Was I ever anything but this? *Her.*

∽

Tom Gilmore starts up, coughing. Something in his dream has made its way into the waking world. Through the window, it's red in the east, but surely it's not yet dawn. He presses palms against the freezing glass, leaving white ghosts. The sky is red above Rawblood. But Rawblood burned months ago... He was dreaming of fire. Or red hair, perhaps. His mind is heavy with it still. Orange, red, roaring. The dream world and this lie atop one another. Red hair. Fire.

Go and dig the grave. Go. The long white bugles of funeral flowers. Lilies.

Since demobilization, he's been adrift in the vast sea. He only just keeps afloat. Each day, only just. The bewildering profusion of everyday things. The farm. Taxes. The calf with the broken leg. He feels at once too young for it all to be expected of him and too weary to care about it. Everyday things and the other, darker matters, lurking always just below. He was managing. After a fashion.

But last night, she was there. In the coffin, and also in the dark, outside the narrow light of the barn door. Within, without. Below him, before him. Dead. Not dead. Pale, awful. Drawn. He felt it like a blow to the throat or the heart. He felt the deep pull of the tide. How to stay afloat?

He could arrange for burial at Manaton, a churchyard, anywhere. Legal and safe and done. But it's not what she would have wanted. He knows what's being asked of him. There's no means of knowing the cost. He thinks bitterly of all they took from him, the Villarcas. Why should he go?

Before the war, he thought you could withstand things. You would recover and replenish yourself. Now, he knows that it's not true. What little reserves you have—of pity, kindness, courage, and so on—must be guarded. Stay afloat. Or let go. Drift into the deep. He stands and thinks.

"Right," he says at last and whistles for the dogs.

ᴓ

The wind's up on the moor. The pony raises her nose. She snorts at the gale, at the ghosts of horses on the air. Tom walks beside her, hand on her neck, eyes watering. The tarp on the cart flutters. Underneath are picks, a shovel, stout ropes, and pegs. And the long box. The dogs race ahead of the cart and back again, long pink tongues out, wild eyes. They're brown, brindled lurchers with great tails like masts. They pant, joyous. They were messenger dogs in the trenches. They don't know that they're farm dogs now. They're still bewildered by the land, the light. One of them is deaf, the other half blind. They have no names.

He is going inexorably toward something. Perhaps he'll not come back. The wind buffets. He's exhilarated, despite it all.

Rawblood in the distance, blackened and broken.

✑

Someone is calling. It's faint at first. It's a name, or something like it. Once, I knew.

I am seized, as if by the scruff of the neck. I land hard on the flags of Rawblood in a haze of firelight. Something dark and dreadful on my hands. I wipe them clean as best I can. What have I done? Someone is calling.

She sits by the cavernous hearth, hair red and burning like the fire before her. I come close to look at her, really look at her. I have never seen a picture. I do not believe there are any. But I know her; I would know her anywhere. Face intent like a cat glimpsing prey. In the uncertain light, I see the wet rims of her pond-green eyes. Not intent. Sad.

Come, I say. *I'll show you my eyes.*

She flings her hand up. *You must stop*, she says. The world coils and uncoils with power. The lines and colors of her shiver in the air. I am stopped in my tracks. She's not a memory. She's here, in one way or another.

Let me go, I say. *What does it matter? It was all long ago.* I do not want to think of the things I've done.

She looks at me. Cold, green, intelligent. *It matters. You burned the house, did you not?*

Papa said to burn it, I say. *Didn't work. We go around and around and around and around. No way out of the circle.*

Did Tom Gilmore dig the grave?

The question is meaningless, enraging. *I don't care*, I say. *Why? How has this happened to me?*

I went to the cave when the time came, she says. *To let you into the world. It is an old place. Too old, perhaps. I should have known. The earth and the stone remember. The cave does. Then Tom Gilmore left your ring on the stone... That the ones you love may never die, they say. Foolish to dismiss old tales. So how are you here? How do we come to such things? I do not know, except that it is by slow degrees and unknowing. And it is all connected. My daughter. Her hand light on my face, her look. It brings the scent of fresh grass, the memory of sunshine. You can get out. If Tom Gilmore digs the grave. I told your father to look after him. He forgot.* Some feeling in her face I can't read. *He is the only one of us left now.*

Tom's not one of us, I say.

Of course he is, she says. *You made him one. It's love that does it.*

He's forgotten me, I say. Tom. *Everyone's dead or forgotten me...*

Iris.

That's not who I am. I'm not her anymore.

She tuts. *Come*, she says and takes my hand. The front of her cambric nightgown. The gentle swell. I am somehow both here and there, warm inside her and alone in the cold dark. She puts her hand over mine. The love that moves then between my mother and I is as tangible as a shared road or a ribbon. It fills the spaces between us. We sit together on the cold stone floor before the dying fire.

I can't stop, I tell her. *And I can't get out.*

I'll give you a memory, she says. And she does. It's of warmth and Papa and the scent of iodine. The ache of bruises. It was a bad day, but then the fire cracked in the grate, and I was safe in the sheets, and he read to me of a grave, and a woman, and a sword.

Somewhere in the distance, the keening of old hinges. A door, swinging open.

Tom stands irresolute among the ruins of Rawblood. Black spires of charred wood rise in the afternoon air. Winter sun pours through the ruined windows. Behind is the gray land. The great curving staircase is gone; the slate roof is gone. The hall is open to the sky. The vast marble mantel remains above the hearth, blackened and cracked. Once, there flowed cherubs and devils in its chilly white folds. He said he would never come here again. But you can't escape some debts.

It was a year ago the house burned. In Dartmeet, they say the fire raged for three days. Everything obliterated in a great welter of flame. All gone. No cause for it to be found. Some said they saw a blazing figure running through the house, setting it alight with burning brands. To hear others tell it, a flaming sword. Starved, bald, with eyes afire. Of course, Rawblood has been haunted always. The old man Shakes was sleeping in the stable, as he always had. He never woke. Or so it must be assumed, for there was no trace of him after. People are sorry about Shakes in Dartmeet and all around. He was well known in these parts. They're not sorry about the Villarcas.

The dogs circle on the grass. They turn elegantly and make no sound. The soft incessant patter of their feet tells their distress. The dogs know fear and death; they're accustomed. But they won't set foot in what's left of Rawblood. They don't like it. They tell Tom this with upturned brown eyes, quivering bodies.

He goes to the place, already chosen, under the cedar tree. He paces out the hard ground. Eight feet long. Four wide. Eight deep, at least. He recalls a night in a cave, talk of a murdered girl beneath the cedar... An old tale. This is now.

What's in the box seems to have nothing to do with her. A scarred, hungry thing, died in its sleep. "We never had a chance," he says to the air. "Not a chance." He's surprised by his fury. Deep, sudden.

He breaks ground. The pick rings as if on metal. The earth resists, then breaks open. He sinks into the rhythm of it. Wintry light sits on him. His straining arms, the shovel, the dogs' worried faces.

It takes most of the afternoon. He stops when he thinks he should. He's not tired. He pours water into the shallow of a shovel for the dogs and the pony. They all drink noisily.

When at last it's done, he lets the coffin down gently into the hole. It's difficult. His arms and back hum with weariness. The sun's low now in the sky. Not long till dark. That old story she loved. The graves opened like doors to yield their dead.

∽

The great tree murmurs at my back. The moon falls through the leaves. Dappled shade. It's not a cedar now, but something older. The branches are dark and knotty, the leaves shaped like blades. The tree and the cave. They call to one another. The same people made them and for the same purpose.

There has always been a tree here on this hill. They hung sacrifices from the branches. Pieces of bread, amber beads, lengths of perfect linen, oxen hearts. They hung the children dressed in white. The blood ran down the bark. The man who does it is wizened, small, and ancient. Face like cooling lava. He treats them gently. He soothes them as he slips the noose about their necks. Then the knife. The old man does it in *her* name. Places remember. Rawblood. Not such a gentle name after all.

The grave's half in shadow under the spreading branches. It lies quiet, newly dug. A pile of earth beside it. There has always been a tree here and beneath it a grave. Someone buries me here. Will bury me here. Has buried me here. Comes to the same thing. How are ghosts set free? Graves are doors too.

A circle of lamplight blooms soft beneath the tree. Someone stands by the grave. Was he always there? Blue eyes. Scarred face solemn in the shifting light.

Tom throws a handful of cold earth. It scatters on the thin coffin wood. The dark is coming, and the air is cold. The sky is a blazing orange line behind the ruins of the house.

He unhitches the pony from the cart. "Go now," he tells her and the dogs. "Go on. Bugger off home." The pony goes gladly with a ladylike kick of her heels. The dogs don't want to leave him, but in the end, they go too, trotting across the fading land.

He lights the lamp. It throws a warm circle on the winter ground. He leans on the spade. He waits. He thinks, *We made each other who we are.* He thinks of her and all the times. A crack is opening in him, or the world. *Forward or back?* he thinks. Something races through him like color or approaching thunder. Forward or back? The sun is nearly down. He wills the night on. The air is uncertain, lustrous. He looks about him sharply. In the dark, beyond the lamplight, something gently stirs.

"Iris," he says.

"She died," says a voice like stone grinding upon stone. Like the death of hope, like battlements falling.

"She died," I say. "I'm not her anymore."

"Iris." The light's warm on his face, young beneath its river of scars. He's afraid.

"You gave me up," I say. "Forgot."

"No," he says. "That's the problem. Can't forget it. All our lives."

I try to think what he means, but it's so distant, removed. Tiny, lit-up scenes, caught in time.

I say, "Put out the light." The winter night rises about us. Multitudes of cold, cold stars. He comes toward me in the dark, breath white and fine-spun in the air.

"Those days," he says. "Won't let me go. You and I."

The black is rising, a tide. I welcome it in.

"You think you know me," I say. "But I am more dangerous than you could dream." The thoughts come fast and lovely like thrown knives. His ignorance, his obstinacy. He did this somehow; he put the ring on the stone. My every fiber burns with the dark. Sweet singing in my bones and my veins. I am made of malice and full of power. I am made of nothing. *Look at me. This is who I am.* I show him my eyes.

He breathes me in. The sickness. The despair washes in, bitter. It rots and curdles his insides. It runs through him, spoiling everything it touches. He coughs. Blood swells within his lower lip, spills to his chin in a thin, eager line. He's afraid, of course, like all the others.

"Go on," he says fiercely. "If you have to."

I curl about his bones. I show him everything.

He stares. Blank, blue look. Without warning, he reaches out and passes a hand over my head. His palm warm on my bare skull. His fingers touch the ridges of the scars, which cover the broken holes. "Oh," he says sadly. Years since anyone touched me in kindness.

"Get away," I say. "Get off." The black scatters. I release him. I come back into myself with a thump.

He doubles over, coughing, rubs his chest through his thin, patched shirt. He pounds his heart with a fist.

"You all right?" I ask.

"Lungs," he says briefly. "Gas did for me. Hold on." He coughs.

"We're quite the pair," I say.

He says, "What was done to you, Iris?"

I tell him. The words taste of tin. "I can't be this anymore," I say.

A pause, and then he says, "What, then?"

I think of Hervor and the door of the dead. "At dawn," I say, and it's me who's frightened now, "I think I go." I look at the horizon, and I see: the line of Rawblood is wrong against the sky. Unfamiliar. Jagged, broken. Twisted, skeletal angles. I peer into the dark. Heavy scent of old, old ash.

"Did it burn?" I ask. "Tom, did Rawblood burn?"

"Yes," he says, wary. "It's gone. Burned last summer."

"I set it on fire," I say. "Last night." It worked after all. Rawblood, my home, my prison. I look at its shattered silhouette. It wells up strong in me still. That love. Even now.

I think I could stay, if I wanted. Burned or not, I could wake beside the fire in the great hall. Go through the endless doors. Do what has already been done and give in. Forget. Rawblood will always be there. All I've done.

I touch the paper in my pocket. Creased, soft. "I had a letter from you," I say to Tom.

"Well," he says, "I must have sent a hundred."

"If you've anything to tell me," I say, "it'd best be now."

"All right," he says. The night wheels on. The shape of his head against the stars.

∽

The skyline's blue and burgeoning. Shapes are stronger by the moment. I can see him, just, in the silver light that comes before the sun. He's tired, pale. Memory surges through me. Afternoon heat, blue serge, his hand touching mine as we ride home. Hooves clipping the road, the song of bees, happiness so thick it's a warm stupor, as if someone has taken our minds. I'm filled with simple knowledge. I touch his shoulder. Through the thin shirt, it's good and damp and real. "I thought it was my father," I say to him. "I thought I came back for Rawblood, for *her*... But after all, it wasn't those things. In the end, it wasn't them I came for."

Tom looks at me and I at him. The first reddish beam of day falls across us. Behind him, the sun crests the hill, a blazing line. Above us, the tree is wreathed in light. Each winter branch is lacework against the sky.

I'm not ready. We've barely begun. I reach for his hands; he grasps mine tight. *No*, he says. *Pest...* The red disc of the sun rears up; the sky runs blood then orange then amber. The light strengthens. I say, *No, wait.* I hold to him. Warm, familiar. *Wait.* His fingers slip through mine. He's gone.

I'm alone in burning light. I close my eyes, but the sun is in them still; behind my lids, there dance eons, planets, stars. All the moments and beginnings and endings. The faces of the dead. Rustle of silk, the thud of a boot. Flash of my father's eye blinking, great and brown. Centuries unroll; the colors are staggering. Indigo, white, yellow. Burning wheat fields, the light caught on battle blades, blood, blood, and everywhere, the sound of trees growing.

The ground creeps up over my boots, my legs. Earth about my shoulders, my head. The ground closes above me like water. A grass snake winds smoothly past my cheek. Creatures and things move in the earth about me; it is so alive. I sink down, past the old stone foundations of Rawblood. The house by the bridge over flowing water. My fingers brush the stinking fur of a fox where it sleeps in its earth. It bares its teeth but doesn't wake. Down through a cold river, bound deep in the rock.

A quick flash of a green shining cave, two children crouched on the rocky floor. They speak to one another, faces intent. I know her, of course, and him. How strange: how tender, distant. The candle stub flickers bravely, casts light and shadow. I yearn toward them. None of it had happened yet then...although, of course, it had.

The little girl looks at me. Horror on her small white face, and fear. She puts her thin child's body between me and him. The white worms crawl in my eyes. She pulls the boy up and runs, scattering shale and shards of brown glass.

The cave walls flicker. There's a woman in a bloodstained dress. She weeps, and her huge belly undulates. A knotted old man crouches by her, eyes milky. I want to touch her, to comfort her and be comforted... but they're gone.

The shining green cave is shadowed, empty. A gold ring sits on the altar stone. Red and white gems gleam in the cool light.

I sink. Down.

Down through other caves where blind fish swim and calcified minerals bleed from the ceilings in glittering pointed spikes. Down into the deep inside of the land. To where nothing is anymore. I come to rest. There are many arms about me in the dark—kind arms. They hold, and their voices are in my ear, my family; I see their faces and their lives laid out like a road through the centuries, like a ribbon. I see my part in it and the choices that were their own, in the end. The sadness brims, fills me like a cup. I will drown in it, surely, and that will be welcome. They speak long and low, and I see, like the crack of breaking bone, that I am so very small in the placement of earth and hill and rock, in the placement of things. And I see that I am forgiven.

They leave me. They slip away like smoke.

I am alone on a great plain. Fire leaps from deep holes. Scent of lilies, of rot. Something approaching. Dark, boiling, rolling closer, huge and terrible under the fiery sky. *No. I've made a mistake.* I turn to run. It rolls over me, hits me like a torrent. I am shattered in a slow explosion. The pain is beyond anything. It's knowledge, time, all racing through me like horses. I am broken, disassembled. The brawling noise, high wind. I flow out into the little rivulets under the world.

~

The day rises through the bare tree. Tom pushes the last of the earth into the grave. Something stirs the air behind him. He throws the shovel aside, turns quickly. A flock of starlings rises, iridescent in the morning light. They flow about the ruins of Rawblood. Shining, cackling. He makes fists of his hands to stop the shaking. He is alone.

∽

Light, somewhere. It could be fire in a great hall. Sunshine in a blue nursery. Morning light, beneath a tree. Or something I have never known.

READING GROUP GUIDE

1. *The Girl from Rawblood* jumps back and forth between many characters and time periods. How did this different method of storytelling affect your journey through the book?

2. How do the females of Rawblood provide a peephole into the struggle of women in England during these time periods, and how do they push against their limitations? Do you encounter similar themes and challenges in today's society?

3. Is there a character in *The Girl from Rawblood* that resonates more strongly with you than others? If so, why?

4. Shakes is a constant presence at Rawblood and seems to have personal connections to the family and the house. Why has he been so loyal, despite the curse?

5. Charles Danforth is clinical and aloof, even when it comes to the welfare of his sister, Meg; yet the experiments on the rabbits were

enough to disturb even him. Was it similarly hard for you to read about such cruelty, and what feelings did it incite?

6. Meg is one of the only characters gifted with sympathetic insight into the dark past of *her*. As you read the horrific consequences of the curse and discover the identity of the ghost, how was it easy or difficult to "forgive" its intentions, as Meg tries to do?

7. Have you ever had a supernatural encounter? What happened, and how did it diminish or expand your beliefs and outlooks?

8. If you had the choice of facing the curse at Rawblood or dying slowly away from Dartmoor, which would you choose and why?

9. The loss of eyesight is a theme that recurs throughout the book, including Meg's preeclampsia and Don Villarca's accident. What are some possible interpretations of blindness throughout the story?

10. Tom and Iris never let go of their love and find their way back to each other in the end. How would the story be different had Iris followed her father's rules?

11. Did you guess the identity of *her* before the end of the book, and if so, what are the clues that led you to your conclusion?

12. Have you ever loved a physical place so much that something inside you felt connected (or trapped) in a way that would always lead you back or tie you down?

13. Where do you think Iris goes at the end? And what do you hope happens to Tom?

A CONVERSATION
WITH THE AUTHOR

What was your inspiration for writing *The Girl from Rawblood*?

Writing this novel was an exorcism of sorts, for me.

During my childhood and adolescence, my family moved from the United States to Kenya, to Madagascar, then to Yemen, Morocco, and back to the United States. We returned each summer to a seventeenth-century stone cottage tucked into a valley beneath the swooping heights of Hamel Down on Dartmoor. The house was surrounded by little old oak woodlands, heather, hills. After the tropics, Dartmoor was exotic, with its mists and bogs; a bleak, grand landscape.

The cottage was partly built on the foundations of an older Devon longhouse and partly on some that were even older. There is a dwelling marked on that site in the *Domesday Book*. The walls were solid granite, seven feet thick. The hearth could have comfortably accommodated an ox. In that house, I rarely lasted the length of a night in my own bedroom. My sister awoke, most mornings, to find me curled up on her floor.

I was continually troubled by something in my room. A presence.

It didn't take any recognizable form but was vaguely rhomboid and spun with color. It would hover before my face, red and seething. Occasionally, this presence would shove me out of bed with a firm hand in the small of my back. An overwhelming intent emanated from it. The dark air was alive with its will, a vast sense of purpose—but no indication of what that purpose might be, whether I was a part of it, or an obstacle to it, or irrelevant.

It was a particular kind of terror, which seemed to belong entirely to the night. I've yet to encounter its daylight counterpart. It's all-consuming while you're in the grips of it: neither a rational, intellectual fear nor an instinctive, animal one. It touches the deep roots of the soul.

This went on for six years. I never grew accustomed. Each night, the fear was as paralyzing as the first time. Eventually, we moved house. The presence didn't follow us.

It was a great relief. At that age, one is very plastic and forgets easily. I grew up, and the experience faded until I thought of it rarely, and then not at all. Until one day in my late twenties, I sat down, and I found myself writing about a girl, and a house on a sunlit moor, and something that came in the night... It possessed me, once I had started. The Villarca family had all been waiting in the wings, and they came in fully formed.

Did you grow up reading ghost stories, and if so, which were your favorites? What about ghost stories captured your imagination?

I love ghost stories and always have. You might think my early experiences would have put me off, but it's quite the opposite. Ghost stories and horror give you permission to mine the darker parts of the psyche and explore those places in safety.

The first ghost story I remember reading was "The Monkey's Paw" by W. W. Jacobs. The tale reaches its climax as a mother and father cower away from a pounding at the front door, which they know to be their son, risen from the grave.

I was afraid and suitably thrilled. But most of all, I recognized a mode of storytelling that gave expression to the fear I felt in the night. It is fear that cannot be explicitly described and is more awful for it. *The Girl from Rawblood* owes its heritage to the literature of the uncanny: M. R. James, Charles Dickens, Sheridan Le Fanu, Robert Aickman to Stephen King, Susan Hill, Kelly Link, Hilary Mantel, Shirley Jackson, Jeremy Dyson, and many others.

People often ask me if I believe in ghosts, and even after everything, I am not sure. I think that is the most frightening position to be in. Because a world where ghosts definitely *do* exist is a world where ghosts are normalized. That's not frightening. Nor is a world in which ghosts definitely *don't* exist. But a world where they *might* exist... *might* is terrifying. This is the uncertainty that all uncanny literature wanders through.

Many of the moments and characters are connected in some way, either distantly or intimately. Was it your intention to write a book the reader could put together like a puzzle? Did you map it out beforehand, or did the stories weave themselves together as you wrote?

It was a combination of the two. At first, I thought it was a fairly simple story about a girl and her father. But it spiraled out and out. More characters came in, more connections. I worked out the ending, the reveal of *her*, fairly early on, but how to get there? I planned each section but pretty loosely and mapped it back into the structure of the novel as I went. I was only ever a bare half step ahead of the narrative, really. I don't write much down or make notes when I'm planning. I agree with Stephen King that there's a certain Darwinian process to ideas—if you still have the thought in the morning, then it might be a go. If you've lost it, then perhaps it's for the best.

It was only as I was writing the ending, sending Iris through the rooms of Rawblood, through time and space, that I understood what the novel had been moving toward, what *The Girl from Rawblood* wanted to be and was really about: family and love. These things light us on our way.

The women of Rawblood are wonderfully strong, but many find themselves tragically at the mercy of their environments. How did these limitations shape the journey, and would Iris's story have been different today?

Quite. The women of this novel—Iris, Mary, Hephzibah, Meg, Lottie—are resourceful and ingenious. They have to be, to negotiate the limitations of the times they live in. The women in *The Girl from Rawblood* are, to varying degrees, politically and socially powerless. Iris's story is, of necessity, the cruelest in the novel. I placed her in the most powerless situation I could contrive.

Perhaps the events of *The Girl from Rawblood* could have been different today. Perhaps Iris would never have been so wronged, so *she* would never have come to exist. I'm not sure. Fanatical belief, torture, and cruelty turn Iris into *her*. We haven't eradicated those evils from our societies by any means.

Or, again, perhaps if all the women of Rawblood had lived in different times, they could have carved out other destinies than marriage or children. They would have obeyed the prohibition, and the Villarca line would have simply ended. But deep down, I suspect that, whatever the age they lived in, Rawblood would have sung all the Villarcas back, somehow, and *she* would have had her way with them.

Dartmoor is so stunningly realized throughout the book that it's almost a character in itself. Do you still have a personal connection to that part of the United Kingdom?

I think I will always feel a connection with it. When I was growing up, wherever my family went in the world, we came back to Dartmoor every year. It has been the single point of continuity in my life. My parents now live there permanently, and whenever inspiration is elusive, I go and visit. The landscape has made its way into my subconscious, as it has done with many other writers. It's one of Britain's last remaining wild places—but you can also see layers of human history laid out before you, half buried in the grass. The medieval village at Hound Tor, the stone circles at Scorehill, the drowned mineshaft behind Hay Tor, the airman's memorial on Hamel Down. Dartmoor breathes age and history, as well as being achingly beautiful. It's the perfect setting for uncanny happenings, a natural literary home for demonic hounds, ghosts, murder; dark, solitary acts. A fertile breeding ground for the imagination.

What research did you do to add depth to the cold and clinical scientific society of Victorian England?

Medicine is more than a shared interest, more than a profession to Charles and Alonso—it frames all their thoughts and feelings. It is a means of expression between them. So it was really important to get the medicine right in a factual sense, but also for Charles's thoughts to have authority and authenticity. I needed to know how doctors talked to one another. The *British Medical Journal* has digitized its archive from 1850 onward, and that was an invaluable resource in this respect. The letters pages of the *BMJ* became a forum for debate and indignant exchanges… "My *dear* sir!" You can see that medicine was a discourse of personalities, as well as of science.

The late nineteenth century is such an interesting point of intersection in scientific thought—wildly experimental, and yet retaining some very odd, almost medieval ideas. It's fascinating. W. F. Bynum's *Science and the Practice of Medicine in the Nineteenth Century* is a wonderful introduction to the period. I live in London, which holds extraordinary collections, archives, and resources on the history of medicine in Great

Britain. The Wellcome Collection has a standing exhibition on medical history. The Hunterian Museum is another gem.

Would you risk the curse for the sake of real love? Can you blame any of your characters for trying?

I think one probably would risk it. That's the tragic mechanism at the heart of this novel—death doesn't really hold any reality for us in our everyday lives. It can't, or we'd spend all our time cowering in terror. A scene that I wrote very early on is the incident where Alonso is singing a coin along the rim of a glass. No one in the bar hears the whistling—can't, until it breaks the glass. We don't hear the song of mortality, but it has been there, all along, behind the human babble. The glass always breaks.

I can't blame any of my characters for risking the curse in order to live full, emotional lives. If the head and the heart are at odds, the heart is almost sure to win in the end.

As a debut author, what was the most surprising discovery you found on your journey to becoming published?

I am still adjusting to being a published author. I spent so many long years working on *The Girl from Rawblood* in private, and it still seems unreal that it is now published all over the world. That is probably the most surprising aspect of all this!

One thing I hadn't anticipated was the number of ghost stories that I am told now, wherever I go. Everyone has one, it seems. I am now a walking almanac of hauntings... Oddly, many people preface these stories by telling me they don't believe in ghosts.

What I have really enjoyed is meeting readers, speaking at book-shops and literary festivals. It is unadulterated pleasure—to talk with like-minded people, not just about *The Girl from Rawblood*, but about books and reading.

What piece of advice would you give to aspiring writers?

I spent six years writing *The Girl from Rawblood*, and a lot of that time was spent learning how to write, which you can only do through practice and grievous error. So practice! Find readers who are honest with you and listen to them. It's impossible to judge your own work at times, and you are writing to be read, after all. You can also ignore them sometimes. You will know when.

Read! The best teacher for a novelist is another author's excellent writing. Read as many different genres, periods, and styles as you can. You will develop.

I did a creative writing master's at the University of East Anglia in the UK. The workshops gave me a much-needed forum in which to discuss work, not only my own, but that of others in the group. You learn a lot from that. So while a master's isn't possible or necessarily desirable for everyone, joining a writing group could be an invaluable experience.

Enjoy it. Writing is heartrending and laborious, and it can be very badly paid. But it is also a great pleasure. Building an imagined world until it becomes something you have wandered into, rather than created… It's wonderful. If you really must do it, put everything you have into it, and enjoy.

Besides writing, what else are you passionate about?

My father has worked in the developing world all my life, in Madagascar, the Gaza Strip, Uganda, Egypt, Morocco, Yemen, and many other places, often on water scarcity and the problems of social and economic justice that crisis brings with it… My parents are people of great conscience, and they have always tried to instill that in their daughters. During the years I was writing *The Girl from Rawblood*, I was lucky enough to work for the Bianca Jagger Human Rights Foundation in London as a writer and researcher. It was a wonderful experience that taught me a great deal.

I love my family: my mother, father, sister. And my friends. I love horse riding and cold wine on a hot night. I am a feminist.

I was lucky enough to grow up all over the world, surrounded by natural beauty. In Madagascar, we explored coral reefs teeming with life and walked in the rain forest. One of my happiest early memories is of a small island off the coast where the lemurs have russet or black fur and vivid yellow eyes. Because they have no predators on the island, they are fearless and very happy to climb all over you. Their hands are small, velvety, and cool. The landscapes and biodiversity of Madagascar are astonishing. But it is rapidly being destroyed. Already, some of the sights I grew up with have been lost to climate change and deforestation.

If there's one thing you'd like readers to take away from *The Girl from Rawblood*, what would it be?

Some people find *The Girl from Rawblood* to be a sad book. It's surprising to me, because I think it's quite a romantic novel. Whatever trouble and suffering befall the Villarcas, they always live passionately and love strongly. What more can you ask for in life?

ACKNOWLEDGMENTS

My parents, Christopher and Isabelle Ward, have all my thanks for their love, help, and support through the years.

Heartfelt thanks go to my partner, Edward McGown, who is wonderful in ways too many to number.

I am deeply indebted to Sam Copeland for his guidance, enthusiasm, and support, and to everyone at Rogers, Coleridge & White.

I am very grateful to my amazing UK editor, Arzu Tahsin, for gently steering me right, and to Rebecca Gray, Jennifer Kerslake, Craig Lye, and the wonderful team at Weidenfeld & Nicolson.

Many thanks to Grace Menary-Winefield for championing *The Girl from Rawblood* and for all her editorial insight. Thank you to the lovely people at Sourcebooks, who brought Iris to the United States.

I am grateful to everyone who read and commented on the manuscript, including Kate Burdette, Emily Cavendish, Susan Civale, William St. Clair, Natalie Dormer, Emma Healey, Alex Learmont, Andy Morwood,

Eugene Noone, Catherine Shepherd, Alice Slater, Mike Walden, Philip Womack, and Anna Wood.

Thank you to Henry Sutton, Giles Foden, Andrew Cowan, and my tutors and classmates at UEA.

Thank you to my lovely sister, Antonia Ward, and to Oriana Elia, Belinda Stewart-Wilson, and Bianca Jagger for all their support.

ABOUT THE AUTHOR

Catriona Ward was born in Washington, DC, and grew up in the United States, Kenya, Madagascar, Yemen, and Morocco. She studied English at St. Edmund Hall, Oxford, followed by a master's in creative writing from the University of East Anglia. After living in New York for four years, where she trained as an actor, she now works for a human rights foundation and lives in London.

Photo credit: Robert Hollingworth